Jane Austen, James Edward Austen-Leigh

# A Memoir of Jane Austen

Jane Austen, James Edward Austen-Leigh

**A Memoir of Jane Austen**

ISBN/EAN: 9783337092863

Printed in Europe, USA, Canada, Australia, Japan

Cover: Foto ©Raphael Reischuk / pixelio.de

More available books at **www.hansebooks.com**

# A MEMOIR OF JANE AUSTEN

TOGETHER WITH

## 'LADY SUSAN': A NOVEL

&c.

PRINTED BY
SPOTTISWOODE AND CO., NEW-STREET SQUARE
LONDON

# A MEMOIR

### OF

# JANE AUSTEN

BY HER NEPHEW

## J. E. AUSTEN-LEIGH

*SIXTH EDITION*

*TO WHICH IS ADDED*

# LADY SUSAN

*AND FRAGMENTS OF*

*TWO OTHER UNFINISHED* **TALES** *BY MISS AUSTEN*

## LONDON

**RICHARD BENTLEY & SON, NEW BURLINGTON STREET**

Publishers in Ordinary to Her Majesty the Queen

1886

# PREFACE.

THE MEMOIR of my Aunt, JANE AUSTEN, has
been received with more favour than I had
ventured to expect.  The notices taken of it
in the periodical press, as well as letters addressed to me by many with whom I am not
personally acquainted, show that an unabated
interest is still taken in every particular that
can be told about her.  I am thus encouraged
not only to offer a Second Edition of the
Memoir, but also to enlarge it with some additional matter which I might have scrupled to
intrude on the public if they had not thus seemed
to call for it.  In the present Edition, the narrative is somewhat enlarged, and a few more
letters are added ; with a short specimen of her
childish stories.  The cancelled chapter of 'Persuasion' is given, in compliance with wishes
both publicly and privately expressed.  A fragment of a story entitled 'The Watsons' is

printed ; and extracts are given from a novel which she had begun a few months before her death ; but the chief addition is a short tale never before published, called 'Lady Susan.' I regret that the little which I have been able to add could not appear in my First Edition ; as much of it was either unknown to me, or not at my command, when I first published ; and I hope that I may claim some indulgent allowance for the difficulty of recovering little facts and feelings which had been merged half a century deep in oblivion.

NOVEMBER 17, 1870.

# CONTENTS.



a

## CHAPTER VI.



## CHAPTER VII.



## CHAPTER VIII.



## CHAPTER IX.



## CHAPTER X.



## CHAPTER XI.



## CHAPTER XII.

## CHAPTER XIII.

' He knew of no one **but himself** who was inclined to **the work.**
**This is no** uncommon motive.  A man **sees** something **to be**
done, **knows** of no **one** who will do it **but** himself, **and so is**
driven to the enterprise.'

**HELPS'** *Life of Columbus*, ch. i.

# A MEMOIR

## OF

# JANE AUSTEN.

## CHAPTER I.

*Introductory Remarks—Birth of Jane Austen—Her Family Connections—Their Influence on her Writings.*

ORE than half a century has passed away since I, the youngest of the mourners,* attended the funeral of my dear aunt Jane in Winchester Cathedral; and now, in my old age, I am asked whether my memory will serve to rescue from oblivion any events of her life or any traits of her character to satisfy the enquiries of a generation of readers who have been born since she died. Of events her life was singularly barren: few changes and no great crisis ever broke the smooth current of its course. Even her fame may be said to have been posthumous: it did

---

* I went to represent my father, who was too unwell to attend himself, and thus I was the only one of my generation present.

not attain to any vigorous life till she had ceased to
exist. Her talents did not introduce her to the
notice of other writers, or connect her with the literary world, or in any degree pierce through the
obscurity of her domestic retirement. I have therefore scarcely any materials for a detailed life of my
aunt; but I have a distinct recollection of her person
and character; and perhaps many may take an interest in a delineation, if any such can be drawn, of
that prolific mind whence sprung the Dashwoods
and Bennets, the Bertrams and Woodhouses, the
Thorpes and Musgroves, who have been admitted
as familiar guests to the firesides of so many families,
and are known there as individually and intimately
as if they were living neighbours. Many may care
to know whether the moral rectitude, the correct
taste, and the warm affections with which she invested her ideal characters, were really existing in
the native source whence those ideas flowed, and
were actually exhibited by her in the various relations of life. I can indeed bear witness that there
was scarcely a charm in her most delightful characters that was not a true reflection of her own sweet
temper and loving heart. I was young when we lost
her; but the impressions made on the young are
deep, and though in the course of fifty years I have
forgotten much, I have not forgotten that 'Aunt
Jane' was the delight of all her nephews and nieces.
We did not think of her as being clever, still less as
being famous; but we valued her as one always kind,
sympathising, and amusing. To all this I am a

living witness, **but** whether **I** can sketch out such a faint outline of this excellence as shall be perceptible to others may be reasonably doubted. **Aided,** however, by **a** few survivors* who knew **her, I** will not refuse to make the attempt. I am the more inclined to undertake the task from a conviction that, however little **I** may have to tell, no **one** else **is** left who could tell **so** much of her.

Jane Austen was **born on** December 16, 1775, at the Parsonage House of **Steventon** · in Hampshire. Her father, the Rev. George Austen, was of a family long established **in** the neighbourhood of Tenterden and Sevenoaks in Kent. I believe that early in **the** seventeenth century they **were** clothiers. Hasted, **in** his history of Kent, says: 'The clothing business was exercised by persons who possessed most of **the** landed property in the Weald, insomuch that almost all the ancient families **of** these parts, now of large estates and genteel rank in life, and some of **them** ennobled by titles, are sprung from ancestors who have used this great staple manufacture, now almost unknown here.' **In** his list of these families Hasted places the Austens, and he adds that these clothiers 'were usually called the Gray Coats **of** Kent; and

* My chief assistants have been my sisters, Mrs. B. Lefroy and Miss **Austen,** whose recollections of our aunt are, on some points, more vivid than my **own.** I have not only been indebted to their memory for facts, but have sometimes used their words. Indeed **some** passages towards the end of the work were entirely written by the latter.

I have also **to thank some** of my cousins, and especially the daughters of Admiral Charles Austen, for the use of letters and **papers** which had passed into their hands, without which this Memoir, **scanty** as it is, could not have been written.

were a body so numerous and united that at county elections whoever had their vote and interest was almost certain of being elected.' The family still retains a badge of this origin; for their livery is of that peculiar mixture of light blue and white called Kentish gray, which forms the facings of the Kentish militia.

Mr. George Austen had lost both his parents before he was nine years old. He inherited no property from them; but was happy in having a kind uncle, Mr. Francis Austen, a successful lawyer at Tunbridge, the ancestor of the Austens of Kippington, who, though he had children of his own, yet made liberal provision for his orphan nephew. The boy received a good education at Tunbridge School, whence he obtained a scholarship, and subsequently a fellowship, at St. John's College, Oxford. In 1764 he came into possession of the two adjoining Rectories of Deane and Steventon in Hampshire; the former purchased for him by his generous uncle Francis, the latter given by his cousin Mr. Knight. This was no very gross case of plurality, according to the ideas of that time, for the two villages were little more than a mile apart, and their united populations scarcely amounted to three hundred. In the same year he married Cassandra, youngest daughter of the Rev. Thomas Leigh, of the family of Leighs of Warwickshire, who, having been a fellow of All Souls, held the College living of Harpsden, near Henley-upon-Thames. Mr. Thomas Leigh was a younger brother of Dr. Theophilus Leigh, a personage well known at Oxford in his day, and his day was not a short one, for he lived to be ninety, and held the Mastership of Balliol College for above half a century. He was a man more famous for his sayings than his doings, overflowing with puns and witticisms and sharp retorts ; but his most serious joke was his practical one of living much longer than had been expected or intended. He was a fellow of Corpus, and the story is that the Balliol men, unable to agree in electing one of their own number to the Mastership, chose him, partly under the idea that he was in weak health and likely soon to cause another vacancy. It was afterwards said that his long incumbency had been a judgment on the Society for having elected an *Out-College Man.** I imagine that the front of Balliol towards Broad Street which has recently been pulled down must have been built, or at least restored, while he was Master, for the Leigh arms were placed under the cornice at the corner nearest to Trinity gates. The beautiful building lately erected has destroyed this record, and thus 'monuments themselves memorials need.'

His fame for witty and agreeable conversation extended beyond the bounds of the University. Mrs. Thrale, in a letter to Dr. Johnson, writes thus : 'Are you acquainted with Dr. Leigh,† the Master of Balliol College, and are you not delighted with his gaiety of

---

* There seems to have been some doubt as to the validity of this election ; for Hearne says that it was referred to the Visitor, who confirmed it. (Hearne's *Diaries*, **v. 2.**)

† Mrs. Thrale writes Dr. *Lee*, but there can be no doubt of the identity of person.

manners and youthful vivacity, now that he is eighty-
six years of age? I never heard a more perfect or
excellent pun than his, when some one told him how,
in a late dispute among the Privy Councillors, the
Lord Chancellor struck the table with such violence
that he split it. "No, no, no," replied the Master;
"I can hardly persuade myself that he *split the table*,
though I believe he *divided* the *Board*."'

Some of his sayings of course survive in family
tradition. He was once calling on a gentleman
notorious for never opening a book, who took him
into a room overlooking the Bath Road, which was
then a great thoroughfare for travellers of every class,
saying rather pompously, 'This, Doctor, I call my
study.' The Doctor, glancing his eye round the
room, in which no books were to be seen, replied,
'And very well named too, sir, for you know Pope
tells us, "The proper *study* of mankind is *Man*."'
When my father went to Oxford he was honoured
with an invitation to dine with this dignified cousin.
Being a raw undergraduate, unaccustomed to the
habits of the University, he was about to take off his
gown, as if it were a great coat, when the old man,
then considerably turned eighty, said, with a grim
smile, 'Young man, you need not strip: we are not
going to fight.' This humour remained in him so
strongly to the last that he might almost have supplied Pope with another instance of 'the ruling passion
strong in death,' for only three days before he expired,
being told that an old acquaintance was lately married,
having recovered from a long illness by eating eggs,

and that the wits said that he **had** been egged on to matrimony, **he** immediately trumped the joke, saying, 'Then **may the yoke sit easy** on him.' I do not know **from** what common ancestor **the** Master of **Balliol and** his great-niece Jane Austen, **with some** others **of** the family, may have derived **the** keen sense of humour **which** they certainly possessed.

Mr. and Mrs. **George** Austen resided first at Deane, but removed in 1771 to Steventon, which was their residence for about thirty **years.** They commenced their married **life with the** charge **of a little** child, a son of the celebrated Warren **Hastings, who** had **been** committed to the care of Mr. Austen **before his** marriage, probably through **the influence** of his **sister, Mrs.** Hancock, whose husband at **that** time **held some office** under Hastings in India. **Mr.** Gleig, in his '**Life of** Hastings,' **says** that his **son** George, the offspring **of** his first marriage, **was sent** to England in 1761 **for** his education, but **that** he **had** never been able **to** ascertain **to whom** this precious charge **was** entrusted, nor what became of him. **I am** able **to** state, from family **tradition,** that **he died** young, of **what was** then **called** putrid sore throat; **and** that **Mrs.** Austen **had become so** much attached **to** him **that** she always declared that his death had been as **great a** grief to her as if he had been a child **of her** own.

About this **time,** the grandfather of Mary Russell Mitford, **Dr. Russell, was** Rector of **the** adjoining parish **of Ashe ; so that the** parents **of** two popular female writers **must have been** intimately acquainted with each **other.**

As my subject carries me back about a hundred years, it will afford occasions for observing many changes gradually effected in the manners and habits of society, which I may think it worth while to mention. They may be little things, but time gives a certain importance even to trifles, as it imparts a peculiar flavour to wine. The most ordinary articles of domestic life are looked on with some interest, if they are brought to light after being long buried; and we feel a natural curiosity to know what was done and said by our forefathers, even though it may be nothing wiser or better than what we are daily doing or saying ourselves. Some of this generation may be little aware how many conveniences, now considered to be necessaries and matters of course, were unknown to their grandfathers and grandmothers. The lane between Deane and Steventon has long been as smooth as the best turnpike road; but when the family removed from the one residence to the other in 1771, it was a mere cart track, so cut up by deep ruts as to be impassable for a light carriage. Mrs. Austen, who was not then in strong health, performed the short journey on a feather-bed, placed upon some soft articles of furniture in the waggon which held their household goods. In those days it was not unusual to set men to work with shovel and pickaxe to fill up ruts and holes in roads seldom used by carriages, on such special occasions as a funeral or a wedding. Ignorance and coarseness of language also were still lingering even upon higher levels of society than might have been expected to retain such mists. About this time, a neighbouring squire, a man of many acres, referred the following difficulty to Mr. Austen's decision : 'You know all about these sort of things. Do tell us. Is Paris in France, or France in Paris? for my wife has been disputing with me about it.' The same gentleman, narrating some conversation which he had heard between the rector and his wife, represented the latter as beginning her reply to her husband with a round oath ; and when his daughter called him to task, reminding him that Mrs. Austen never swore, he replied, ' Now, Betty, why do you pull me up for nothing ? that's neither here nor there; you know very well that's only *my way of telling the story.* Attention has lately been called by a celebrated writer to the inferiority of the clergy to the laity of England two centuries ago. The charge no doubt is true, if the rural clergy are to be compared with that higher section of country gentlemen who went into parliament, and mixed in London society, and took the lead in their several counties ; but it might be found less true if they were to be compared, as in all fairness they ought to be, with that lower section with whom they usually associated. The smaller landed proprietors, who seldom went farther from home than their county town, from the squire with his thousand acres to the yeoman who cultivated his hereditary property of one or two hundred, then formed a numerous class—each the aristocrat of his own parish; and there was probably a greater difference in manners and refinement between this class and that immediately above them than could now be found between any two persons who rank as gentlemen. For in the progress of civilisation, though all orders may make some progress, yet it is most perceptible in the lower. It is a process of 'levelling up;' the rear rank 'dressing up,' as it were, close to the front rank. When Hamlet mentions, as something which he had 'for *three years taken* note of,' that 'the toe of the peasant comes so near the heel of the courtier,' it was probably intended by Shakspeare as a satire on his own times; but it expressed a principle which is working at all times in which society makes any progress. I believe that a century ago the improvement in most country parishes began with the clergy; and that in those days a rector who chanced to be a gentleman and a scholar found himself superior to his chief parishioners in information and manners, and became a sort of centre of refinement and politeness.

Mr. Austen was a remarkably good-looking man, both in his youth and his old age. During his year of office at Oxford he had been called 'the handsome Proctor;' and at Bath, when more than seventy years old, he attracted observation by his fine features and abundance of snow-white hair. Being a good scholar he was able to prepare two of his sons for the University, and to direct the studies of his other children, whether sons or daughters, as well as to increase his income by taking pupils.

In Mrs. Austen also was to be found the germ of much of the ability which was concentrated in Jane, but of which others of her children had a share. She united strong **common** sense with a lively imagination, and often expressed herself, both in writing and in conversation, with epigrammatic force and point. **She** lived, like many of her family, to an advanced **age.** During the last years of her life she endured continual pain, not only patiently but with characteristic cheerfulness. She once said to me, 'Ah, my dear, you find me just where you left me—on the sofa. I sometimes think that God Almighty must have forgotten me ; but I dare say He will come for me in His own good time.' She died and was buried at Chawton, January 1827, aged eighty-eight.

Her own family were so much, and the rest of the world so little, to Jane Austen, that some brief mention of her brothers and sister is necessary in order to give any idea of the objects which principally occupied her thoughts and filled her heart, especially as **some of** them, from their characters or professions **in** life, may be supposed to have had more or less influence on her writings : though I feel some reluctance in bringing before public notice persons and circumstances essentially private.

Her eldest brother James, my own father, had, when a very young man, at St. John's College, Oxford, been the originator and chief supporter of a periodical paper called 'The Loiterer,' written somewhat on **the** plan **of** the 'Spectator' and its successors, but nearly confined to subjects connected with the University. **In** after life he used to speak very slightingly of this early work, which he had the better right to do, as, whatever may have been the degree of their merits, the best papers had certainly been written by himself.   He was well read in English literature, had a correct taste, and wrote readily and happily, both in prose and verse.   He was more than ten years older than Jane, and had, I believe, a large share in directing her reading and forming her taste.

Her second brother, Edward, had been a good deal separated from the rest of the family, as he was early adopted by his cousin, Mr. Knight, of Godmersham Park in Kent and Chawton House in Hampshire; and finally came into possession both of the property and the name.   But though a good deal separated in childhood, they were much together in after life, and Jane gave a large share of her affections to him and his children.   Mr. Knight was not only a very amiable man, kind and indulgent to all connected with him, but possessed also a spirit of fun and liveliness, which made him especially delightful to all young people.

Her third brother, Henry, had great conversational powers, and inherited from his father an eager and sanguine disposition.   He was a very entertaining companion, but had perhaps less steadiness of purpose, certainly less success in life, than his brothers. He became a clergyman when middle-aged; and an allusion to his sermons will be found in one of Jane's letters.   At one time he resided in London, and was useful in transacting his sister's business with her publishers.

Her two youngest brothers, Francis and Charles, were sailors during that glorious period of the British navy which comprises **the close of** the last and the beginning of the present century, when it was impossible **for an** officer to **be** almost always **afloat,** as these brothers were, without seeing service **which, in** these days, would **be** considered distinguished. Accordingly, **they** were continually engaged in actions of **more or less** importance, and sometimes gained **promotion by their** success. Both rose to the rank of Admiral, **and** carried **out** their flags to distant stations.

Francis lived to attain the very summit of his profession, having died, **in** his ninety-third **year,** G.C.B. **and** Senior **Admiral of** the Fleet, **in 1865.** He possessed great firmness of character, with **a** strong **sense** of duty, whether due **from** himself to others, **or from** others **to** himself. **He was** consequently **a strict** disciplinarian; but, as **he** was a very religious man, it was remarked of **him** (for in those **days,** at least, **it** was remarkable) **that** he maintained **this** discipline **without ever** uttering an oath or permitting one **in** his presence. On one occasion, when ashore in a seaside town, **he was** spoken of as ' *the* officer **who** kneeled at church ;' **a** custom which now happily would not **be** thought peculiar.

Charles was generally serving in frigates or sloops; blockading harbours, driving the ships of the enemy ashore, boarding gun-boats, and frequently making **small** prizes. At **one time** he was **absent** from England **on such** services **for** seven years together. In later life **he** commanded **the** Bellerophon, at the bombardment of St. Jean d'Acre in 1840. In 1850 he

went out in the Hastings, in command of the East
India and China station, but on the breaking out of
the Burmese war he transferred his flag to a steam
sloop, for the purpose of getting up the shallow
waters of the Irrawaddy, on board of which he died
of cholera in 1852, in the seventy-fourth year of his
age. His sweet temper and affectionate disposition,
in which he resembled his sister Jane, had secured to
him an unusual portion of attachment, not only from
his own family, but from all the officers and common
sailors who served under him. One who was with
him at his death has left this record of him : ' Our
good Admiral won the hearts of all by his gentleness
and kindness while he was struggling with disease,
and endeavouring to do his duty as Commander-in-
chief of the British naval forces in these waters. His
death was a great grief to the whole fleet. I know
that I cried bitterly when I found he was dead.' The
Order in Council of the Governor-General of India,
Lord Dalhousie, expresses ' admiration of the staunch
high spirit which, notwithstanding his age and previous sufferings, had led the Admiral to take his part
in the trying service which has closed his career.'

These two brothers have been dwelt on longer than
the others because their honourable career accounts
for Jane Austen's partiality for the Navy, as well as
for the readiness and accuracy with which she wrote
about it. She was always very careful not to meddle
with matters which she did not thoroughly understand.
She never touched upon politics, law, or medicine,
subjects which some novel writers have ventured on

rather too boldly, and have treated, perhaps, with
more brilliancy than accuracy. But with ships and
sailors she felt herself at home, or at least could
always trust to a brotherly critic to keep her right.
I believe that no flaw has ever been found in her
seamanship either in 'Mansfield Park' or in 'Persuasion.'

But dearest of all to the heart of Jane was her
sister Cassandra, about three years her senior. Their
sisterly affection for each other could scarcely be exceeded. Perhaps it began on Jane's side with the
feeling of deference natural to a loving child towards
a kind elder sister. Something of this feeling always
remained; and even in the maturity of her powers,
and in the enjoyment of increasing success, she would
still speak of Cassandra as of one wiser and better
than herself. In childhood, when the elder was sent
to the school of a Mrs. Latournelle, in the Forbury
at Reading, the younger went with her, not because
she was thought old enough to profit much by the
instruction there imparted, but because she would
have been miserable without her sister; her mother
observing that 'if Cassandra were going to have her
head cut off, Jane would insist on sharing her fate.'
This attachment was never interrupted or weakened.
They lived in the same home, and shared the same
bed-room, till separated by death. They were not
exactly alike. Cassandra's was the colder and calmer
disposition; she was always prudent and well judging,
but with less outward demonstration of feeling and
less sunniness of temper than Jane possessed. It was

remarked in her family that 'Cassandra had the *merit* of having her temper always under command, but that Jane had the *happiness* of a temper that never required to be commanded.' When 'Sense and Sensibility' came out, some persons, who knew the family slightly, surmised that the two elder Miss Dashwoods were intended by the author for her sister and herself; but this could not be the case. Cassandra's character might indeed represent the '*sense*' of Elinor, but Jane's had little in common with the '*sensibility*' of Marianne. The young woman who, before the age of twenty, could so clearly discern the failings of Marianne Dashwood, could hardly have been subject to them herself.

This was the small circle, continually enlarged, however, by the increasing families of four of her brothers, within which Jane Austen found her wholesome pleasures, duties, and interests, and beyond which she went very little into society during the last ten years of her life. There was so much that was agreeable and attractive in this family party that its members may be excused if they were inclined to live somewhat too exclusively within it. They might see in each other much to love and esteem, and something to admire. The family talk had abundance of spirit and vivacity, and was never troubled by disagreements even in little matters, for it was not their habit to dispute or argue with each other: above all, there was strong family affection and firm union, never to be broken but by death. It cannot be doubted that all this had its influence on the author in the construction of her stories, in which a family party usually supplies the narrow stage, while the interest is made to revolve round a few actors.

It will be seen also that though her circle of society was small, yet she found in her neighbourhood persons of good taste and cultivated minds. Her acquaintance, in fact, constituted the very class from which she took her imaginary characters, ranging from the member of parliament, or large landed proprietor, to the young curate or younger midshipman of equally good family ; and I think that the influence of these early associations may be traced in her writings, especially in two particulars. First, that she is entirely free from the vulgarity, which is so offensive in some novels, of dwelling on the outward appendages of wealth or rank, as if they were things to which the writer was unaccustomed ; and, secondly, that she deals as little with very low as with very high stations in life. She does not go lower than the Miss Steeles, Mrs. Elton, and John Thorpe, people of bad taste and underbred manners, such as are actually found sometimes mingling with better society. She has nothing resembling the Brangtons, or Mr. Dubster and his friend Tom Hicks, with whom Madame D'Arblay loved to season her stories, and to produce striking contrasts to her well bred characters.

## CHAPTER II.

*Description of Steventon—Life at Steventon—Changes of Habits and
Customs in the last Century.*

As the first twenty-five years, more than half of the
brief life of Jane Austen, were spent in the parsonage
of Steventon, some description of that place ought to
be given.   Steventon is a small rural village upon the
chalk hills of north Hants, situated in a winding
valley about seven miles from Basingstoke.   The
South-Western railway  crosses it by a short embank-
ment, and, as it curves round, presents a good view of
it on the left hand to those who are travelling down
the line, about three miles before entering the tunnel
under Popham Beacon.   It may be known to some
sportsmen, as lying in one of the best portions of the
Vine Hunt.   It is certainly not a picturesque country ;
it presents no grand or extensive views ; but the
features are small rather than plain.   The surface
continually swells and sinks, but the hills are not
bold, nor the valleys deep ; and though it is sufficiently
well clothed with woods and hedgerows, yet the
poverty of the soil in most places prevents the timber
from attaining a large size.   Still it has its beauties.
The lanes wind along in a natural curve, continually

fringed with irregular borders of native turf, and lead
to pleasant nooks **and** corners. One who knew and
loved it well very happily expressed its quiet charms,
when he wrote

> **True** taste is not fastidious, nor rejects,
> Because they may not come within the rule
> Of composition pure and picturesque,
> Unnumbered simple scenes which fill the leaves
> Of Nature's sketch book.

Of this somewhat tame country, Steventon, from
the fall of the ground, and the abundance of its timber,
is certainly one of the prettiest spots; **yet** one cannot
be surprised that, when Jane's mother, **a** little before
her marriage, was shown the scenery of her future
home, she should have thought it unattractive, compared with the broad river, the rich valley, and the
noble hills which she had been accustomed to behold
at her native home near Henley-upon-Thames.

**The** house itself stood in a shallow valley, surrounded by sloping meadows, well sprinkled with elm
trees, at the **end of** a small village of cottages, each
well provided with a **garden,** scattered about prettily
on either side of the road. It was sufficiently commodious to hold pupils in addition **to a** growing
family, and was in those times considered to be above
the average of parsonages; but the rooms were
finished with less elegance than would now be found
in the most ordinary dwellings. **No** cornice marked
the junction of wall and ceiling; while **the** beams
which supported the upper floors projected into the
rooms below in all their naked simplicity, **covered**

only by a coat of paint or whitewash : accordingly it has since been considered unworthy of being the Rectory house of a family living, and about forty-five years ago it was pulled down for the purpose of erecting a new house in a far better situation on the opposite side of the valley.

North of the house, the road from Deane to Pop-ham Lane ran at a sufficient distance from the front to allow a carriage drive, through turf and trees.  On the south side the ground rose gently, and was occu-pied by one of those old-fashioned gardens in which vegetables and flowers are combined, flanked and protected on the east by one of the thatched mud walls common in that country, and overshadowed by fine elms.  Along the upper or southern side of this garden, ran a terrace of the finest turf, which must have been in the writer's thoughts when she described Catharine Morland's childish delight in ' rolling down the green slope at the back of the house.'

But the chief beauty of Steventon consisted in its hedgerows.  A hedgerow, in that country, does not mean a thin formal line of quickset, but an irregular border of copse-wood and timber, often wide enough to contain within it a winding footpath, or a rough cart track.  Under its shelter the earliest primroses, anemones, and wild hyacinths were to be found ; sometimes, the first bird's-nest ; and, now and then, the unwelcome adder.  Two such hedgerows radiated, as it were, from the parsonage garden.  One, a con-tinuation of the turf terrace, proceeded westward, forming the southern boundary of the home meadows ;

and was formed into a rustic shrubbery, **with** occasional seats, **entitled** 'The Wood Walk.' **The** other ran **straight** up the hill, under the name **of** 'The Church Walk,' because **it** led to **the** parish **church, as** well **as** to a fine old manor-house, **of** Henry **VIII.**'s time, occupied by a family named Digweed, who have for more than a century rented it, together with the chief farm in the parish. The church itself—I speak of **it** as it **then** was, before **the** improvements made **by the present rector—**

A little spireless fane,<br>Just seen above the woody lane,

might have appeared **mean** and uninteresting **to an** ordinary observer; but the adept in church architecture would **have** known that it must have stood there some seven centuries, and would have found beauty in the very narrow early English windows, as well **as** in the general proportions of its little chancel; while its solitary position, far from the hum of the village, and within sight of no habitation, except **a** glimpse of the gray manor-house through its circling screen **of** sycamores, has in **it** something solemn and appropriate to the last resting-place of the silent dead. Sweet violets, both purple and white, **grow in** abundance beneath its south **wall.** One may imagine for how **many** centuries **the** ancestors of those little flowers **have** occupied **that** undisturbed, sunny nook, and **may** think how few living families can boast of as ancient **a** tenure **of their** land. **Large** elms protrude their rough branches; old hawthorns shed their annual blossoms over the graves; and the hollow yew-tree must be at least coeval with the church.

But whatever may be the beauties or defects of the surrounding scenery, this was the residence of Jane Austen for twenty-five years. This was the cradle of her genius. These were the first objects which inspired her young heart with a sense of the beauties of nature. In strolls along those wood-walks, thick-coming fancies rose in her mind, and gradually assumed the forms in which they came forth to the world. In that simple church she brought them all into subjection to the piety which ruled her in life, and supported her in death.

The home at Steventon must have been, for many years, a pleasant and prosperous one. The family was unbroken by death, and seldom visited by sorrow. Their situation had some peculiar advantages beyond those of ordinary rectories. Steventon was a family living. Mr. Knight, the patron, was also proprietor of nearly the whole parish. He never resided there, and consequently the rector and his children came to be regarded in the neighbourhood as a kind of representatives of the family. They shared with the principal tenant the command of an excellent manor, and enjoyed, in this reflected way, some of the consideration usually awarded to landed proprietors. They were not rich, but, aided by Mr. Austen's powers of teaching, they had enough to afford a good education to their sons and daughters, to mix in the best society of the neighbourhood, and to exercise a liberal hospitality to their own relations and friends. A carriage and a pair of horses were kept. This might imply a higher style of living in our days than it did in theirs. There were then no assessed taxes. The carriage, once bought, entailed little further expense ; and the horses probably, like Mr. Bennet's, were often employed on farm work. Moreover, it should be remembered that a pair of horses in those days were almost necessary, if ladies were to move about at all ; for neither the condition of the roads nor the style of carriage-building admitted of any comfortable vehicle being drawn by a single horse. When one looks at the few specimens still remaining of coach-building in the last century, it strikes one that the chief object of the builders must have been to combine the greatest possible weight with the least possible amount of accommodation.

The family lived in close intimacy with two cousins, Edward and Jane Cooper, the children of Mrs. Austen's eldest sister, and Dr. Cooper, the vicar of Sonning, near Reading. The Coopers lived for some years at Bath, which seems to have been much frequented in those days by clergymen retiring from work. I believe that Cassandra and Jane sometimes visited them there, and that Jane thus acquired the intimate knowledge of the topography and customs of Bath, which enabled her to write ' Northanger Abbey ' long before she resided there herself. After the death of their own parents, the two young Coopers paid long visits at Steventon. Edward Cooper did not live undistinguished. When an undergraduate at Oxford, he gained the prize for Latin hexameters on

'Hortus Anglicus' in 1791 ; and in later life he was known by a work on prophecy, called 'The Crisis,' and other religious publications, especially for several volumes of Sermons, much preached in many pulpits in my youth. Jane Cooper was married from her uncle's house at Steventon, to Captain, afterwards Sir Thomas Williams, under whom Charles Austen served in several ships. She was a dear friend of her namesake, but was fated to become a cause of great sorrow to her, for a few years after the marriage she was suddenly killed by an accident to her carriage.

There was another cousin closely associated with them at Steventon, who must have introduced greater variety into the family circle. This was the daughter of Mr. Austen's only sister, Mrs. Hancock. This cousin had been educated in Paris, and married to a Count de Feuillade, of whom I know little more than that he perished by the guillotine during the French Revolution. Perhaps his chief offence was his rank; but it was said that the charge of 'incivism,' under which he suffered, rested on the fact of his having laid down some arable land into pasture—a sure sign of his intention to embarrass the Republican Government by producing a famine! His wife escaped through dangers and difficulties to England, was received for some time into her uncle's family, and finally married her cousin Henry Austen. During the short peace of Amiens, she and her second husband went to France, in the hope of recovering some of the Count's property, and there narrowly escaped being included amongst the *détenus*. Orders had been given by Buonaparte's government to detain all English travellers, but at the post-houses Mrs. Henry Austen gave the necessary orders herself, and her French was so perfect that she passed everywhere for a native, and her husband escaped under this protection.

She was a clever woman, and highly accomplished, after the French rather than the English mode; and in those days, when intercourse with the Continent was long interrupted by war, such an element in the society of a country parsonage must have been a rare acquisition. The sisters may have been more indebted to this cousin than to Mrs. La Tournelle's teaching for the considerable knowledge of French which they possessed. She also took the principal parts in the private theatricals in which the family several times indulged, having their summer theatre in the barn, and their winter one within the narrow limits of the dining-room, where the number of the audience must have been very limited. On these occasions, the prologues and epilogues were written by Jane's eldest brother, and some of them are very vigorous and amusing. Jane was only twelve years old at the time of the earliest of these representations, and not more than fifteen when the last took place. She was, however, an early observer, and it may be reasonably supposed that some of the incidents and feelings which are so vividly painted in the Mansfield Park theatricals are due to her recollections of these entertainments.

Some time before they left Steventon, one great

affliction came upon the family. Cassandra was engaged to be married to a young clergyman. He had not sufficient private fortune to permit an immediate union ; but the engagement was not likely to be a hopeless or a protracted one, for he had a prospect of early preferment from a nobleman with whom he was connected both by birth and by personal friendship. He accompanied this friend to the West Indies, as chaplain to his regiment, and there died of yellow fever, to the great concern of his friend and patron, who afterwards declared that, if he had known of the engagement, he would not have permitted him to go out to such a climate. This little domestic tragedy caused great and lasting grief to the principal sufferer, and could not but cast a gloom over the whole party. The sympathy of Jane was probably, from her age, and her peculiar attachment to her sister, the deepest of all.

Of Jane herself I know of no such definite tale of love to relate. Her reviewer in the 'Quarterly' of January 1821 observes, concerning the attachment of Fanny Price to Edmund Bertram : ' The silence in which this passion is cherished, the slender hopes and enjoyments by which it is fed, the restlessness and jealousy with which it fills a mind naturally active, contented, and unsuspicious, the manner in which it tinges every event, and every reflection, are painted with a vividness and a detail of which we can scarcely conceive any one but a female, and we should almost add, a female writing from recollection, capable.' This conjecture, however probable, was wide of the mark. The picture was drawn from the intuitive perceptions of genius, not from personal experience. In no circumstance of her life was there any similarity between herself and her heroine in 'Mansfield Park.' She did not indeed pass through life without being the object of **warm** affection. In her youth she had declined **the** addresses of a gentleman who had the recommendations of good character, and connections, and position **in** life, **of** everything, in **fact,** except the subtle power of touching her heart. There is, however, one passage of romance in her history with which I am imperfectly acquainted, and **to** which I am unable to assign name, or date, or place, though I have it on sufficient authority. Many years after her death, some circumstances **induced** her sister **Cassandra to** break through her habitual reticence, and to speak of it. She said that, while staying **at** some **seaside** place, **they** became acquainted with **a** gentleman, whose charm of person, mind, and **manners was** such **that** Cassandra thought **him** worthy to possess and likely to win her sister's **love.** When they parted, he expressed his intention of soon seeing them again ; and Cassandra felt no doubt as to his motives. But they **never** again met. Within a short time they heard **of** his sudden death. I believe that, if Jane ever loved, **it was** this unnamed gentleman ; but the acquaintance **had** been short, and I am unable to say whether her feelings were of such a nature **as to** affect her happiness.

Any description that I might attempt of the family life at Steventon, which closed soon after I was born,

could be little better than a fancy-piece.   There is
no doubt that if we look into the households of the
clergy and the small gentry of that period, we should
see some things which would seem strange to us, and
should miss many more to which we are accustomed.
Every hundred years, and especially a century like
the last, marked by an extraordinary advance in
wealth, luxury, and refinement of taste, as well as in
the mechanical arts which embellish our houses, must
produce a great change in their aspect.  These
changes are always at work ; they are going on now,
but so silently that we take no note of them.  Men
soon forget the small objects which they leave behind
them as they drift down the stream of life.  As Pope
says—

> Nor does life's stream for observation stay ;
> It hurries all too fast to mark their way.

Important inventions, such as the applications of
steam, gas, and electricity, may find their places in
history ; but not so the alterations, great as they may
be, which have taken place in the appearance of our
dining and drawing-rooms.  Who can now record the
degrees by which the custom prevalent in my youth
of asking each other to take wine together at dinner
became obsolete?  Who will be able to fix, twenty
years hence, the date when our dinners began to be
carved and handed round by servants, instead of
smoking before our eyes and noses on the table?  To
record such little matters would indeed be ' to chro-
nicle small beer.'  But, in a slight memoir like this,

I may be allowed to note some of those changes in social habits which give **a** colour **to** history, but which the historian has the greatest difficulty **in** recovering.

**At** that time the dinner-table presented **a far** less splendid appearance than it does now. It was appropriated to solid food, rather than to flowers, fruits, and decorations. Nor was there much glitter of plate upon it; for the early dinner hour rendered candlesticks unnecessary, and silver forks had not come into general use: while the broad rounded end of the knives indicated the substitute generally used instead of them.*

The dinners too were more homely, though not less plentiful and savoury ; and the bill of fare **in one** house would not be so like that in another **as it is** now, for family receipts were held in high estimation. **A** grandmother of culinary talent could bequeath **to** her descendant fame for some particular dish, and

---

* The celebrated Beau Brummel, who was so intimate with George IV. as to be able to quarrel with him, was born in 1771. It is reported that when he was questioned about his parents, he replied that it was long since he had heard of them, but that he imagined the worthy couple must have cut their own throats by that time, because when he last saw them they were eating peas with their knives. Yet Brummel's father had probably lived in good society ; and was certainly able to put his son into a fashionable regiment, and to leave him 30,000*l.*[1] Raikes believes that he had been Secretary to Lord North. Thackeray's idea that he had been a footman cannot stand against the authority of **Raikes,** who was intimate with the son.

---

[1] Raikes's *Memoirs,* vol. ii. p. 207.

might influence the family dinner for many generations.

**Dos est** magna parentium
**Virtus.**

One house would pride itself on its ham, another on its game-pie, and a third on its superior furmity, or tansey-pudding.  Beer and home-made wines, especially mead, were more largely consumed.  Vegetables were less plentiful and less various.  Potatoes were used, but not so abundantly as now; and there was an idea that they were to be eaten only with roast meat.  They were novelties to a tenant's wife who was entertained at Steventon Parsonage, certainly less than a hundred years ago; and when Mrs. Austen advised her to plant them in her own garden, she replied, ‘No, no; they are very well for you gentry, but they must be terribly *costly to rear.*’

But a still greater difference would be found in the furniture of the rooms, which would appear to us lamentably scanty.  There was a general deficiency of carpeting in sitting-rooms, bed-rooms, and passages. A pianoforte, or rather a spinnet or harpsichord, was by no means a necessary appendage.  It was to be found only where there was a decided taste for music, not so common then as now, or in such great houses as would probably contain a billiard-table.  There would often be but one sofa in the house, and that a stiff, angular, uncomfortable article.  There were no deep easy-chairs, nor other appliances for lounging; for to lie down, or even to lean back, was a luxury permitted only to old persons or invalids. It was said of a nobleman, a personal friend of George III. and a model gentleman of his day, that **he** would have **made the** tour of Europe **without** ever touching the back of his travelling carriage. But perhaps we should be most struck with the total absence of those elegant little articles which now embellish and encumber our drawing-room tables. We should miss the sliding bookcases and picture-stands, the letter-weighing machines and envelope cases, the periodicals and illustrated newspapers—above all, the countless swarm of photograph books which now threaten to swallow up all space. A small writing-desk, with a smaller **work-box,** or netting-case, was all that each young **lady** contributed **to** occupy the table; for the large family work-basket, though often produced in the parlour, lived in the closet.

There must have been more dancing throughout the country in those days than **there is now: and it** seems to have sprung up more spontaneously, as if it were a natural production, with less fastidiousness as to the quality of music, lights, and floor. Many country towns had a monthly ball throughout the winter, in some of which the same apartment served for dancing and tea-room. Dinner parties more frequently ended with an extempore dance on the carpet, to the music of a harpsichord in the house, or a fiddle from the village. This was always supposed to be **for** the entertainment of the young people, but many, who had little pretension to youth, were very ready to join in it. There can be no doubt that

Jane herself enjoyed dancing, for she attributes this taste to her favourite heroines ; in most of her works, a ball or a private dance is mentioned, and made of importance.

Many things connected with the ball-rooms of those days have now passed into oblivion. The barbarous law which confined the lady to one partner throughout the evening must indeed have been abolished before Jane went to balls. It must be observed, however, that this custom was in one respect advantageous to the gentleman, inasmuch as it rendered his duties more practicable. He was bound to call upon his partner the next morning, and it must have been convenient to have only one lady for whom he was obliged

> To gallop all the country over,
> The last night's partner to behold,
> And humbly hope she caught no cold.

But the stately minuet still reigned supreme; and every regular ball commenced with it. It was a slow and solemn movement, expressive of grace and dignity, rather than of merriment. It abounded in formal bows and courtesies, with measured paces, forwards, backwards and sideways, and many complicated gyrations. It was executed by one lady and gentleman, amidst the admiration, or the criticism, of surrounding spectators. In its earlier and most palmy days, as when Sir Charles and Lady Grandison delighted the company by dancing it at their own wedding, the gentleman wore a dress sword, and the lady was armed with a fan of nearly equal dimensions. Addison observes that 'women are armed with fans, as men with swords, and sometimes do more execution with them.' The graceful carriage of each weapon was considered a test of high breeding. The clownish man was in danger of being tripped up by his sword getting between his legs : the fan held clumsily looked more of a burden than an ornament; while in the hands of an adept it could be made to speak a language of its own.* It was not everyone who felt qualified to make this public exhibition, and I have been told that those ladies who intended to dance minuets, used to distinguish themselves from others by wearing a particular kind of lappet on their head-dress. I have heard also of another curious proof of the respect in which this dance was held. Gloves immaculately clean were considered requisite for its due performance, while gloves a little soiled were thought good enough for a country dance; and accordingly some prudent ladies provided themselves with two pairs for their several purposes. The minuet expired with the last century : but long after it had ceased to be danced publicly it was taught to boys and girls, in order to give them a graceful carriage.

* See 'Spectator,' No. 102, on the Fan Exercise. Old gentlemen who had survived the fashion of wearing swords were known to regret the disuse of that custom, because it put an end to one way of distinguishing those who had, from those who had not, been used to good society. To wear the sword easily was an art which, like swimming and skating, required to be learned in youth. Children could practise it early with their toy swords adapted to their size.

Hornpipes, cotillons, and reels, were occasionally danced; but the chief occupation of the evening was the interminable country dance, in which all could join. This dance presented a great show of enjoyment, but it was not without its peculiar troubles. The ladies and gentlemen were ranged apart from each other in opposite rows, so that the facilities for flirtation, or interesting intercourse, were not so great as might have been desired by both parties. Much heart-burning and discontent sometimes arose as to *who* should stand above *whom*, and especially as to who was entitled to the high privilege of calling and leading off the first dance: and no little indignation was felt at the lower end of the room when any of the leading couples retired prematurely from their duties, and did not condescend to dance up and down the whole set. We may rejoice that these causes of irritation no longer exist; and that if such feelings as jealousy, rivalry, and discontent ever touch celestial bosoms in the modern ball-room they must arise from different and more recondite sources.

I am tempted to add a little about the difference of personal habits. It may be asserted as a general truth, that less was left to the charge and discretion of servants, and more was done, or superintended, by the masters and mistresses. With regard to the mistresses, it is, I believe, generally understood, that at the time to which I refer, a hundred years ago, they took a personal part in the higher branches of cookery, as well as in the concoction of home-made wines, and distilling of herbs for domestic medicines, which are nearly allied to the same art. Ladies did not disdain to spin the thread of which the household linen was woven. Some ladies liked to wash with their own hands their choice china **after** breakfast **or tea.** In one **of** my earliest child's **books, a** little girl, the daughter of a gentleman, is taught **by** her mother to make her own bed **before** leaving **her** chamber. It was not so much that they had not servants to do all these things for them, as that they took an interest in such occupations. And it must be borne in mind how many sources of interest enjoyed by this generation were then closed, or very scantily opened to ladies. A very small minority of them cared much for literature or science. Music was not a very common, and drawing was **a still** rarer, accomplishment ; needlework, in some form or other, was their chief sedentary employment.

But **I** doubt whether the rising generation are equally aware how much gentlemen also did for themselves in those times, and whether some things that **I can** mention will not be a surprise to them. Two homely proverbs were held in higher estimation in my early days than they are now—'The master's eye makes the horse fat ;' and, ' If you would be well served, serve yourself.' Some gentlemen took pleasure in being their own gardeners, performing all the scientific, and some of the manual, work themselves. Well-dressed young men of my acquaintance, who had their coat from a London tailor, would always brush their evening suit themselves, rather than entrust it to the carelessness of a rough servant, and to the risks of dirt and grease in the kitchen ; for in

those days servants' halls were not common in the
houses of the clergy and the smaller country gentry.
It was quite natural that Catherine Morland should
have contrasted the magnificence of the offices at
Northanger Abbey with the few shapeless pantries
in her father's parsonage.  A young man who expected to have his things packed or unpacked for him
by a servant, when he travelled, would have been
thought exceptionally fine, or exceptionally lazy.
When my uncle undertook to teach me to shoot, his
first lesson was how to clean my own gun.  It was
thought meritorious on the evening of a hunting day,
to turn out after dinner, lanthorn in hand, and visit
the stable, to ascertain that the horse had been well
cared for.  This was of the more importance, because,
previous to the introduction of clipping, about the
year 1820, it was a difficult and tedious work to make
a long-coated hunter dry and comfortable, and was
often very imperfectly done.  Of course, such things
were not practised by those who had gamekeepers,
and stud-grooms, and plenty of well-trained servants;
but they were practised by many who were unequi-
vocally gentlemen, and whose grandsons, occupying
the same position in life, may perhaps be astonished
at being told that ' *such things were.*'

I have drawn pictures for which my own experience, or what I heard from others in my youth,
have supplied the materials.  Of course, they cannot
be universally applicable.  Such details varied in
various circles, and were changed very gradually; nor
can I pretend to tell how much of what I have said

is descriptive of the family life **at Steventon in Jane** Austen's **youth.** I am sure that the **ladies** there had nothing **to do with** the mysteries **of the** stew-pot **or** the preserving-pan ; **but it is** probable that their way **of** life differed a little from ours, and would have appeared **to us more** homely. It may be that useful articles, which would not now be produced in drawing-rooms, were hemmed, and marked, and darned in the old-fashioned parlour. But all this concerned only the outer life ; **there** was as much cultivation and **re-**finement of mind as now, with probably more studied courtesy and ceremony of manner to visitors ; whilst certainly **in** that family literary pursuits **were** not neglected.

I remember to have heard of only two **little** things different from modern customs. One was, that **on** hunting mornings the young men usually took their hasty breakfast **in** the kitchen. **The** early hour at which hounds then met may account for this ; and probably the custom began, if it did not end, when they were boys ; for they hunted at an early age, **in a** scrambling sort **of way,** upon any pony **or** donkey that they could procure, or, in default of such luxuries, on foot. **I have been** told that Sir Francis Austen, when seven years old, **bought** on his own account, it must be supposed with his father's permission, **a** pony for a guinea and a half; **and** after riding him with great **success** for two seasons, sold him for a guinea more. One may wonder how the child could have **so** much money, and how **the** animal could have been obtained **for** so little. **The** same authority informs

me that his first cloth suit was made from a scarlet
habit, which, according to the fashion of the times,
had been his mother's usual morning dress. If all
this is true, the future admiral of the British Fleet
must have cut a conspicuous figure in the hunting-
field. The other peculiarity was that, when the roads
were dirty, the sisters took long walks in pattens.
This defence against wet and dirt is now seldom seen.
The few that remain are banished from good society,
and employed only in menial work; but a hundred
and fifty years ago they were celebrated in poetry,
and considered so clever a contrivance that Gay, in
his 'Trivia,' ascribes the invention to a god stimulated
by his passion for a mortal damsel, and derives the
name 'Patten' from 'Patty.'

> The patten now supports each frugal dame,
> Which from the blue-eyed Patty takes the name.

But mortal damsels have long ago discarded the
clumsy implement. First it dropped its iron ring and
became a clog; afterwards it was fined down into the
pliant galoshe—lighter to wear and more effectual to
protect—a no less manifest instance of gradual improvement than Cowper indicates when he traces
through eighty lines of poetry his 'accomplished sofa'
back to the original three-legged stool.

As an illustration of the purposes which a patten
was intended to serve, I add the following epigram,
written by Jane Austen's uncle, Mr. Leigh Perrot, on
reading in a newspaper the marriage of Captain Foote
to Miss Patten :—

> Through the rough paths of life, with a patten your guard,
>   May you safely and pleasantly jog ;
> May the knot never slip, nor the ring press too hard,
>   Nor the *Foot* find the *Patten* a **clog.**

At the time when Jane Austen lived at Steventon, a work was carried on in the neighbouring cottages which ought to be recorded, because it has long ceased to exist.

Up to the beginning of the present century, poor women found profitable employment in spinning flax or wool. This was a better occupation for them than straw plaiting, inasmuch as it was carried on **at** the family hearth, and did not admit of gadding and gossiping about the village. **The** implement used was **a** long narrow machine **of** wood, raised **on legs,** furnished at one end with **a large** wheel, and **at** the other with a spindle on which the flax or wool was loosely wrapped, connected together by **a** loop of string. One hand turned the wheel, while the other formed the thread. The outstretched arms, the advanced foot, the sway of the whole figure backwards and forwards, produced picturesque attitudes, and displayed whatever of grace or beauty **the** work-woman might possess.* Some ladies were **fond** of spinning, but they worked in **a** quieter manner, sitting at **a** neat little machine **of** varnished wood, like Tunbridge ware, generally turned by the **foot,** with a **basin** of water at hand **to supply** the moisture required **for** forming the thread, **which** the cottager took by a **more** direct and

---

* Mrs. Gaskell, in her tale **of** 'Sylvia's Lovers,' declares that this hand-spinning rivalled harp-playing in its gracefulness.

natural process from her own mouth.  I remember
two such elegant little wheels in our own family.

It may be observed that this hand-spinning is the
most primitive of female accomplishments, and can
be traced back to the earliest times.  Ballad poetry
and fairy tales are full of allusions to it.  The term
' spinster ' still testifies to its having been the ordinary
employment of the English young woman.  It was
the labour assigned to the ejected nuns by the rough
earl who said, 'Go spin, ye jades, go spin.'  It was
the employment at which Roman matrons and Gre-
cian princesses presided amongst their handmaids.
Heathen mythology celebrated it in the three Fates
spinning and measuring out the thread of human
life.  Holy Scripture honours it in those ' wise-hearted
women ' who ' did spin with their hands, and brought
that which they had spun ' for the construction of the
Tabernacle in the wilderness: and an old English
proverb carries it still farther back to the time ' when
Adam delved and Eve span.'  But, at last, this time-
honoured domestic manufacture is quite extinct
amongst us—crushed by the power of steam, over-
borne by a countless host of spinning jennies, and I
can only just remember some of its last struggles for
existence in the Steventon cottages.

# CHAPTER III.

*Early Compositions—Friends at Ashe—A very old Letter—Lines on the Death of Mrs. Lefroy—Observations on Jane Austen's Letter-writing —Letters.*

I KNOW little of Jane Austen's childhood. Her mother followed a custom, not unusual in those days, though it seems strange to us, of putting out her babies to be nursed in a cottage in the village. The infant was daily visited by one or both of its parents, and frequently brought to them at the parsonage, but the cottage was its home, and must have remained so till it was old enough to run about and talk; for I know that one of them, in after life, used to speak of his foster mother as 'Movie,' the name by which he had called her in his infancy. It may be that the contrast between the parsonage house and the best class of cottages was not quite so extreme then as it would be now, that the one was somewhat less luxurious, and the other less squalid. It would certainly seem from the results that it was a wholesome and invigorating system, for the children were all strong and healthy. Jane was probably treated like the rest in this respect. In childhood every available opportunity of instruction was made use of. According to the ideas of the time, she was well educated, though

not highly accomplished, and she certainly enjoyed
that important element of mental training, associating
at home with persons of cultivated intellect.  It cannot be doubted that her early years were bright and
happy, living, as she did, with indulgent parents, in a
cheerful home, not without agreeable variety of society.
To these sources of enjoyment must be added the first
stirrings of talent within her, and the absorbing interest of original composition.  It is impossible to say
at how early an age she began to write.  There are
copy books extant containing tales some of which
must have been composed while she was a young girl,
as they had amounted to a considerable number by
the time she was sixteen.  Her earliest stories are of
a slight and flimsy texture, and are generally intended
to be nonsensical, but the nonsense has much spirit
in it.  They are usually preceded by a dedication of
mock solemnity to some one of her family.  It would
seem that the grandiloquent dedications prevalent in
those days had not escaped her youthful penetration.
Perhaps the most characteristic feature in these early
productions is that, however puerile the matter, they
are always composed in pure simple English, quite
free from the over-ornamented style which might be
expected from so young a writer.  One of her juvenile
effusions is given, as a specimen of the kind of tran-
sitory amusement which Jane was continually supplying to the family party.

# THE MYSTERY.

## AN UNFINISHED COMEDY.

## DEDICATION.

### To the Rev. George Austen.

Sir,—I humbly solicit your patronage to the following Comedy, which, though an unfinished one, is, I flatter myself, as complete a *Mystery* as any of its kind.

I am, Sir, your most humble Servant,

The Author.

## THE MYSTERY, A COMEDY.

*DRAMATIS PERSONÆ.*

| *Men.* | *Women.* |
|---|---|
| Col. Elliott. | Fanny Elliott. |
| Old Humbug. | Mrs. Humbug |
| Young Humbug. | *and* |
| Sir Edward Spangle | Daphne. |
| *and* | |
| Corydon. | |

## ACT I.

Scene I.—*A Garden.*

*Enter* Corydon.

*Corydon.* But hush: I am interrupted. [*Exit* Corydon.

*Enter* Old Humbug *and his* Son, *talking.*

*Old Hum.* It is for that reason that I wish you to follow my advice. Are you convinced of its propriety?

*Young Hum.* I am, sir, and will certainly act in the manner you have pointed out to me.

*Old Hum.* Then let us return to the house.  [*Exeunt.*

Scene II.—*A parlour in* Humbug's *house.* Mrs. Humbug and Fanny *discovered at work.*

*Mrs. Hum.* You understand me, my love ?

*Fanny.* Perfectly, ma'am : pray continue your narration.

*Mrs. Hum.* Alas! it is nearly concluded ; for I have nothing more to say on the subject.

*Fanny.* Ah ! here is Daphne.

*Enter* Daphne.

*Daphne.* My dear Mrs. Humbug, how d'ye do? Oh ! Fanny, it is all over.

*Fanny.* Is it indeed !

*Mrs. Hum.* I'm very sorry to hear it.

*Fanny.* Then 'twas to no purpose that I——

*Daphne.* None upon earth.

*Mrs. Hum.* And what is to become of ——?

*Daphne.* Oh ! 'tis all settled. (*Whispers* Mrs. Humbug.)

*Fanny.* And how is it determined ?

*Daphne.* I'll tell you. (*Whispers* Fanny.)

*Mrs. Hum.* And is he to——?

*Daphne.* I'll tell you all I know of the matter. (*Whispers* Mrs. Humbug *and* Fanny.)

*Fanny.* Well, now I know everything about it, I'll go away.

*Mrs. Hum.*  
*Daphne.*  } And so will I.    [*Exeunt.*

Scene III.—*The curtain rises, and discovers* Sir Edward Spangle *reclined in an elegant attitude on a sofa fast asleep.*

*Enter* Col. Elliott.

*Col. E.* My daughter is not here, I see. There lies Sir

Edward.  Shall I tell him the secret?  No, he'll certainly blab it.  But he's asleep, and won't hear me ;—so I'll e'en venture.  (*Goes **up** to* Sir EDWARD, *whispers him, and exit.*)

END OF THE FIRST ACT.

FINIS.

Her own mature opinion of the desirableness of such an early habit of composition is given in the following words of a niece :—

'As I grew older, my aunt would talk to me more seriously of my reading and my amusements.  I had taken early to writing verses and stories, and I am sorry to think how I troubled her with reading them. She was very kind about it, and always had some praise to bestow, but at last she warned me against spending too much time upon them.  She said—how well I recollect it!—that she knew writing stories was a great amusement, and *she* thought a harmless one, though many people, she was aware, thought otherwise ; but that at my age it would be bad for me to be much taken up with my own compositions.  Later still—it was after she had gone to Winchester—she sent me a message to this effect, that if I would take her advice I should cease writing till I was sixteen ; that she had herself often wished she had read more, and written less in the corresponding years of her own life.'  As this niece was only twelve years old at the time of her aunt's death, these words seem to imply that the juvenile tales to which I have referred had, some of them at least, been written in her childhood.

But between these childish effusions, and the composition of her living works, there intervened another stage of her progress, during which she produced some stories, not without merit, but which she never considered worthy of publication. During this preparatory period her mind seems to have been working in a very different direction from that into which it ultimately settled. Instead of presenting faithful copies of nature, these tales were generally burlesques, ridiculing the improbable events and exaggerated sentiments which she had met with in sundry silly romances. Something of this fancy is to be found in 'Northanger Abbey,' but she soon left it far behind in her subsequent course. It would seem as if she were first taking note of all the faults to be avoided, and curiously considering how she ought *not* to write before she attempted to put forth her strength in the right direction. The family have, rightly, I think, declined to let these early works be published. Mr. Shortreed observed very pithily of Walter Scott's early rambles on the borders, ' He was makin' himsell a' the time ; but he didna ken, may be, what he was about till years had passed. At first he thought of little, I dare say, but the queerness and the fun.' And so, in a humbler way, Jane Austen was 'makin' hersell,' little thinking of future fame, but caring only for ' the queerness and the fun ;' and it would be as unfair to expose this preliminary process to the world, as it would be to display all that goes on behind the curtain of the theatre before it is drawn up.

It was, however, at Steventon that the real foundations of her fame were laid.   There some of her most successful writing was composed at such an early age as to make it surprising that so young a woman could 'have acquired the insight into character, and the nice observation of manners which they display.  'Pride and Prejudice,' which some consider the most brilliant of her novels, was the first finished, **if not** the first begun.   She began it in October 1796, before she was twenty-one years old, and completed it in about ten months, in August 1797.   The title then intended for it was 'First Impressions.'  'Sense and Sensibility' was begun, **in** its present form, immediately after **the** completion of **the** former, in November 1797 ; but something similar **in** story **and** character had been written earlier under the title **of** ' Elinor and Marianne ; ' **and** if, as is probable, **a** good deal of this earlier production was retained, it must form the earliest specimen of her writing that has been given to the world.  'Northanger Abbey,' though not prepared for the press till 1803, was certainly first composed in 1798.

Amongst the most valuable neighbours of the Austens were Mr. and Mrs. Lefroy and their family. He was rector **of** the adjoining parish of Ashe ; she was sister to Sir Egerton Brydges, to whom we are indebted for the earliest notice of Jane Austen that exists.  **In** his autobiography, speaking of his visits at Ashe, he writes thus : ' The nearest neighbours of the Lefroys were the Austens of Steventon.   I remember Jane Austen, the novelist, as a little child.

She was very intimate with Mrs. Lefroy, and much encouraged by her. Her mother was a Miss Leigh, whose paternal grandmother was sister to the first Duke of Chandos. Mr. Austen was of a Kentish family, of which several branches have been settled in the Weald of Kent, and some are still remaining there. When I knew Jane Austen, I never suspected that she was an authoress; but my eyes told me that she was fair and handsome, slight and elegant, but with cheeks a little too full.' One may wish that Sir Egerton had dwelt rather longer on the subject of these memoirs, instead of being drawn away by his extreme love for genealogies to her great-grandmother and ancestors. That great-grandmother however lives in the family records as Mary Brydges, a daughter of Lord Chandos, married in Westminster Abbey to Theophilus Leigh of Addlestrop in 1698. When a girl she had received a curious letter of advice and reproof, written by her mother from Constantinople. Mary, or ' Poll,' was remaining in England with her grandmother, Lady Bernard, who seems to have been wealthy and inclined to be too indulgent to her granddaughter. This letter is given. Any such authentic document, two hundred years old, dealing with domestic details, must possess some interest. This is remarkable, not only as a specimen of the homely language in which ladies of rank then expressed themselves, but from the sound sense which it contains. Forms of expression vary, but good sense and right principles are the same in the nineteenth that they were in the seventeenth century.

‘ MY DEARES POLL,

‘ Yʳ letters by Cousin Robbert Serle arrived here not before the 27ᵗʰ of Aprill, yett were they hartily wellcome to us, bringing yᵉ joyful news which a great while we had longed for of my most dear Mother & all other relations & friends good health which I beseech God continue to you all, & as I observe in yʳˢ to yʳ Sister Betty yᵉ extraordinary kindness of (as I may truly say) the best Mothʳ & Gⁿᵈ Mothʳ in the world in pinching herself to make you fine, so I cannot but admire her great good Housewifry in affording you so very plentifull an allowance, & yett to increase her Stock at the rate I find she hath done ; & think I can never sufficiently mind you how very much it is yʳ duty on all occasions to pay her yʳ gratitude in all humble submission & obedience to all her commands soe long as you live. I must tell you ’tis to her bounty & care in yᵉ greatest measure you are like to owe yʳ well living in this world, & as you cannot but be very sensible you are an extra- ordinary charge to her so it behoves you to take par- ticular heed thᵗ in yᵉ whole course of yʳ life, you render her a proportionable comfort, especially since ’tis yᵉ best way you can ever hope to make her such amends as God requires of yʳ hands. but Poll! it grieves me a little & yᵗ I am forced to take notice of & reprove you for some vaine expressions in yʳ lettʳˢ to yʳ Sister—you say concerning yʳ allowance “you aime to bring yʳ bread & cheese even ” in this I do not discommend you, for a foule shame indeed it would be should you out run the Constable having

soe liberall a provision made you for yr maintenance
—but ye reason you give for yr resolution I cannot at
all approve for you say "to spend more you can't"
thats because you have it not to spend, otherwise it
seems you would. So yt 'tis yr Grandmoth{rs} discretion & not yours th{t} keeps you from extravagancy,
which plainly appears in ye close of yr sentence, saying yt you think it simple covetousness to save out of
y{rs} but 'tis my opinion if you lay all on yr back 'tis
ten tymes a greater sin & shame th{n} to save some
what out of soe large an allowance in yr purse to
help you at a dead lift. Child, we all know our
beginning, but who knows his end? Ye best use th{t}
can be made of fair weath{r} is to provide against foule
& 'tis great discretion & of noe small commenda-
tions for a young woman betymes to shew herself
housewifly & frugal. Yr Mother neither Maide nor
wife ever yett bestowed forty pounds a yeare on
herself & yett if you never fall und{r} a worse reputation in ye world th{n} she (I thank God for it) hath
hitherto done, you need not repine at it, & you cannot be ignorant of ye difference th{t} was between my
fortune & what you are to expect. You ought likewise to consider th{t} you have seven brothers & sisters
& you are all one man's children & therefore it is
very unreasonable that one should expect to be preferred in finery soe much above all ye rest for 'tis
impossible you should soe much mistake yr ffather's
condition as to fancy he is able to allow every one of
you forty pounds a yeare a piece, for such an allowance with the charge of their diett over and above

will amount to at least five hundred pounds **a** yeare, a sum **y**ʳ poor ffather can ill spare, besides doe but bethink yʳself what a ridiculous sight it will be when yʳ grandmothʳ & you come to us **to** have noe less thⁿ seven waiting gentlewomen in one house, for what reason can you give why every one of yʳ Sistʳˢ should not have every one **of yᵐ a** Maide as well as you, & though you may spare to pay yʳ maide's wages out of yʳ allowance yett you take no care of yᵉ unnecessary charge you put yʳ ffathʳ to **in** yʳ increase of his family, whereas if it were not a piece of pride to have yᵉ name of keeping yʳ maide she yᵗ waits on yʳ good Grandmother might easily doe **as** formerly you know she hath done, all yᵉ business **you** have for a maide unless as you grow oldʳ you grow **a** veryer Foole which God forbid !

'**Poll,** you live in a place where you see great plenty & splendour but let not yᵉ allurements **of** earthly pleasures tempt you to forget or neglect **yᵉ** duty of a good Christian in dressing yʳ bettʳ part which is yʳ soule, as will best please God. I am not against yʳ going decent & neate as becomes yʳ ffathers daughter but to clothe yʳself rich & be running into every gaudy fashion can never become yʳ circumstances & instead of doing you creditt & getting you **a** good preferⁿᵗ it is yᵉ readiest way you can take to fright all sober men from ever thinking of matching thᵐselves with women that live above thyʳ fortune, & **if** this be a wise way of spending money judge you ! & besides, doe but reflect what an od

sight it will be to a stranger that comes to our house
to see y^r Grandmoth^r y^r Moth^r & all y^r Sisters in a
plane dress & you only trick^d up like a bartlemew-
babby—you know what sort of people those are th^t
can't faire well but they must cry rost meate now
what effect could you imagine y^r writing in such a
high straine to y^r Sisters could have but eithe^r to pro-
voke th^m to envy you or murmur against us.   I must
tell you neith^r of y^r Sisters have ever had twenty
pounds a yeare allowance from us yett, & yett they^r
dress hath not disparaged neith^r th^m nor us & without
incurring y^e censure of simple covetousness they will
have some what to shew out of their saving that will
doe th^m creditt & I expect y^t you th^t are theyr elder
Sister sh^d rather sett th^m examples of y^e like nature
th^n tempt th^m from treading in y^e steps of their good
Grandmoth^r & poor Moth^r.  This is not half what
might be saide on this occasion but believing thee to
be a very good natured dutyfull child I sh^d have
thought it a great deal too much but y^t having in my
coming hither past through many most desperate
dangers I cannot forbear thinking & preparing myself for all events, & therefore not knowing how it
may please God to dispose of us I conclude it my
duty to God & thee my d^r child to lay this matter
as home to thee as I could, assuring you my daily
prayers are not nor shall not be wanting that God
may give you grace always. to remember to make
a right use of this truly affectionate counsell of
y^r poor Moth^r. & though I speak very plaine downright english to you yett I would not have you doubt

but that I love you as hartily as **any** child **I have &**
if you serve God **and take** good courses I promise
you my kindness **to** you shall **be** according to y<sup>r</sup>
own **hart's** desire, for you **may be certain I** can aime
at nothing in **what I** have now writ **but y<sup>r</sup> real good**
which to promote shall **be y<sup>e</sup>** study & care day & night

   ' Of my dear Poll
  ' **thy** truly affectionate Moth<sup>r</sup>.
     ' ELIZA CHANDOS.

' Pera of Galata, May y<sup>e</sup> 6th **1686.**

' **P.S.**—Thy ffath<sup>r</sup> & **I** send **thee our** blessing, **&
all** thy broth<sup>rs</sup> & sist<sup>rs</sup> they<sup>r</sup> service. Our harty &
affectionate service to my **broth<sup>r</sup> & sist<sup>r</sup>** Childe & **all**
my dear cozens. When you **see my Lady** Worster
**& cozen** Howlands pray present **th<sup>m</sup> my** most humble
service.'

This **letter shows that the** wealth acquired **by trade**
was already manifesting itself **in** contrast **with** the
straitened circumstances **of** some of **the** nobility.
Mary Brydges's ' poor **ffather,'** in whose household
economy was **necessary, was the** King of England's
ambassador **at** Constantinople ; the grandmother,
who lived in ' great plenty **and** splendour,' was the
widow of a Turkey merchant. But **then,** as now,
**it** would seem, rank had the power of attracting and
absorbing wealth.

At Ashe also Jane **became acquainted with a**
member **of the** Lefroy family, who **was** still living
when I began these memoirs, **a few** months ago ; the
Right Hon. Thomas Lefroy, late Chief Justice of

Ireland.  One must look back more than seventy
years to reach the time when these two bright young
persons were, for a short time, intimately acquainted
with each other, and then separated on their several
courses, never to meet again ; both destined to attain
some distinction in their different ways, one to survive the other for more than half a century, yet in his
extreme old age to remember and speak, as he sometimes did, of his former companion, as one to be
much admired, and not easily forgotten by those who
had ever known her.

Mrs. Lefroy herself was a remarkable person.  Her
rare endowments of goodness, talents, graceful person,
and engaging manners, were sufficient to secure her a
prominent place in any society into which she was
thrown; while her enthusiastic eagerness of disposition rendered her especially attractive to a clever and
lively girl.  She was killed by a fall from her horse
on Jane's birthday, Dec. 16, 1804.  The following
lines to her memory were written by Jane four years
afterwards, when she was thirty-three years old.
They are given, not for their merits as poetry, but to
show how deep and lasting was the impression made
by the elder friend on the mind of the younger :—

TO THE MEMORY OF MRS. LEFROY.

I.

The day returns again, my natal day ;
    What mix'd emotions in my mind arise !
Beloved Friend ; four years have passed away
    Since thou wert snatched for ever from our eyes.

### 2.

The day commemorative of my birth,
　Bestowing life, and light, and hope **to me**,
Brings back the hour which was thy last **on earth.**
　O ! bitter pang of torturing memory !

### 3.

Angelic woman ! past my power to praise
　In language meet thy talents, temper, mind,
Thy solid worth, thy captivating grace,
　Thou friend and ornament of human kind.

### 4.

But come, fond Fancy, thou indulgent power ;
　Hope is desponding, chill, severe, to thee :
Bless thou this little portion of an hour ;
　Let me behold her as she used **to be.**

### 5.

**I see her** here with all her smiles benign,
　**Her** looks of eager love, her accents sweet,
That voice and countenance almost divine,
　Expression, harmony, alike complete.

### 6.

Listen !　It is not sound **alone, 'tis sense,**
　'Tis genius, taste, and tenderness of soul :
'Tis genuine warmth of heart without pretence,
　And purity of mind **that crowns** the whole.

### 7.

She speaks !　'Tis eloquence, that grace of tongue,
　So rare, so lovely, never misapplied
By her, **to** palliate vice, **or** deck a wrong :
　She speaks and argues but **on** virtue's side.

8.

Hers is the energy of soul sincere ;
    Her Christian spirit, ignorant to feign,
Seeks but to comfort, heal, enlighten, cheer,
    Confer a pleasure or prevent a pain.

9.

Can aught enhance such goodness? yes, to me
    Her partial favour from my earliest years
Consummates all : ah ! give me but to see
    Her smile of love!   The vision disappears.

10.

'Tis past and gone.   We meet no more below.
    Short is the cheat of Fancy o'er the tomb.
Oh ! might I hope to equal bliss to go,
    To meet thee, angel, in thy future home.

11.

Fain would I feel an union with thy fate :
    Fain would I seek to draw an omen fair
From this connection in our earthly date.
    Indulge the harmless weakness.   Reason, spare.

The loss of their first home is generally a great grief to young persons of strong feeling and lively imagination; and Jane was exceedingly unhappy when she was told that her father, now seventy years of age, had determined to resign his duties to his eldest son, who was to be his successor in the Rectory of Steventon, and to remove with his wife and daughters to Bath.  Jane had been absent from home when this resolution was taken; and, as her father was always **rapid** both in forming his resolutions and in acting **on** them, she had little time to reconcile herself **to the** change.

A wish has sometimes been expressed that some of Jane Austen's letters should be published. Some entire letters, and many extracts, will be given in this memoir ; but the reader must **be** warned not to expect too much from them. With regard to accuracy of language indeed every word of them might be printed without correction. The style is always clear, and generally animated, while a vein **of** humour continually gleams through the whole ; **but** the materials may be thought inferior **to the** execution, for they **treat only** of the details of domestic life. There **is in** them no notice of politics or public events ; scarcely any discussions **on** literature, **or** other subjects of general interest. They may be said **to** resemble **the** nest which some little bird builds **of** the materials nearest at hand, of the twigs and mosses supplied by the tree in which it is placed ; curiously constructed out of the simplest matters.

Her letters have **very** seldom the date of the year, or the signature of her christian name at **full** length ; but it has been easy to ascertain their dates, either **from** the post-mark, or from their contents.

The two following letters **are** the earliest that I have seen. They **were** both written **in** November 1800 ; before the family removed **from** Steventon. Some of the same circumstances are referred to **in both.**

The first is to her sister Cassandra, who was then staying with their brother Edward at Godmersham Park, Kent:—

‘ Steventon, Saturday evening, **Nov. 8th.**

My dear Cassandra,

‘I thank you for so speedy a return to my two last, and particularly thank you for your anecdote of Charlotte Graham and her cousin, Harriet Bailey, which has very much amused both my mother and myself. If you can learn anything farther of that interesting affair, I hope you will mention it. I have two messages; let me get rid of them, and then my paper will be my own. Mary fully intended writing to you by Mr. Chute's frank, and only happened entirely to forget it, but will write soon; and my father wishes Edward to send him a memorandum of the price of the hops. The tables are come, and give general contentment. I had not expected that they would so perfectly suit the fancy of us all three, or that we should so well agree in the disposition of them; but nothing except their own surface can have been smoother. The two ends put together form one constant table for everything, and the centre piece stands exceedingly well under the glass, and holds a great deal most commodiously, without looking awkwardly. They are both covered with green baize, and send their best love. The Pembroke has got its destination by the sideboard, and my mother has great delight in keeping her money and papers locked up. The little table which used to stand there has most conveniently taken itself off into the best bedroom;

and we are **now in** want only of the chiffonniere,
is neither finished nor come. So much for that subject ; **I** now come to another, of a **very** different
nature, **as** other subjects are very apt **to be.** Earle
Harwood has been again giving uneasiness to his
family and talk to the neighbourhood ; in the present
instance, however, he is only unfortunate, and not in
fault.

' About ten days ago, in cocking a pistol in the
guard-room at Marcau, he accidentally shot himself
through the thigh. Two young Scotch surgeons in
the island were polite enough to propose taking off
**the** thigh at once, but to that he would not consent ;
and accordingly in his wounded state was put on
**board a cutter and** conveyed **to** Haslar Hospital, at
Gosport, where the bullet was extracted, and where
he now is, I hope, in a fair way of doing well. The
surgeon **of the** hospital wrote to the family on the
occasion, and John Harwood went down to him immediately, attended by James,* whose object in going
was to be **the** means of bringing back the earliest
intelligence to Mr. and Mrs. Harwood, whose anxious
sufferings, particularly those of the latter, have of
course been dreadful. They went down on Tuesday,
**and** James came back the next day, bringing such
favourable accounts as greatly to lessen the distress of
the family at Deane, though it will probably be a long
while before Mrs. Harwood can be quite at ease. *One*
**most material** comfort, however, they have ; the assurance of its being really an accidental wound, which is
not only positively declared **by** Earle himself, but is

* James, the **writer's** eldest brother.

likewise testified by the particular direction of the bullet. Such a wound could not have been received in a duel. At present he is going on very well, but the surgeon will not declare him to be in no danger.* Mr. Heathcote met with a genteel little accident the other day in hunting. He got off to lead his horse over a hedge, or a house, or something, and his horse in his haste trod upon his leg, or rather ancle, I believe, and it is nct certain whether the small bone is not broke. Martha has accepted Mary's invitation for Lord Portsmouth's ball. He has not yet sent out his own invitations, but *that* does not signify; Martha comes, and a ball there is to be. I think it will be too early in her mother's absence for me to return with her.

' *Sunday Evening.*—We have had a dreadful storm of wind in the fore part of this day, which has done a great deal of mischief among our trees. I was sitting alone in the dining-room when an odd kind of crash startled me—in a moment afterwards it was repeated. I then went to the window, which I reached just in time to see the last of our two highly valued elms descend into the Sweep!!!!! The other, which had fallen, I suppose, in the first crash, and which was the nearest to the pond, taking a more easterly direction, sunk among our screen of chestnuts and firs, knocking down one spruce-fir, beating off the head of another, and stripping the two corner chestnuts of several branches in its fall. This is not all. One large elm out of the two on the left-hand side as you

* The limb was saved.

enter what I call the elm walk, was likewise blown
down ; the maple bearing the weathercock was **broke**
in **two, and** what **I regret** more than **all the** rest is,
that all the three **elms** which grew in **Hall's** meadow,
**and gave such** ornament to it, are gone ; two were
**blown** down, and the other so much injured that it
cannot stand. **I am** happy **to** add, however, that no
greater evil than the **loss of** trees has been the consequence **of** the storm **in** this place, or in our immediate neighbourhood. We grieve, **therefore, in** some
comfort.

'I am yours **ever,**        '**J. A.**'

**The next letter,** written **four** days **later** than **the**
former, **was** addressed **to Miss** Lloyd, **an** intimate
friend, whose sister (my mother) was married to
Jane's eldest brother :—

'Steventon, Wednesday evening, Nov. 12th.

'MY DEAR MARTHA,

'I did **not receive your** note yesterday **till after**
Charlotte had left Deane, or I would have sent **my**
answer by her, instead of being the means, **as I** now
must be, of lessening the elegance of your new dress
**for** the Hurstbourne **ball by** the value of 3*d*. You
**are** very good **in** wishing to see me **at** Ibthorp so
soon, and I am equally good in wishing to come **to**
**you. I believe our** merit **in that** respect is much
upon **a par, our** self-denial **mutually** strong. Having
paid this tribute of praise **to** the virtue **of** both, I
shall here have done with panegyric, and proceed to

plain matter of fact. In about a fortnight's time I hope to be with you. I have two reasons for not being able to come before. I wish so to arrange my visit as to spend some days with you after your mother's return. In the 1st place, that I may have the pleasure of seeing her, and in the 2nd, that I may have a better chance of bringing you back with me. Your promise in my favour was not quite absolute, but if your will is not perverse, you and I will do all in our power to overcome your scruples of conscience. I hope we shall meet next week to talk all this over, till we have tired ourselves with the very idea of my visit before my visit begins. Our invitations for the 19th are arrived, and very curiously are they worded.* Mary mentioned to you yesterday poor Earle's unfortunate accident, I dare say. He does not seem to be going on very well. The two or three last posts have brought less and less favourable accounts of him. John Harwood has gone to Gosport again to-day. We have two families of friends now who are in a most anxious state ; for though by a note from Catherine this morning there seems now to be a revival of hope at Manydown, its continuance may be too reasonably doubted. Mr. Heathcote,† however, who has

---

* The invitation, the ball dress, and some other things in this and the preceding letter refer to a ball annually given at Hurstbourne Park, on the anniversary of the Earl of Portsmouth's marriage with his first wife. He was the Lord Portsmouth whose eccentricities afterwards became notorious, and the invitations, as well as other arrangements about these balls, were of a peculiar character.

† The father of Sir William Heathcote, of Hursley, who was married to a daughter of Mr. Bigg Wither, of Manydown, and lived in the neighbourhood.

broken the small bone **of** his leg, is so good as to be going on **very** well. It would be really too much to have three people to care for.

'You distress me cruelly by your request about books. I cannot think of any to bring with me, nor have I any idea of our wanting them. I come to you to be talked to, not to read or hear reading; I can do that at home; and indeed I am now laying in a stock of intelligence to pour out on you as my share of the conversation. I am reading Henry's History of England, which I will repeat to you in any manner you may prefer, either in a loose, desultory, unconnected stream, or dividing my recital, as the historian divides **it** himself, into seven parts:—The Civil and Military: Religion: Constitution: Learning and Learned Men: Arts **and** Sciences: Commerce, Coins, and Shipping: and Manners. So that for every evening in the week there will be a different subject. The Friday's lot— Commerce, Coins, and Shipping—you will find the least entertaining; **but** the next evening's portion will make amends. With such a provision on my part, if you will do yours by repeating the French Grammar, and Mrs. Stent* will now and then ejaculate some wonder about the cocks and hens, what can we want? Farewell for a short time. **We all unite in** best love, and I am your very affectionate

'J. A.'

The two next letters must have been written early in 1801, after the removal from Steventon had been

---

* A **very** dull old lady, then residing with Mrs. Lloyd.

decided on, but before it had taken place. They
refer to the two brothers who were at sea, and give
some idea of a kind of anxieties and uncertainties to
which sisters are seldom subject in these days of
peace, steamers, and electric telegraphs. At that time
ships were often windbound or becalmed, or driven
wide of their destination; and sometimes they had
orders to alter their course for some secret service;
not to mention the chance of conflict with a vessel of
superior power—no improbable occurrence before the
battle of Trafalgar. Information about relatives on
board men-of-war was scarce and scanty, and often
picked up by hearsay or chance means; and every
scrap of intelligence was proportionably valuable:—

'MY DEAR CASSANDRA,

'I should not have thought it necessary to write to
you so soon, but for the arrival of a letter from Charles
to myself. It was written last Saturday from off the
Start, and conveyed to Popham Lane by Captain
Boyle, on his way to Midgham. He came from Lisbon
in the "Endymion." I will copy Charles's account of
his conjectures about Frank: "He has not seen my
brother lately, nor does he expect to find him arrived,
as he met Captain Inglis at Rhodes, going up to take
command of the 'Petrel,' as he was coming down;
but supposes he will arrive in less than a fortnight
from this time, in some ship which is expected to
reach England about that time with dispatches from
Sir Ralph Abercrombie." The event must show what
sort of a conjuror Captain Boyle is. The "Endy-

mion" has not been plagued with any more prizes. Charles spent three pleasant days in Lisbon.

'They were very well satisfied with their royal passenger,* whom they found jolly and affable, who talks of Lady Augusta as his wife, and seems much attached to her.

'When this letter was written, the "Endymion" was becalmed, but Charles hoped to reach Portsmouth by Monday or Tuesday. He received my letter, communicating our plans, before he left England; was much surprised, of course, but is quite reconciled to them, and means to come to Steventon once more while Steventon is ours.'

From a letter written later in the same year:—

'Charles has received 30*l.* for his share of the privateer, and expects 10*l.* more; but of what avail is it to take prizes if he lays out the produce in presents to his sisters? He has been buying gold chains and topaze crosses for us. He must be well scolded. The "Endymion" has already received orders for taking troops to Egypt, which I should not like at all if I did not trust to Charles being removed from her somehow or other before she sails. He knows nothing of his own destination, he says, but desires me to write directly, as the "Endymion" will probably sail in three or four days. He will receive my yesterday's letter, and I shall write again by this post to thank and reproach him. We shall be unbearably fine.'

* The Duke of Sussex, son of George III., married, without royal consent, to the Lady Augusta Murray.

## CHAPTER IV.

*Removal from Steventon—Residences at Bath and at Southampton—
Settling at Chawton.*

THE family removed to Bath in the spring of 1801,
where they resided first at No. 4 Sydney Terrace,
and afterwards in Green Park Buildings. I do not
know whether they were at all attracted to Bath by
the circumstance that Mrs. Austen's only brother,
Mr. Leigh Perrot, spent part of every year there. The
name of Perrot, together with a small estate at Northleigh in Oxfordshire, had been bequeathed to him by
a great uncle. I must devote a few sentences to this
very old and now extinct branch of the Perrot family ;
for one of the last survivors, Jane Perrot, married to a
Walker, was Jane Austen's great grandmother, from
whom she derived her Christian name. The Perrots
were settled in Pembrokeshire at least as early as the
thirteenth century. They were probably some of the
settlers whom the policy of our Plantagenet kings
placed in that county, which thence acquired the
name of 'England beyond Wales,' for the double
purpose of keeping open a communication with
Ireland from Milford Haven, and of overawing the
Welsh. One of the family seems to have carried out

this latter purpose very vigorously; for it is recorded of him that he slew *twenty-six* **men** of Kemaes, a district of Wales, and *one wolf*. The manner in which the two kinds of game are classed together, and the disproportion of numbers, **are** remarkable; but probably at that time the wolves had been so closely killed down, that *lupicide* was become a more rare and distinguished exploit than *homicide*. The last of this family died about 1778, and their property was divided between Leighs and Musgraves, **the** larger portion going to the latter. Mr. Leigh Perrot pulled down **the** mansion, and sold the estate to **the** Duke of Marlborough, **and** the name of these Perrots is now to be found only on some monuments in the church of Northleigh.

Mr. Leigh **Perrot was** also **one of several** cousins to whom a life interest in **the** Stoneleigh **property in** Warwickshire was **left,** after the extinction **of the** earlier Leigh peerage, **but** he compromised his claim **to** the succession **in** his lifetime. He married a niece **of** Sir Montague Cholmeley of Lincolnshire. He was **a** man of considerable natural power, with much **of the** wit of his uncle, the Master of Balliol, and wrote clever epigrams and riddles, **some** of which, though without his name, found their **way** into print; but he lived a **very** retired life, **dividing** his time between Bath **and his** place in Berkshire called Scarlets. Jane's letters from Bath **make** frequent mention of this uncle and aunt.

The unfinished story, **now** published under the title **of** 'The Watsons,' must **have** been written during

the author's residence in Bath.   In the autumn of
1804 she spent some weeks at Lyme, and became
acquainted with the Cobb, which she afterwards
made memorable for the fall of Louisa Musgrove.
In February 1805, her father died at Bath, and
was buried at Walcot Church.   The widow and
daughters went into lodgings for a few months, and
then removed to Southampton.   The only records
that I can find about her during those four years are
the three following letters to her sister; one from
Lyme, the others from Bath.   They shew that she
went a good deal into society, in a quiet way, chiefly
with ladies; and that her eyes were always open to
minute traits of character in those with whom she
associated :—

*Extract from a letter from Jane Austen to her Sister.*

'Lyme, Friday, Sept. 14 (1804).

'MY DEAR CASSANDRA,—I take the first sheet of
fine striped paper to thank you for your letter from
Weymouth, and express my hopes of your being at
Ibthorp before this time.   I expect to hear that you
reached it yesterday evening, being able to get as far
as Blandford on Wednesday.   Your account of Weymouth contains nothing which strikes me so forcibly
as there being no ice in the town.   For every other
vexation I was in some measure prepared, and particularly for your disappointment in not seeing the
Royal Family go on board on Tuesday, having
already heard from Mr. Crawford that he had seen
you in the very act of being too late.   But for there

being no ice, what could prepare me! You found my letter at Andover, I hope, yesterday, and have now for many hours been satisfied that your kind anxiety on my behalf was as much thrown away as kind anxiety usually is. I continue quite well; in proof of which I have bathed again this morning. It was absolutely necessary that I should have the little fever and indisposition which I had : it has been all the fashion this week in Lyme. We are quite settled in our lodgings by this time, as you may suppose, and everything goes on in the usual order. The servants behave very well, and make no difficulties, though nothing certainly can exceed the inconvenience of the offices, except the general dirtiness of the house and furniture, and all its inhabitants. I endeavour, as far as I can, to supply your place, and be useful, and keep things in order. I detect dirt in the water decanters, as fast as I can, and keep everything as it was under your administration. . . . The ball last night was pleasant, but not full for Thursday. My father staid contentedly till half-past nine (we went a little after eight), and then walked home with James and a lanthorn, though I believe the lanthorn was not lit, as the moon was up; but sometimes this lanthorn may be a great convenience to him. My mother and I staid about an hour later. Nobody asked me the two first dances ; the two next I danced with Mr. Crawford, and had I chosen to stay longer might have danced with Mr. Granville, Mrs. Granville's son, whom my dear friend Miss A. introduced to me, or with a new

odd-looking man who had been eyeing me for some
time, and at last, without any introduction, asked me
if I meant to dance again.　I think he must be Irish
by his ease, and because I imagine him to belong to
the hon^bl B.'s, who are son, and son's wife of an Irish
viscount, bold queer-looking people, just fit to be
quality at Lyme.　I called yesterday morning (ought
it not in strict propriety to be termed yester-morn-
ing ?) on Miss A. and was introduced to her father
and mother.　Like other young ladies she is considerably genteeler than her parents.　Mrs. A. sat
darning a pair of stockings the whole of my visit.
But do not mention this at home, lest a warning
should act as an example.　We afterwards walked
together for an hour on the Cobb ; she is very con-
verseable in a common way ; I do not perceive wit
or genius, but she has sense and some degree of
taste, and her manners are very engaging.　She
seems to like people rather too easily.

'Yours affect^ly,

'J. A.'

Letter from Jane Austen to her sister Cassandra at
Ibthorp, alluding to the sudden death of Mrs. Lloyd
at that place :—

'25 Gay Street (Bath), Monday,

'April 8, 1805.

'MY DEAR CASSANDRA,—Here is a day for you.
Did Bath or Ibthorp ever see such an 8th of April ?
It is March and April together ; the glare of the one
and the warmth of the other.　We do nothing but

walk **about**. As far as your means will admit, I hope you profit by such weather too. I dare say you are already the better **for** change of place. We were out again last night. Miss Irvine invited us, when I met **her in** the Crescent, to drink tea with them, but I rather declined it, having no idea that my mother would be disposed **for** another evening visit there so **soon** ; but when **I gave** her the message, I found her very well inclined to go ; and accordingly, on leaving Chapel, we walked to Lansdown. This morning we have been to see Miss Chamberlaine look hot on horseback. Seven years and four months ago we went to the same riding-house to see Miss Lefroy's performance !* What **a** different set are we now moving in ! But seven years, I suppose, are enough to change every pore of one's skin and every feeling of one's mind. We did not walk long in the Crescent yesterday. **It** was hot and not crowded enough ; so we went into the field, and passed close by S. T. and **Miss** S.† again. I have not yet seen her face, but neither her dress nor air have anything of the dash or stylishness which the Browns talked of; quite the contrary ; indeed, her dress is not even smart, and her appearance very quiet. Miss Irvine says she is never speaking a word. Poor wretch ; I am afraid she is *en pénitence.* Here has been that excellent Mrs. Coulthart calling, while my mother was out, and I was believed to be so. I always respected her, as a

---

* **Here is** evidence that Jane **Austen was** acquainted with Bath before it became her residence in 1801. **See p.** 23.

† A gentleman and lady lately engaged to be married.

good-hearted friendly woman.  And the Browns have
been here; I find their affidavits on the table.  The
"Ambuscade" reached Gibraltar on the 9th of March,
and found all well; so say the papers.  We have had
no letters from anybody, but we expect to hear from
Edward to-morrow, and from you soon afterwards.
How happy they are at Godmersham now!  I shall be
very glad of a letter from Ibthorp, that I may know
how you all are, but particularly yourself.  This is
nice weather for Mrs. J. Austen's going to Speen, and
I hope she will have a pleasant visit there.  I expect
a prodigious account of the christening dinner; perhaps it brought you at last into the company of Miss
Dundas again.

' *Tuesday.*—I received your letter last night, and
wish it may be soon followed by another to say that
all is over; but I cannot help thinking that nature
will struggle again, and produce a revival.  Poor
woman!  May her end be peaceful and easy as the
exit we have witnessed!  And I dare say it will.  If
there is no revival, suffering must be all over; even the
consciousness of existence, I suppose, was gone when
you wrote.  The nonsense I have been writing in this
and in my last letter seems out of place at such a
time, but I will not mind it; it will do you no harm,
and nobody else will be attacked by it.  I am heartily
glad that you can speak so comfortably of your own
health and looks, though I can scarcely comprehend
the latter being really approved.  Could travelling
fifty miles produce such an immediate change?  You
were looking very poorly here, and everybody seemed

sensible **of it. Is there a** charm **in a** hack postchaise? But if there **were, Mrs. Craven's** carriage might have undone **it all. I am much** obliged to you for the time and trouble **you** have bestowed **on** Mary's cap, and **am** glad **it pleases her ; but it** will prove a useless gift **at** present, I suppose. Will not she leave Ibthorp **on her** mother's death? **As** a companion you are **all** that Martha can be supposed **to want,** and **in** that light, under these circumstances, your visit will **indeed have** been **well** timed.

'*Thursday.*—I was not able to **go on** yesterday ; all my **wit and** leisure **were** bestowed **on** letters to Charles and **Henry. To the former I wrote in** consequence of my mother's having seen **in the** papers **that** the "Urania" **was** waiting **at** Portsmouth for the convoy for Halifax. This is nice, as it is only three weeks ago that you wrote by the "Camilla." I wrote **to** Henry because I had a letter from him in which he desired **to hear** from me very soon. His to me **was** most affectionate **and** kind, as **well as** entertaining ; there is no merit **to** him in *that* ; he cannot help being amusing. **He offers to meet us on** the **sea** coast, if the plan of which Edward gave him some hint takes place. Will **not this** be making the execution of such a plan **more** desirable and delightful than ever? He talks of the rambles we took together **last** summer with pleasing affection.

'Yours ever,

**'J. A.'**

*From the same to the same.*

'Gay St. Sunday Evening,
'April 21 (1805).

'MY DEAR CASSANDRA,—I am much obliged to you for writing to me again so soon; your letter yesterday was quite an unexpected pleasure. Poor Mrs. Stent! it has been her lot to be always in the way; but we must be merciful, for perhaps in time we may come to be Mrs. Stents ourselves, unequal to anything, and unwelcome to everybody. . . . My morning engagement was with the Cookes, and our party consisted of George and Mary, a Mr. L., Miss B., who had been with us at the concert, and the youngest Miss W. Not Julia; we have done with her; she is very ill; but Mary. Mary W.'s turn is actually come to be grown up, and have a fine complexion, and wear great square muslin shawls. I have not expressly enumerated myself among the party, but there I was, and my cousin George was very kind, and talked sense to me every now and then, in the intervals of his more animated fooleries with Miss B., who is very young, and rather handsome, and whose gracious manners, ready wit, and solid remarks, put me somewhat in mind of my old acquaintance L. L. There was a monstrous deal of stupid quizzing and common-place nonsense talked, but scarcely any wit; all that bordered on it or on sense came from my cousin George, whom altogether I like very well. Mr. B. seems nothing more than a tall young man. My evening engagement and walk was with Miss A.,

who had called on me the day before, and gently up-
braided me in her turn with a change of manners to
**her** since she had been in Bath, or **at** least of late.
Unlucky me! that my notice should be of such consequence, and my manners so bad!  She was so well
disposed, and so reasonable, that I soon forgave her,
and made this engagement with **her** in proof of it.
She is really an agreeable girl, so I think I may like
her; and her great want of a companion at home,
which may well make any tolerable acquaintance important to her, gives her another claim on my attention.
I shall endeavour as much as possible to keep my
intimacies **in** their proper place, and prevent their
clashing.  Among so many friends, **it** will be **well** if **I**
do not get **into** a scrape; **and** now here is Miss
Blashford come.  I should have gone distracted if the
Bullers had staid. . . . **When I** tell you I **have** been
visiting a countess this morning, you will immediately,
with great justice, **but no** truth, guess it **to be** Lady
Roden.  No: it **is Lady Leven, the** mother of Lord
Balgonie.  On receiving a message from Lord and
Lady Leven through the Mackays, declaring their
intention of waiting on us, we thought it right to go
to them.  I hope we have not done too much, but the
friends and admirers of Charles must be attended to.
They seem very reasonable, good sort of people, very
civil, and full of his praise.*  We were shewn at first
into an empty drawing-room, and presently in came

---

* It seems that Charles Austen, then first lieutenant of the 'Endymion,' had had an opportunity of shewing attention and kindness to
some of Lord Leven's family.

his lordship, not knowing who we were, to apologise for the servant's mistake, and to say himself what was untrue, that Lady Leven was not within. He is a tall gentlemanlike looking man, with spectacles, and rather deaf. After sitting with him ten minutes we walked away; but Lady Leven coming out of the dining parlour as we passed the door, we were obliged to attend her back to it, and pay our visit over again. She is a stout woman, with a very handsome face. By this means we had the pleasure of hearing Charles's praises twice over. They think themselves excessively obliged to him, and estimate him so highly as to wish Lord Balgonie, when he is quite recovered, to go out to him. There is a pretty little Lady Marianne of the party, to be shaken hands with, and asked if she remembered Mr. Austen. . . .

'I shall write to Charles by the next packet, unless you tell me in the meantime of your intending to do it.

'Believe me, if you chuse,

'Y<sup>r</sup> aff<sup>te</sup> Sister.'

Jane did not estimate too highly the 'Cousin George' mentioned in the foregoing letter; who might easily have been superior in sense and wit to the rest of the party. He was the Rev. George Leigh Cooke, long known and respected at Oxford, where he held important offices, and had the privilege of helping to form the minds of men more eminent than himself. As Tutor in Corpus Christi College, he became instructor to some of the most distinguished undergraduates of that time : amongst others to Dr. Arnold, the **Rev. John** Keble, **and** Sir John Coleridge. The latter has mentioned him in terms **of** affectionate regard, both in his Memoir **of** Keble, **and** in a letter which appears in Dean Stanley's 'Life of Arnold.' Mr. Cooke was also an impressive preacher of earnest awakening sermons. **I** remember to have heard **it** observed by some **of my** undergraduate friends **that,** after all, there was more good to be got from George Cooke's plain sermons than from much **of the more** laboured oratory of the University pulpit. **He** was frequently Examiner in the schools, and occupied the chair **of** the Sedleian Professor of Natural Philosophy, **from 1810 to** 1853.

Before **the end** of 1805, **the little** family party removed to Southampton. They resided **in** a commodious old-fashioned house **in** a corner of Castle Square.

I have **no letters of my** aunt, **nor any** other record **of** her, during **her four years'** residence **at** Southampton ; and though **I now** began **to** know, and, **what** was the **same** thing, **to** love **her** myself, **yet** my observations **were** only those **of a** young boy, and were not capable **of** penetrating her character, **or** estimating her powers. I **have,** however, **a** lively recollection of some local circumstances **at** South**ampton,** and **as** they refer chiefly to things which have been long ago swept away, I will record them. My grandmother's house had a pleasant garden, bounded **on one** side by the old city walls ; **the** top of this wall was sufficiently wide to afford a pleasant walk, with an extensive view, easily accessible to ladies by steps. This must have been a part of the identical walls which witnessed the embarkation of Henry V. before the battle of Agincourt, and the detection of the conspiracy of Cambridge, Scroop, and Grey, which Shakspeare has made so picturesque; when, according to the chorus in Henry V., the citizens saw

> The well-appointed King at Hampton Pier
> Embark his royalty.

Among the records of the town of Southampton, they have a minute and authentic account, drawn up at that time, of the encampment of Henry V. near the town, before his embarkment for France. It is remarkable that the place where the army was encamped, then a low level plain, is now entirely covered by the sea, and is called Westport.* At that time Castle Square was occupied by a fantastic edifice, too large for the space in which it stood, though too small to accord well with its castellated style, erected by the second Marquis of Lansdowne, half-brother to the well-known statesman, who succeeded him in the title. The Marchioness had a light phaeton, drawn by six, and sometimes by eight little ponies, each pair decreasing in size, and becoming lighter in colour, through all the grades of dark brown, light brown, bay, and chestnut, as it was placed farther away from the carriage. The two leading pairs were managed by two boyish postilions, the two pairs nearest to the

---

* See Wharton's note to Johnson and Steevens' Shakspeare.

carriage were driven in hand. It was a delight to me to look down from the window and see this fairy equipage put together; **for** the premises of this castle were so contracted that the whole process went on in the little space that remained of the open square. Like other fairy works, however, it all proved evanescent. Not only carriage **and** ponies, but castle itself, soon vanished away, 'like the baseless fabric **of a** vision.' **On the death** of the Marquis in 1809, the castle **was** pulled down. Few probably remember its existence; and **any one who** might visit **the** place **now** would wonder how it ever could have stood there.

**In** 1809 **Mr.** Knight was **able to** offer **his** mother the choice of two houses **on** his property; one near his usual residence at Godmersham Park **in Kent;** the other near Chawton **House,** his occasional residence in Hampshire. The latter **was** chosen; and in that year the mother **and** daughters, together with Miss Lloyd, **a** near connection **who lived with** them, settled themselves at Chawton Cottage.

Chawton **may be** called the *second,* as **well as the** *last* home of Jane Austen; for during the temporary residences of the party at **Bath** and Southampton she **was** only a sojourner in a **strange** land; but here she **found a** real home amongst **her own** people. It so happened that during her residence at Chawton circumstances brought several of her brothers and their families within easy distance of the house. Chawton must also be considered the **place** most closely connected with **her** career as **a** writer; for there it was that, in the maturity of **her** mind, she either wrote or rearranged, and prepared for publication the books by which she has become known to the world.  This was the home where, after a few years, while still in the prime of life, she began to droop and wither away, and which she left only in the last stage of her illness, yielding to the persuasion of friends hoping against hope.

This house stood in the village of Chawton, about a mile from Alton, on the right hand side, just where the road to Winchester branches off from that to Gosport.  It was so close to the road that the front door opened upon it ; while a very narrow enclosure, paled in on each side, protected the building from danger of collision with any runaway vehicle.  I believe it had been originally built for an inn, for which purpose it was certainly well situated.  Afterwards it had been occupied by Mr. Knight's steward ; but by some additions to the house, and some judicious planting and skreening, it was made a pleasant and commodious abode.  Mr. Knight was experienced and adroit at such arrangements, and this was a labour of love to him.  A good-sized entrance and two sitting-rooms made the length of the house, all intended originally to look upon the road, but the large drawing-room window was blocked up and turned into a book-case, and another opened at the side which gave to view only turf and trees, as a high wooden fence and hornbeam hedge shut out the Winchester road, which skirted the whole length of the little domain.  Trees were planted each side to form a shrubbery walk, carried round the enclosure, which gave a sufficient space for ladies' exercise. There was a pleasant irregular mixture of hedgerow, and gravel walk, and orchard, and long grass for mowing, arising from two or three little enclosures having been thrown together. The house itself was quite as good as the generality of parsonage-houses then were, and much in the same style ; and was capable of receiving other members of the family as frequent visitors. It was sufficiently well furnished ; everything inside and out was kept in good repair, and it was altogether a comfortable and ladylike establishment, though the means which supported it were not large.

I give this description because some interest is generally taken in the residence of a popular writer. Cowper's unattractive house in the street of Olney has been pointed out to visitors, and has even attained the honour of an engraving in Southey's edition of his works : but I cannot recommend any admirer of Jane Austen to undertake a pilgrimage to this spot. The building indeed still stands, but it has lost all that gave it its character. After the death of Mrs. Cassandra Austen, in 1845, it was divided into tenements for labourers, and the grounds reverted to ordinary uses.

# CHAPTER V.

*Description of Jane Austen's person, character, and taste.*

As my memoir has now reached the period when I
saw a great deal of my aunt, and was old enough to
understand something of her value, I will here attempt a description of her person, mind, and habits.
In person she was very attractive; her figure was
rather tall and slender, her step light and firm, and
her whole appearance expressive of health and ani-
mation.  In complexion she was a clear brunette
with a rich colour; she had full round cheeks, with
mouth and nose small and well formed, bright hazel
eyes, and brown hair forming natural curls close
round her face.  If not so regularly handsome as her
sister, yet her countenance had a peculiar charm of
its own to the eyes of most beholders.  At the time
of which I am now writing, she never was seen, either
morning or evening, without a cap; I believe that
she and her sister were generally thought to have
taken to the garb of middle age earlier than their
years or their looks required; and that, though remarkably neat in their dress as in all their ways, they
were scarcely sufficiently regardful of the fashionable,
or the becoming.

She was **not** highly accomplished according to the present standard. Her **sister** drew well, and it **is** from a drawing of hers that the likeness prefixed to this **volume** has been taken. **Jane** herself was fond of music, and **had** a sweet voice, both in singing and in conversation ; **in** her youth she had received some instruction on **the** pianoforte ; and at Chawton she practised daily, chiefly before breakfast. I believe she did so partly that she might not disturb the rest **of the** party who were less fond of music. **In** the evening she would sometimes sing, **to** her own accompaniment, some simple old songs, the words and **airs of** which, **now never** heard, still linger **in my** memory.

She read French with facility, and knew something of Italian. **In** those days German was **no** more thought of than Hindostanee, as part **of a** lady's education. In history she followed the old guides— Goldsmith, Hume, and Robertson. Critical enquiry into the usually received **statements** of the old historians was scarcely begun. The history of the early kings **of** Rome had not yet been dissolved into legend. Historic characters **lay** before the reader's eyes in broad light or shade, **not** much broken up by details. **The** virtues of King Henry VIII. were yet undiscovered, nor had much light been thrown on the inconsistencies of Queen Elizabeth ; **the** one was held to be an unmitigated tyrant, and an embodied Blue Beard ; the **other a** perfect model **of** wisdom and policy. Jane, when a girl, **had** strong political opinions, especially about the affairs of the sixteenth and seventeenth centuries. She was a vehement defender of Charles I. and his grandmother Mary; but I think it was rather from an impulse of feeling than from any enquiry into the evidences by which they must be condemned or acquitted. As she grew up, the politics of the day occupied very little of her attention, but she probably shared the feeling of moderate Toryism which prevailed in her family. She was well acquainted with the old periodicals from the 'Spectator' downwards. Her knowledge of Richardson's works was such as no one is likely again to acquire, now that the multitude and the merits of our light literature have called off the attention of readers from that great master. Every circumstance narrated in Sir Charles Grandison, all that was ever said or done in the cedar parlour, was familiar to her; and the wedding days of Lady L. and Lady G. were as well remembered as if they had been living friends. Amongst her favourite writers, Johnson in prose, Crabbe in verse, and Cowper in both, stood high. It is well that the native good taste of herself and of those with whom she lived, saved her from the snare into which a sister novelist had fallen, of imitating the grandiloquent style of Johnson. She thoroughly enjoyed Crabbe; perhaps on account of a certain resemblance to herself in minute and highly finished detail; and would sometimes say, in jest, that, if she ever married at all, she could fancy being Mrs. Crabbe; looking on the author quite as an abstract idea, and ignorant and regardless what manner of man he might be. Scott's

poetry gave her great pleasure; she did not live to
make much acquaintance with his novels. Only three
of them were published before her death; but it will
be seen by the following extract from one of her
letters, that she was quite prepared to admit the
merits of 'Waverley'; and it is remarkable that, living,
as she did, far apart from the gossip of the literary
world, she should even then have spoken so confidently of his being the author of it :—

'Walter Scott has no business to write novels;
especially good ones. It is not fair. He has fame
and profit enough as a poet, and ought not to be
taking the bread out of other people's mouths. I do
not mean to like "Waverley," if I can help it, but I
fear I must. I am quite determined, however, not to
be pleased with Mrs. ———'s, should I ever meet with
it, which I hope I may not. I think I can be stout
against anything written by her. I have made up my
mind to like no novels really, but Miss Edgeworth's,
E.'s, and my own.'

It was not, however, what she *knew*, but what she
*was*, that distinguished her from others. I cannot
better describe the fascination which she exercised
over children than by quoting the words of two of
her nieces. One says :—

'As a very little girl I was always creeping up to
aunt Jane, and following her whenever I could, in the
house and out of it. I might not have remembered
this but for the recollection of my mother's telling me
privately, that I must not be troublesome to my aunt.
Her first charm to children was great sweetness of

manner. She seemed to love you, and you loved her in return. This, as well as I can now recollect, was what I felt in my early days, before I was old enough to be amused by her cleverness. But soon came the delight of her playful talk. She could make everything amusing to a child. Then, as I got older, when cousins came to share the entertainment, she would tell us the most delightful stories, chiefly of Fairyland, and her fairies had all characters of their own. The tale was invented, I am sure, at the moment, and was continued for two or three days, if occasion served.'

Again : 'When staying at Chawton, with two of her other nieces, we often had amusements in which my aunt was very helpful. She was the one to whom we always looked for help. She would furnish us with what we wanted from her wardrobe ; and she would be the entertaining visitor in our make-believe house. She amused us in various ways. Once, I remember, in giving a conversation as between myself and my two cousins, supposing we were all grown up, the day after a ball.'

Very similar is the testimony of another niece :— 'Aunt Jane was the general favourite with children ; her ways with them being so playful, and her long circumstantial stories so delightful. These were continued from time to time, and were begged for on all possible and impossible occasions ; woven, as she proceeded, out of nothing but her own happy talent for invention. Ah! if but one of them could be recovered! And again, as I grew older, when the original seventeen years between our ages seemed to shrink to seven, or to nothing, it comes back to me now how strangely I missed her. It had become so much a habit with me to put by things in my mind with a reference to her, and to say to myself, I shall keep this for aunt Jane.'

A nephew of hers used to observe that his visits to Chawton, after the death of his aunt Jane, were always a disappointment to him. From old associations he could not help expecting to be particularly happy in that house ; and never till he got there could he realise to himself how all its peculiar charm was gone. It was not only that the chief light in the house was quenched, but that the loss of it had cast a shade over the spirits of the survivors. Enough has been said to show her love for children, and her wonderful power of entertaining them ; but her friends of all ages felt her enlivening influence. Her unusually quick sense of the ridiculous led her to play with all the common-places of everyday life, whether as regarded persons or things ; but she never played with its serious duties or responsibilities, nor did she ever turn individuals into ridicule. With all her neighbours in the village she was on friendly, though not on intimate, terms. She took a kindly interest in all their proceedings, and liked to hear about them. They often served for her amusement ; but it was her own nonsense that gave zest to the gossip. She was as far as possible from being censorious or satirical. She never abused them or *quizzed* them—*that* was the word of the day ; an ugly word, now obsolete ; and the ugly practice which it expressed is much less prevalent now than it was then.  The laugh which she occasionally raised was by imagining for her neighbours, as she was equally ready to imagine for her friends or herself, impossible contingencies, or by relating in prose or verse some trifling anecdote coloured to her own fancy, or in writing a fictitious history of what they were supposed to have said or done, which could deceive nobody.

The following specimens may be given of the liveliness of mind which imparted an agreeable flavour both to her correspondence and her conversation :—

ON READING IN THE NEWSPAPERS THE MARRIAGE OF MR. GELL TO MISS GILL, OF EASTBOURNE.

At Eastbourne Mr. Gell, From being perfectly well,
Became dreadfully ill, For love of Miss Gill.
So he said, with some sighs, I'm the slave of your *iis* ;
Oh, restore, if you please, By accepting my *ees.*

ON THE MARRIAGE OF A MIDDLE-AGED FLIRT WITH A MR. WAKE, WHOM, IT WAS SUPPOSED, SHE WOULD SCARCELY HAVE ACCEPTED IN HER YOUTH.

Maria, good-humoured, and handsome, and tall,
For a husband was at her last stake ;
And having in vain danced at many a ball,
Is now happy to *jump at a Wake.*

' We were all at the play last night to see Miss O'Neil in Isabella.  I do not think she was quite equal to my expectation.  I fancy I want something more than can be.  Acting seldom satisfies me.  I took two pockethandkerchiefs, but had very little occasion for either.   She is an elegant creature, however, and hugs Mr. Young delightfully.'

'So, Miss B. is actually married, but I have never seen it in the papers ; and one may as well be single if the wedding is not to be in print.'

Once, too, she took it into her head to write the following mock panegyric on a young friend, who really was clever and handsome :—

### 1.

In measured verse I'll now rehearse
   The charms of lovely Anna :
And, first, her mind is unconfined
   Like any vast savannah.

### 2.

Ontario's lake may fitly speak
   Her fancy's ample bound :
Its circuit may, on strict survey
   Five hundred miles be found.

### 3.

Her wit descends on foes and friends
   Like famed Niagara's Fall ;
And travellers gaze in wild amaze,
   And listen, one and all.

### 4.

Her judgment sound, thick, black, profound,
   Like transatlantic groves,
Dispenses aid, and friendly shade
   To all that in it roves.

5.

If thus her mind to be defined
   America exhausts,
And all that's grand in that great land
   In similes it costs—

6.

Oh how can I her person try
   To image and portray?
How paint the face, the form how trace
   In which those virtues lay?

7.

Another world must be unfurled,
   Another language known,
Ere tongue or sound can publish round
   Her charms of flesh and bone.

I believe that all this nonsense was nearly extempore, and that the fancy of drawing the images from America arose at the moment from the obvious rhyme which presented itself in the first stanza.

The following extracts are from letters addressed to a niece who was at that time amusing herself by attempting a novel, probably never finished, certainly never published, and of which I know nothing but what these extracts tell. They show the good-natured sympathy and encouragement which the aunt, then herself occupied in writing 'Emma,' could give to the less matured powers of the niece. They bring out incidentally some of her opinions concerning compositions of that kind :—

*Extracts.*

'Chawton, **Aug.** 10, 1814.

'Your aunt C. does **not** like desultory novels, and
**is** rather fearful that yours will be too much so ; that
there will be too frequent a change from one set of
people to another, **and** that circumstances will be
sometimes introduced, of apparent consequence, which
will lead to nothing.  **It will not** be so great an objection **to me.**  I allow much more latitude than she
does, and think nature and spirit cover many sins of
a wandering story.  And people in general do **not**
care much about it, for your **comfort. . . .**'

'Sept. 9.

'**You are** now **collecting your** people delightfully,
getting them exactly **into such a** spot as is the delight
of my life.  Three **or** four families in a country village is the very thing to work on ; and I hope you
will write a great deal more, and make full use of
them while they are so very favourably arranged.'

'Sept. **28.**

'Devereux Forrester being ruined by **his vanity is**
very good : but I wish you would not let him plunge
into a "vortex of dissipation."  I do not object to the
thing, but I cannot **bear** the expression : **it is** such
thorough novel slang ; **and so old that I** dare say
Adam met with it in the first novel **that he** opened.'

'Hans Place (Nov. 1814).

'I have been very far from finding your book an evil, I assure you. I read it immediately, and with great pleasure. Indeed, I do think you get on very fast. I wish other people of my acquaintance could compose as rapidly. Julian's history was quite a surprise to me. You had not very long known it yourself, I suspect; but I have no objection to make to the circumstance; it is very well told, and his having been in love with the aunt gives Cecilia an additional interest with him. I like the idea; a very proper compliment to an aunt! I rather imagine, indeed, that nieces are seldom chosen but in compliment to some aunt or other. I dare say your husband was in love with me once, and would never have thought of you if he had not supposed me dead of a scarlet fever.'

Jane Austen was successful in everything that she attempted with her fingers. None of us could throw spilikins in so perfect a circle, or take them off with so steady a hand. Her performances with cup and ball were marvellous. The one used at Chawton was an easy one, and she has been known to catch it on the point above an hundred times in succession, till her hand was weary. She sometimes found a resource in that simple game, when unable, from weakness in her eyes, to read or write long together. A specimen of her clear strong handwriting is here given. Happy would the compositors for the press be if they had always so legible a manuscript to work from. But the writing was not the only part of her letters which showed ʋ superior handiwork. In those days there was an art in folding and sealing. No adhesive envelopes made all easy. Some people's letters always looked loose and untidy; but her paper was sure to take the right folds, and her sealing-wax to drop into the right place. Her needlework both plain and ornamental was ex- cellent, and might almost have put a sewing machine to shame. She was considered especially great in satin stitch. She spent much time in these occupations, and some of her merriest talk was over clothes which she and her companions were making, sometimes for themselves, and sometimes for the poor. There still remains a curious specimen of her needlework made for a sister-in-law, my mother. In a very small bag is deposited a little rolled up housewife, furnished with minikin needles and fine thread. In the housewife is a tiny pocket, and in the pocket is enclosed a slip of paper, on which, written as with a crow quill, are these lines :—

> This little bag, I hope, will prove
> To be not vainly made ;
> For should you thread and needles want,
> It will afford you aid.
>
> And, as we are about to part,
> 'T will serve another end :
> For, when you look upon this bag,
> You'll recollect your friend.

It is the kind of article that some benevolent fairy might be supposed to give as a reward to a diligent little girl.  The whole is of flowered silk, and having been never used and carefully preserved, it is as fresh and bright as when it was first made seventy years ago ; and shows that the same hand which painted so exquisitely with the pen could work as delicately with the needle.

I have collected some of the bright qualities which shone, as it were, on the surface of Jane Austen's character, and attracted most notice ; but underneath them there lay the strong foundations of sound sense and judgment, rectitude of principle, and delicacy of feeling, qualifying her equally to advise, assist, or amuse.  She was, in fact, as ready to comfort the unhappy, or to nurse the sick, as she was to laugh and jest with the light-hearted.  Two of her nieces were grown up, and one of them was married, before she was taken away from them.  As their minds became more matured, they were admitted into closer intimacy with her, and learned more of her graver thoughts ; they know what a sympathising friend and judicious adviser they found her to be in many little difficulties and doubts of early womanhood.

I do not venture to speak of her religious principles : that is a subject on which she herself was more inclined to *think* and *act* than to *talk*, and I shall imitate her reserve ; satisfied to have shown how much of Christian love and humility abounded in her heart, without presuming to lay bare the roots whence those graces grew.  Some little insight, however, into these deeper recesses of the heart must be given, when we come to speak of her death.

# CHAPTER VI.



IT may seem extraordinary that Jane Austen should
have written so little during the years that elapsed
between leaving Steventon and settling at Chawton ;
especially when this cessation from work is contrasted
with her literary activity both before and after that
period.  It might rather have been expected that fresh
scenes and new acquaintance would have called forth
her powers ; while the quiet life which the family led
both at Bath and Southampton must have afforded
abundant leisure for composition ; but so it was that
nothing which I know of, certainly nothing which the
public have seen, was completed in either of those
places.  I can only state the fact, without assigning any
cause for it ; but as soon as she was fixed in her second
home, she resumed the habits of composition which
had been formed in her first, and continued them to
the end of her life.  The first year of her residence
at Chawton seems to have been devoted to revising
and preparing for the press ' Sense and Sensibility,'
and ' Pride and Prejudice '; but between February
1811 and August 1816, she began and completed
' Mansfield Park,' ' Emma,' and ' Persuasion,' so that
the last five years of her life produced the same

number of novels with those which had been written
in her early youth. How she was able to effect all
this is surprising, for she had no separate study to
retire to, and most of the work must have been done
in the general sitting-room, subject to all kinds of
casual interruptions. She was careful that her occupation should not be suspected by servants, or visitors,
or any persons beyond her own family party. She
wrote upon small sheets of paper which could easily
be put away, or covered with a piece of blotting
paper. There was, between the front door and the
offices, a swing door which creaked when it was
opened ; but she objected to having this little inconvenience remedied, because it gave her notice when
anyone was coming. She was not, however, troubled
with companions like her own Mrs. Allen in ' Northanger Abbey,' whose ' vacancy of mind and incapacity
for thinking were such that, as she never talked a
great deal, so she could never be entirely silent ; and
therefore, while she sat at work, if she lost her needle,
or broke her thread, or saw a speck of dirt on her
gown, she must observe it, whether there were any
one at leisure to answer her or not.' In that well
occupied female party there must have been many
precious hours of silence during which the pen was
busy at the little mahogany writing-desk,* while
Fanny Price, or Emma Woodhouse, or Anne Elliott
was growing into beauty and interest. I have no
doubt that I, and my sisters and cousins, in our visits

* This mahogany desk, which has done good service to the public, is
now in the possession of my sister, Miss Austen.

to Chawton, frequently disturbed this mystic process, without having any idea of the mischief that we were doing ; certainly we never should have guessed it by any signs of impatience or irritability in the writer.

As so much had been previously prepared, when once she began to publish, her works came out in quick succession. 'Sense and Sensibility' was published in 1811, 'Pride and Prejudice' at the beginning of 1813, 'Mansfield Park' in 1814, 'Emma' early in 1816; 'Northanger Abbey' and 'Persuasion' did not appear till, after her death, in 1818. It will be shown farther on why 'Northanger Abbey,' though amongst the first written, was one of the last published. Her first three novels were published by Egerton, her last three by Murray. The profits of the four which had been printed before her death had not at that time amounted to seven hundred pounds.

I have no record of the publication of 'Sense and Sensibility,' nor of the author's feelings at this her first appearance before the public; but the following extracts from three letters to her sister give a lively picture of the interest with which she watched the reception of 'Pride and Prejudice,' and show the carefulness with which she corrected her compositions, and rejected much that had been written :—

'Chawton, Friday, January 29 (1813).

'I hope you received my little parcel by J. Bond on Wednesday evening, my dear Cassandra, and that you will be ready to hear from me again on Sunday, for I feel that I must write to you to-day. I want to tell

H

you that I have got my own darling child from London.  On Wednesday I received one copy sent down by Falkener, with three lines from Henry to say that he had given another to Charles and sent a third by the coach to Godmersham. . . . The advertisement is in our paper to-day for the first time : 18*s.* He shall ask 1*l.* 1*s.* for my two next, and 1*l.* 8*s.* for my stupidest of all.  Miss B. dined with us on the very day of the book's coming, and in the evening we fairly set at it, and read half the first vol. to her, prefacing that, having intelligence from Henry that such a work would soon appear, we had desired him to send it whenever it came out, and I believe it passed with her unsuspected.  She was amused, poor soul! *That* she could not help, you know, with two such people to lead the way, but she really does seem to admire Elizabeth.  I must confess that I think her as delightful a creature as ever appeared in print, and how I shall be able to tolerate those who do not like *her* at least I do not know.  There are a few typical errors ; and a " said he," or a " said she," would sometimes make the dialogue more immediately clear ; but " I do not write for such dull elves " as have not a great deal of ingenuity themselves.  The second volume is shorter than I could wish, but the difference is not so much in reality as in look, there being a larger proportion of narrative in that part.  I have lop't and crop't so successfully, however, that I imagine it must be rather shorter than " Sense and Sensibility " altogether.  Now I will try and write of something else.'

'Chawton, Thursday, **February** 4 (1813).

'MY DEAR CASSANDRA,—Your letter was truly welcome, and I am much obliged to you for all your praise; it came at a right time, for I had had some fits of disgust. Our second evening's reading to Miss B. had not pleased me so **well, but** I believe something must be attributed to my mother's **too rapid way** of getting on: though she perfectly **understands the** characters herself, **she cannot** speak **as** they ought. **Upon** the whole, **however, I am** quite vain enough **and well** satisfied **enough. The** work is rather too light, and bright, **and** sparkling; it wants shade; it wants to be stretched out here and there with a long chapter of sense, if it could be had; if not, of solemn specious nonsense, about something unconnected with the **story; an** essay **on writing, a** critique **on Walter** Scott, **or** the history **of** Buonaparté, **or** something that would form a contrast, and bring **the** reader with increased delight to **the** playfulness and epigrammatism of **the** general style. . . . The greatest **blunder in** the printing that I have met with is in page **220, v. 3, where** two speeches are made into one. There might as well be no suppers **at** Longbourn; but I **suppose** it was the remains of Mrs. Bennett's old Meryton habits.'

The following letter seems **to** have been written soon after the last two: in February 1813 :—

'This will be a quick return **for** yours, my dear Cassandra ; **I** doubt its having much else to recommend it; but there is no saying; it may turn out to be a very long and delightful letter. I am exceedingly pleased that you can say what you do, after having gone through the whole work, and Fanny's praise is very gratifying.　My hopes were tolerably strong of *her*, but nothing like a certainty.　Her liking Darcy and Elizabeth is enough.　She might hate all the others, if she would.　I have her opinion under her own hand this morning, but your transcript of it, which I read first, was not, and is not, the less acceptable.　To *me* it is of course all praise, but the more exact truth which she sends *you* is good enough. . . . . Our party on Wednesday was not unagreeable, though we wanted a master of the house less anxious and fidgety, and more conversible.　Upon Mrs. ——'s mentioning that she had sent the rejected addresses to Mrs. H., I began talking to her a little about them, and expressed my hope of their having amused her.　Her answer was, " Oh dear yes, very much, very droll indeed, the opening of the house, and the striking up of the fiddles !"　What she meant, poor woman, who shall say?　I sought no farther.　As soon as a whist party was formed, and a round table threatened, I made my mother an excuse and came away, leaving just as many for *their* round table as there were at Mrs. Grant's.*　I wish they might be as agreeable a set.　My mother is very well, and finds great amusement in glove-knitting, and at present wants no other work. We quite run over with books.　She has got Sir John Carr's " Travels in Spain," and I am reading a Society octavo, an " Essay on the Military Police and Institutions of the British Empire," by Capt. Pasley of

* At this time, February 1813, 'Mansfield Park' was nearly finished.

the Engineers, a book which I protested against at first, but which upon trial I find delightfully written and highly entertaining.  I am as much in love with the author as I ever was with Clarkson or Buchanan, or even the two Mr. Smiths of the city.  The first soldier I ever sighed for; but he does write with extraordinary force and spirit.  Yesterday, moreover, brought us "Mrs. Grant's Letters," with Mr. White's compliments; but I have disposed of them, compliments and all, to Miss P., and amongst so many readers or retainers of books as we have in Chawton, I dare say there will be no difficulty in getting rid of them for another fortnight, if necessary.  I have disposed of Mrs. Grant for the second fortnight to Mrs. ——.  It can make no difference to *her* which of the twenty-six fortnights in the year the 3 vols. lie on her table.  I have been applied to for information as to the oath taken in former times of Bell, Book, and Candle, but have none to give.  Perhaps you may be able to learn something of its origin where you now are.  Ladies who read those enormous great stupid thick quarto volumes which one always sees in the breakfast parlour there must be acquainted with everything in the world.  I detest a quarto.  Capt. Pasley's book is too good for their society.  They will not understand a man who condenses his thoughts into an octavo.  I have learned from Sir J. Carr that there is no Government House at Gibraltar.  I must alter it to the Commissioner's.'

The following letter belongs to the same year, but

treats of a different subject. It describes a journey
from Chawton to London, in her brother's curricle,
and shows how much could be seen and enjoyed in
course of a long summer's day by leisurely travelling
amongst scenery which the traveller in an express
train now rushes through in little more than an hour,
but scarcely sees at all :—

'Sloane Street, Thursday, May 20 (1813).

'MY DEAR CASSANDRA,

' Before I say anything else, I claim a paper full of
halfpence on the drawing-room mantel-piece ; I put
them there myself, and forgot to bring them with me.
I cannot say that I have yet been in any distress for
money, but I chuse to have my due, as well as the
Devil. How lucky we were in our weather yesterday!
This wet morning makes one more sensible of it. We
had no rain of any consequence. The head of the
curricle was put half up three or four times, but our
share of the showers was very trifling, though they
seemed to be heavy all round us, when we were on
the Hog's-back, and I fancied it might then be raining
so hard at Chawton as to make you feel for us much
more than we deserved. Three hours and a quarter
took us to Guildford, where we staid barely two hours,
and had only just time enough for all we had to do
there ; that is, eating a long and comfortable breakfast,
watching the carriages, paying Mr. Harrington, and
taking a little stroll afterwards. From some views
which that stroll gave us, I think most highly of the
situation of Guildford. We wanted all our brothers

and sisters **to be standing** with us in the bowling-green, **and** looking towards Horsham. I was very lucky in my gloves—got **them at** the first shop I went to, though I went **into it** rather because it was near than because it looked at all like a glove shop, and gave only four shillings for **them** ; after which everybody at Chawton will be hoping and predicting that they cannot be good for anything, and their worth certainly remains to be proved ; but I think they look very well. We left Guildford at twenty minutes before twelve **(I** hope somebody cares for these minutiæ), and were at Esher in about two hours more. I was very much pleased with the country **in** general. Between Guildford and Ripley I thought it particularly pretty, also **about** Painshill ; and from a Mr. Spicer's grounds **at Esher, which we walked** into before dinner, the views were beautiful. **I** cannot say what **we did** *not* see, but I should think there could not be a wood, or a meadow, or palace, **or** remarkable spot in England that was not spread out before us on one side **or** other. Claremont is going to be sold : a Mr. Ellis has it now. It is a house that seems **never** to **have** prospered. After dinner we walked forward to be overtaken at the coachman's time, and before he did overtake us we were very near Kingston. I fancy it was about half-past six when we reached this house—a twelve hours' business, and the horses did not appear more than reasonably tired. I was very tired too, and glad to get to bed early, **but am** quite well to-day. I am very snug in **the** front drawing-room all to myself, and would not say "thank you" for

any company but you.  The quietness of it does me
good.  I have contrived to pay my two visits, though
the weather made me a great while about it, and left
me only a few minutes to sit with Charlotte Craven.*
She looks very well, and her hair is done up with
an elegance to do credit to any education.  Her
manners are as unaffected and pleasing as ever.  She
had heard from her mother to-day.  Mrs. Craven
spends another fortnight at Chilton.  I saw nobody
but Charlotte, which pleased me best.  I was shewn
upstairs into a drawing-room, where she came to me,
and the appearance of the room, so totally unschool-
like, amused me very much; it was full of modern
elegancies.

'Yours very affec^tly,          'J. A.'


The next letter, written in the following year,
contains an account of another journey to London,
with her brother Henry, and reading with him the
manuscript of 'Mansfield Park':—

'Henrietta Street, Wednesday, March 2 (1814).

'MY DEAR CASSANDRA,

'You were wrong in thinking of us at Guildford
last night: we were at Cobham.  On reaching G.
we found that John and the horses were gone on.
We therefore did no more than we had done at
Farnham—sit in the carriage while fresh horses were
put in, and proceeded directly to Cobham, which we

* The present Lady Pollen, of Redenham, near Andover, then at a
school in London.

reached by seven, **and about** eight were sitting down **to a very nice roast fowl, &c.** We had altogether a very good journey, **and** everything **at** Cobham was comfortable. **I could** not pay **Mr.** Harrington! That was the only alas! of the business. **I** shall therefore return his bill, and my mother's **2*l.*,** that you may try your luck. We did not begin reading till Bentley Green. Henry's approbation **is** hitherto even equal to **my** wishes. He says it is different from the other two, but does not appear to think it at all inferior. He has only married Mrs. R. **I** am afraid **he has** gone through the most entertaining part. **He** took **to** Lady B. and **Mrs.** N. most kindly, and gives great praise **to the drawing of the** characters. He understands **them all,** likes Fanny, and, I think, foresees how it will all be. I finished the " Heroine " last night, **and was** very much amused **by it.** I wonder James did **not like it** better. **It** diverted me exceedingly. **We** went to bed at ten. **I was** very tired, but slept to a miracle, and **am lovely to-day,** and at present Henry seems **to have** no complaint. We left Cobham at half-past eight, stopped to bait and breakfast at Kingston, **and** were in this house considerably before two. Nice smiling **Mr.** Barlowe **met us at the door** and, in reply to enquiries after **news, said that** peace was generally expected. **I have taken** possession of my bedroom, unpacked my bandbox, sent Miss P.'s two letters to the twopenny post, **been** visited by M^d. B., and am now writing by myself at the new table in **the** front **room.** It is snowing. We had some snowstorms yesterday, and **a** smart frost at night, which

gave us a hard road from Cobham to Kingston ; but
as it was then getting dirty and heavy, Henry had a
pair of leaders put on to the bottom of Sloane St.
His own horses, therefore, cannot have had hard work.
I watched for *veils* as we drove through the streets,
and had the pleasure of seeing several upon vulgar
heads.   And now, how do you all do ?—you in particular, after the worry of yesterday and the day
before.   I hope Martha had a pleasant visit again,
and that you and my mother could eat your beef-
pudding.   Depend upon my thinking of the chimney-
sweeper as soon as I wake to-morrow.   Places are
secured at Drury Lane for Saturday, but so great is
the rage for seeing Kean that only a third and fourth
row could be got ; as it is in a front box, however, I
hope we shall do pretty well—Shylock, a good play
for Fanny—she cannot be much affected, I think
Mrs. Perigord has just been here.   She tells me that
we owe her master for the silk-dyeing.   My poor
old muslin has never been dyed yet.   It has been
promised to be done several times.   What wicked
people dyers are.   They begin with dipping their
own souls in scarlet sin.   It is evening.   We have
drank tea, and I have torn through the third vol. of
the " Heroine."   I do not think it falls off.   It is a
delightful burlesque, particularly on the Radcliffe
style.   Henry is going on with " Mansfield Park."   He
admires H. Crawford : I mean properly, as a clever,
pleasant man.   I tell you all the good I can, as I
know how much you will enjoy it.   We hear that
Mr. Kean is more admired than ever.   There are no

good places to **be** got in Drury Lane for the next fortnight, **but** Henry means to secure some for Saturday fortnight, when you **are** reckoned upon. Give my **love to** little Cass. I hope she found my bed comfortable last night. I have seen nobody in **London** yet with such **a** long chin as Dr. Syntax, **nor** anybody quite so large as Gogmagolicus.

'Yours aff<sup>ly</sup>.,

'J. AUSTEN.'

# CHAPTER VII.

*Seclusion from the literary world—Notice from the Prince Regent— Correspondence with Mr. Clarke—Suggestions to alter her style of writing.*

JANE AUSTEN lived in entire seclusion from the literary world: neither by correspondence, nor by personal intercourse was she known to any contemporary authors. It is probable that she never was in company with any person whose talents or whose celebrity equalled her own; so that her powers never could have been sharpened by collision with superior intellects, nor her imagination aided by their casual suggestions. Whatever she produced was a genuine home-made article. Even during the last two or three years of her life, when her works were rising in the estimation of the public, they did not enlarge the circle of her acquaintance. Few of her readers knew even her name, and none knew more of her than her name. I doubt whether it would be possible to mention any other author of note, whose personal obscurity was so complete. I can think of none like her, but of many to contrast with her in that respect. Fanny Burney, afterwards Madame D'Arblay, was at an early age petted by Dr. Johnson,

and introduced to the wits and scholars of the day
at the tables of Mrs. Thrale and Sir Joshua Reynolds. Anna Seward, in her self-constituted shrine
at Lichfield, would have been miserable, had she not
trusted that the eyes of all lovers of poetry were
devoutly fixed on her. Joanna Baillie and Maria
Edgeworth were indeed far from courting publicity;
they loved the privacy of their own families, one with
her brother and sister in their Hampstead villa, the
other in her more distant retreat in Ireland; but
fame pursued them, and they were the favourite correspondents of Sir Walter Scott. Crabbe, who was
usually buried in a country parish, yet sometimes
visited London, and dined at Holland House, and was
received as a fellow-poet by Campbell, Moore, and
Rogers; and on one memorable occasion he was
Scott's guest at Edinburgh, and gazed with wondering eyes on the incongruous pageantry with which
George IV. was entertained in that city. Even those
great writers who hid themselves amongst lakes and
mountains associated with each other; and though
little seen by the world were so much in its thoughts
that a new term, 'Lakers,' was coined to designate
them. The chief part of Charlotte Brontë's life was
spent in a wild solitude compared with which Steventon and Chawton might be considered to be in
the gay world; and yet she attained to personal
distinction which never fell to Jane's lot. When she
visited her kind publisher in London, literary men
and women were invited purposely to meet her:
Thackeray bestowed upon her the honour of his

notice; and once in Willis's Rooms,* she had to walk shy and trembling through an avenue of lords and ladies, drawn up for the purpose of gazing at the author of 'Jane Eyre.' Miss Mitford, too, lived quietly in 'Our Village,' devoting her time and talents to the benefit of a father scarcely worth of her; but she did not live there unknown. Her tragedies gave her a name in London. She numbered Milman and Talfourd amongst her correspondents; and her works were a passport to the society of many who would not otherwise have sought her. Hundreds admired Miss Mitford on account of her writings for one who ever connected the idea of Miss Austen with the press. A few years ago, a gentleman visiting Winchester Cathedral desired to be shown Miss Austen's grave. The verger, as he pointed it out, asked, 'Pray, sir, can you tell me whether there was anything particular about that lady; so many people want to know where she was buried?' During her life the ignorance of the verger was shared by most people; few knew that 'there was anything particular about that lady.'

It was not till towards the close of her life, when the last of the works that she saw published was in the press, that she received the only mark of distinction ever bestowed upon her; and that was remarkable for the high quarter whence it emanated rather than for any actual increase of fame that it conferred. It happened thus. In the autumn of 1815 she nursed her brother Henry through a dan-

---

* See Mrs. Gaskell's 'Life of Miss Brontë,' vol. ii. p. 215.

gerous fever and slow convalescence at his house in
Hans Place. He was attended by one of the Prince
Regent's physicians. All attempts to keep her name
secret had at this time ceased, and though it had
never appeared on a title-page, all who cared to
know might easily learn it : and the friendly physician was aware that his patient's nurse was the
author of 'Pride and Prejudice.' Accordingly he
informed her one day that the Prince was a great
admirer of her novels ; that he read them often, and
kept a set in every one of his residences ; that he
himself therefore had thought it right to inform his
Royal Highness that Miss Austen was staying in
London, and that the Prince had desired Mr. Clarke,
the librarian of Carlton House, to wait upon her.
The next day Mr. Clarke made his appearance, and
invited her to Carlton House, saying that he had
the Prince's instructions to show her the library and
other apartments, and to pay her every possible attention. The invitation was of course accepted, and
during the visit to Carlton House Mr. Clarke declared himself commissioned to say that if Miss
Austen had any other novel forthcoming she was at
liberty to dedicate it to the Prince. Accordingly such
a dedication was immediately prefixed to 'Emma,'
which was at that time in the press.

Mr. Clarke was the brother of Dr. Clarke, the
traveller and mineralogist, whose life has been written
by Bishop Otter. Jane found in him not only a very
courteous gentleman, but also a warm admirer of her
talents ; though it will be seen by his letters that he

did not clearly apprehend the limits of her powers, or the proper field for their exercise. The following correspondence took place between them.

Feeling some apprehension lest she should make a mistake in acting on the verbal permission which she had received from the Prince, Jane addressed the following letter to Mr. Clarke :—

'Nov. 15, 1815.

'SIR,—I must take the liberty of asking you a question. Among the many flattering attentions which I received from you at Carlton House on Monday last was the information of my being at liberty to dedicate any future work to His Royal Highness the Prince Regent, without the necessity of any solicitation on my part. Such, at least, I believed to be your words; but as I am very anxious to be quite certain of what was intended, I entreat you to have the goodness to inform me how such a permission is to be understood, and whether it is incumbent on me to show my sense of the honour by inscribing the work now in the press to His Royal Highness; I should be equally concerned to appear either presumptuous or ungrateful.'

The following gracious answer was returned by Mr. Clarke, together with a suggestion which must have been received with some surprise :—

'Carlton House, Nov. 16, 1815.

'DEAR MADAM,—It is certainly not *incumbent* on you to dedicate your work now in the press to His

Royal Highness ; but if you wish to do the Regent that honour either now or at any future period I am happy to send you that permission, which need not require any more trouble or solicitation on your part.

'Your late works, Madam, and in particular "Mansfield Park," reflect the highest honour on your genius and your principles. In every new work your mind seems to increase its energy and power of discrimination. The Regent has read and admired all your publications.

'Accept my best thanks for the pleasure your volumes have given me. In the perusal of them I felt a great inclination to write and say so. And I also, dear Madam, wished to be allowed to ask you to delineate in some future work the habits of life, and character, and enthusiasm of a clergyman, who should pass his time between the metropolis and the country, who should be something like Beattie's Minstrel—

> Silent when glad, affectionate tho' shy,
> And in his looks was most demurely sad ;
> And now he laughed aloud, yet none knew why.

Neither Goldsmith, nor La Fontaine in his "Tableau de Famille," have in my mind quite delineated an English clergyman, at least of the present day, fond of and entirely engaged in literature, no man's enemy but his own. Pray, dear Madam, think of these things.

'Believe me at all times with sincerity and respect, your faithful and obliged servant,

'J. S. CLARKE, Librarian.'

I

The following letter, written in reply, will show
how unequal the author of ' Pride and Prejudice'
felt herself to delineating an enthusiastic clergyman
of the present day, who should resemble Beattie's
Minstrel :—

' Dec. 11.

' DEAR SIR,—My " Emma " is now so near publication that I feel it right to assure you of my not
having forgotten your kind recommendation of an
early copy for Carlton House, and that I have Mr.
Murray's promise of its being sent to His Royal
Highness, under cover to you, three days previous to
the work being really out.  I must make use of this
opportunity to thank you, dear Sir, for the very high
praise you bestow on my other novels.  I am too
vain to wish to convince you that you have praised
them beyond their merits.  My greatest anxiety at
present is that this fourth work should not disgrace
what was good in the others.  But on this point I
will do myself the justice to declare that, whatever
may be my wishes for its success, I am strongly
haunted with the idea that to those readers who have
preferred " Pride and Prejudice " it will appear inferior in wit, and to those who have preferred " Mansfield Park " inferior in good sense.  Such as it is,
however, I hope you will do me the favour of accepting a copy.  Mr. Murray will have directions for
sending one.  I am quite honoured by your thinking
me capable of drawing such a clergyman as you gave
the sketch of in your note of Nov. 16th.  But I

assure you I am *not.* The comic part of the character I might be equal **to, but not the** good, the
enthusiastic, the literary. Such a man's conversation
must at times be on subjects of science and philosophy, of which I know nothing; **or at** least be occasionally abundant in quotations and allusions which
a woman who, like me, knows only her own mother
tongue, and **has read little in** that, would **be** totally
without the **power of** giving. A classical education,
or at any rate a very extensive acquaintance **with**
English literature, ancient and modern, appears **to**
me quite indispensable for the **person who** would do
any justice to your clergyman; and **I** think I may
boast myself to be, with all possible vanity, the most
unlearned **and uninformed** female who **ever dared to**
be an authoress.

      ' Believe me, dear Sir,
     ' Your obliged and faithful hum¹¹ Ser¹.
        ' JANE AUSTEN.'*

Mr. Clarke, however, was not to be discouraged
from proposing another subject. He had recently
been appointed chaplain and private English secretary to Prince Leopold, who was then about to
be united to the Princess Charlotte; and when he
again wrote to express the gracious thanks of **the**
Prince Regent for the copy **of** ' Emma ' which had
been presented, he suggests that **' an** historical ro-

---

* It was her pleasure to boast of greater ignorance than she had any
just claim to. She knew more than her mother tongue, for she knew a
good deal of French and a little of Italian.

mance illustrative of the august House of Cobourg would just now be very interesting,' and might very properly be dedicated to Prince Leopold.  This was much as if Sir William Ross had been set to paint a great battle-piece ; and it is amusing to see with what grave civility she declined a proposal which must have struck her as ludicrous, in the following letter :—

'MY DEAR SIR,—I am honoured by the Prince's thanks and very much obliged to yourself for the kind manner in which you mention the work.  I have also to acknowledge a former letter forwarded to me from Hans Place.  I assure you I felt very grateful for the friendly tenor of it, and hope my silence will have been considered, as it was truly meant, to proceed only from an unwillingness to tax your time with idle thanks.  Under every interesting circumstance which your own talents and literary labours have placed you in, or the favour of the Regent bestowed, you have my best wishes.  Your recent appointments I hope are a step to something still better.  In my opinion, the service of a court can hardly be too well paid, for immense must be the sacrifice of time and feeling required by it.

'You are very kind in your hints as to the sort of composition which might recommend me at present, and I am fully sensible that an historical romance, founded on the House of Saxe Cobourg, might be much more to the purpose of profit or popularity than such pictures of domestic life in country villages as I deal in. **But I** could **no** more write a romance than **an epic** poem. I could not sit seriously down to write **a** serious romance under any other motive than to save my life; and if it were indispensable for me to keep it up and never relax into laughing at myself **or** at other people, **I** am sure **I** should be hung before **I** had finished the first chapter. No, I must keep **to** my **own** style and go on in my own way; and though **I may** never succeed again in that, **I am** convinced that I should totally fail in any other.

'I remain, my dear Sir,

'Your very much obliged, and sincere **friend,**

'J. AUSTEN.

'Chawton, near Alton, April 1, 1816.'

**Mr.** Clarke should have recollected **the** warning of the wise man, '**Force not** the course **of** the river.' If you divert it from **the** channel in which nature taught it to flow, and **force it into** one arbitrarily cut by yourself, you will lose its grace and beauty.

> But when his free course is not hindered,
> He makes sweet music with the enamelled stones,
> Giving a gentle kiss to every sedge
> He overtaketh in his pilgrimage :
> And so by many winding nooks he strays
> With willing sport.

**All** writers **of** fiction, **who have** genius strong enough to work out a course **of their** own, resist every attempt to interfere with **its** direction. No two writers could **be** more unlike each other than Jane Austen and Charlotte Brontë; so much so that the latter was unable to understand why the former was admired, and confessed that she herself ‘should hardly like to live with her ladies and gentlemen, in their elegant but confined houses ;’ but each writer equally resisted interference with her own natural style of composition.    Miss Brontë, in reply to a friendly critic, who had warned her against being too melo-dramatic, and had ventured to propose Miss Austen's works to her as a study, writes thus :—

‘Whenever I *do* write another book, I think I will have nothing of what you call “melodrama.”  I *think* so, but I am not sure.  I *think*, too, I will endeavour to follow the counsel which shines out of Miss Aus-ten's “mild eyes,” to finish more, and be more sub-dued ; but neither am I sure of that.  When authors write best, or, at least, when they write most fluently, an influence seems to waken in them which becomes their master—which will have its way—putting out of view all behests but its own, dictating certain words, and insisting on their being used, whether vehement or measured in their nature, new moulding characters, giving unthought of turns to incidents, rejecting carefully elaborated old ideas, and suddenly creating and adopting new ones.  Is it not so ?  And should we try to counteract this influence ?  Can we indeed counteract it ?’ *

The playful raillery with which the one parries an attack on her liberty, and the vehement eloquence of the other in pleading the same cause and maintaining the independence of genius, are very characteristic of the minds of the respective writers.

* Mrs. Gaskell's ‘Life of Miss Brontë,’ vol. ii. p. 53.

The suggestions which Jane received **as to the sort** of story that **she** ought **to write** were, however, an amusement **to her,** though they were not likely to prove useful ; and she has **left** amongst her papers one entitled, 'Plan of a novel according to hints from various quarters.' The names of some of those **advisers** are written on the margin of the manuscript opposite to their respective suggestions.

'Heroine to be **the** daughter **of** a clergyman, who after having lived much in the world had retired from it, **and** settled on a curacy with a very small fortune of his own. **The most** excellent man that can be imagined, perfect **in** character, temper, and manner, without the smallest drawback or peculiarity to prevent his being the most delightful companion to his daughter from one year's **end to** the other. Heroine faultless in character, beautiful in person, and possessing every possible accomplishment. Book to open with father and daughter conversing in long speeches, elegant language, and a tone of high serious sentiment. The father induced, **at** his daughter's earnest request, to relate to her the past events of his life. Narrative to reach through the greater part of the first volume ; **as** besides all the circumstances of his attachment to her mother, and their marriage, it will comprehend his going to sea as chaplain to a distinguished naval character about **the** court ; and his going afterwards to court himself, which involved him in many interesting situations, concluding with his opinion of the benefits of tithes being done away with. . . . From this outset the story will proceed, and contain a striking variety of adventures. Father an exemplary parish priest, and devoted to literature; but heroine and father never above a fortnight in one place: he being driven from his curacy by the vile arts of some totally unprincipled and heartless young man, desperately in love with the heroine, and pursuing her with unrelenting passion. No sooner settled in one country of Europe, than they are compelled to quit it, and retire to another, always making new acquaintance, and always obliged to leave them. This will of course exhibit a wide variety of character. The scene will be for ever shifting from one set of people to another, but there will be no mixture, all the good will be unexceptionable in every respect. There will be no foibles or weaknesses but with the wicked, who will be completely depraved and infamous, hardly a resemblance of humanity left in them. Early in her career, the heroine must meet with the hero: all perfection, of course, and only prevented from paying his addresses to her by some excess of refinement. Wherever she goes, somebody falls in love with her, and she receives repeated offers of marriage, which she refers wholly to her father, exceedingly angry that *he* should not be the first applied to. Often carried away by the anti-hero, but rescued either by her father or the hero. Often reduced to support herself and her father by her talents, and work for her bread; continually cheated, and defrauded of her hire; worn down to a skeleton, and now and then starved to death. At last, hunted out of civilised society, denied the poor shelter of the humblest cottage, they are compelled to retreat into Kamtschatka, where the poor father quite worn down, finding his end approaching, throws himself on the ground, and after four or five hours of tender advice and parental admonition to his miserable child, expires in a fine burst of literary enthusiasm, intermingled with invectives against the holders of tithes. Heroine inconsolable for some time, but afterwards crawls back towards her former country, having at least twenty narrow escapes of falling into the hands of anti-hero; and at last, in the very nick of time, turning a corner to avoid him, runs into the arms of the hero himself, who, having just shaken off the scruples which fettered him before, was at the very moment setting off in pursuit of her. The tenderest and completest *éclaircissement* takes place, and they are happily united. Throughout the whole work heroine to be in the most elegant society, and living in high style.'

Since the first publication of this memoir, Mr. Murray of Albemarle Street has very kindly sent to me copies of the following letters, which his father received from Jane Austen, when engaged in the publication of 'Emma.' The increasing cordiality of the letters shows that the author felt that her interests were duly cared for, and was glad to find herself in the hands of a publisher whom she could consider as a friend.

Her brother had addressed to Mr. Murray a strong complaint of the tardiness of a printer :—

'23 Hans Place, Thursday, November 23 (1815).

'SIR,—My brother's note last Monday has been so fruitless, that I am afraid there can be but little chance of my writing to any good effect ; but yet I am so very much disappointed and vexed by the delays of the printers, that I cannot help begging to know whether there is no hope of their being quickened.  Instead of the work being ready by the end of the present month, it will hardly, at the rate we now proceed, be finished by the end of the next ; and as I expect to leave London early in December, it is of consequence that no more time should be lost.  Is it likely that the printers will be influenced to greater dispatch and punctuality by knowing that the work is to be dedicated, by permission, to the Prince Regent ?  If you can make that circumstance operate, I shall be very glad.  My brother returns 'Waterloo' with many thanks for the loan of it.  We have heard much of Scott's account of Paris.*  If it be not incompatible with other arrangements, would you favour us with it, supposing you have any set already opened ?  You may depend upon its being in careful hands.

'I remain, Sir, your ob' humble Se'

'J. AUSTEN.'

'Hans Place, December 11 (1815).

'DEAR SIR,—As I find that "Emma" is advertised for publication as early as Saturday next, I think it best to lose no time in settling all that remains to be

* This must have been 'Paul's Letters to his Kinsfolk.'

settled on the subject, and adopt this method as involving the smallest tax on your time.

'In the first place, I beg you to understand that I leave the terms on which the trade should be supplied with the work entirely to your judgment, entreating you to be guided in every such arrangement by your own experience of what is most likely to clear off the edition rapidly. I shall be satisfied with whatever you feel to be best. The title-page must be "Emma, dedicated by permission to H.R.H. the Prince Regent." And it is my particular wish that one set should be completed and sent to H.R.H. two or three days before the work is generally public. It should be sent under cover to the Rev. J. S. Clarke, Librarian, Carlton House. I shall subjoin a list of those persons to whom I must trouble you to forward also a set each, when the work is out ; all unbound, with " From the Authoress " in the first page.

'I return you, with very many thanks, the books you have so obligingly supplied me with. I am very sensible, I assure you, of the attention you have paid to my convenience and amusement. I return also " Mansfield Park," as ready for a second edition, I believe, as I can make it. I am in Hans Place till the 16th. From that day inclusive, my direction will be Chawton, Alton, Hants.

'I remain, dear Sir,<br>'Y<sup>r</sup> faithful humb. Serv<sup>t</sup><br>'J. AUSTEN.

'I wish you would have the goodness to send a line

by the bearer, stating *the day* on which the set will be ready for the Prince Regent.'

'Hans Place, December 11 (1815).

'DEAR SIR,—I am much obliged by yours, and very happy to feel everything arranged to our mutual satisfaction. As to my direction about the title-page, it was arising from my ignorance only, and from my having never noticed the proper place for a dedication. I thank you for putting me right. Any deviation from what is usually done in such cases is the last thing I should wish for. I feel happy in having a friend to save me from the ill effect of my own blunder.

'Yours, dear Sir, &c.

'J. AUSTEN.'

'Chawton, April 1, 1816.

'DEAR SIR,—I return you the "Quarterly Review" with many thanks. The Authoress of "Emma" has no reason, I think, to complain of her treatment in it, except in the total omission of "Mansfield Park." I cannot but be sorry that so clever a man as the Reviewer of "Emma" should consider it as unworthy of being noticed. You will be pleased to hear that I have received the Prince's thanks for the *handsome* copy I sent him of "Emma." Whatever he may think of *my* share of the work, yours seems to have been quite right.

'In consequence of the late event in Henrietta Street, I must request that if you should at any time have anything to communicate by letter, you will be so good as to write by the post, directing to me (Miss J. Austen), Chawton, near Alton ; and that for anything of a larger bulk, you will add to the same direction, by *Collier's Southampton coach.*

'I remain, dear Sir,

'Yours very faithfully,

'J. AUSTEN.'

About the same time the following letters passed between the Countess of Morley and the writer of 'Emma.' I do not know whether they were personally acquainted with each other, nor in what this interchange of civilities originated :—

*The Countess of Morley to Miss J. Austen.*

'Saltram, December 27 (1815).

'MADAM,—I have been most anxiously waiting for an introduction to "Emma," and am infinitely obliged to you for your kind recollection of me, which will procure me the pleasure of her acquaintance some days sooner than I should otherwise have had it. I am already become intimate with the Woodhouse family, and feel that they will not amuse and interest me less than the Bennetts, Bertrams, Norrises, and all their admirable predecessors. I can give them no higher praise.

'I am, Madam, your much obliged

'F. MORLEY.'

*Miss J. Austen to the Countess of Morley.*

'MADAM,—Accept my thanks for the honour of
your note, and for your kind disposition in favour of
"Emma." In my present state of doubt as to her reception in the world, it is particularly gratifying to
me to receive so early an assurance of your Ladyship's approbation. It encourages me to depend on the
same share of general good opinion which "Emma's"
predecessors have experienced, and to believe that I
have not yet, as almost every writer of fancy does
sooner or later, overwritten myself.

'I am, Madam,<br>
'Your obliged and faithful Serv<sup>t.</sup><br>
'J. AUSTEN.

'December 31, 1815.'

## CHAPTER VIII.

*Slow growth of her fame—Ill success of first attempts at publication—
Two Reviews of her works contrasted.*

SELDOM has any literary reputation been of such slow growth as that of Jane Austen. Readers of the present day know the rank that is generally assigned to her. They have been told by Archbishop Whately, in his review of her works, and by Lord Macaulay, in his review of Madame D'Arblay's, the reason why the highest place is to be awarded to Jane Austen, as a truthful drawer of character, and why she is to be classed with those who have approached nearest, in that respect, to the great master Shakspeare. They see her safely placed, by such authorities, in her niche, not indeed amongst the highest orders of genius, but in one confessedly her own, in our British temple of literary fame; and it may be difficult to make them believe how coldly her works were at first received, and how few readers had any appreciation of their peculiar merits. Sometimes a friend or neighbour, who chanced to know of our connection with the author, would condescend to speak with moderate approbation of ' Sense and Sensibility,' or ' Pride and Prejudice '; but if they had known that we, in our secret thoughts, classed her with Madame D'Arblay or Miss Edgeworth, or even with some other novel writers of the day whose names are now scarcely remembered, they would have considered it an amusing instance of family conceit.  To the multitude her works appeared tame and commonplace,* poor in colouring, and sadly deficient in incident and interest.  It is true that we were sometimes cheered by hearing that a different verdict had been pronounced by more competent judges: we were told how some great statesman or distinguished poet held these works in high estimation; we had the satisfaction of believing that they were most admired by the best judges, and comforted ourselves with Horace's ' satis est Equitem mihi plaudere.'  So much was this the case, that one of the ablest men of my acquaintance † said, in that kind of jest which has much earnest in it, that he had established it in his own mind, as a new test of ability, whether people *could* or *could not* appreciate Miss Austen's merits.

But though such golden opinions were now and then gathered in, yet the wide field of public taste

---

* A greater genius than my aunt shared with her the imputation of being *commonplace*.  Lockhart, speaking of the low estimation in which Scott's conversational powers were held in the literary and scientific society of Edinburgh, says : ' I think the epithet most in vogue concerning it was "commonplace." '  He adds, however, that one of the most eminent of that society was of a different opinion, 'who, when some glib youth chanced to echo in his hearing the consolatory tenet of local mediocrity, answered quietly, "I have the misfortune to think differently from you—in my humble opinion Walter Scott's *sense* is a still more wonderful thing than his genius." '—Lockhart's *Life of Scott*, vol. iv. chap. v.

† The late Mr. R. H. Cheney.

yielded **no** adequate **return** either in praise **or** profit. Her reward **was not to be** the quick **return** of the cornfield, but **the** slow growth of the **tree** which is **to** endure **to another** generation. Her first attempts **at** publication were very discouraging. **In** November, 1797, **her father wrote** the following letter to **Mr.** Cadell :—

'**SIR**,—**I have** in my possession a manuscript novel, comprising 3 vols., about the length of Miss Burney's "Evelina." As I am well aware of **what** consequence it is that a work **of** this sort sh$^d$ make its first appearance under **a** respectable **name,** I apply **to** you. **I** shall be much obliged therefore if you will inform me whether **you** choose to be concerned in it, what will **be the** expense of publishing **it** at the author's risk, **and** what you will venture **to advance for the** property of **it, if** on perusal **it is** approved **of.** Should **you** give **any** encouragement, **I will send** you the work.

'**I am, Sir,** your humble Servant,

'**GEORGE AUSTEN.**'

'Steventon, near Overton, Hants,
'1st Nov. 1797.'

**This proposal** was declined **by** return of post! The work thus summarily rejected must have been 'Pride and Prejudice.'

The fate of 'Northanger Abbey' was still more humiliating. **It** was sold, in 1803, to a publisher in Bath, for ten pounds, but it found **so** little favour in **his eyes,** that he chose to abide by his first loss rather than risk farther expense by publishing such a work. It seems to have lain for many years unnoticed in his drawers ; somewhat as the first chapters of 'Waverley' lurked forgotten amongst the old fishing-tackle in Scott's cabinet. Tilneys, Thorpes, and Morlands consigned apparently to eternal oblivion ! But when four novels of steadily increasing success had given the writer some confidence in herself, she wished to recover the copyright of this early work. One of her brothers undertook the negotiation. He found the purchaser very willing to receive back his money, and to resign all claim to the copyright. When the bargain was concluded and the money paid, but not till then, the negotiator had the satisfaction of informing him that the work which had been so lightly esteemed was by the author of 'Pride and Prejudice.' 'I do not think that she was herself much mortified by the want of early success. She wrote for her own amusement. Money, though acceptable, was not necessary for the moderate expenses of her quiet home. Above all, she was blessed with a cheerful contented disposition, and an humble mind ; and so lowly did she esteem her own claims, that when she received 150*l*. from the sale of 'Sense and Sensibility,' she considered it a prodigious recompense for that which had cost her nothing. It cannot be supposed, however, that she was altogether insensible to the superiority of her own workmanship over that of some contemporaries who were then enjoying a brief popularity. Indeed a few touches in the following extracts from two of her letters show that she

was as quicksighted **to** absurdities in composition as
to those in living persons.

'Mr. C.'s opinion is gone down in my list; but as
my paper relates only to "Mansfield Park," I may
fortunately excuse myself from entering Mr. D.'s. I
will redeem my credit with him by writing a close
imitation of "Self-Control," as soon as I can. **I will**
improve upon it. My heroine shall not only be wafted
down an American river in a boat by herself. She
shall cross the Atlantic in the same way; and **never**
stop till she reaches Gravesend.'

'We have got "Rosanne" **in** our Society, and **find**
it much as you describe it; very good and clever, but
tedious. **Mrs.** Hawkins' great excellence is on serious
subjects. **There** are some very delightful conversations and reflections on religion: but on lighter
topics I think she falls into many absurdities; and,
as to love, her heroine has very comical feelings.
There **are a** thousand improbabilities **in the** story.
Do **you** remember the two Miss Ormsdens introduced
just at last? Very flat and **unnatural.** Mad^elle.^
Cossart is rather my passion.'

Two notices of her works appeared in the 'Quarterly
Review.' **One** in October 1815, and another, more
than three **years** after her death, in January 1821.
The latter article is known to have been from **the**
pen of Whately, afterwards Archbishop of Dublin.*

* Lockhart had supposed that this article had been written by Scott,
because it exactly accorded with the opinions which Scott had often
been heard to express, but he learned afterwards that it had been written
by Whately; and Lockhart, who became the Editor of the Quarterly,

They differ much from each other in the degree of praise which they award, and I think also it may be said, in the ability with which they are written. The first bestows some approval, but the other expresses the warmest admiration.  One can scarcely be satisfied with the critical acumen of the former writer, who, in treating of ‘Sense and Sensibility,’ takes no notice whatever of the vigour with which many of the characters are drawn, but declares that ‘the interest and *merit* of the piece depends *altogether* upon the behaviour of the elder sister!’  Nor is he fair when, in ‘Pride and Prejudice,’ he represents Elizabeth’s change of sentiments towards Darcy as caused by the sight of his house and grounds.  But the chief discrepancy between the two reviewers is to be found in their appreciation of the commonplace and silly characters to be found in these novels.  On this point the difference almost amounts to a contradiction, such as one sometimes sees drawn up in parallel columns, when it is desired to convict some writer or some statesman of inconsistency.  The Reviewer, in 1815, says : ‘The faults of these works arise from the minute detail which the author’s plan comprehends.  Characters of folly or simplicity, such as those of old Woodhouse and Miss Bates, are ridiculous when first presented, but if too often brought forward, or too long dwelt on, their prosing

must have had the means of knowing the truth.  (See Lockhart’s *Life of Sir Walter Scott*, vol. v. p. 158.)  I remember that, at the time when the review came out, it was reported in Oxford that Whately had written the article at the request of the lady whom he afterwards married.

is apt to become as tiresome in fiction as in real society.' The Reviewer, in 1821, on the contrary, singles out the fools as especial instances of the writer's abilities, and declares that in this respect she shows a regard to character hardly exceeded by Shakspeare himself. These are his words: 'Like him (Shakspeare) she shows as admirable a discrimination in the character of fools as of people of sense; a merit which is far from common. To invent indeed a conversation full of wisdom or of wit requires that the writer should himself possess ability; but the converse does not hold good, it is no fool that can describe fools well; and many who have succeeded pretty well in painting superior characters have failed in giving individuality to those weaker ones which it is necessary to introduce in order to give a faithful representation of real life: they exhibit to us mere folly in the abstract, forgetting that to the eye of the skilful naturalist the insects on a leaf present as wide differences as exist between the lion and the elephant. Slender, and Shallow, and Aguecheek, as Shakspeare has painted them, though equally fools, resemble one another no more than Richard, and Macbeth, and Julius Cæsar; and Miss Austen's * Mrs. Bennet, Mr. Rushworth, and Miss Bates are no more alike than her Darcy, Knightley, and Edmund Bertram. Some have complained indeed of finding her fools too much like nature, and consequently tiresome. There is no disputing about tastes; all we

* In transcribing this passage I have taken the liberty so far to correct it as to spell her name properly with an 'e.'

can say is, that such critics must (whatever deference they may outwardly pay to received opinions) find the " Merry Wives of Windsor " and " Twelfth Night " very tiresome ; and that those who look with pleasure at Wilkie's picture, or those of the Dutch school, must admit that excellence of imitation may confer attraction on that which would be insipid or disagreeable in the reality. Her minuteness of detail has also been found fault with ; but even where it produces, at the time, a degree of tediousness, we know not whether that can justly be reckoned a blemish, which is absolutely essential to a very high excellence. Now it is absolutely impossible, without this, to produce that thorough acquaintance with the characters which is necessary to make the reader heartily interested in them. Let any one cut out from the " Iliad " or from Shakspeare's plays everything (we are far from saying that either might not lose some parts with advantage, but let him reject everything) which is absolutely devoid of importance and interest *in itself* ; and he will find that what is left will have lost more than half its charms. We are convinced that some writers have diminished the effect of their works by being scrupulous to admit nothing into them which had not some absolute and independent merit. They have acted like those who strip off the leaves of a fruit tree, as being of themselves good for nothing, with the view of securing more nourishment to the fruit, which in fact cannot attain its full maturity and flavour without them.'

The world, I think, has endorsed the opinion of

the later writer ; but **it would not** be **fair** to set down
the discrepancy between the two entirely **to** the discredit **of** the former. The fact **is** that, **in the** course
**of the** intervening five years, **these works** had been
**read and** reread by many leaders **in** the literary
world. The public **taste was** forming itself all this
time, **and 'grew by what it** fed on.' These novels
belong to **a** class **which** gain rather **than** lose by frequent perusals, **and it is** probable that each Reviewer
represented **fairly** enough the prevailing opinions of
readers in **the year** when each wrote.

**Since that time, the** testimonies **in favour** of Jane
Austen's works **have been** continual and almost un-
animous. They **are** frequently **referred to** as models ;
nor have **they** lost their first distinction of being
especially acceptable to minds of the highest order.
**I** shall indulge myself by collecting into the next
chapter instances of the homage paid to **her** by such
persons.

# CHAPTER IX.



INTO this list of the admirers of my Aunt's works, I admit those only whose eminence will be universally acknowledged. No doubt the number might have been increased.

Southey, in a letter to Sir Egerton Brydges, says : 'You mention Miss Austen. Her novels are more true to nature, and have, for my sympathies, passages of finer feeling than any others of this age. She was a person of whom I have heard so well and think so highly, that I regret not having had an opportunity of testifying to her the respect which I felt for her.'

It may be observed that Southey had probably heard from his own family connections of the charm of her private character. A friend of hers, the daughter of Mr. Bigge Wither, of Manydown Park near Basingstoke, was married to Southey's uncle, the Rev. Herbert Hill, who had been useful to his nephew in many ways, and especially in supplying him with the means of attaining his extensive knowledge of Spanish and Portuguese literature. Mr. Hill had been Chaplain to the British Factory at Lisbon, where Southey visited

him and **had** the **use of** a library in those languages
which his uncle had collected.  Southey himself con-
**tinually** mentions his uncle Hill **in** terms **of** respect
**and** gratitude.

S. T. Coleridge would sometimes burst out into high
encomiums of Miss Austen's novels as being, 'in their
**way,** perfectly genuine and individual productions.'

I remember Miss Mitford's saying to me : ' I would
almost cut off one **of** my hands, if it would enable me
to write like your aunt with the other.'

The biographer of Sir J. Mackintosh says : 'Something recalled to his mind the traits of **character** which
are so delicately touched in Miss Austen's novels. . .
**He** said that there **was** genius **in sketching out that**
new kind of novel. . . **He was vexed for** the credit of
the " Edinburgh **Review"** that **it had left** her **unnoticed.*** . . The **"Quarterly"** had done **her more**
justice. . . **It was** impossible **for a** foreigner to understand fully the merit of **her works.**  Madame de Staël,
to whom he had recommended one **of** her novels, found
no interest in it ; **and in** her **note to** him **in** reply said
it was "vulgaire" : and yet, he said, nothing could be
**more** true than what **he** wrote in answer: " There is
no book which that word would **so** little suit." . . .
Every village could furnish matter for a novel to Miss
Austen.  She did not need the common materials for
a novel, strong emotions, or strong incidents.' †

**It** was not, **however,** quite impossible for a foreigner

---

* Incidentally she **had** received high praise in Lord Macaulay's
Review of Madame D'Arblay's Works in the ' Edinburgh.'

† *Life of Sir J. Mackintosh,* **vol. ii.** p. 472.

to appreciate these works; for Mons. Guizot writes thus: 'I am a great novel reader, but I seldom read German or French novels. The characters are too artificial. My delight is to read English novels, particularly those written by women. "C'est toute une école de morale." Miss Austen, Miss Ferrier, &c., form a school which in the excellence and profusion of its productions resembles the cloud of dramatic poets of the great Athenian age.'

In the 'Keepsake' of 1825 the following lines appeared, written by Lord Morpeth, afterwards seventh Earl of Carlisle, and Lord-Lieutenant of Ireland, accompanying an illustration of a lady reading a novel.

> Beats thy quick pulse o'er Inchbald's thrilling leaf,
> Brunton's high moral, Opie's deep wrought grief?
> Has the mild chaperon claimed thy yielding heart,
> Carroll's dark page, Trevelyan's gentle art?
> Or is it thou, all perfect Austen? Here
> Let one poor wreath adorn thy early bier,
> That scarce allowed thy modest youth to claim
> Its living portion of thy certain fame!
> Oh! Mrs. Bennet! Mrs. Norris too!
> While memory survives we'll dream of you.
> And Mr. Woodhouse, whose abstemious lip
> Must thin, but not too thin, his gruel sip.
> Miss Bates, our idol, though the village bore;
> And Mrs. Elton, ardent to explore.
> While the dear style flows on without pretence,
> With unstained purity, and unmatched sense:
> Or, if a sister e'er approached the throne,
> She called the rich 'inheritance' her own.

The admiration felt by Lord Macaulay would probably have taken a very practical form, if his life had been prolonged. I have the authority of his sister, Lady Trevelyan, for stating that he had intended to undertake the task upon which I have ventured. He purposed to write a memoir of Miss Austen, with criticisms on her works, to prefix it to a new edition of her novels, and from the proceeds of the sale to erect a monument to her memory in Winchester Cathedral. Oh! that such an idea had been realised! That portion of the plan in which Lord Macaulay's success would have been most certain might have been almost sufficient for his object. A memoir written by him would have been a monument.

I am kindly permitted by Sir Henry Holland to give the following quotation from his printed but unpublished recollections of his past life:—

'I have the picture still before me of Lord Holland lying on his bed, when attacked with gout, his admirable sister, Miss Fox, beside him reading aloud, as she always did on these occasions, some one of Miss Austen's novels, of which he was never wearied. I well recollect the time when these charming novels, almost unique in their style of humour, burst suddenly on the world. It was sad that their writer did not live to witness the growth of her fame.'

My brother-in-law, Sir Denis Le Marchant, has supplied me with the following anecdotes from his own recollections:—

'When I was a student at Trinity College, Cambridge, Mr. Whewell, then a Fellow and afterwards Master of the College, often spoke to me with admiration of Miss Austen's novels. On one occasion I said that I had found "Persuasion" rather dull. He quite fired up in defence of it, insisting that it was the most beautiful of her works. This accomplished philosopher was deeply versed in works of fiction. I recollect his writing to me from Caernarvon, where he had the charge of some pupils, that he was weary of *his* stay, for he had read the circulating library twice through.

'During a visit I paid to Lord Lansdowne, at Bowood, in 1846, one of Miss Austen's novels became the subject of conversation and of praise, especially from Lord Lansdowne, who observed that one of the circumstances of his life which he looked back upon with vexation was that Miss Austen should once have been living some weeks in his neighbourhood without his knowing it.

'I have heard Sydney Smith, more than once, dwell with eloquence on the merits of Miss Austen's novels. He told me he should have enjoyed giving her the pleasure of reading her praises in the "Edinburgh Review." "Fanny Price" was one of his prime favourites.'

I close this list of testimonies, this long 'Catena Patrum,' with the remarkable words of Sir Walter Scott, taken from his diary for March 14, 1826: *
'Read again, for the third time at least, Miss Austen's finely written novel of "Pride and Prejudice." That young lady had a talent for describing the involvements and feelings and characters of ordinary life,

* Lockhart's *Life of Scott*, vol. vi. chap. vii.

which is to me the most wonderful I ever met with. The big Bow-Wow strain I can do myself like any now going; but the exquisite touch which renders ordinary common-place things and characters interesting from the truth of the description and the sentiment is denied to me. What a pity such a gifted creature died so early!' The well-worn condition of Scott's own copy of these works attests that they were much read in his family. When I visited Abbotsford, a few years after Scott's death, I was permitted, as an unusual favour, to take one of these volumes in my hands. One cannot suppress the wish that she had lived to know what such men thought of her powers, and how gladly they would have cultivated a personal acquaintance with her. I do not think that it would at all have impaired the modest simplicity of her character; or that we should have lost our own dear 'Aunt Jane' in the blaze of literary fame.

It may be amusing to contrast with these testimonies from the great, the opinions expressed by other readers of more ordinary intellect. The author herself has left a list of criticisms which it had been her amusement to collect, through means of her friends. This list contains much of warm-hearted sympathising praise, interspersed with some opinions which may be considered surprising.

One lady could say nothing better of 'Mansfield Park,' than that it was ' a mere novel.'

Another owned that she thought 'Sense and Sensibility' and 'Pride and Prejudice' downright non-

sense; but expected to like 'Mansfield Park' better,
and having finished the first volume, hoped that she
had got through the worst.

Another did not like 'Mansfield Park.' Nothing
interesting in the characters. Language poor.

One gentleman read the first and last chapters of
'Emma,' but did not look at the rest, because he had
been told that it was not interesting.

The opinions of another gentleman about 'Emma'
were so bad that they could not be reported to the
author.

'Quot homines, tot sententiæ.'

Thirty-five years after her death there came also a
voice of praise from across the Atlantic. In 1852
the following letter was received by her brother Sir
Francis Austen :—

'Boston, Massachusetts, U. S. A.<br>
6th Jan. 1852.

' Since high critical authority has pronounced the
delineations of character in the works of Jane Austen
second only to those of Shakspeare, transatlantic
admiration appears superfluous; yet it may not be
uninteresting to her family to receive an assurance
that the influence of her genius is extensively recognised in the American Republic, even by the highest
judicial authorities. The late Mr. Chief Justice Marshall, of the supreme Court of the United States, and
his associate Mr. Justice Story, highly estimated and
admired Miss Austen, and to them we owe our introduction to her society. For many years her talents
have brightened our daily path, and her name and

those of her characters are familiar to us as " household words." We have long wished to express to
some of her family the sentiments of gratitude and
affection she has inspired, and request more information relative to her life than is given in the brief
memoir prefixed to her works.

' Having accidentally heard that a brother of Jane
Austen held a high rank in the British Navy, we
have obtained his address from our friend Admiral
Wormley, now resident in Boston, and we trust this
expression of our feeling will be received by her
relations with the kindness and urbanity characteristic of Admirals of *her creation.* Sir Francis Austen,
or one of his family, would confer a great favour by
complying with our request. The autograph of his
sister, or a few lines in her handwriting, would be
placed among our chief treasures.

' The family who delight in the companionship of
Jane Austen, and who present this petition, are of
English origin. Their ancestor held a high rank
among the first emigrants to New England, and
his name and character have been ably represented
by his descendants in various public stations of trust
and responsibility to the present time in the colony
and state of Massachusetts. A letter addressed to
Miss Quincey, care of the Hon^ble Josiah Quincey,
Boston, Massachusetts, would reach its destination.'

Sir Francis Austen returned a suitable reply to
this application ; and sent a long letter of his sister's,
which, no doubt, still occupies the place of honour
promised by the Quincey family.

# CHAPTER X.

*Observations on the Novels.*

IT is not the object of these memoirs to attempt a
criticism on Jane Austen's novels.  Those particulars
only have been noticed which could be illustrated by
the circumstances of her own life ; but I now desire to
offer a few observations on them, and especially on
one point, on which my age renders me a competent
witness—the fidelity with which they represent the
opinions and manners of the class of society in which
the author lived early in this century.  They do this
the more faithfully on account of the very deficiency
with which they have been sometimes charged—
namely, that they make no attempt to raise the
standard of human life, but merely represent it as it
was.  They certainly were not written to support any
theory or inculcate any particular moral, except indeed the great moral which is to be equally gathered
from an observation of the course of actual life—
namely, the superiority of high over low principles,
and of greatness over littleness of mind.  These
writings are like photographs, in which no feature is
softened ; no ideal expression is introduced, all is the
unadorned reflection of the natural object ; and the

value of such a faithful likeness must increase as
time gradually works more and more changes in the
face of society itself. A remarkable instance of this
is to be found in her portraiture of the clergy. She
was the daughter and the sister of clergymen, who
certainly were not low specimens of their order : and
she has chosen three of her heroes from that profession ; but no one in these days can think that
either Edmund Bertram or Henry Tilney had adequate ideas of the duties of a parish minister. Such,
however, were the opinions and practice then prevalent among respectable and conscientious clergymen before their minds had been stirred, first by the
Evangelical, and afterwards by the High Church
movement which this century has witnessed. The
country may be congratulated which, on looking
back to such a fixed landmark, can find that it has
been advancing instead of receding from it.

The long interval that elapsed between the completion of 'Northanger Abbey' in 1798, and the
commencement of 'Mansfield Park' in 1811, may
sufficiently account for any difference of style which
may be perceived between her three earlier and her
three later productions. If the former showed quite
as much originality and genius, they may perhaps be
thought to have less of the faultless finish and high
polish which distinguish the latter. The characters
of the John Dashwoods, Mr. Collins, and the Thorpes
stand out from the canvas with a vigour and originality which cannot be surpassed ; but I think that
in her last three works are to be found a greater

refinement of taste, a more nice sense of propriety, and a deeper insight into the delicate anatomy of the human heart, marking the difference between the brilliant girl and the mature woman. Far from being one of those who have over-written themselves, it may be affirmed that her fame would have stood on a narrower and less firm basis, if she had not lived to resume her pen at Chawton.

Some persons have surmised that she took her characters from individuals with whom she had been acquainted. They were so life-like that it was assumed that they must once have lived, and have been transferred bodily, as it were, into her pages. But surely such a supposition betrays an ignorance of the high prerogative of genius to create out of its own resources imaginary characters, who shall be true to nature and consistent in themselves. Perhaps, however, the distinction between keeping true to nature and servilely copying any one specimen of it is not always clearly apprehended. It is indeed true, both of the writer and of the painter, that he can use only such lineaments as exist, and as he has observed to exist, in living objects ; otherwise he would produce monsters instead of human beings ; but in both it is the office of high art to mould these features into new combinations, and to place them in the attitudes, and impart to them the expressions which may suit the purposes of the artist ; so that they are nature, but not exactly the same nature which had come before his eyes ; just as honey can be obtained only from the natural flowers which the bee has sucked ; yet **it is not** a reproduction of the odour or flavour of any particular flower, **but becomes** something different when it has gone through the process of transformation which that **little** insect is **able to** effect. Hence, in the case **of** painters, arises **the** superiority of original compositions over portrait painting. Reynolds was exercising **a** higher faculty when he designed Comedy and Tragedy contending for Garrick, than when he merely took a likeness of that actor. The same difference exists in writings between the original conceptions of Shakspeare and some other creative geniuses, and such full-length likenesses of individual persons, 'The Talking Gentleman' for instance, as are admirably drawn **by Miss** Mitford. **Jane Austen's** powers, whatever **may** be the degree **in** which **she** possessed them, **were** certainly of that higher order. She did not copy individuals, but she invested her own creations with individuality of character. **A** reviewer **in** the 'Quarterly' speaks of an **acquaintance who,** ever since the publication of 'Pride and Prejudice,' had been called by his friends Mr. Bennet, but the author did not know him. Her own relations never recognised any individual in her characters ; and I can call to mind several of her acquaintance whose peculiarities were very tempting and easy **to** be caricatured of whom there are no traces in her pages. She herself, when questioned on the subject by a friend, expressed a dread of what **she** called such an 'invasion of social proprieties.' She said that she thought it quite fair to note peculiarities and weaknesses, but that it was her desire to create, not to reproduce; ' besides,' she added, ' I am too proud of my gentlemen to admit that they were only Mr. A. or Colonel B.' She did not, however, suppose that her imaginary characters were of a higher order than are to be found in nature ; for she said, when speaking of two of her great favourites, Edmund Bertram and Mr. Knightley : ' They are very far from being what I know English gentlemen often are.'

She certainly took a kind of parental interest in the beings whom she had created, and did not dismiss them from her thoughts when she had finished her last chapter. We have seen, in one of her letters, her personal affection for Darcy and Elizabeth ; and when sending a copy of ' Emma ' to a friend whose daughter had been lately born, she wrote thus: ' I trust you will be as glad to see my " Emma," as I shall be to see your Jemima.' She was very fond of Emma, but did not reckon on her being a general favourite ; for, when commencing that work, she said, ' I am going to take a heroine whom no one but myself will much like.' She would, if asked, tell us many little particulars about the subsequent career of some of her people. In this traditionary way we learned that Miss Steele never succeeded in catching the Doctor ; that Kitty Bennet was satisfactorily married to a clergyman near Pemberley, while Mary obtained nothing higher than one of her uncle Philip's clerks, and was content to be considered a star in the society of Meriton ; that the ' considerable sum ' given by Mrs. Norris to William Price was one pound; that Mr. Woodhouse survived **his** daughter's marriage, and kept **her and** Mr. Knightley **from** settling **at** Donwell, about **two years; and** that **the letters** placed by Frank Churchill before **Jane Fairfax,** which she swept away unread, **contained the word 'pardon.' Of** the good people in 'Northanger Abbey' and 'Persuasion' we know nothing more than what **is** written : for before those works were published their author had been taken away from us, **and** all such amusing communications had ceased **for ever.**

## CHAPTER XI.



EARLY in the year 1816 some family troubles disturbed the usually tranquil course of Jane Austen's life ; and it is probable that the inward malady, which was to prove ultimately fatal, was already felt by her ; for some distant friends,* whom she visited in the spring of that year, thought that her health was somewhat impaired, and observed that she went about her old haunts, and recalled old recollections connected with them in a particular manner, as if she did not expect ever to see them again.   It is not surprising that, under these circumstances, some of her letters were of a graver tone than had been customary with her, and expressed resignation rather than cheerfulness.   In reference to these troubles in a letter to her brother Charles, after mentioning that she had been laid up with an attack of bilious fever, she says : 'I live up stairs for the present and am coddled.   I am the only one of the party who has been so silly, but a weak body must excuse weak nerves.'   And again, to another correspondent : 'But

* The Fowles, of Kintbury, in Berkshire.

I am getting too near complaint ; it has been the appointment of God, however secondary causes may have operated.' But the elasticity of her spirits soon recovered their tone. It was in the latter half of that year that she addressed the two following lively letters to a nephew, one while he was at Winchester School, the other soon after he had left it :—

'Chawton, July 9, 1816.

'MY DEAR E.—Many thanks. A thank for every line, and as many to Mr. W. Digweed for coming. We have been wanting very much to hear of your mother, and are happy to find she continues to mend, but her illness must have been a very serious one indeed. When she is really recovered, she ought to try change of air, and come over to us. Tell your father that I am very much obliged to him for his share of your letter, and most sincerely join in the hope of her being eventually much the better for her present discipline. She has the comfort moreover of being confined in such weather as gives one little temptation to be out. It is really too bad, and has been too bad for a long time, much worse than any one *can* bear, and I begin to think it will never be fine again. This is a *finesse* of mine, for I have often observed that if one writes about the weather, it is generally completely changed before the letter is read. I wish it may prove so now, and that when Mr. W. Digweed reaches Steventon to-morrow, he may find you have had a long series of hot dry weather. We are a small party at present, only

grandmamma, Mary Jane, and myself.   Yalden's
coach cleared off the rest yesterday.   I am glad you
recollected to mention your being come home.*   My
heart began to sink within me when I had got so far
through your letter without its being mentioned.   I
was dreadfully afraid that you might be detained at
Winchester by severe illness, confined to your bed
perhaps, and quite unable to hold a pen, and only
dating from Steventon in order, with a mistaken sort
of tenderness, to deceive me.   But now I have no
doubt of your being at home.   I am sure you would
not say it so seriously unless it actually were so.
We saw a countless number of post-chaises full of
boys pass by yesterday morning †—full of future
heroes, legislators, fools, and villains.   You have
never thanked me for my last letter, which went by
the cheese.   I cannot bear not to be thanked.   You
will not pay us a visit yet of course ; we must not
think of it.   Your mother must get well first, and
you must go to Oxford and *not* be elected ; after that
a little change of scene may be good for you, and
your physicians I hope will order you to the sea, or
to a house by the side of a very considerable pond.‡
Oh! it rains again.   It beats against the window.
Mary Jane and I have been wet through once already

---

* It seems that her young correspondent, after dating from his home,
had been so superfluous as to state in his letter that he was returned
home, and thus to have drawn on himself this banter.

† The road by which many Winchester boys returned home ran close
to Chawton Cottage.

‡ There was, though it exists no longer, a pond close to Chawton
Cottage, at the junction of the Winchester and Gosport roads.

to-day; we set off in the donkey-carriage for Farringdon, as I wanted to see the improvement Mr. Woolls is making, but we were obliged to turn back before we got there, but not soon enough to avoid a pelter all the way home. We met **Mr.** Woolls. I talked of its being bad weather for the hay, and he returned me the comfort of its being much worse for the wheat. We hear that **Mrs.** S. does not quit Tangier: why and wherefore? **Do** you know that our Browning is gone? **You** must prepare for a William when you come, a good-looking lad, civil and quiet, and seeming likely to do. **Good bye.** I am sure Mr. **W.** D.* will be astonished at my writing so much, for the paper is so thin that he will be able to count the lines if not to read them.

'Yours affec<sup>ly</sup>,

'JANE AUSTEN.'

In the next letter will be found her description of her own style of composition, which has already appeared in the notice prefixed to 'Northanger Abbey' and 'Persuasion':—

'Chawton, Monday, **Dec.** 16th (1816).

'**My** DEAR E.,—One reason for my writing to you now is, that I may have the pleasure of directing to you Esq<sup>re.</sup> I give you joy of having left Winchester. Now you may own how miserable you were there; now it will gradually all come out, your crimes and

---

* Mr. **Digweed**, who conveyed the letters to and from Chawton, was the gentleman named in page 21, as renting the old manor-house and the large farm at Steventon.

your miseries—how often you went up by the Mail
to London and threw away fifty guineas at a tavern,
and how often you were on the point of hanging
yourself, restrained only, as some ill-natured aspersion
upon poor old Winton has it, by the want of a tree
within some miles of the city. Charles Knight and
his companions passed through Chawton about 9
this morning; later than it used to be. Uncle
Henry and I had a glimpse of his handsome face,
looking all health and good humour. I wonder
when you will come and see us. I know what I
rather speculate upon, but shall say nothing. We
think uncle Henry in excellent looks. Look at him
this moment, and think so too, if you have not done
it before; and we have the great comfort of seeing
decided improvement in uncle Charles, both as to
health, spirits, and appearance. And they are each
of them so agreeable in their different way, and
harmonise so well, that their visit is thorough enjoyment. Uncle Henry writes very superior sermons.
You and I must try to get hold of one or two, and
put them into our novels: it would be a fine help to
a volume; and we could make our heroine read it
aloud on a Sunday evening, just as well as Isabella
Wardour, in the " Antiquary," is made to read the
" History of the Hartz Demon " in the ruins of St.
Ruth, though I believe, on recollection, Lovell is the
reader. By the bye, my dear E., I am quite concerned for the loss your mother mentions in her
letter. Two chapters and a half to be missing is
monstrous! It is well that *I* have not been at

Steventon lately, and therefore cannot be suspected of purloining them : two strong twigs and a half towards **a nest of** my **own** would have been something. I do not think, however, that any theft of that **sort** would be really very useful to me. What should **I do** with your strong, manly, **vigorous** sketches, full **of** variety and glow? **How** could I possibly join them on to the little **bit (two** inches wide) of ivory on which I work with **so fine a** brush, as produces little effect after much labour?

'**You** will hear from uncle Henry how **well Anna is.** She seems perfectly recovered. Ben **was here on** Saturday, **to ask uncle Charles** and me **to** dine **with** them, as **to-morrow, but I was** forced **to** decline **it,** the walk is **beyond** my **strength** (though I am **otherwise** very well), and this **is not a season for** donkeycarriages ; and as **we do not like to spare** uncle **Charles, he has declined** it **too.** *Tuesday.* Ah, ah ! **Mr. E. I doubt** your seeing **uncle** Henry **at** Steventon to-day. The weather will prevent **your** expecting him, **I** think. Tell your father, with aunt Cass's love **and** mine, that the pickled cucumbers **are** extremely good, **and** tell him also—"tell him what you will." No, don't tell him **what you** will, but tell him that grandmamma **begs him to** make Joseph Hall pay his rent, if **he can.**

'You must not be **tired of** reading the word *uncle,* **for** I **have not** done **with it.** Uncle Charles thanks your mother for her **letter ; it** was a great pleasure to him to know that the parcel was received and gave so much satisfaction, **and** he begs her to be **so** good as to give three shillings for him to Dame Staples, which shall be allowed for in the payment of her debt here.

'Adieu, Amiable! I hope Caroline behaves well to you.

'Yours affec[ly],

'J. AUSTEN.'

I cannot tell how soon she was aware of the serious nature of her malady. By God's mercy it was not attended with much suffering; so that she was able to tell her friends as in the foregoing letter, and perhaps sometimes to persuade herself that, excepting want of strength, she was 'otherwise very well;' but the progress of the disease became more and more manifest as the year advanced. The usual walk was at first shortened, and then discontinued; and air was sought in a donkey-carriage. Gradually, too, her habits of activity within the house ceased, and she was obliged to lie down much. The sitting-room contained only one sofa, which was frequently occupied by her mother, who was more than seventy years old. Jane would never use it, even in her mother's absence; but she contrived a sort of couch for herself with two or three chairs, and was pleased to say that this arrangement was more comfortable to her than a real sofa. Her reasons for this might have been left to be guessed, but for the importunities of a little niece, which obliged her to explain that if she herself had shown any inclination to use the sofa, her mother might have scrupled being on it so much as was good for her.

It is **certain,** however, that the mind did not share in this decay of the bodily strength. 'Persuasion' was not finished before the **middle of** August in that year; and the manner in which **it was then com-**pleted affords proof that neither the critical nor the creative powers of the author were **at all** impaired. The book had **been** brought **to an end in** July; and the re-engagement of the hero and heroine effected in a totally different manner in a scene laid at Admiral Croft's lodgings. But her performance did not satisfy her. **She** thought **it** tame and flat, and was desirous of producing something better. This weighed upon **her mind,** the more so probably **on** account of the **weak state of** her health; so that **one** night **she** retired to rest **in very** low spirits. But such depression was little **in** accordance **with** her **nature, and** was soon **shaken** off. **The next** morning **she** awoke to more cheerful views **and** brighter inspirations : **the** sense **of** power revived; **and** imagination resumed its course. She cancelled **the** condemned chapter, and wrote two others, entirely different, in **its** stead. The result is that we possess the visit of **the** Musgrove party to Bath ; the crowded and animated scenes at the White Hart **Hotel ; and** the charming conversation between Capt. Harville and Anne Elliot, overheard by Capt. Wentworth, by which the two faithful lovers were **at** last led **to** understand each other's feelings. The tenth and eleventh chapters of 'Persuasion' then, rather than the actual winding-up **of the** story, contain the latest **of her** printed compositions, her last contribution **to** the entertainment of the

public.  Perhaps it may be thought that she has
seldom written anything more brilliant; and that,
independent of the original manner in which the
*dénouement* is brought about, the pictures of Charles
Musgrove's goodnatured boyishness and of his wife's
jealous selfishness would have been incomplete without
these finishing strokes.  The cancelled chapter exists
in manuscript.  It is certainly inferior to the two
which were substituted for it: but it was such as
some writers and some readers might have been contented with ; and it contained touches which scarcely
any other hand could have given, the suppression of
which may be almost a matter of regret.*

The following letter was addressed to her friend
Miss Bigg, then staying at Streatham with her
sister, the wife of the Reverend Herbert Hill, uncle
of Robert Southey.  It appears to have been written
three days before she began her last work, which will
be noticed in another chapter ; and shows that she
was not at that time aware of the serious nature of
her malady :—

' Chawton, January 24, 1817.

'MY DEAR ALETHEA,—I think it time there
should be a little writing between us, though I believe the epistolary debt is on *your* side, and I hope
this will find all the Streatham party well, neither
carried away by the flood, nor rheumatic through
the damps.  Such mild weather is, you know, de-

---

* This cancelled chapter is now printed, in compliance with the
requests addressed to me from several quarters.

lightful **to** *us,* **and though we** have **a** great many ponds, and **a** fine running stream through the meadows on the **other** side of the road, it is nothing but what beautifies us and does to talk **of.** *I* have certainly gained strength through the winter and am not far **from** being well; **and I** think **I** understand **my** own case now so **much** better **than I** did, as **to be** able by care **to keep off any** serious return of illness. I am convinced **that** *bile* **is at** the bottom of all **I** have suffered, which makes it easy **to know how** to treat myself. You will **be** glad to hear **thus** much of me, I am sure. We have just had a **few** days' visit from Edward, who brought **us a** good account of his father, and the very circumstance **of his** coming **at** all, of his father's being able to spare him, **is itself a** good **account.** He grows **still,** and still improves **in** appearance, at least in **the** estimation **of** his aunts, who **love** him better and better, as they **see the** sweet temper and warm affections **of the** boy confirmed in the young man : I tried **hard to** persuade him that he **must** have some message for William,* but in vain. . . . This is not a time of year **for** donkey-carriages, and our donkeys are necessarily having so long a run of luxurious idleness that **I** suppose we shall find they have forgotten much of their education when we use them again. We do **not** use two at once however ; don't imagine such excesses. . . Our own new clergyman † is expected here **very** soon, perhaps in time to

---

* Miss Bigg's nephew, the present Sir William Heathcote, of Hursley.

† Her brother Henry, who had been ordained late in life.

assist Mr. Papillon on Sunday.　I shall be very glad
when the first hearing is over.　It will be a nervous
hour for our pew, though we hear that he acquits himself with as much ease and collectedness, as if he had
been used to it all his life.　We have no chance we
know of seeing you between Streatham and Winchester: you go the other road and are engaged to
two or three houses ; if there should be any change,
however, you know how welcome you would be. . . .
We have been reading the " Poet's Pilgrimage to
Waterloo," and generally with much approbation.
Nothing will please all the world, you know ; but
parts of it suit me better than much that he has
written before.　The opening—*the proem* I believe
he calls it—is very beautiful.　Poor man ! one cannot but grieve for the loss of the son so fondly described.　Has he at all recovered it ?　What do Mr.
and Mrs. Hill know about his present state ?

' Yours aff^{ly},

' J. AUSTEN.

' The real object of this letter is to ask you for a
receipt, but I thought it genteel not to let it appear
early.　We remember some excellent orange wine at
Manydown, made from Seville oranges, entirely or
chiefly.　I should be very much obliged to you for
the receipt, if you can command it within a few
weeks.'

On the day before, January 23rd, she had written
to her niece in the same hopeful tone : ' I feel myself
getting stronger than I was, and can so perfectly walk

*to* Alton, **or** back again without fatigue, that **I** hope
to be able to do *both* when summer comes.'

Alas! summer came **to** her only **on her** death-
bed. March 17th **is** the last date **to be** found in the
manuscript on which she was engaged; and as the
watch of the drowned man indicates **the** time of his
death, so does this final date seem to fix the period
when her mind could **no** longer pursue its accustomed
course.

And here **I** cannot **do** better **than quote** the words
of the niece to whose private records **of** her **aunt's**
life and character I have been so often indebted:—
'**I** do not know how early the alarming symptoms **of**
her malady **came on.** It **was in** the following March
that **I** had the first idea of her being seriously ill. It
had been settled that about **the** end of **that** month, **or**
the beginning **of April, I should** spend **a** few days at
Chawton, **in** the absence of **my** father and mother,
who were just then engaged with Mrs. Leigh Perrot in
arranging her late husband's affairs; **but** Aunt Jane
became too ill to have **me in** the house, and so **I**
went instead to my sister Mrs. Lefroy at Wyards'.
The next day we walked over to Chawton to make
enquiries after our aunt. **She** was then keeping her
room, but said she would **see** us, and we **went** up to
her. She was in her dressing gown, and was sitting
quite like an invalid in **an** arm-chair, **but** she got up
and kindly greeted us, **and** then, pointing to seats
which had been arranged for us **by** the fire, she said,
"There is a chair for the married lady, and a little

stool for you, Caroline." * It is strange, but those trifling words were the last of hers that I can remember, for I retain no recollection of what was said by anyone in the conversation that ensued. I was struck by the alteration in herself. She was very pale, her voice was weak and low, and there was about her a general appearance of debility and suffering; but I have been told that she never had much acute pain. She was not equal to the exertion of talking to us, and our visit to the sick room was a very short one, Aunt Cassandra soon taking us away. I do not suppose we stayed a quarter of an hour; and I never saw Aunt Jane again.'

In May 1817 she was persuaded to remove to Winchester, for the sake of medical advice from Mr. Lyford. The Lyfords have, for some generations, maintained a high character in Winchester for medical skill, and the Mr. Lyford of that day was a man of more than provincial reputation, in whom great London practitioners expressed confidence. Mr. Lyford spoke encouragingly. It was not, of course, his business to extinguish hope in his patient, but I believe that he had, from the first, very little expectation of a permanent cure. All that was gained by the removal from home was the satisfaction of having done the best that could be done, together with such alleviations of suffering as superior medical skill could afford.

Jane and her sister Cassandra took lodgings in College Street. They had two kind friends living

---

* The writer was at that time under twelve years old.

in the Close, Mrs. Heathcote and Miss Bigg, the mother **and** aunt of the present Sir Wm. Heathcote of Hursley, between whose family and ours a close friendship has existed for several generations. These friends did all that they could to promote the comfort of the sisters, during that sad sojourn **in** Winchester, both by their society, and by supplying those little conveniences in which a lodging-house was likely to be deficient. It was shortly after settling in these lodgings that she wrote to a nephew the following characteristic letter, no longer, alas! in her former strong, clear hand.

'**Mrs.** David's, College St., Winton,
Tuesday, May 27th.

'There is no better way, **my** dearest E., of thanking you for your affectionate concern for me during my illness than by telling **you** myself, as soon **as** possible, that I continue **to** get better. I will not boast of my handwriting; neither that **nor** my face have yet recovered **their** proper beauty, but in other respects I gain strength **very fast.** I **am** now out of bed from 9 in the morning **to** 10 at **night : upon** the sofa, it **is** true, **but I eat** my meals **with aunt** Cassandra in **a** rational way, and can employ myself, and walk from one room to another. Mr. Lyford says he will cure me, and if he fails, I shall draw up a memorial and lay it before the Dean and Chapter, and have **no** doubt **of** redress from **that** pious, learned, and disinterested body. Our lodgings are very comfortable. We have **a** neat little drawing-room with a bow window overlooking Dr. Gabell's garden.* Thanks to the kindness of your father and mother in sending me their carriage, my journey hither on Saturday was performed with very little fatigue, and had it been a fine day, I think I should have felt none; but it distressed me to see uncle Henry and Wm. Knight, who kindly attended us on horseback, riding in the rain almost the whole way. We expect a visit from them to-morrow, and hope they will stay the night; and on Thursday, which is a confirmation and a holiday, we are to get Charles out to breakfast. We have had but one visit from *him*, poor fellow, as he is in sick-room, but he hopes to be out to-night. We see Mrs. Heathcote every day, and William is to call upon us soon. God bless you, my dear E. If ever you are ill, may you be as tenderly nursed as I have been. May the same blessed alleviations of anxious, sympathising friends be yours: and may you possess, as I dare say you will, the greatest blessing of all in the consciousness of not being unworthy of their love. *I* could not feel this.

'Your very affec<sup>te</sup> Aunt,

'J. A.'

The following extract from a letter which has been before printed, written soon after the former, breathes the same spirit of humility and thankfulness :—

'I will only say further that my dearest sister, my tender, watchful, indefatigable nurse, has not been

---

* It was the corner house in College Street, at the entrance to Commoners.

made ill by her exertions  As to what I owe her,
and the anxious affection of all my beloved family
on this occasion, I can only cry over it, and pray
God to bless them more and more.'

Throughout her illness she was nursed by her
sister, often assisted by her sister-in-law, my mother.
Both were with her when she died. Two of her
brothers, who were clergymen, lived near enough to
Winchester to be in frequent attendance, and to ad-
minister the services suitable for a Christian's death-
bed. While she used the language of hope to her
correspondents, she was fully aware of her danger,
though not appalled by it. It is true that there was
much to attach her to life. She was happy in her
family; she was just beginning to feel confidence in
her own success; and, no doubt, the exercise of her
great talents was an enjoyment in itself. We may
well believe that she would gladly have lived longer;
but she was enabled without dismay or complaint to
prepare for death. She was a humble, believing
Christian. Her life had been passed in the performance of home duties, and the cultivation of domestic
affections, without any self-seeking or craving after
applause. She had always sought, as it were by
instinct, to promote the happiness of all who came
within her influence, and doubtless she had her reward in the peace of mind which was granted her in
her last days. Her sweetness of temper never failed.
She was ever considerate and grateful to those who
attended on her. At times, when she felt rather
better, her playfulness of spirit revived, and she

amused them even in their sadness. Once, when she thought herself near her end, she said what she imagined might be her last words to those around her, and particularly thanked her sister-in-law for being with her, saying: 'You have always been a kind sister to me, Mary.' When the end at last came, she sank rapidly, and on being asked by her attendants whether there was anything that she wanted, her reply was, '*Nothing but death.*' These were her last words. In quietness and peace she breathed her last on the morning of July 18, 1817.

On the 24th of that month she was buried in Winchester Cathedral, near the centre of the north aisle, almost opposite to the beautiful chantry tomb of William of Wykeham. A large slab of black marble in the pavement marks the place. Her own family only attended the funeral. Her sister returned to her desolated home, there to devote herself, for ten years, to the care of her aged mother; and to live much on the memory of her lost sister, till called many years later to rejoin her. Her brothers went back sorrowing to their several homes. They were very fond and very proud of her. They were attached to her by her talents, her virtues, and her engaging manners; and each loved afterwards to fancy a resemblance in some niece or daughter of his own to the dear sister Jane, whose perfect equal they yet never expected to see.

# CHAPTER XII.

*The Cancelled Chapter (Chap. X.) of ‘ Persuasion.’*

WITH all this knowledge of Mr. Elliot and this authority to impart it, Anne left Westgate Buildings, her mind deeply busy in revolving what she had heard, feeling, thinking, recalling, and foreseeing everything, shocked at Mr. Elliot, sighing over future Kellynch, and pained for Lady Russell, whose confidence in him had been entire. The embarrassment which must be felt from this hour in his presence! How to behave to him? How to get rid of him? What to do by any of the party at home? Where to be blind? Where to be active? It was altogether a confusion of images and doubts—a perplexity, an agitation which she could not see the end of. And she was in Gay Street, and still so much engrossed that she started on being addressed by Admiral Croft, as if he were a person unlikely to be met there. It was within a few steps of his own door.

‘You are going to call upon my wife,’ said he. ‘She will be very glad to see you.’

Anne denied it.

‘No! she really had not time, she was in her way home ;’ but while she spoke the Admiral had stepped back and knocked at the door, calling out,

'Yes, yes; do go in; she is all alone; go in and rest yourself.'

Anne felt so little disposed at this time to be in company of any sort, that it vexed her to be thus constrained, but she was obliged to stop.

'Since you are so very kind,' said she, 'I will just ask Mrs. Croft how she does, but I really cannot stay five minutes. You are sure she is quite alone?'

The possibility of Captain Wentworth had occurred; and most fearfully anxious was she to be assured—either that he was within, or that he was not—*which* might have been a question.

'Oh yes! quite alone, nobody but her mantua-maker with her, and they have been shut up together this half-hour, so it must be over soon.'

'Her mantuamaker! Then I am sure my calling now would be most inconvenient. Indeed you must allow me to leave my card and be so good as to explain it afterwards to Mrs. Croft.'

'No, no, not at all—not at all—she will be very happy to see you. Mind, I will not swear that she has not something particular to say to you, but *that* will all come out in the right place. I give no hints. Why, Miss Elliot, we begin to hear strange things of you (smiling in her face). But you have not much the look of it, as grave as a little judge!'

Anne blushed.

'Aye, aye, that will do now, it is all right. I thought we were not mistaken.'

She was left to guess at the direction of his suspicions; the first wild idea had been of some disclosure from his brother-in-law, but she was ashamed the next moment, and felt how far more probable it was that he should be meaning Mr. Elliot. The door was opened, and the man evidently beginning to *deny* his mistress, when the sight of his master stopped him. The Admiral enjoyed the joke exceedingly. Anne thought his triumph over Stephen rather too long. At last, however, he was able to invite her up stairs, and stepping before her said, ' I will just go up with you myself and show you in. I cannot stay, because I must go to the Post-Office, but if you will only sit down for five minutes I am sure Sophy will come, and you will find nobody to disturb you—there is nobody but Frederick here,' opening the door as he spoke. Such a person to be passed over as nobody to *her*! After being allowed to feel quite secure, indifferent, at her ease, to have it burst on her that she was to be the next moment in the same room with him! No time for recollection! for planning behaviour or regulating manners! There was time only to turn pale before she had passed through the door, and met the astonished eyes of Captain Wentworth, who was sitting by the fire, pretending to read, and prepared for no greater surprise than the Admiral's hasty return.

Equally unexpected was the meeting on each side. There was nothing to be done, however, but to stifle feelings, and to be quietly polite, and the Admiral was too much on the alert to leave any troublesome pause. He repeated again what he had said before about his wife and everybody, insisted on Anne's sitting down and being perfectly comfortable—was sorry he must leave her himself, but was sure Mrs. Croft would be down very soon, and would go up-stairs and give her notice directly. Anne *was* sitting down, but now she arose, again to entreat him not to interrupt Mrs. Croft and re-urge the wish of going away and calling another time. But the Admiral would not hear of it ; and if she did not return to the charge with unconquerable perseverance, or did not with a more passive determination walk quietly out of the room (as certainly she might have done), may she not be pardoned ? If she *had* no horror of a few minutes' tête-à-tête with Captain Wentworth, may she not be pardoned for not wishing to give him the idea that she had ? She reseated herself, and the Admiral took leave, but on reaching the door, said—

'Frederick, a word with *you* if you please.'

Captain Wentworth went to him, and instantly, before they were well out of the room, the Admiral continued—

'As I am going to leave you together, it is but fair I should give you something to talk of ; and so, if you please——'

Here the door was very firmly closed, she could guess by which of the two—and she lost entirely what immediately followed, but it was impossible for her not to distinguish parts of the rest, for the Admiral, on the strength of the door's being shut, was speaking without any management of voice, though she could hear his companion trying to check him. She could not doubt their being speaking of her. She heard her own name and Kellynch repeatedly. She **was** very much disturbed. She knew not what to do, or what to expect, and among other agonies felt the possibility of Captain Wentworth's not returning into **the room at** all, which, after her consenting to stay, would have been—too bad for language. They seemed to be talking of the Admiral's **lease of** Kellynch. She heard him say something of the lease being signed—or not signed—*that* was not likely to be a very agitating subject, but then followed—

' I hate to be at an uncertainty. I must know at once. Sophy thinks the same.'

Then in a lower tone Captain Wentworth seemed remonstrating, wanting to be excused, wanting to put something off.

' Phoo, phoo,' answered the Admiral, 'now is the time; if you will not speak, I will stop and speak myself.'

' Very well, sir, very well, sir,' followed with **some** impatience from his companion, opening the door as he spoke—

' You will then, you promise you will ?' replied the Admiral in all the power of his natural voice, unbroken even by one thin door.

' Yes, sir, **yes.**' And **the** Admiral **was** hastily left, the door was closed, and the moment arrived in which Anne was alone with Captain Wentworth.

She could not attempt to see how he looked, but he walked immediately to a window as **if** irresolute

and embarrassed, and for about the space of five
seconds she repented what she had done—censured
it as unwise, blushed over it as indelicate. She
longed to be able to speak of the weather or the
concert, but could only compass the relief of taking a
newspaper in her hand. The distressing pause was
over, however ; he turned round in half a minute, and
coming towards the table where she sat, said in a voice
of effort and constraint—

'You must have heard too much already, Madam,
to be in any doubt of my having promised Admiral
Croft to speak to you on a particular subject, and
this conviction determines me to do so, however re-
pugnant to my—to all my sense of propriety to be
taking so great a liberty! You will acquit me of
impertinence I trust, by considering me as speaking
only for another, and speaking by necessity ; and the
Admiral is a man who can never be thought imperti-'
nent by one who knows him as you do. His intentions are always the kindest and the best, and you
will perceive he is actuated by none other in the
application which I am now, with—with very peculiar feelings—obliged to make.' He stopped, but
merely to recover breath, not seeming to expect any
answer. Anne listened as if her life depended on the
issue of his speech. He proceeded with a forced
alacrity :—

'The Admiral, Madam, was this morning confidently informed that you were—upon my soul, I am
quite at a loss, ashamed (breathing and speaking
quickly)—the awkwardness of *giving* information of

this kind to one of the parties—you can be at no loss
to understand me.  It was very confidently said that
Mr. Elliot—that everything was settled in the family
for a union between Mr. Elliot and yourself.  It was
added that you were to live at Kellynch—that
Kellynch was to be given up.  This the Admiral
knew could not be correct.  But it occurred to
him that it might be the *wish* of the parties.  And
my commission from him, Madam, is to say, that
if the family wish is such, his lease of Kellynch
shall be cancelled, and he and my sister will provide
themselves with another home, without imagining
themselves to be doing anything which under similar
circumstances would not be done for *them.*  This is
all, Madam.  A very few words in reply from you
will be sufficient.  That *I* should be the person
commissioned on this subject is extraordinary ! and
believe me, Madam, it is no less painful.  A very
few words, however, will put an end to the awkwardness and distress we may *both* be feeling.'

Anne spoke a word or two, but they were unintel-
ligible ; and before she could command herself, he
added, 'If you will only tell me that the Admiral
may address a line to Sir Walter, it will be enough.
Pronounce only the words, *he may*, and I shall immediately follow him with your message.'

'No, Sir,' said Anne ; 'there is no message.  You
are misin—the Admiral is misinformed.  I do justice
to the kindness of his intentions, but he is quite mistaken.  There is no truth in any such report.'

He was a moment silent.  She turned her eyes

towards him for the first time since his re-entering the room.   His colour was varying, and he was looking at her with all the power and keenness which she believed no other eyes than his possessed.

‘No truth in any such report?’ he repeated.   ‘No truth in any *part* of it ?’

‘None.’

He had been standing by a chair, enjoying the relief of leaning on it, or of playing with it.   He now sat down, drew it a little nearer to her, and looked with an expression which had something more than penetration in it—something softer.   Her countenance did not discourage.   It was a silent but a very powerful dialogue ;  on his supplication, on hers acceptance. Still a little nearer, and a hand taken and pressed ; and ‘Anne, my own dear Anne !’ bursting forth in all the fulness of exquisite feeling,—and all suspense and indecision were over.   They were re-united.   They were restored to all that had been lost.   They were carried back to the past with only an increase of attachment and confidence, and only such a flutter of present delight as made them little fit for the interruption of Mrs. Croft when she joined them not long afterwards.   *She*, probably, in the observations of the next ten minutes saw something to suspect ;  and though it was hardly possible for a woman of her description to wish the mantuamaker had imprisoned her longer, she might be very likely wishing for some excuse to run about the house, some storm to break the windows above, or a summons to the Admiral's shoemaker below.   Fortune favoured them all, however, in another way, in a gentle, steady rain, just happily set in as the Admiral returned and Anne rose to go. She was earnestly invited to stay dinner. A note was despatched to Camden Place, and she staid—staid till ten **at night** ; and during that time the **husband** and wife, either by **the** wife's contrivance, or **by** simply going on in their usual way, were frequently out of the room together—gone upstairs to **hear** a noise, or downstairs to settle their accounts, **or** upon the landing to **trim the lamp.** And these precious moments were turned to so good an account that all the most anxious feelings of the past were gone through. Before they **parted at** night, Anne had the felicity **of** being assured that in the first **place** (so far from being altered for the worse), **she** had gained inexpressibly in personal loveliness ; **and** that as to character, hers was now fixed on his mind as *perfection* itself, maintaining **the** just medium **of** fortitude and gentleness—that he had never ceased **to love** and prefer her, though **it** had been only at Uppercross that **he** had learnt to do her justice, and only at Lyme that he had begun to understand his own feelings ; that at Lyme he had received lessons of more than one kind—the passing admiration of Mr. Elliot had at least *roused* him, and the scene on the Cobb, and at Captain Harville's, had fixed her superiority. In his preceding attempts to attach himself to Louisa Musgrove (the attempts of anger and pique), he protested that he had continually felt the impossibility of really caring for Louisa, though till *that day*, till the **leisure for** reflection which followed it, he had not under-

stood the perfect excellence of the mind with which
Louisa's could so ill bear comparison ; or the perfect,
the unrivalled hold it possessed over his own.   There
he had learnt to distinguish between the steadiness of
principle and the obstinacy of self-will, between the
darings of heedlessness and the resolution of a collected mind ; there he had seen everything to exalt in
his estimation the woman he had lost, and there had
begun to deplore the pride, the folly, the madness of
resentment, which had kept him from trying to regain
her when thrown in his way.  From that period to the
present had his penance been the most severe.   He
had no sooner been free from the horror and remorse
attending the first few days of Louisa's accident, no
sooner had begun to feel himself alive again, than he
had begun to feel himself, though alive, not at liberty.

He found that he was considered by his friend Harville an engaged man.   The Harvilles entertained
not a doubt of a mutual attachment between him and
Louisa; and though this to a degree was contradicted
instantly, it yet made him feel that perhaps by *her*
family, by everybody, by *herself* even, the same idea
might be held, and that he was not *free* in honour,
though if such were to be the conclusion, too free alas !
in heart.   He had never thought justly on this subject before, and he had not sufficiently considered
that his excessive intimacy at Uppercross must have
its danger of ill consequence in many ways ; and that
while trying whether he could attach himself to either
of the girls, he might be exciting unpleasant reports
if not raising unrequited regard.

He found too late that he had entangled himself, and that precisely as he became thoroughly satisfied of his not *caring* for Louisa at all, he must regard himself as bound to her if her feelings for him were what the Harvilles supposed. It determined him to leave Lyme, and await her perfect recovery elsewhere. He would gladly weaken by any *fair* means whatever sentiment or speculations concerning them might exist; and he went therefore into Shropshire, meaning after a while to return to the Crofts at Kellynch, and act as he found requisite.

He had remained in Shropshire, lamenting the blindness of his own pride and the blunders of his own calculations, till at once released from Louisa by the astonishing felicity of her engagement with Benwick.

Bath—Bath had instantly followed in *thought*, and not long after in *fact*. To Bath—to arrive with hope, to be torn by jealousy at the first sight of Mr. Elliot; to experience all the changes of each at the concert; to be miserable by the morning's circumstantial report, to be now more happy than language could express, or any heart but his own be capable of.

He was very eager and very delightful in the description of what he had felt at the concert; the evening seemed to have been made up of exquisite moments. The moment of her stepping forward in the octagon room to speak to him, the moment of Mr. Elliot's appearing and tearing her away, and one or two subsequent moments, marked by returning hope or increasing despondency, were dwelt on with energy.

'To see you,' cried he, 'in the midst of those who could not be my well-wishers; to see your cousin close by you, conversing and smiling, and feel all the horrible eligibilities and proprieties of the match! To consider it as the certain wish of every being who could hope to influence you! Even if your own feelings were reluctant or indifferent, to consider what powerful support would be his! Was it not enough to make the fool of me which I appeared? How could I look on without agony? Was not the very sight of the friend who sat behind you; was not the recollection of what had been, the knowledge of her influence, the indelible, immovable impression of what persuasion had once done—was it not all against me?'

'You should have distinguished,' replied Anne. 'You should not have suspected me now; the case so different, and my age so different. If I was wrong in yielding to persuasion once, remember it was to persuasion exerted on the side of safety, not of risk. When I yielded, I thought it was to duty; but no duty could be called in aid here. In marrying a man indifferent to me, all risk would have been incurred, and all duty violated.'

'Perhaps I ought to have reasoned thus,' he replied; 'but I could not. I could not derive benefit from the late knowledge I had acquired of your character. I could not bring it into play; it was overwhelmed, buried, lost in those earlier feelings which I had been smarting under year after year. I could think of you only as one who had yielded, who had given me up, **who** had been influenced by anyone rather than **by me.** I saw you with the very person who had guided you in that year of misery. I had no reason to believe her of less authority now. **The** force of habit was to be added.'

' I should have thought,' said Anne, ' that my manner to yourself might have spared you much or **all** of this.'

'No, no! Your manner might be only the ease which your engagement to another man would give. I left you in this belief; and yet—I was determined to see you again. My spirits rallied with the morning, and I felt that I had still a motive for remaining here. The Admiral's news, indeed, was a revulsion; since that moment **I have been** divided what to do, and had it been confirmed, **this** would have been my last day in Bath.'

There was time **for all this to pass,** with such interruptions only as enhanced **the** charm of the communication, and Bath could hardly **contain any** other two beings **at once** so rationally and so rapturously happy as during that evening occupied **the** sofa of Mrs. Croft's drawing-room in Gay Street.

Captain Wentworth **had** taken care to meet **the** Admiral as he returned into the house, to satisfy **him as** to Mr. Elliot and Kellynch; and the delicacy of **the** Admiral's good-nature kept him from saying another word on the subject **to Anne.** He **was** quite concerned lest he might have **been** giving her pain by touching **on a** tender part—who could **say?** She might be liking her cousin better than he liked her;

and, upon recollection, if they had been to marry at all, why should they have waited so long? When the evening closed, it is probable that the Admiral received some new ideas from his wife, whose particularly friendly manner in parting with her gave Anne the gratifying persuasion of her seeing and approving. It had been such a day to Anne; the hours which had passed since her leaving Camden Place had done so much! She was almost bewildered—almost too happy in looking back. It was necessary to sit up half the night, and lie awake the remainder, to comprehend with composure her present state, and pay for the overplus of bliss by headache and fatigue.

Then follows Chapter XI., *i.e.* XII. in the published book and at the end is written—

Finis, July 18, 1816.

# CHAPTER XIII.

*The last Work.*

JANE AUSTEN was taken from us: how much un-exhausted talent perished with her, how largely she might yet have contributed to the entertainment of her readers, if her life had been prolonged, cannot be known; but it is certain that the mine at which she had so long laboured was not worked out, and that she was still diligently employed in collect-ing fresh materials from it. 'Persuasion' had been finished in August 1816; some time was probably given to correcting it for the press; but on the 27th of the following January, according to the date on her own manuscript, she began a new novel, and worked at it up to the 17th of March. The chief part of this manuscript is written in her usual firm and neat hand, but some of the latter pages seem to have been first traced in pencil, probably when she was too weak to sit long at her desk, and written over in ink afterwards. The quantity produced does not indicate any decline of power or industry, for in those seven weeks twelve chapters had been com-pleted. It is more difficult to judge of the quality of a work so little advanced. It had received no name; there was scarcely any indication what the course of the story was to be, nor was any heroine yet perceptible, who, like Fanny Price, or Anne Elliot, might draw round her the sympathies of the reader. Such an unfinished fragment cannot be presented to the public; but I am persuaded that some of Jane Austen's admirers will be glad to learn something about the latest creations which were forming themselves in her mind; and therefore, as some of the principal characters were already sketched in with a vigorous hand, I will try to give an idea of them, illustrated by extracts from the work.

The scene is laid at Sanditon, a village on the Sussex coast, just struggling into notoriety as a bathing-place, under the patronage of the two principal proprietors of the parish, Mr. Parker and Lady Denham.

Mr. Parker was an amiable man, with more enthusiasm than judgment, whose somewhat shallow mind overflowed with the one idea of the prosperity of Sanditon, together with a jealous contempt of the rival village of Brinshore, where a similar attempt was going on. To the regret of his much-enduring wife, he had left his family mansion, with all its ancestral comforts of gardens, shrubberies, and shelter, situated in a valley some miles inland, and had built a new residence—a Trafalgar House—on the bare brow of the hill overlooking Sanditon and the sea, exposed to every wind that blows; but he will confess to no discomforts, nor suffer his family to feel any from the change. The following extract brings him before the reader, mounted on his hobby :—

' He wanted to secure the promise of a visit, and to get as many of the family as his own house would hold to follow him to Sanditon as soon as possible ; and, healthy as all the Heywoods undeniably were, he foresaw that every one of them would be bene- fitted by the sea. **He** held it indeed as certain that no person, however upheld for the present by **for**tuitous aids of exercise **and spirit in a** semblance of health, could be really **in a state of** secure and per- manent health without spending at least six weeks by the sea every year. The sea air and sea-bathing together were nearly infallible ; one or other of them being a match for every disorder of **the** stomach, the lungs, **or** the blood. They were anti-spasmodic, anti- pulmonary, anti-bilious, **and** anti-rheumatic. Nobody could catch cold by the **sea ;** nobody wanted appe- tite by the sea; nobody wanted **spirits ;** nobody wanted strength. They were healing, **softening,** re- laxing, fortifying, and bracing, seemingly just as was wanted ; sometimes one, sometimes the other. If the sea breeze failed, the sea-bath **was** the certain corrective ; and when bathing disagreed, the sea breeze was evidently designed by nature for the cure. His eloquence, however, could not prevail. Mr. and Mrs. Heywood never left home. . . . . The mainten- ance, education, and fitting out of fourteen children demanded a very quiet, settled, careful course of life ; and obliged them to **be** stationary and healthy at Willingden. What **prudence** had at first enjoined **was now** rendered pleasant **by habit.** They never left home, and they had a gratification in saying so.'

Lady Denham's was a very different character. She was a rich vulgar widow, with a sharp but narrow mind, who cared for the prosperity of Sanditon only so far as it might increase the value of her own property. She is thus described :—

'Lady Denham had been a rich Miss Brereton, born to wealth, but not to education. Her first husband had been a Mr. Hollis, a man of considerable property in the country, of which a large share of the parish of Sanditon, with manor and mansion-house, formed a part. He had been an elderly man when she married him; her own age about thirty. Her motives for such a match could be little understood at the distance of forty years, but she had so well nursed and pleased Mr. Hollis that at his death he left her everything—all his estates, and all at her disposal. After a widowhood of some years she had been induced to marry again. The late Sir Harry Denham, of Denham Park, in the neighbourhood of Sanditon, succeeded in removing her and her large income to his own domains; but he could not succeed in the views of permanently enriching his family which were attributed to him. She had been too wary to put anything out of her own power, and when, on Sir Harry's death, she returned again to her own house at Sanditon, she was said to have made this boast, "that though she had *got* nothing but her title from the family, yet she had *given* nothing for it." For the title it was to be supposed that she married.

'Lady Denham was indeed a great lady, beyond the

common **wants of** society; for she had many thousands **a year to** bequeath, **and** three distinct sets of people **to be courted by**:—her own relations, who might very **reasonably** wish for her original thirty thousand pounds among **them**; the legal heirs of Mr. Hollis, who might hope to be more indebted to *her* sense of justice than he had allowed them to **be** to *his*; and those members **of** the Denham family for whom her second husband **had** hoped to make a good bargain. By all these, or by branches of them, she had, **no** doubt, been long and still continued to be well attacked; and **of** these three divisions Mr. Parker did not hesitate **to** say that Mr. Hollis's kindred were the least in favour, and **Sir** Harry Denham's the most. The former, he believed, had done themselves irremediable harm by expressions of very unwise resentment at the time of **Mr.** Hollis's death: **the** latter, to the advantage of being the remnant of **a** connection which she certainly **valued,** joined those **of** having been known to her from their childhood, and **of** being always at hand **to** pursue their interests by seasonable attentions. But another claimant was now to be taken into account: **a** young female relation whom **Lady** Denham had been induced to receive into her family. After having always protested against any such addition, and often enjoyed the repeated defeat she had given to every attempt **of** her own relations to introduce 'this young lady, or that young lady,' **as a** companion at Sanditon House, she **had** brought back with her from London last Michaelmas a Miss **Clara** Brereton, who bid fair to **vie** in favour with Sir Edward Denham, and to secure for herself and her family that share of the accumulated property which they had certainly the best right to inherit.'

Lady Denham's character comes out in a conversation which takes place at Mr. Parker's tea-table.

'The conversation turned entirely upon Sanditon, its present number of visitants, and the chances of a good season. It was evident that Lady Denham had more anxiety, more fears of loss than her coadjutor. She wanted to have the place fill faster, and seemed to have many harassing apprehensions of the lodgings being in some instances underlet. To a report that a large boarding-school was expected she replies, 'Ah, well, no harm in that. They will stay their six weeks, and out of such a number who knows but some may be consumptive, and want asses' milk; and I have two milch asses at this very time. But perhaps the little Misses may hurt the furniture. I hope they will have a good sharp governess to look after them.' But she wholly disapproved of Mr. Parker's wish to secure the residence of a medical man amongst them. 'Why, what should we do with a doctor here? It would only be encouraging our servants and the poor to fancy themselves ill, if there was a doctor at hand. Oh, pray let us have none of that tribe at Sanditon: we go on very well as we are. There is the sea, and the downs, and my milch asses: and I have told Mrs. Whitby that if anybody enquires for a chamber horse, they may be supplied at a fair rate (poor Mr. Hollis's chamber horse, as good as new); and what can people want more? I have lived seventy good years in the world, and never took physic, except twice: and never saw the face of a doctor in all my life on my own account; and I really believe if my poor dear Sir Harry had never seen one neither, he would have been alive now. Ten fees, one after another, did the men take who sent him out of the world. I beseech you, Mr. Parker, no doctors here.'

This lady's character comes out more strongly in a conversation with Mr. Parker's guest, Miss Charlotte Heywood. Sir **Edward** Denham with his sister Esther **and** Clara Brereton have just left them.

'Charlotte accepted an invitation from Lady **Den**ham to remain with her on the terrace, when the others adjourned to the library. Lady Denham, like a **true** great lady, talked, **and** talked only of her own concerns, **and** Charlotte listened. Taking hold **of** Charlotte's arm with the ease of one who felt that any notice from her was a favour, and communicative from the same sense of importance, or from a natural love **of** talking, she immediately said **in** a tone of great satisfaction, and with a look of arch sagacity :—

'Miss Esther wants me to invite her and her brother to spend a week with me at Sanditon House, as I did last summer, but I shan't. She has been trying to get round me every way with her praise of this and her praise of that ; but I saw what she was about. I saw through it all. I am not very easily taken in, my dear.'

Charlotte could think of nothing more harmless to **be** said than the simple enquiry of, 'Sir Edward and Miss Denham ?'

'Yes, my dear; *my young folks,* as I call them,

sometimes: for I take them very much by the hand,
and had them with me last summer, about this time,
for a week—from Monday to Monday—and very
delighted and thankful they were.   For they are very
good young people, my dear.   I would not have you
think that I only notice them for poor dear Sir Harry's
sake.   No, no; they are very deserving themselves,
or, trust me, they would not be so much in my
company.   I am not the woman to help anybody
blindfold.   I always take care to know what I am
about, and who I have to deal with before I stir a
finger.   I do not think I was ever overreached in my
life ; and that is a good deal for a woman to say that
has been twice married.   Poor dear Sir Harry (between
ourselves) thought at first to have got more, but (with
a bit of a sigh) he is gone, and we must not find fault
with the dead.   Nobody could live happier together
than us : and he was a very honourable man, quite
the gentleman, of ancient family ; and when he died I
gave Sir Edward his gold watch.'

This was said with a look at her companion which
implied its right to produce a great impression ; and
seeing no rapturous astonishment in Charlotte's coun··
tenance, she added quickly,

'He did not bequeath it to his nephew, my dear;
it was no bequest ; it was not in the will.   He only
told me, and *that* but *once*, that he should wish his
nephew to have his watch ; but it need not have been
binding, if I had not chose it.'

'Very kind indeed, very handsome!' said Charlotte, absolutely forced to affect admiration.

'Yes, my dear; and it is not the only kind thing I have done by him. I have been a very liberal friend to Sir Edward; and, poor young man, he needs it bad enough. For, though I am only the dowager, my dear, and he is the heir, things do not stand between us in the way they usually do between those two parties. Not a shilling do I receive from the Denham estate. Sir Edward has no payments to make *me*. *He* don't stand uppermost, believe me; it is *I* that help *him*.'

'Indeed! he is a very fine young man, and particularly elegant in his address.'

This was said chiefly for the sake of saying something; but Charlotte directly saw that it was laying her open to suspicion, by Lady Denham's giving a shrewd glance at her, and replying,

'Yes, yes; he's very well to look at; and it is to be hoped that somebody of large fortune will think so; for Sir Edward *must* marry for money. He and I often talk that matter over. A handsome young man like him will go smirking and smiling about, and paying girls compliments, but he knows he *must* marry for money. And Sir Edward is a very steady young man, in the main, and has got very good notions.'

'Sir Edward Denham,' said Charlotte, 'with such personal advantages, may be almost sure of getting a woman of fortune, if he chooses it.'

This glorious sentiment seemed quite to remove suspicion.

'Aye, my dear, that is very sensibly said; and

if we could but get a young heiress to Sanditon!
But heiresses are monstrous scarce!  I do not think
we have had an heiress here, nor even a *Co.*, since
Sanditon has been a public place.  Families come
after families, but, as far as I can learn, it is not one
in a hundred of them that have any real property,
landed or funded.  An income, perhaps, but no property.  Clergymen, may be, or lawyers from town,
or half-pay officers, or widows with only a jointure;
and what good can such people do to anybody?
Except just as they take our empty houses, and
(between ourselves) I think they are great fools for
not staying at home.  Now, if we could get a young
heiress to be sent here for her health, and, as soon as
she got well, have her fall in love with Sir Edward!
And Miss Esther must marry somebody of fortune,
too.  She must get a rich husband.  Ah! young
ladies that have no money are very much to be
pitied.'  After a short pause: 'If Miss Esther thinks
to talk me into inviting them to come and stay
at Sanditon House, she will find herself mistaken.
Matters are altered with me since last summer, you
know: I have Miss Clara with me now, which makes
a great difference.  I should not choose to have my
two housemaids' time taken up all the morning in
dusting out bedrooms.  They have Miss Clara's room
to put to rights, as well as mine, every day.  If they
had hard work, they would want higher wages.'

Charlotte's feelings were divided between amusement and indignation.  She kept her countenance,
and kept a civil silence; but without attempting to

listen any longer, and only conscious that Lady Denham was still talking in the same way, allowed her own thoughts **to** form themselves into **such** meditation as this :—' She is thoroughly mean ; I had no expectation of anything so bad. Mr. Parker spoke too mildly of her. He is too kind-hearted to **see** clearly, and their very connection misleads him. He has persuaded her to engage in the same speculation, and because they have so far the same object in view, he fancies that she feels like **him in other** things ; but she is very, very mean. **I can see** no good in her. Poor Miss Brereton ! And **it** makes everybody **mean** about her. This poor Sir Edward **and his** sister ! **how far nature** meant them to be respectable **I cannot** tell ; but they are obliged to **be** mean in their servility to her ; and I am **mean, too,** in giving her my attention **with** the appearance of coinciding with her. Thus it is when **rich** people **are** sordid.'

Mr. Parker has **two** unmarried sisters of singular character. They live together ; Diana, the younger, always takes the lead, and the elder follows in the same track. It is their pleasure to fancy themselves invalids **to** a degree and in a manner never experienced by others ; but, from **a** state of exquisite pain and utter prostration, Diana Parker can always rise to **be** officious in the concerns of all her acquaintance, and to make incredible exertions where they are not wanted.

It would seem that they must be always either very busy for the good of others, or else extremely ill themselves. Some natural delicacy of constitution, in fact, with an unfortunate turn for medicine, especially quack medicine, had given them an early tendency at various times to various disorders. The rest of their suffering was from their own fancy, the love of distinction, and the love of the wonderful. They had charitable hearts and many amiable feelings ; but a spirit of restless activity, and the glory of doing more than anybody else, had a share in every exertion of benevolence, and there was vanity in all they did, as well as in all they endured.

These peculiarities come out in the following letter of Diana Parker to her brother :—

' MY DEAR TOM,—We were much grieved at your accident, and if you had not described yourself as having fallen into such very good hands, I should have been with you at all hazards the day after receipt of your letter, though it found me suffering under a more severe attack than usual of my old grievance, spasmodic bile, and hardly able to crawl from my bed to the sofa. But how were you treated ? Send me more particulars in your next. If indeed a simple sprain, as you denominate it, nothing would have been so judicious as friction—friction by the hand alone, supposing it could be applied *immediately*. Two years ago I happened to be calling on Mrs. Sheldon, when her coachman sprained his foot, as he was cleaning the carriage, and could hardly limp into the house ; but by the immediate use of friction alone, steadily persevered in (I rubbed his ancle with my **own** hands **for** four hours without intermission), he **was** well **in three** days. . . . **Pray** never **run** into **peril** again **in** looking for an apothecary **on** our account; **for** had **you the** most experienced man in his line **settled at** Sanditon, it would be **no** recommendation to us. We have entirely done with the whole medical tribe. We have consulted physician after physician **in** vain, till **we** are quite convinced **that** they can do nothing **for us,** and that we **must trust to** our knowledge **of** our own wretched constitutions **for any** relief; but **if you** think it advisable for the interests **of the** *place* **to get a** medical man there, I will undertake the **commission** with pleasure, and **have no doubt** of succeeding. I **could soon put** the necessary irons **in the fire. As** for getting **to Sanditon** myself, **it is an** impossibility. I grieve **to say that I** cannot attempt it, **but my** feelings tell me **too plainly** that in **my present** state the **sea-air** would probably be the death **of me;** and in truth I doubt whether Susan's nerves would be equal to the effort. She has been suffering much from headache, and six leeches a day, for ten days together, relieved her so little that **we** thought it right to change our measures; and being convinced on examination **that** much of the evil lay in her gums, **I** persuaded **her to** attack **the** disorder there. She has accordingly **had** three teeth drawn, and is decidedly **better**; but her nerves are a good deal deranged, she can **only** speak **in** a whisper, and fainted away this morning **on** poor Arthur's trying to suppress **a** cough.'

O

Within a week of the date of this letter, in spite
of the impossibility of moving, and of the fatal effects
to be apprehended from the sea-air, Diana Parker
was at Sanditon with her sister.  She had flattered
herself that by her own indefatigable exertions, and
by setting at work the agency of many friends, she
had induced two large families to take houses at
Sanditon.   It was to expedite these politic views that
she came; and though she met with some disappointment of her expectation, yet she did not suffer in
health.

Such were some of the *dramatis personæ*, ready
dressed and prepared for their parts.  They are at
least original and unlike any that the author had
produced before.  The success of the piece must
have depended on the skill with which these parts
might be played ; but few will be inclined to distrust the skill of one who had so often succeeded.
If the author had lived to complete her work, it is
probable that these personages might have grown
into as mature an individuality of character, and
have taken as permanent a place amongst our familiar
acquaintance, as Mr. Bennet, or John Thorp, Mary
Musgrove, or Aunt Norris herself.

194

If your Uncle were at home
he would send his best Love,
but I will not impose any
base, fictitious remembrance
on you. — Mine I can honestly
give, & remain Yr. affec: Aunt
J. Austen

23. Hans Place

Mrs B. Lefroy

Hendon

# CHAPTER XIV.

*Postscript.*

WHEN first I was asked to put together a memoir of my aunt, I saw reasons for declining the attempt. It was not only that, having passed the three score years and ten usually allotted to man's strength, and being unaccustomed to write for publication, I might well distrust my ability to complete the work, but that I also knew the extreme scantiness of the materials out of which it must be constructed. The grave closed over my aunt fifty-two years ago; and during that long period no idea of writing her life had been entertained by any of her family. Her nearest relatives, far from making provision for such a purpose, had actually destroyed many of the letters and papers by which it might have been facilitated. They were influenced, I believe, partly by an extreme dislike to publishing private details, and partly by never having assumed that the world would take so strong and abiding an interest in her works as to claim her name as public property. It was therefore necessary for me to draw upon recollections rather than on written documents for my materials; while the subject itself supplied me with nothing striking or prominent with which to arrest the attention of the reader. It has been said that the happiest individuals, like nations during their happiest periods, —have no history. In the case of my aunt, it was not only that her course of life was unvaried, but that her own disposition was remarkably calm and even. There was in her nothing eccentric or angular; no ruggedness of temper; no singularity of manner; none of the morbid sensibility or exaggeration of feeling, which not unfrequently accompanies great talents, to be worked up into a picture. Hers was a mind well balanced on a basis of good sense, sweetened by an affectionate heart, and regulated by fixed principles; so that she was to be distinguished from many other amiable and sensible women only by that peculiar genius which shines out clearly enough in her works, but of which a biographer can make little use. The motive which at last induced me to make the attempt is exactly expressed in the passage prefixed to these pages. I thought that I saw something to be done: knew of no one who could do it but myself, and so was driven to the enterprise. I am glad that I have been able to finish my work. As a family record it can scarcely fail to be interesting to those relatives who must ever set a high value on their connection with Jane Austen, and to them I especially dedicate it; but as I have been asked to do so, I also submit it to the censure of the public, with all its faults both of deficiency and redundancy. I know that its value in their eyes must depend, not on any merits of its own, but on the degree of estimation in which my aunt's works may still be held ; and indeed I shall esteem it one of the strongest testimonies ever borne to her talents, if for her sake an interest can be taken in so poor a sketch as I have been able to draw.

BRAY VICARAGE:
 *Sept.* 7, 1869.

# LADY SUSAN.

# PREFACE.

I HAVE lately received permission to print the following tale from the author's niece, Lady Knatchbull, of Provender, in Kent, to whom the autograph copy was given. I am not able to ascertain when it was composed. Her family have always believed it to be an early production. Perhaps she wrote it as an experiment in conducting a story by means of letters. It was not, however, her only attempt of that kind; for 'Sense and Sensibility' was first written in letters; but as she afterwards re-wrote one of these works and never published the other, it is probable that she was not quite satisfied with the result. The tale itself is scarcely one on which a literary reputation could have been founded: but though, like some plants, it may be too slight to stand alone, it may, perhaps, be supported by the strength of her more firmly rooted works. At any rate, it cannot diminish Jane Austen's reputation as a writer; for even if it should be judged unworthy of the publicity now given to it, the censure must fall on him who has put it forth, not on her who kept it locked up in her desk.

# LADY SUSAN.

## I.

*Lady Susan Vernon to Mr. Vernon.*

Langford, Dec.

Y DEAR BROTHER,—I can no longer re-
fuse myself the pleasure of profiting by
your kind invitation when we last parted
of spending some weeks with you at
Churchhill, and, therefore, if quite convenient to you
and Mrs. Vernon to receive me at present, I shall
hope within a few days to be introduced to a
sister whom I have so long desired to be acquainted
with. My kind friends here are most affectionately
urgent with me to prolong my stay, but their hospitable and cheerful dispositions lead them too much
into society for my present situation and state of
mind; and I impatiently look forward to the hour
when I shall be admitted into your delightful retirement.

I long to be made known to your dear little children,
in whose hearts I shall be very eager to secure an
interest. I shall soon have need for all my fortitude,

as I am on the point of separation from my own
daughter. The long illness of her dear father prevented my paying her that attention which duty and
affection equally dictated, and I have too much reason
to fear that the governess to whose care I consigned
her was unequal to the charge. I have therefore
resolved on placing her at one of the best private
schools in town, where I shall have an opportunity of
leaving her myself in my way to you. I am determined, you see, not to be denied admittance at
Churchhill. It would indeed give me most painful
sensations to know that it were not in your power to
receive me.

Your most obliged and affectionate Sister,<br>
S. VERNON.

## II.

### *Lady Susan Vernon to Mrs. Johnson.*

Langford.

You were mistaken, my dear Alicia, in supposing
me fixed at this place for the rest of the winter : it
grieves me to say how greatly you were mistaken,
for I have seldom spent three months more agreeably
than those which have just flown away. At present,
nothing goes smoothly ; the females of the family
are united against me. You foretold how it would be
when I first came to Langford, and Mainwaring is so
uncommonly pleasing that I was not without apprehensions for myself. I remember saying to myself,
as I drove to the house, ‘I like this man, pray

Heaven no harm come of it!' But I was determined to be discreet, to bear in mind my being only four months a widow, and to be as quiet as possible: and I have been so, my dear creature; I have admitted no one's attentions but Mainwaring's. I have avoided all general flirtation whatever; I have distinguished no creature besides, of all the numbers resorting hither, except Sir James Martin, on whom I bestowed a little notice, in order to detach him from Miss Mainwaring; but, if the world could know my motive *there* they would honour me. I have been called an unkind mother, but it was the sacred impulse of maternal affection, it was the advantage of my daughter that led me on; and if that daughter were not the greatest simpleton on earth, I might have been rewarded for my exertions as I ought.

Sir James did make proposals to me for Frederica; but Frederica, who was born to be the torment of my life, chose to set herself so violently against the match that I thought it better to lay aside the scheme for the present. I have more than once repented that I did not marry him myself; and were he but one degree less contemptibly weak I certainly should: but I must own myself rather romantic in that respect, and that riches only will not satisfy me. The event of all this is very provoking: Sir James is gone, Maria highly incensed, and Mrs. Mainwaring insupportably jealous; so jealous, in short, and so enraged against me, that, in the fury of her temper, I should not be surprised at her appealing to her guardian, if she had the liberty of addressing him: but there your husband stands my friend ; and the kindest, most amiable action of his life was his throwing her off for ever on her marriage. Keep up his resentment, therefore, I charge you. We are now in a sad state; no house was ever more altered; the whole party are at war, and Mainwaring scarcely dares speak to me. It is time for me to be gone; I have therefore determined on leaving them, and shall spend, I hope, a comfortable day with you in town within this week. If I am as little in favour with Mr. Johnson as ever, you must come to me at 10 Wigmore Street; but I hope this may not be the case, for as Mr. Johnson, with all his faults, is a man to whom that great word 'respectable' is always given, and I am known to be so intimate with his wife, his slighting me has an awkward look.

I take London in my way to that insupportable spot, a country village ; for I am really going to Churchhill. Forgive me, my dear friend, it is my last resource. Were there another place in England open to me I would prefer it. Charles Vernon is my aversion, and I am afraid of his wife. At Churchhill, however, I must remain till I have something better in view. My young lady accompanies me to town, where I shall deposit her under the care of Miss Summers, in Wigmore Street, till she becomes a little more reasonable. She will make good connections there as the girls are all of the best families. The price is immense, and much beyond what I can ever attempt to pay.

Adieu, I will send you a line as soon as I arrive in town.

Yours ever,

S. VERNON.


## III.

*Mrs. Vernon to Lady De Courcy.*

Churchhill.

My dear Mother,—I am very sorry to tell you that it will **not** be in our power to keep our promise of spending our Christmas **with** you ; and we are prevented that happiness by a circumstance which is not likely **to make** us any amends. Lady Susan, **in a** letter to her brother-in-law, has declared her intention of visiting us almost immediately ; and as such a visit is in all probability merely an affair of convenience, it is impossible to conjecture **its** length. I was by **no** means prepared for such **an event, nor can I now ac-**count for her ladyship's conduct; Langford appeared so exactly the place for her in every respect, as well from the elegant and expensive style of living there, as from her particular attachment to Mr. Mainwaring, that **I** was very far from expecting so speedy a distinction, though I always imagined from her increasing friendship for us since her husband's death that we should, at some future period, be obliged to receive her. Mr. Vernon, **I** think, was a great deal too kind to her when he was in Staffordshire ; her behaviour to him, independent of her general character, has been so inexcusably artful and ungenerous since our marriage was first in agitation that no one less amiable and mild than himself could have overlooked it all; and though, as his brother's widow, and in narrow circumstances, it was proper to render her pecuniary assistance, I cannot help thinking his pressing invitation to her to visit us at Churchhill perfectly unnecessary. Disposed, however, as he always is to think the best of everyone, her display of grief, and professions of regret, and general resolutions of prudence, were sufficient to soften his heart and make him really confide in her sincerity; but, as for myself, I am still unconvinced, and plausibly as her ladyship has now written, I cannot make up my mind till I better understand her real meaning in coming to us. You may guess, therefore, my dear madam, with what feelings I look forward to her arrival. She will have occasion for all those attractive powers for which she is celebrated to gain any share of my regard; and I shall certainly endeavour to guard myself against their influence, if not accompanied by something more substantial. She expresses a most eager desire of being acquainted with me, and makes very gracious mention of my children, but I am not quite weak enough to suppose a woman who has behaved with inattention, if not with unkindness to her own child, should be attached to any of mine. Miss Vernon is to be placed at a school in London before her mother comes to us, which I am glad of, for her sake and my own. It must be to her advantage to be separated from her mother, and a girl of sixteen who has received so wretched an education, could not be a very desirable companion here. Reginald **has** long wished, **I** know, to **see the** captivating **Lady** Susan, **and we** shall **depend on his** joining **our party soon. I am glad to** hear **that** my father continues so **well ; and am,** with **best love, &c,**

CATHERINE VERNON.

IV.

*Mr. De Courcy to Mrs. Vernon.*

Parklands.

My dear Sister,—I congratulate **you and Mr.** Vernon on being **about to** receive **into** your family the most accomplished coquette **in** England. **As a** very distinguished flirt **I have always been** taught to consider her, but it has lately **fallen in my way to hear some** particulars of her **conduct at** Langford, **which prove** that **she** does not **confine herself to that sort of honest** flirtation which satisfies most people, **but** aspires **to** the more delicious gratification of **making** a **whole** family miserable. By her behaviour **to** Mr. Mainwaring she gave jealousy and wretchedness to his wife, and by her attentions **to a young man** previously attached **to** Mr. Mainwaring's sister deprived an amiable girl **of her lover.**

I learnt **all** this from M**r.** Smith, now in this neighbourhood **(I** have dined with him, at Hurst and Wilford), **who** is just come **from** Langford where he was **a** fortnight with her ladyship, and who is therefore well qualified to make the communication.

What **a** woman she must **be ! I** long to see her, and

shall certainly accept your kind invitation, that I may form some idea of those bewitching powers which can do so much—engaging at the same time, and in the same house, the affections of two men, who were neither of them at liberty to bestow them—and all this without the charm of youth! I am glad to find Miss Vernon does not accompany her mother to Churchhill, as she has not even manners to recommend her; and, according to Mr. Smith's account, is equally dull and proud. Where pride and stupidity unite there can be no dissimulation worthy notice, and Miss Vernon shall be consigned to unrelenting contempt; but by all that I can gather Lady Susan possesses a degree of captivating deceit which it must be pleasing to witness and detect. I shall be with you very soon, and am ever,

Your affectionate Brother,<br>
R. DE COURCY.

## V.

*Lady Susan Vernon to Mrs. Johnson.*

Churchhill.

I received your note, my dear Alicia, just before I left town, and rejoice to be assured that Mr. Johnson suspected nothing of your engagement the evening before. It is undoubtedly better to deceive him entirely, and since he will be stubborn he must be tricked. I arrived here in safety, and have no reason to complain of my reception from Mr. Vernon; but I confess myself not equally satisfied with the behaviour of his lady. **She is** perfectly well-bred, indeed, and has the air of a woman of fashion, but her manners are not such as can persuade me of her being pre-possessed in my favour. I wanted **her** to be delighted at seeing me. I was as amiable as possible on the occasion, but all in vain. She does not like me. To be sure when we consider that I *did* take some pains to prevent my brother-in-law's marrying her, this want **of** cordiality is not very surprising, and **yet it** shows an illiberal and vindictive spirit to resent **a** project which influenced me six years ago, and which never succeeded at last.

I am sometimes disposed to repent **that** I did **not** let Charles buy Vernon Castle, when we were obliged **to** sell it ; but it was a trying circumstance, especially as the sale took place exactly **at** the time of his marriage ; and everybody ought to respect the delicacy of those feelings which could not endure that my husband's dignity should be lessened by his younger brother's having possession **of** the family estate. Could matters have been so arranged as to prevent the necessity of our leaving the castle, could we have lived with Charles and kept him single, **I** should have been very far from persuading my husband to dispose of it elsewhere ; **but** Charles was on the point of marrying Miss De Courcy, and the event has justified me. Here **are** children in abundance, and what benefit could have accrued to me from his purchasing Vernon ? My having prevented it may perhaps have given his wife an unfavourable impression, but where there is a disposition to dislike, a motive will never be wanting; and as to money matters it has not withheld him from being very useful to me. I really have a regard for him, he is so easily imposed upon! The house is a good one, the furniture fashionable, and everything announces plenty and elegance. Charles is very rich I am sure; when a man has once got his name in a banking-house he rolls in money; but they do not know what to do with it, keep very little company, and never go to London but on business. We shall be as stupid as possible. I mean to win my sister-in-law's heart through the children; I know all their names already, and am going to attach myself with the greatest sensibility to one in particular, a young Frederic, whom I take on my lap and sigh over for his dear uncle's sake.

Poor Mainwaring! I need not tell you how much I miss him, how perpetually he is in my thoughts. I found a dismal letter from him on my arrival here, full of complaints of his wife and sister, and lamentations on the cruelty of his fate. I passed off the letter as his wife's, to the Vernons, and when I write to him it must be under cover to you.

Ever yours,<br>S. VERNON.

## VI.

*Mrs. Vernon to Mr. De Courcy.*

Churchhill.

Well, my dear Reginald, I have seen this dangerous creature, and must give you some description of her, though I hope you will soon be able to form your own judgment. She is really excessively pretty;

however you may choose to question **the allurements of** a lady no longer young, **I must,** for my own part, **declare** that **I** have seldom **seen so** lovely a woman as Lady Susan. She is delicately fair, with fine grey eyes and dark eyelashes; and from her appearance one would not suppose her more than five and twenty, though she must in fact be ten years older. I was certainly not disposed to admire her, though always hearing she was beautiful; but I cannot help feeling that she possesses **an** uncommon union of symmetry, brilliancy, and **grace.** Her address to me was **so** gentle, frank, and even affectionate, that, if **I had not** known **how** much **she** has always disliked **me** for marrying Mr. Vernon, and that we **had** never met before, I should have imagined her **an** attached friend. **One is** apt, I believe, **to** connect assurance of manner with coquetry, **and to** expect **that an** impudent address will naturally attend an impudent mind; **at** least I was myself prepared for an improper degree of confidence in Lady Susan; but her countenance is absolutely sweet, and her voice **and** manner winningly mild. I am sorry **it** is so, for what is this but deceit? Unfortunately, one knows her too well. She is clever and agreeable, has all that knowledge **of** the world which makes conversation easy, and talks very well, with **a** happy command **of** language, which is too often used, I believe, **to** make black appear white. **She** has already almost persuaded **me** of her being warmly attached to her daughter, though I have been **so** long convinced to the contrary. She speaks of her with **so** much tenderness and anxiety, lamenting so bitterly the neglect of her education, which she represents however as wholly unavoidable, that I am forced to recollect how many successive springs her ladyship spent in town, while her daughter was left in Staffordshire to the care of servants, or a governess very little better, to prevent my believing what she says.

If her manners have so great an influence on my resentful heart, you may judge how much more strongly they operate on Mr. Vernon's generous temper. I wish I could be as well satisfied as he is, that it was really her choice to leave Langford for Churchhill; and if she had not stayed there for months before she discovered that her friend's manner of living did not suit her situation or feelings, I might have believed that concern for the loss of such a husband as Mr. Vernon, to whom her own behaviour was far from unexceptionable, might for a time make her wish for retirement. But I cannot forget the length of her visit to the Mainwarings, and when I reflect on the different mode of life which she led with them from that to which she must now submit, I can only suppose that the wish of establishing her reputation by following though late the path of propriety, occasioned her removal from a family where she must in reality have been particularly happy. Your friend Mr. Smith's story, however, cannot be quite correct, as she corresponds regularly with Mrs. Mainwaring. At any rate it must be exaggerated. It is scarcely possible that two men should be so grossly deceived by her at once.

Yours, &c., CATHERINE VERNON.

# VII.

### *Lady Susan Vernon to Mrs. Johnson.*

Churchhill.

My dear Alicia,—You are very good in taking notice of Frederica, and I am grateful for it as a mark of your friendship; but as I cannot have any doubt of the warmth of your affection, I am far from exacting so heavy a sacrifice. She is a stupid girl, and has nothing to recommend her. I would not, therefore, on my account, have you encumber one moment of your precious time by sending for her to Edward Street, especially as every visit is so much deducted from the grand affair of education, which I really wish to have attended to while she remains at Miss Summers'. I want her to play and sing with some portion of taste and a good deal of assurance, as she has my hand and arm and a tolerable voice. I was so much indulged in my infant years that I was never obliged to attend to anything, and consequently am without the accomplishments which are now necessary to finish a pretty woman. Not that I am an advocate for the prevailing fashion of acquiring a perfect knowledge of all languages, arts, and sciences. It is throwing time away to be mistress of French, Italian, and German: music, singing, and drawing, &c., will gain a woman some applause, but will not add one lover to her list—grace and manner, after all, are of the greatest importance. I do not mean, therefore, that Frederica's acquirements should be more than superficial,

and I flatter myself that she will not remain long
enough at school to understand anything thoroughly.
I hope to see her the wife of Sir James within a
twelvemonth.  You know on what I ground my hope,
and it is certainly a good foundation, for school
must be very humiliating to a girl of Frederica's age.
And, by-the-by, you had better not invite her any
more on that account, as I wish her to find her situation as unpleasant as possible.  I am sure of Sir
James at any time, and could make him renew his
application by a line.  I shall trouble you meanwhile
to prevent his forming any other attachment when he
comes to town.  Ask him to your house occasionally,
and talk to him of Frederica, that he may not forget
her.  Upon the whole, I commend my own conduct
in this affair extremely, and regard it as a very happy
instance of circumspection and tenderness.  Some
mothers would have insisted on their daughter's accepting so good an offer on the first overture ; but I
could not reconcile it to myself to force Frederica into
a marriage from which her heart revolted, and instead
of adopting so harsh a measure merely propose to
make it her own choice, by rendering her thoroughly
uncomfortable till she does accept him—but enough
of this tiresome girl.  You may well wonder how I
contrive to pass my time here, and for the first week
it was insufferably dull.  Now, however, we begin to
mend, our party is enlarged by Mrs. Vernon's brother,
a handsome young man, who promises me some
amusement.  There is something about him which
rather interests me, a sort of sauciness and familiarity

which I shall teach him to correct. He is lively, and seems clever, and when I have inspired him with greater respect for me than his sister's kind offices have implanted, he may be an agreeable flirt. There is exquisite pleasure in subduing an insolent spirit, in making a person predetermined to dislike acknowledge one's superiority. I have disconcerted him already by my calm reserve, and it shall be my endeavour to humble the pride of these self-important De Courcys still lower, to convince Mrs. Vernon that her sisterly cautions have been bestowed in vain, and to persuade Reginald that she has scandalously belied me. This project will serve at least to amuse me, and prevent my feeling so acutely this dreadful separation from you and all whom I love.

Yours ever,

S. VERNON

## VIII.

*Mrs. Vernon to Lady De Courcy.*

Churchhill.

My dear Mother,—You must not expect Reginald back again for some time. He desires me to tell you that the present open weather induces him to accept Mr. Vernon's invitation to prolong his stay in Sussex, that they may have some hunting together. He means to send for his horses immediately, and it is impossible to say when you may see him in Kent. I will not disguise my sentiments on this change from you, my dear mother, though I think you had better

not communicate them to my father, whose excessive
anxiety about Reginald would subject him to an
alarm which might seriously affect his health and
spirits.   Lady Susan has certainly contrived, in the
space of a fortnight, to make my brother like her.   In
short, I am persuaded that his continuing here beyond
the time originally fixed for his return is occasioned
as much by a degree of fascination towards her, as by
the wish of hunting with Mr. Vernon, and of course I
cannot receive that pleasure from the length of his
visit which my brother's company would otherwise give
me.   I am, indeed, provoked at the artifice of this
unprincipled woman; what stronger proof of her dangerous abilities can be given than this perversion of
Reginald's judgment, which when he entered the
house was so decidedly against her?   In his last letter
he actually gave me some particulars of her behaviour
at Langford, such as he received from a gentleman
who knew her perfectly well, which, if true, must raise
abhorrence against her, and which Reginald himself
was entirely disposed to credit.   His opinion of her,
I am sure, was as low as of any woman in England;
and when he first came it was evident that he considered her as one entitled neither to delicacy nor respect, and that he felt she would be delighted with
the attentions of any man inclined to flirt with her.
Her behaviour, I confess, has been calculated to do
away with such an idea; I have not detected the
smallest impropriety in it—nothing of vanity, of pretension, of levity; and she is altogether so attractive
that I should not wonder at his being delighted with

her, had he known nothing of her previous to this personal acquaintance; but, against reason, against conviction, to be so well pleased with her, as I am sure he is, does really astonish me. His admiration was at first very strong, but no more than was natural, and I did not wonder at his being much struck by the gentleness and delicacy of her manners; but when he has mentioned her of late it has been in terms of more extraordinary praise; and yesterday he actually said that he could not be surprised at any effect produced on the heart of man by such loveliness and such abilities; and when I lamented, in reply, the badness of her disposition, he observed that whatever might have been her errors they were to be imputed to her neglected education and early marriage, and that she was altogether a wonderful woman. This tendency to excuse her conduct, or to forget it, in the warmth of admiration, vexes me; and if I did not know that Reginald is too much at home at Churchhill to need an invitation for lengthening his visit, I should regret Mr. Vernon's giving him any. Lady Susan's intentions are of course those of absolute coquetry, or a desire of universal admiration; I cannot for a moment imagine that she has anything more serious in view; but it mortifies me to see a young man of Reginald's sense duped by her at all.

I am, &c.,

CATHERINE VERNON.

## IX.

*Mrs. Johnson to Lady S. Vernon.*

Edward Street.

My dearest Friend,—I congratulate you on Mr. De Courcy's arrival, and I advise you by all means to marry him ; his father's estate is, we know, considerable, and I believe certainly entailed. Sir Reginald is very infirm, and not likely to stand in your way long. I hear the young man well spoken of ; and though no one can really deserve you, my dearest Susan, Mr. De Courcy may be worth having. Mainwaring will storm of course, but you may easily pacify him ; besides, the most scrupulous point of honour could not require you to wait for *his* emancipation. I have seen Sir James ; he came to town for a few days last week, and called several times in Edward Street. I talked to him about you and your daughter, and he is so far from having forgotten you, that I am sure he would marry either of you with pleasure. I gave him hopes of Frederica's relenting, and told him a great deal of her improvements. I scolded him for making love to Maria Mainwaring ; he protested that he had been only in joke, and we both laughed heartily at her disappointment ; and, in short, were very agreeable. He is as silly as ever.

Yours faithfully,

ALICIA.

## X.

*Lady Susan Vernon* **to Mrs.** *Johnson.*

Churchhill.

I am much obliged to you, my dear friend, for your advice respecting Mr. De Courcy, which I know was given with the full conviction of its expediency, though I am not quite determined on following it. I cannot easily resolve on anything so serious as marriage; especially as I am not at present in want of money, and might perhaps, till the old gentleman's death, be very little benefited by the match. It is true that I am vain enough to believe it within my reach. I have made him sensible of my power, and can now enjoy the pleasure of triumphing over a mind prepared to dislike me, and prejudiced against all my past actions. His sister, too, is, I hope, convinced how little the ungenerous representations of anyone to the disadvantage of another will avail when opposed by the immediate influence of intellect and manner. I see plainly that she is uneasy at my progress in the good opinion of her brother, and conclude that nothing will be wanting on her part to counteract me; but having once made him doubt the justice of her opinion of me, I think I may defy her. It has been delightful to me to watch his advances towards intimacy, especially to observe his altered manner in consequence of my repressing by the cool dignity of my deportment his insolent approach to direct familiarity. My conduct has been

equally guarded from the first, and I never behaved
less like a coquette in the whole course of my life,
though perhaps my desire of dominion was never
more decided. I have subdued him entirely by
sentiment and serious conversation, and made him,
I may venture to say, at least *half* in love with me,
without the semblance of the most commonplace
flirtation. Mrs. Vernon's consciousness of deserving
every sort of revenge that it can be in my power to
inflict for her ill-offices could alone enable her to
perceive that I am actuated by any design in behaviour so gentle and unpretending. Let her think
and act as she chooses, however. I have never yet
found that the advice of a sister could prevent a
young man's being in love if he chose. We are
advancing now to some kind of confidence, and in
short are likely to be engaged in a sort of platonic
friendship. On my side you may be sure of its never
being more, for if I were not attached to another
person as much as I can be to anyone, I should
make a point of not bestowing my affection on a
man who had dared to think so meanly of me.
Reginald has a good figure and is not unworthy
the praise you have heard given him, but is still
greatly inferior to our friend at Langford. He is less
polished, less insinuating than Mainwaring, and is
comparatively deficient in the power of saying those
delightful things which put one in good humour with
oneself and all the world. He is quite agreeable
enough, however, to afford me amusement, and to
make many of those hours pass very pleasantly

which would otherwise be spent in endeavouring to overcome my sister-in-law's reserve, and listening to the insipid talk of her husband. Your account of Sir James is most satisfactory, **and** I mean to **give** Miss Frederica **a** hint of my intentions very soon.

Yours, &c.,

S. VERNON.

## XI.

### *Mrs. Vernon to Lady De Courcy.*

Churchhill.

I really grow quite uneasy, my dearest mother, about Reginald, from witnessing the very rapid increase of Lady Susan's influence. They are now on terms **of** the most particular friendship, frequently engaged **in** long conversations together; **and** she has **contrived** by the most artful coquetry **to** subdue **his** judgment **to** her **own purposes. It is** impossible **to** see the intimacy **between** them so **very** soon established without some alarm, though I can hardly suppose that Lady Susan's plans extend to marriage. I wish you could get Reginald home again on **any** plausible pretence; he is not at all disposed to leave us, and I have given him as many hints of my father's precarious state of health as common decency will allow me to do in my own house. Her power over him must now be boundless, as she has entirely effaced all his former ill-opinion, and persuaded him not merely **to** forget but **to** justify her conduct. Mr. Smith's account of **her** proceedings at Langford, where he accused her of having made Mr. Mainwaring and a young man engaged to Miss Mainwaring distractedly in love with her, which Reginald firmly believed when he came here, is now, he is persuaded, only a scandalous invention. He has told me so with a warmth of manner which spoke his regret at having believed the contrary himself. How sincerely do I grieve that she ever entered this house! I always looked forward to her coming with uneasiness; but very far was it from originating in anxiety for Reginald. I expected a most disagreeable companion for myself, but could not imagine that my brother would be in the smallest danger of being captivated by a woman with whose principles he was so well acquainted, and whose character he so heartily despised If you can get him away it will be a good thing.

Yours, &c.,<br>CATHERINE VERNON.

## XII.

*Sir Reginald De Courcy to his Son.*

Parklands.

I know that young men in general do not admit of any enquiry even from their nearest relations into affairs of the heart, but I hope, my dear Reginald, that you will be superior to such as allow nothing for a father's anxiety, and think themselves privileged to refuse him their confidence and slight his advice. You must be sensible that as an only son, and the representative of an ancient family, your conduct in

life is most interesting **to your** connections; **and in**
the very important **concern of** marriage especially,
there is everything at stake—your own happiness,
that of your parents, and the credit **of your** name.  I
do not suppose **that** you would deliberately form **an**
absolute engagement of that nature without acquaint-
ing your mother and myself, **or at** least, without
being convinced that we **should approve** of your
choice ; but **I** cannot help fearing **that you** may be
drawn in, **by** the lady who has lately attached you,
to a marriage which **the whole** of your family, far
and near, must highly reprobate.  Lady Susan's age
is itself a material objection, but her **want of** character **is one** so much more serious, that the difference
of even twelve years becomes in comparison **of** small
amount.  **Were** you not blinded by a **sort of** fascination, **it** would **be** ridiculous **in** me to repeat **the**
instances **of** great misconduct **on** her **side so very**
generally known.

Her neglect of her husband, her encouragement
of other men, her extravagance and dissipation, were
**so** gross and notorious that no one could be ignorant
of them **at** the time, nor **can** now have forgotten
them.  **To our** family she has always been represented in softened colours by **the** benevolence of Mr.
Charles Vernon, and yet, in spite of his generous endeavours to excuse her, **we** know that she did, from
the most selfish motives, take **all** possible pains to
prevent his marriage with Catherine.

My years and increasing infirmities make me very
desirous of seeing you settled in the world.  To the

fortune of a wife, the goodness of my own will make
me indifferent, but her family and character must be
equally unexceptionable.  When your choice is fixed
so that no objection can be made to it, then I can
promise you a ready and cheerful consent; but it is
my duty to oppose a match which deep art only
could render possible, and must in the end make
wretched.  It is possible her behaviour may arise only
from vanity, or the wish of gaining the admiration of
a man whom she must imagine to be particularly
prejudiced against her; but it is more likely that she
should aim at something further.  She is poor, and
may naturally seek an alliance which must be advantageous to herself; you know your own rights,
and that it is out of my power to prevent your
inheriting the family estate.  My ability of distressing you during my life would be a species of revenge
to which I could hardly stoop under any circumstances.

I honestly tell you my sentiments and intentions:
I do not wish to work on your fears, but on your
sense and affection.  It would destroy every comfort
of my life to know that you were married to Lady
Susan Vernon; it would be the death of that honest
pride with which I have hitherto considered my son;
I should blush to see him, to hear of him, to think of
him.  I may perhaps do no good but that of reliev-
ing my own mind by this letter, but I felt it my duty
to tell you that your partiality for Lady Susan is no
secret to your friends, and to warn you against her.
I should be glad to hear your reasons for disbelieving

Mr. Smith's intelligence ; **you had no** doubt of its authenticity **a** month ago. **If** you can give **me** your assurance of having no design beyond enjoying the conversation **of** a clever woman for **a** short period, and of yielding admiration only to her beauty and abilities, without being blinded by them to her faults, you will restore me to happiness ; but, if you cannot do this, explain to me, at least, what has occasioned so great an alteration in your opinion of her.

I am, &c., &c.,

Reginald De Courcy.

## XIII.

### *Lady De Courcy to Mrs. Vernon.*

Parklands.

**My dear** Catherine,—Unluckily I was confined to my room when your last letter came, by **a** cold which affected my eyes so much **as to** prevent my reading it myself, so I could not refuse your father when he offered to read it to me, by which means he became acquainted, to my great vexation, **with** all your fears about **your** brother. **I had intended to** write **to** Reginald myself as soon **as** my eyes would let me, to point out, as well as I could, the danger of an intimate acquaintance, with **so** artful a woman as Lady Susan, to **a** young **man** of his age, and high expectations. I meant, **moreover,** to have reminded him of our being quite alone **now,** and very much in need of him to keep up our spirits these long winter evenings. Whether it would have done any good

can never be settled now, but I am excessively vexed
that Sir Reginald should know anything of a matter
which we foresaw would make him so uneasy.  He
caught all your fears the moment he had read your
letter, and I am sure he has not had the business
out of his head since.  He wrote by the same post
to Reginald a long letter full of it all, and particularly asking an explanation of what he may have
heard from Lady Susan to contradict the late shock-
ing reports.  His answer came this morning, which I
shall enclose to you, as I think you will like to see
it.  I wish it was more satisfactory; but it seems
written with such a determination to think well of
Lady Susan, that his assurances as to marriage, &c.,
do not set my heart at ease.  I say all I can, however, to satisfy your father, and he is certainly less
uneasy since Reginald's letter.  How provoking it
is, my dear Catherine, that this unwelcome guest of
yours should not only prevent our meeting this
Christmas, but be the occasion of so much vexation
and trouble!  Kiss the dear children for me.

Your affectionate mother,

C. DE COURCY.

## XIV.

*Mr. De Courcy to Sir Reginald.*

Churchhill.

My dear Sir,—I have this moment received your
letter, which has given me more astonishment than I

ever felt **before.** I am to thank my sister, I suppose, for having represented **me in such** a light as to injure me in **your** opinion, and **give you** all this alarm. I know **not** why **she** should choose to make herself and her family uneasy by apprehending an event which no **one** but herself, I can affirm, would ever have thought possible. To impute such a design to Lady Susan would **be** taking from her every claim **to** that excellent understanding which her bitterest enemies have never denied her; **and** equally low **must** sink my pretensions to common sense if I am suspected of matrimonial views **in my** behaviour to **her.** Our difference **of age must be an** insuperable objection, and I entreat **you, my dear** father, to quiet **your** mind, and no longer harbour **a** suspicion which cannot be more injurious to **your own** peace **than to our** understandings. I can have no **other view in** remaining with Lady Susan, than to enjoy for a short time (as you **have** yourself expressed **it)** the conversation of **a** woman of high intellectual powers. **If** Mrs. Vernon would allow something to **my** affection **for** herself and her husband **in** the length **of** my visit, she would do more justice **to us** all; but **my** sister is unhappily prejudiced beyond **the** hope of conviction against Lady Susan. **From** an attachment to her husband, which in itself does honour **to** both, she cannot forgive the endeavours **at** preventing their union, which have been attributed to selfishness **in** Lady Susan; but in this case, **as** well **as in many** others, the world has most grossly injured that lady, by supposing the worst where the motives of her conduct have been doubtful. Lady Susan had heard something so materially to the disadvantage of my sister as to persuade her that the happiness of Mr. Vernon, to whom she was always much attached, would be wholly destroyed by the marriage. And this circumstance, while it explains the true motives of Lady Susan's conduct, and removes all the blame which has been so lavished on her, may also convince us how little the general report of anyone ought to be credited; since no character, however upright, can escape the malevolence of slander. If my sister, in the security of retirement, with as little opportunity as inclination to do evil, could not avoid censure, we must not rashly condemn those who, living in the world and surrounded with temptations, should be accused of errors which they are known to have the power of committing.

I blame myself severely for having so easily believed the slanderous tales invented by Charles Smith to the prejudice of Lady Susan, as I am now convinced how greatly they have traduced her. As to Mrs. Mainwaring's jealousy it was totally his own invention, and his account of her attaching Miss Mainwaring's lover was scarcely better founded. Sir James Martin had been drawn in by that young lady to pay her some attention; and as he is a man of fortune, it was easy to see *her* views extended to marriage. It is well known that Miss M. is absolutely on the catch for a husband, and no one therefore can pity her for losing, by the superior attractions of another woman, the chance of being able to make a worthy man completely wretched. Lady Susan was far from intending such a conquest, and on finding how warmly Miss Mainwaring resented her lover's defection, determined, in spite of Mr. and Mrs. Mainwaring's most urgent entreaties, to leave the family. I have reason to imagine she did receive serious proposals from Sir James, but her removing to Langford immediately on the discovery of his attachment, must acquit her on that article with any mind of common candour. You will, I am sure, my dear Sir, feel the truth of this, and will hereby learn to do justice to the character of a very injured woman. I know that Lady Susan in coming to Churchhill was governed only by the most honourable and amiable intentions; her prudence and economy are exemplary, her regard for Mr. Vernon equal even to *his* deserts; and her wish of obtaining my sister's good opinion merits a better return than it has received. As a mother she is unexceptionable; her solid affection for her child is shown by placing her in hands where her education will be properly attended to; but because she has not the blind and weak partiality of most mothers, she is accused of wanting maternal tenderness. Every person of sense, however, will know how to value and commend her well-directed affection, and will join me in wishing that Frederica Vernon may prove more worthy than she has yet done of her mother's tender care. I have now, my dear father, written my real sentiments of Lady Susan; you will know from this letter how highly I admire her abilities, and esteem her character; but if you are not equally convinced by my full and solemn assurance that your fears have been most idly created, you will deeply mortify and distress me.

I am, &c., &c.,

R. DE COURCY.

## XV.

*Mrs. Vernon to Lady De Courcy.*

Churchhill.

My dear Mother,—I return you Reginald's letter, and rejoice with all my heart that my father is made easy by it : tell him so, with my congratulations ; but, between ourselves, I must own it has only convinced *me* of my brother's having no *present* intention of marrying Lady Susan, not that he is in no danger of doing so three months hence. He gives a very plausible account of her behaviour at Langford ; I wish it may be true, but his intelligence must come from herself, and I am less disposed to believe it than to lament the degree of intimacy subsisting between them implied by the discussion of such a subject. I am sorry to have incurred his displeasure, but can expect nothing better while he is so very eager in Lady Susan's justification. He is very severe against me indeed, and yet I hope I have not been hasty in my judgment of her. Poor woman ! though I have reasons enough for my dislike, I cannot help pitying her at present, as she is in real distress, and with too much cause. She had this morning a letter from the lady with whom she has placed her daughter, to request that Miss Vernon might be immediately removed, as she had been detected in an attempt to run away. Why, or whither she intended to go, does not appear; but, as her situation seems to have been unexceptionable, it is a sad thing, and of course highly distressing to Lady Susan. Frederica must be as much as sixteen, and ought to know better; but from what her mother insinuates, I am afraid she is a perverse girl. She has been sadly neglected, however, and her mother ought to remember it. Mr. Vernon set off for London as soon as she had determined what should be done. He is, if possible, to prevail on Miss Summers to let Frederica continue with her; and if he cannot succeed, to bring her to Churchhill for the present, till some other situation can be found for her. Her ladyship is comforting herself meanwhile by strolling along the shrubbery with Reginald, calling forth all his tender feelings, I suppose, on this distressing occasion. She has been talking a great deal about it to me. She talks vastly well; I am afraid of being ungenerous, or I should say, *too* well to feel so very deeply; but I will not look for faults; she may be Reginald's wife! Heaven forbid it! but why should I be quicker-sighted than anyone else? Mr. Vernon declares that he never saw deeper distress than hers, on the receipt of the letter; and is his judgment inferior to mine? She was very unwilling that Frederica should be allowed to come to Churchhill, and justly enough, as it seems a sort of reward to behaviour deserving very differently; but it was impossible to take her anywhere else, and she is not to remain here long. 'It will be absolutely **necessary**,' said she, 'as you, my dear sister, must be sensible, to treat my daughter with some severity while she is here ; a most painful necessity, but I will *endeavour* to submit to it. I am afraid I have often been too indulgent, but my poor Frederica's temper could never bear opposition well : you must support and encourage me ; you must urge the necessity of reproof if you see me too lenient.' All this sounds very reasonably. Reginald is so incensed against the poor silly girl! Surely it is not to Lady Susan's credit that he should be so bitter against her daughter ; his idea of her must be drawn from the mother's description. Well, whatever may be his fate, we have the comfort of knowing that we have done our utmost to save him. We must commit the event to a higher power.

Yours ever, &c.<br>CATHERINE VERNON.

## XVI.

### *Lady Susan to Mrs. Johnson.*

Churchhill.

Never, my dearest Alicia, was I so provoked in my life as by a letter this morning from Miss Summers. That horrid girl of mine has been trying to run away. I had not a notion of her being such a little devil before, she seemed to have all the Vernon milkiness ; but on receiving the letter in which I declared my intention about Sir James, she actually attempted to elope ; at **least, I cannot** otherwise account **for** her doing it. She **meant, I** suppose, to go to the Clarks in Staffordshire, for she has no other acquaintances. But she shall be punished, she *shall* have him. **I** have sent Charles to town to make matters up if **he** can, **for I do** not **by any** means want her here. **If** Miss Summers will not keep her, you must find me out another school, unless **we** can **get** her married immediately. **Miss S. writes** word that she could not get **the** young lady to assign any cause for her extraordinary conduct, which confirms me in my own previous explanation of it. Frederica **is too** shy, I think, and **too** much in awe of me to tell tales, but if the mildness **of** her uncle should get anything out of **her,** I am not afraid. I trust I shall be able to make my story as good as **hers.** **If I** am vain of anything, it **is of** my eloquence. Consideration and esteem as surely follow command **of** language **as** admiration waits on beauty, and here **I** have opportunity enough for the exercise **of** my talent, **as** the chief of my time is spent in conversation.

Reginald is never easy unless we **are by** ourselves, and when the weather is tolerable, we pace the shrubbery for hours together. I like him **on** the whole very well; **he is** clever **and** has a good deal to say, but he is sometimes impertinent and troublesome. There is **a** sort **of** ridiculous delicacy about him which requires the fullest explanation of whatever he may have heard to **my** disadvantage, and is never satisfied till he thinks **he** has ascertained the beginning and end of everything. This is **one** sort of love, but I confess it does not particularly recommend itself to me.　I infinitely prefer the tender and liberal spirit of Mainwaring, which, impressed with the deepest conviction of my merit, is satisfied that whatever I do must be right ; and look with a degree of contempt on the inquisitive and doubtful fancies of that heart which seems always debating on the reasonableness of its emotions.　Mainwaring is indeed, beyond all compare, superior to Reginald—superior in everything but the power of being with me !　Poor fellow ! he is much distracted by jealousy, which I am not sorry for, as I know no better support of love. He has been teazing me to allow of his coming into this country, and lodging somewhere near *incog.*; but I forbade everything of the kind.　Those women are inexcusable who forget what is due to themselves, and the opinion of the world.

Yours ever,

S. VERNON.

## XVII.

### *Mrs. Vernon to Lady De Courcy.*

Churchhill.

My dear Mother,—Mr. Vernon returned on Thursday night, bringing his niece with him.　Lady Susan had received a line from him by that day's post, informing her that Miss Summers had absolutely refused to allow of Miss Vernon's continuance in her academy; we were therefore prepared for her arrival, and expected them impatiently the whole evening.

They came while we were at tea, and I never saw any creature look so frightened as Frederica when she entered the room. Lady Susan, who had been shedding tears before, and showing great agitation at the idea of the meeting, received her with perfect self-command, and without betraying the least tenderness of spirit. She hardly spoke to her, and on Frederica's bursting into tears as soon as we were seated, took her out of the room, and did not return for some time. When she did, her eyes looked very red, and she was as much agitated as before. We saw no more of her daughter. Poor Reginald was beyond measure concerned to see his fair friend in such distress, and watched her with so much tender solicitude, that I, who occasionally caught her observing his countenance with exultation, was quite out of patience. This pathetic representation lasted the whole evening, and so ostentatious and artful a display has entirely convinced me that she did in fact feel nothing. I am more angry with her than ever since I have seen her daughter ; the poor girl looks so unhappy that my heart aches for her. Lady Susan is surely too severe, for Frederica does not seem to have the sort of temper to make severity necessary. She looks perfectly timid, dejected, and penitent. She is very pretty, though not so handsome as her mother, nor at all like her. Her complexion is delicate, but neither so fair nor so blooming as Lady Susan's, and she has quite the Vernon cast of countenance, the oval face and mild dark eyes, and there is peculiar sweetness in her look when she speaks either to her uncle or me, for as we behave kindly to her we have of course engaged her gratitude.

Her mother has insinuated that her temper is intractable, but I never saw a face less indicative of any evil disposition than hers ; and from what I can see of the behaviour of each to the other, the invariable severity of Lady Susan and the silent dejection of Frederica, I am led to believe as heretofore that the former has no real love for her daughter, and has never done her justice or treated her affectionately. I have not been able to have any conversation with my niece ; she is shy, and I think I can see that some pains are taken to prevent her being much with me. Nothing satisfactory transpires as to her reason for running away. Her kind-hearted uncle, you may be sure, was too fearful of distressing her to ask many questions as they travelled. I wish it had been possible for me to fetch her instead of him. I think I should have discovered the truth in the course of a thirty-mile journey. The small pianoforte has been removed within these few days, at Lady Susan's request, into her dressing-room, and Frederica spends great part of the day there, practising as it is called ; but I seldom hear any noise when I pass that way ; what she does with herself there I do not know. There are plenty of books, but it is not every girl who has been running wild the first fifteen years of her life, that can or will read. Poor creature ! the prospect from her window is not very instructive, for that room overlooks the lawn, you know, with the shrubbery on one side, where she may see her mother walking for an hour together in earnest conversation with Reginald. A girl of Frederica's age must be childish indeed, if such things do not strike her. Is it not inexcusable to give such an example to a daughter? Yet Reginald still thinks Lady Susan the best of mothers, and still condemns Frederica as a worthless girl! He is convinced that her attempt to run away proceeded from no justifiable cause, and had no provocation. I am sure I cannot say that it *had*, but while Miss Summers declares that Miss Vernon showed no signs of obstinacy or perverseness during her whole stay in Wigmore Street, till she was detected in this scheme, I cannot so readily credit what Lady Susan has made him, and wants to make me believe, that it was merely an impatience of restraint and a desire of escaping from the tuition of masters which brought on the plan of an elopement. O Reginald, how is your judgment enslaved! He scarcely dares even allow her to be handsome, and when I speak of her beauty, replies only that her eyes have no brilliancy! Sometimes he is sure she is deficient in understanding, and at others that her temper only is in fault. In short, when a person is always to deceive, it is impossible to be consistent. Lady Susan finds it necessary that Frederica should be to blame, and probably has sometimes judged it expedient to excuse her of ill-nature and sometimes to lament her want of sense. Reginald is only repeating after her ladyship.

I remain, &c., &c.,
CATHERINE VERNON.

# XVIII.



*From the same to the same.*

Churchhill.

My dear Mother,—I am very glad to find that my description of Frederica Vernon has interested you, for I do believe her truly deserving of your regard; and when I have communicated a notion which has recently struck me, your kind impressions in her favour will, I am sure, be heightened. I cannot help fancying that she is growing partial to my brother. I so very often see her eyes fixed on his face with a remarkable expression of pensive admiration. He is certainly very handsome; and yet more, there is an openness in his manner that must be highly prepossessing, and I am sure she feels it so. Thoughtful and pensive in general, her countenance always brightens into a smile when Reginald says anything amusing; and, let the subject be ever so serious that he may be conversing on, I am much mistaken if a syllable of his uttering escapes her. I want to make him sensible of all this, for we know the power of gratitude on such a heart as his; and could Frederica's artless affection detach him from her mother, we might bless the day which brought her to Churchhill. I think, my dear mother, you would not disapprove of her as a daughter. She is extremely young, to be sure, has had a wretched education, and a dreadful example of levity in her mother; but yet I can pronounce her disposition to be excellent, and her natural abilities very good. Though totally without accomplishments, she **is** by **no** means so ignorant as **one** might expect **to** find her, being fond of books and spending **the chief** of her time in reading. Her **mother** leaves her more **to** herself than she did, **and** I have her with me **as much** as possible, **and** have **taken** great pains to overcome her timidity. **We** are **very** good friends, **and** though she never opens her lips before her mother, she talks enough when alone with me to make it clear that, if properly **treated by** Lady Susan, she would always appear to much **greater** advantage. There cannot be a more gentle, **affec**tionate heart ; **or** more obliging manners, when **acting** without **restraint ;** and her little cousins **are all very** fond of **her.**

Your affectionate Daughter,<br>C. VERNON.

## XIX.

*Lady Susan **to Mrs.** Johnson.*

Churchhill.

You will be eager, **I** know, to hear **something** further of Frederica, and perhaps **may think me** negligent for not writing before. She **arrived with her** uncle last Thursday fortnight, when, **of** course, **I lost no** time in demanding the cause of her behaviour ; and soon found myself to have been perfectly right in attributing it to my own letter. The prospect **of** it frightened her so thoroughly, that, with a mixture of **true** girlish perverseness and folly, she resolved on getting out of the **house and** proceeding directly by the stage **to** her friends, the Clarkes ; **and** had really got as far as the length of two streets in her journey when she was fortunately missed, pursued, and over-taken. Such was the first distinguished exploit of Miss Frederica Vernon; and, if we consider that it was achieved at the tender age of sixteen, we shall have room for the most flattering prognostics of her future renown. I am excessively provoked, however, at the parade of propriety which prevented Miss Summers from keeping the girl; and it seems so extraordinary a piece of nicety, considering my daughter's family connections, that I can only suppose the lady to be governed by the fear of never getting her money. Be that as it may, however, Frederica is returned on my hands; and, having nothing else to employ her, is busy in pursuing the plan of romance begun at Langford. She is actually falling in love with Reginald De Courcy! To disobey her mother by refusing an unexceptionable offer is not enough; her affections must also be given without her mother's approbation. I never saw a girl of her age bid fairer to be the sport of mankind. Her feelings are tolerably acute, and she is so charmingly artless in their display as to afford the most reasonable hope of her being ridiculous, and despised by every man who sees her.

Artlessness will never do in love matters; and that girl is born a simpleton who has it either by nature or affectation. I am not yet certain that Reginald sees what she is about, nor is it of much conse-quence. She is now an object of indifference to him, and she would be one of contempt were he to understand her emotions. Her beauty is much admired by the Vernons, but it has no effect on him. She is in high favour with her aunt altogether, because she is so little like myself, of course. She is exactly the companion for Mrs. Vernon, who dearly loves to be first, and to have all the sense and all the wit of the conversation to herself: Frederica will never eclipse her. When she first came I was at some pains to prevent her seeing much of her aunt; but I have relaxed, as I believe I may depend on her observing the rules I have laid down for their discourse. But do not imagine that with all this lenity I have for a moment given up my plan of her marriage. No; I am unalterably fixed on this point, though I have not yet quite decided on the manner of bringing it about. I should not choose to have the business brought on here, and canvassed by the wise heads of Mr. and Mrs. Vernon; and I cannot just now afford to go to town. Miss Frederica must therefore wait a little.

Yours ever,<br>S. VERNON.

## XX.

*Mrs. Vernon to Lady De Courcy.*

Churchhill.

We have a very unexpected guest with us at present, my dear mother: he arrived yesterday. I heard a carriage at the door, as I was sitting with my children while they dined; and supposing I should be wanted, left the nursery soon afterwards, and was half-way down stairs, when Frederica, as pale as ashes, came running up, and rushed by me into her own room.  I instantly followed, and asked her what was the matter.  'Oh!' said she, 'he is come—Sir James is come, and what shall I do?'  This was no explanation; I begged her to tell me what she meant.  At that moment we were interrupted by a knock at the door: it was Reginald, who came, by Lady Susan's direction, to call Frederica down.  'It is Mr. De Courcy!' said she, colouring violently.  'Mamma has sent for me; I must go.'  We all three went down together; and I saw my brother examining the terrified face of Frederica with surprise.  In the breakfast-room we found Lady Susan, and a young man of gentlemanlike appearance, whom she introduced by the name of Sir James Martin—the very person, as you may remember, whom it was said she had been at pains to detach from Miss Mainwaring; but the conquest, it seems, was not designed for herself, or she has since transferred it to her daughter; for Sir James is now desperately in love with Frederica, and with full encouragement from mamma.  The poor girl, however, I am sure, dislikes him ; and though his person and address are very well, he appears, both to Mr. Vernon and me, a very weak young man.  Frederica looked so shy, so confused, when we entered the room, that I felt for her exceedingly.  Lady Susan behaved with great attention to her visitor; and yet I thought I could perceive that she had no particular pleasure in seeing him.  Sir James talked a great deal, and made many civil excuses to me for the liberty he had taken in coming to Churchhill—mixing more frequent **laughter** with his discourse than the subject required—said **many** things over **and** over again, **and** told Lady Susan three times that he had seen Mrs. Johnson a few evenings before. He **now** and **then** addressed Frederica, but more frequently her mother. The poor girl sat all this time without opening her lips—her eyes cast down, and her colour varying every instant; while Reginald observed all that passed in perfect silence. At length Lady Susan, weary, I believe, of her situation, proposed walking ; and we left the two gentlemen together, to put on our pelisses. As we went upstairs Lady Susan begged permission **to attend me for a few** moments **in my** dressing-room, as **she** was anxious **to** speak with me in private. I led her thither accordingly, and as soon as the door was closed, she said : **' I** was never more surprised **in my life than by** Sir James's arrival, **and** the suddenness **of it requires some** apology **to** you, my dear sister ; though **to** *me*, as a mother, it is highly flattering. **He is so** extremely attached **to** my daughter that **he** could **not** exist longer without seeing her. Sir James is a young **man** of an amiable disposition and excellent character ; a little too much of the rattle, perhaps, but a year **or two** will rectify *that* : and **he is in** other respects so **very** eligible a match **for** Frederica, **that** I have always observed his attachment with the greatest pleasure ; and am per- suaded that you and **my** brother will give the alliance your hearty approbation. I have never before men- tioned the likelihood **of** its taking place to anyone, because **I** thought that whilst Frederica continued at school it had better not be known to exist; but now, as I am convinced that Frederica is too old ever to submit to school confinement, and have, therefore, begun to consider her union with Sir James as not very distant, I had intended within a few days to acquaint yourself and Mr. Vernon with the whole business. I am sure, my dear sister, you will excuse my remaining silent so long, and agree with me that such circumstances, while they continue from any cause in suspense, cannot be too cautiously concealed. When you have the happiness of bestowing your sweet little Catherine, some years hence, on a man who in connection and character is alike unexceptionable, you will know what I feel now; though, thank Heaven, you cannot have all my reasons for rejoicing in such an event. Catherine will be amply provided for, and not, like my Frederica, indebted to a fortunate establishment for the comforts of life.' She concluded by demanding my congratulations. I gave them somewhat awkwardly, I believe; for, in fact, the sudden disclosure of so important a matter took from me the power of speaking with any clearness. She thanked me, however, most affectionately, for my kind concern in the welfare of herself and daughter; and then said: 'I am not apt to deal in professions, my dear Mrs. Vernon, and I never had the convenient talent of affecting sensations foreign to my heart; and therefore I trust you will believe me when I declare, that much as I had heard in your praise before I knew you, I had no idea that I should ever love you as I now do; and I must further say that your friendship towards me is more particularly gratifying because I have reason to **believe** that some attempts **were made to** prejudice **you** against me. I only wish **that they,** whoever they are, to whom **I am** indebted **for** such kind intentions, could see the terms on which **we now** are together, and understand the real affection we feel for each other; **but I** will not detain you any longer. God bless **you, for** your goodness to me and my girl, and continue to you all your present happiness.' What can one say of such a woman, my dear mother? Such earnestness, such solemnity of expression! **and** yet I cannot help suspecting **the** truth of everything she **says.** As for Reginald, **I** believe **he** does **not** know **what to make** of **the matter.** When Sir James came, **he** appeared **all** astonishment **and** perplexity; the folly of the young **man** and the confusion of Frederica entirely engrossed **him; and** though a little private discourse with Lady Susan has since had its effect, **he is** still hurt, **I** am sure, at her allowing of such a man's attentions to her daughter. Sir James invited himself **with great** composure to remain here a few days—hoped **we** would not think it odd, was aware of its being very impertinent, but **he** took the liberty of a relation; **and** concluded by wishing, with **a** laugh, that he might be really one very soon. Even Lady Susan seemed a little disconcerted by this forwardness; in her heart I am persuaded she sincerely wished him gone. But something must be done for this poor girl, **if** her feelings are such as both I and **her** uncle believe them to be. She must not be sacrificed to policy or ambition, and she must not be left to suffer from the dread of it. The girl whose heart can distinguish Reginald De Courcy, deserves, however he may slight her, a better fate than to be Sir James Martin's wife. As soon as I can get her alone, I will discover the real truth; but she seems to wish to avoid me. I hope this does not proceed from anything wrong, and that I shall not find out I have thought too well of her. Her behaviour to Sir James certainly speaks the greatest consciousness and embarrassment, but I see nothing in it more like encouragement. Adieu, my dear mother.

Yours, &c.

C. VERNON.

## XXI.

### *Miss Vernon to Mr. De Courcy.*

Sir,—I hope you will excuse this liberty; I am forced upon it by the greatest distress, or I should be ashamed to trouble you. I am very miserable about Sir James Martin, and have no other way in the world of helping myself but by writing to you, for I am forbidden even speaking to my uncle and aunt on the subject; and this being the case, I am afraid my applying to you will appear no better than equivocation, and as if I attended to the letter and not the spirit of mamma's commands. But if you do not take my part and persuade her to break it off, I shall be half distracted, for I cannot bear him. No human being but *you* could have any chance of prevailing with her.

If you will, therefore, have **the** unspeakably great kindness of taking my part with her, and persuading her to send Sir James away, **I** shall be more obliged to you than it is possible for me **to** express. I always disliked him from the first: **it is** not a sudden fancy, I assure you, sir; I always thought him silly and impertinent and disagreeable, and now he is grown worse than ever. I would rather work for my bread than marry him. **I do not** know **how** to apologise enough for this letter ; I know it is taking so great a liberty. I am aware how dreadfully angry it will make mamma, but I remember **the risk.**

I am, Sir, your most humble servant,

**F. S. V.**

## XXII.

### *Lady Susan to Mrs. Johnson.*

**Churchhill.**

This is insufferable ! My dearest friend, I was never so enraged before, and must relieve myself **by** writing to you, who I know will enter into **all** my feelings. **Who** should come on Tuesday but **Sir** James Martin ! Guess **my** astonishment, and vexation—for, as you well know, I never wished him to be seen **at** Church-hill. What a pity that **you** should not have known his intentions ! Not content with coming, he actually invited himself **to** remain here a few days. I could **have** poisoned him ! **I made** the best of it, however, **and told** my story with great success to Mrs. Vernon, who, whatever might **be** her real sentiments, said nothing in opposition to mine. I made a point also of Frederica's behaving civilly to Sir James, and gave her to understand that I was absolutely determined on her marrying him. She said something of her misery, but that was all. I have for some time been more particularly resolved on the match from seeing the rapid increase of her affection for Reginald, and from not feeling secure that a knowledge of such affection might not in the end awaken a return. Contemptible as a regard founded only on compassion must make them both in my eyes, I felt by no means assured that such might not be the consequence. It is true that Reginald had not in any degree grown cool towards me; but yet he has lately mentioned Frederica spontaneously and unnecessarily, and once said something in praise of her person. *He* was all astonishment at the appearance of my visitor, and at first observed Sir James with an attention which I was pleased to see not unmixed with jealousy; but unluckily it was impossible for me really to torment him, as Sir James, though extremely gallant to me, very soon made the whole party understand that his heart was devoted to my daughter. I had no great difficulty in convincing De Courcy, when we were alone, that I was perfectly justified, all things considered, in desiring the match; and the whole business seemed most comfortably arranged. They could none of them help perceiving that Sir James was no Solomon; but I had positively forbidden Frederica complaining to Charles Vernon or his wife, and they had therefore no pretence for interference; though my impertinent

sister, **I believe,** wanted **only** opportunity for doing
so. Everything, however, was going on calmly and
quietly ; **and,** though I counted **the** hours of Sir James's
stay, my mind was entirely satisfied with the posture
of affairs. Guess, then, what I must feel at the sudden
disturbance of all my **schemes ;** and that, too, from a
quarter where I had least reason to expect it. Reginald
came this morning into my dressing-room with a very
unusual solemnity of countenance, and after some
preface informed me in so many words that **he** wished
to reason with me on the impropriety and unkindness
of allowing Sir James Martin to address my daughter
contrary to **her** inclinations. I was all amazement.
When I found that he was not to be laughed out of his
design, **I calmly** begged an explanation, and desired
**to** know **by what** he was impelled, and **by whom**
commissioned, to reprimand me. He then told **me,**
mixing in his speech a few insolent compliments **and**
ill-timed expressions of tenderness, to which I listened
with perfect indifference, that **my** daughter had acquainted him with some circumstances concerning
herself, Sir James, and me which had given him **great**
uneasiness. In short, I found that she **had in** the first
place actually written to him to request his interference,
and that, on receiving her letter, he had conversed
with her on the subject of it, in order to understand
the particulars, and to assure himself of her real
wishes. I have not a doubt but that the girl took
this opportunity of making downright love to him.
I am convinced of it by the manner in which he spoke
of her. Much good may such love do him ! I shall

ever despise the man who can be gratified by the
passion which he never wished to inspire, nor solicited
the avowal of.   I shall always detest them both.   He
can have no true regard for me, or he would not have
listened to her; and *she*, with her little rebellious
heart and indelicate feelings, to throw herself into the
protection of a young man with whom she has scarcely
ever exchanged two words before!   I am equally con-
founded at *her* impudence and *his* credulity.   How
dared he believe what she told him in my disfavour!
Ought he not to have felt assured that I must have
unanswerable motives for all that I had done?   Where
was his reliance on my sense and goodness then?
Where the resentment which true love would have
dictated against the person defaming me—that person,
too, a chit, a child, without talent or education, whom
he had been always taught to despise?   I was calm
for some time; but the greatest degree of forbearance
may be overcome, and I hope I was afterwards sufficiently keen.   He endeavoured, long endeavoured, to
soften my resentment; but that woman is a fool
indeed who, while insulted by accusation, can be
worked on by compliments.   At length he left me,
as deeply provoked as myself; and he showed his
anger more.   I was quite cool, but he gave way to
the most violent indignation; I may therefore expect
it will the sooner subside, and perhaps his may
be vanished for ever, while mine will be found still
fresh and implacable.   He is now shut up in his
apartment, whither I heard him go on leaving mine.
How unpleasant, one would think, must be his reflec-

tions! but **some** people's feelings **are** incomprehensible. I have **not** yet tranquillised myself enough to see Frederica. *She* shall not **soon** forget **the occurrences of this** day; she shall find that she has poured forth her tender tale of **love** in vain, **and** exposed herself for ever to the contempt of the whole world, and the severest resentment **of** her injured mother.

Your affectionate

S. VERNON.

## XXIII.

### *Mrs. Vernon to Lady De Courcy.*

Churchhill.

Let me congratulate you, my dearest mother! **The** affair which **has** given us so **much** anxiety is drawing to a happy conclusion. Our prospect is most delightful, and since matters have now taken so favourable a turn, I am quite sorry that **I** ever imparted my apprehensions to you; for the **pleasure of** learning that the danger is over is perhaps **dearly purchased** by all that **you** have previously suffered. **I am** so much agitated by delight that **I** can scarcely **hold a** pen; but am determined to send you a few short lines **by** James, that you may have some explanation of what must so greatly astonish you, **as** that Reginald should be returning **to** Parklands. I was sitting about half-an-hour ago with Sir James **in the** breakfast parlour, **when** my brother called me **out of** the room. I instantly saw that something **was the** matter; his complexion was raised, and he spoke with great emotion; **you** know his eager manner, my dear mother, when his mind is interested. 'Catherine,' said he, 'I am going home to-day; I am sorry to leave you, but I must go: it is a great while since I have seen my father and mother. I am going to send James forward with my hunters immediately; if you have any letter, therefore, he can take it. I shall not be at home myself till Wednesday or Thursday, as I shall go through London, where I have business; but before I leave you,' he continued, speaking in a lower tone, and with still greater energy, 'I must warn you of one thing—do not let Frederica Vernon be made unhappy by that Martin. He wants to marry her; her mother promotes the match, but she cannot endure the idea of it. Be assured that I speak from the fullest conviction of the truth of what I say; I *know* that Frederica is made wretched by Sir James's continuing here. She is a sweet girl, and deserves a better fate. Send him away immediately; he is only a fool: but what her mother can mean, Heaven only knows! Good bye,' he added, shaking my hand with earnestness; 'I do not know when you will see me again; but remember what I tell you of Frederica; you *must* make it your business to see justice done her. She is an amiable girl, and has a very superior mind to what we have given her credit for.' He then left me, and ran upstairs. I would not try to stop him, for I know what his feelings must be. The nature of mine, as I listened to him, I need not attempt to describe; for a minute or two I remained in the same spot, overpowered by wonder of a most agreeable sort indeed; yet it required some consideration to be tranquilly happy. In about ten minutes after my return to the parlour Lady Susan entered the room. I concluded, of course, that she and Reginald had been quarrelling; and looked with anxious curiosity for a confirmation of my belief in her face. Mistress of deceit, however, she appeared perfectly unconcerned, and after chatting on indifferent subjects for a short time, said to me, ' I find from Wilson that we are going to lose Mr. De Courcy —is it true that he leaves Churchhill this morning?' I replied that it was. ' He told us nothing of all this last night,' said she, laughing, ' or even this morning at breakfast; but perhaps he did not know it himself. Young men are often hasty in their resolutions, and not more sudden in forming than unsteady in keeping them. I should not be surprised if he were to change his mind at last, and not go.' She soon afterwards left the room. I trust, however, my dear mother, that we have no reason to fear an alteration of his present plan; things have gone too far. They must have quarrelled, and about Frederica, too. Her calmness astonishes me. What delight will be yours in seeing him again; in seeing him still worthy your esteem, still capable of forming your happiness! When I next write I shall be able to tell you that Sir James is gone, Lady Susan vanquished, and Frederica at peace. We have much to do, but it shall be done. I am all impatience to hear how this astonishing change was effected. I finish as I began, with the warmest congratulations.

Yours ever, &c.,<br>CATH. VERNON.

## XXIV.

*From the same to the same.*

Churchhill.

Little did I imagine, my dear mother, when I sent off my last letter, that the delightful perturbation of spirits I was then in would undergo so speedy, so melancholy a reverse. I never can sufficiently regret that I wrote to you at all. Yet who could have foreseen what has happened? My dear mother, every hope which made me so happy only two hours ago has vanished. The quarrel between Lady Susan and Reginald is made up, and we are all as we were before. One point only is gained. Sir James Martin is dismissed. What are we now to look forward to? I am indeed disappointed; Reginald was all but gone, his horse was ordered and all but brought to the door; who would not have felt safe? For half an hour I was in momentary expectation of his departure. After I had sent off my letter to you, I went to Mr. Vernon, and sat with him in his room talking over the whole matter, and then determined to look for Frederica, whom I had not seen since breakfast. I met her on the stairs, and saw that she was crying. ' My dear aunt,' said she, ' he is going—Mr. De Courcy is going, and it is all my fault. I am afraid you will be very angry with me, but indeed I had no idea it would end so.' ' My love,' I replied, ' do not think it necessary to apologise to me on that account. I shall feel myself under an obligation to anyone who is the means of sending my brother home, because,' recol-

lecting myself, ' I **know my** father wants very much
to see him. But what is it **you** have done to occasion
all this ? ' She blushed deeply as she answered : ' **I**
was **so** unhappy about Sir **James** that **I** could **not**
help—I have **done** something very wrong, I know ;
but you have not an idea of the misery I have been
in : and mamma had ordered me never to speak to you
**or** my uncle about it, and—' ' You therefore spoke to
my brother to engage his interference,' said I, to save
her the explanation. '**No,** but I wrote **to** him—I
did indeed, I got up this morning before it was light,
and was two hours about **it ;** and when my letter
**was** done I thought I never should have courage **to**
give it. After breakfast, however, **as** I was going to **my
room, I** met him in the passage, **and** then, as **I knew**
that everything must depend on that moment, I forced
myself to **give it. He** was so good as **to** take it immediately. I dared **not** look at him, and ran away directly.
I was in such a **fright I could** hardly breathe. My dear
**aunt,** you do not **know how** miserable **I have been.'**
' Frederica,' said **I,** ' you ought to have told me all your
distresses. You would have found in me a friend always
ready to assist you. Do **you** think that your uncle
**or I** should not have espoused your cause as warmly
as my brother ? ' ' Indeed, I did not doubt your kindness,' said she, colouring again, ' but I thought Mr.
**De** Courcy **could do** anything with my mother ; but
I was mistaken : they have had **a** dreadful quarrel
about it, **and he** is going **away.** Mamma will never
forgive me, and **I shall** be worse off than ever.' ' No,
you shall not,' I replied ; ' **in** such a point as this your

mother's prohibition ought not to have prevented your speaking to me on the subject. She has no right to make you unhappy, and she shall *not* do it. Your applying, however, to Reginald can be productive only of good to all parties. I believe it is best as it is. Depend upon it that you shall not be made unhappy any longer.' At that moment how great was my astonishment at seeing Reginald come out of Lady Susan's dressing-room. My heart misgave me instantly. His confusion at seeing me was very evident. Frederica immediately disappeared. 'Are you going?' I said ; 'you will find Mr. Vernon in his own room.' 'No, Catherine,' he replied, 'I am not going. Will you let me speak to you a moment?' We went into my room. 'I find,' he continued, his confusion increasing as he spoke, 'that I have been acting with my usual foolish impetuosity. I have entirely misunderstood Lady Susan, and was on the point of leaving the house under a false impression of her conduct. There has been some very great mistake ; we have been all mistaken, I fancy. Frederica does not know her mother. Lady Susan means nothing but her good, but she will not make a friend of her. Lady Susan does not always know, therefore, what will make her daughter happy. Besides, I could have no right to interfere. Miss Vernon was mistaken in applying to me. In short, Catherine, everything has gone wrong, but it is now all happily settled. Lady Susan, I believe, wishes to speak to you about it, if you are at leisure.' ' Certainly,' I replied, deeply sighing at the recital of so lame a story. I made no **comments,** however, **for words would have** been vain.

Reginald was glad to get away, and I went **to** Lady Susan, curious, indeed, **to hear her** account of **it.** '**Did I not** tell you,' **said** she with a smile, 'that your brother would not leave us after all?' 'You did, indeed,' replied I very gravely; 'but I flattered myself you would be mistaken.' 'I should not have hazarded such an opinion,' returned she, '**if** it had not at that moment occurred to me that his resolution of going might be occasioned by a conversation in which we had been this morning engaged, and which had ended very much to his dissatisfaction, from our not rightly understanding each other's meaning. This idea struck me at the moment, and I instantly determined that an accidental dispute, in which **I** might probably be as much to blame as himself, should not deprive you of your brother. If you remember, I left the room almost immediately. **I** was resolved to lose no time in clearing up those mistakes as far as I could. The case was this—Frederica had set herself violently against marrying Sir James.' 'And can your lady-ship wonder that she should?' cried **I** with some warmth; 'Frederica has an excellent understanding, and Sir **James** has none.' 'I am at least very far from regretting it, my dear sister,' said she; '**on** the contrary, **I am** grateful for **so** favourable a sign of my daughter's sense. Sir James is certainly below par (**his** boyish **manners** make him appear worse); and had Frederica possessed **the** penetration and the abilities which I could have wished in my daughter, or had I even known her to possess as much as she does, I should not have been anxious for the match.' 'It is odd that you should alone be ignorant of your daughter's sense!' 'Frederica never does justice to herself; her manners are shy and childish, and besides she is afraid of me. During her poor father's life she was a spoilt child; the severity which it has since been necessary for me to show has alienated her affection; neither has she any of that brilliancy of intellect, that genius or vigour of mind which will force itself forward.' 'Say rather that she has been unfortunate in her education!' 'Heaven knows, my dearest Mrs. Vernon, how fully I am aware of that; but I would wish to forget every circumstance that might throw blame on the memory of one whose name is sacred with me.' Here she pretended to cry; I was out of patience with her. 'But what,' said I, 'was your ladyship going to tell me about your disagreement with my brother?' 'It originated in an action of my daughter's, which equally marks her want of judgment and the unfortunate dread of me I have been mentioning—she wrote to Mr. De Courcy.' 'I know she did; you had forbidden her speaking to Mr. Vernon or to me on the cause of her distress; what could she do, therefore, but apply to my brother?' 'Good God!' she exclaimed, 'what an opinion you must have of me! Can you possibly suppose that I was aware of her unhappiness? that it was my object to make my own child miserable, and that I had forbidden her speaking to you on the subject from a fear of your interrupting the diabolical scheme? Do you think me destitute of every honest, every natural feeling? Am I capable of consigning *her* to everlasting misery whose welfare it is my first earthly duty to promote? The idea is horrible!' 'What, then, was your intention when you insisted on her silence?' 'Of what use, my dear sister, could be any application to you, however the affair might stand? Why should I subject you to entreaties which I refused to attend to myself? Neither for your sake nor for hers, nor for my own, could such a thing be desirable. When my own resolution was taken I could not wish for the interference, however friendly, of another person. I was mistaken, it is true, but I believed myself right.' 'But what was this mistake to which your ladyship so often alludes? from whence arose so astonishing a misconception of your daughter's feelings? Did you not know that she disliked Sir James?' 'I knew that he was not absolutely the man she would have chosen, but I was persuaded that her objections to him did not arise from any perception of his deficiency. You must not question me, however, my dear sister, too minutely on this point,' continued she, taking me affectionately by the hand; 'I honestly own that there is something to conceal. Frederica makes me very unhappy! Her applying to Mr. De Courcy hurt me particularly.' 'What is it you mean to infer,' said I, 'by this appearance of mystery? If you think your daughter at all attached to Reginald, her objecting to Sir James could not less deserve to be attended to than if the cause of her objecting had been a consciousness of his folly; and why should

your ladyship, at any rate, quarrel with my brother
for an interference which, you must know, it is not in
his nature to refuse when urged in such a manner?'

' His disposition, you know, is warm, and he came
to expostulate with me ; his compassion all alive for
this ill-used girl, this heroine in distress !  We misunderstood each other : he believed me more to
blame than I really was ; I considered his interference less excusable than I now find it.  I have a
real regard for him, and was beyond expression mortified to find it, as I thought, so ill bestowed.  We
were both warm, and of course both to blame.  His
resolution of leaving Churchhill is consistent with his
general eagerness.  When I understood his intention,
however, and at the same time began to think that
we had been perhaps equally mistaken in each other's
meaning, I resolved to have an explanation before
it was too late.  For any member of your family I
must always feel a degree of affection, and I own it
would have sensibly hurt me if my acquaintance with
Mr. De Courcy had ended so gloomily.  I have now
only to say further, that as I am convinced of
Frederica's having a reasonable dislike to Sir James,
I shall instantly inform him that he must give up
all hope of her.  I reproach myself for having even,
though innocently, made her unhappy on that score.
She shall have all the retribution in my power to
make ; if she value her own happiness as much as I
do, if she judge wisely, and command herself as she
ought, she may now be easy.  Excuse me, my dearest
sister, for thus trespassing on your time, but I owe it

to my own character; and after this explanation I trust I am **in no** danger of sinking in **your opinion.'** I could have said, ' Not much, indeed !' but I left her almost in silence. It **was** the greatest stretch **of for-** bearance I could practise. I could not have **stopped** myself had I begun. **Her** assurance ! her deceit ! **but I** will not allow **myself to** dwell on them ; they will strike you sufficiently. My heart sickens within me. As soon as **I** was tolerably composed **I** returned **to the** parlour. Sir James's carriage was **at the** door, and he, merry as usual, **soon** afterwards **took** his leave. How easily does **her** ladyship encourage **or** dismiss **a lover!** In spite **of this** release, Frederica still looks **unhappy:** still **fearful,** perhaps, of **her** mother's anger; **and** though dreading my brother's departure, **jealous, it may** be, of his staying. **I see** how closely **she observes him and** Lady Susan, poor girl! I have now **no hope for** her. There is not a chance **of her** affection being returned. **He** thinks very differently of **her** from what **he used to do ;** he does her some justice, but his **reconciliation with her** mother precludes every dearer **hope.** Prepare, **my dear** mother, for the worst! **The** probability of their marrying is surely heightened! He is more securely **hers** than **ever.** When that wretched event takes place, Frederica must belong wholly to us. I am thankful that my last letter will precede this by **so** little, as every moment **that you can** be saved **from** feeling a joy which **leads** only to disappointment **is** of consequence.

Yours ever, &c.<br>
CATHERINE VERNON.

# XXV.

## *Lady Susan to Mrs. Johnson.*

Churchhill.

I call on you, dear Alicia, for congratulations : I am my ownself, gay and triumphant ! When I wrote to you the other day I was, in truth, in high irritation, and with ample cause. Nay, I know not whether I ought to be quite tranquil now, for I have had more trouble in restoring peace than I ever intended to submit to — a spirit, too, resulting from a fancied sense of superior integrity, which is peculiarly in- solent ! I shall not easily forgive him, I assure you. He was actually on the point of leaving Churchhill ! I had scarcely concluded my last, when Wilson brought me word of it. I found, therefore, that some- thing must be done ; for I did not choose to leave my character at the mercy of a man whose passions are so violent and so revengeful. It would have been trifling with my reputation to allow of his de- parting with such an impression in my disfavour ; in this light, condescension was necessary. I sent Wilson to say that I desired to speak with him before he went ; he came immediately. The angry emotions which had marked every feature when we last parted were partially subdued. He seemed astonished at the summons, and looked as if half wishing and half fearing to be softened by what I might say. If my countenance expressed what I aimed at, it was com- posed and dignified ; and yet, with a degree of pen- siveness which might convince him that I was not quite happy. ' I beg your pardon, sir, **for the** liberty I have taken in sending for you,' said I ; ' but as **I** have just learnt your intention of **leaving** this place to-day, I feel it my duty to entreat that you will **not** on **my** account shorten **your** visit here even an **hour.** I **am** perfectly aware that after what has passed between us it would ill suit the feelings of either to remain longer **in** the same house : so very great, so total a change from **the** intimacy of friendship must render **any** future intercourse the severest punish-ment; **and** your resolution of quitting Churchhill is undoubtedly **in** unison with our situation, and with those lively feelings which I know you to possess. But, at the same time, it is not for me to suffer such **a** **sacrifice as it** must be to leave relations to whom you **are** so much attached, and are so dear. My remaining here cannot give that pleasure to Mr. and Mrs. Vernon which your society must ; and my visit has already perhaps been too long. My removal, therefore, which **must,** at any rate, **take place** soon, may, **with** perfect convenience, be hastened ; **and I** make it **my** particular request that I may not in any way **be** instrumental in separating a family so affectionately attached to each other. Where I go is of no consequence to any-**one** ; of very little **to** myself; **but** you are of im-portance to all your connections.' Here I concluded, and **I** hope you will be satisfied with my speech. Its effect **on** Reginald justifies some portion of vanity, for **it was** no less favourable than instantaneous. Oh, how delightful it **was** to watch the variations of his countenance while **I** spoke ! to see the struggle between returning tenderness and the remains of displeasure. There is something agreeable in feelings so easily worked on; not that I envy him their possession, nor would, for the world, have such myself; but they are very convenient when one wishes to influence the passions of another. And yet this Reginald, whom a very few words from me softened at once into the utmost submission, and rendered more tractable, more attached, more devoted than ever, would have left me in the first angry swelling of his proud heart without deigning to seek an explanation. Humbled as he now is, I cannot forgive him such an instance of pride, and am doubtful whether I ought not to punish him by dismissing him at once after this reconciliation, or by marrying and teazing him for ever. But these measures are each too violent to be adopted without some deliberation; at present my thoughts are fluctuating between various schemes. I have many things to compass: I must punish Frederica, and pretty severely too, for her application to Reginald; I must punish him for receiving it so favourably, and for the rest of his conduct. I must torment my sister-in-law for the insolent triumph of her look and manner since Sir James has been dismissed; for, in reconciling Reginald to me, I was not able to save that ill-fated young man; and I must make myself amends for the humiliation to which I have stooped within these few days. To effect all this I have various plans. I have also an idea of being soon in town; and whatever may be my determination as to the rest, I shall probably put *that* project in execution ; for London will be always the fairest field of action, however my views may be directed ; and at any rate I shall there be rewarded by your society, and a little dissipation, for a ten weeks' penance at Churchhill. I believe I owe it to my character to complete the match between my daughter and Sir James after having so long intended it. Let me know your opinion on this point. Flexibility of mind, a disposition easily biassed by others, is an attribute which you know I am not very desirous of obtaining ; nor has Frederica any claim to the indulgence of her notions at the expense of her mother's inclinations. Her idle love for Reginald, too ! It is surely my duty to discourage such romantic nonsense. All things considered, therefore, it seems incumbent on me to take her to town and marry her immediately to Sir James. When my own will is effected contrary to his, I shall have some credit in being on good terms with Reginald, which at present, in fact, I have not ; for though he is still in my power, I have given up the very article by which our quarrel was produced, and at best the honour of victory is doubtful. Send me your opinion on all these matters, my dear Alicia, and let me know whether you can get lodgings to suit me within a short distance of you.

Your most attached<br>S. VERNON.

## XXVI.

### *Mrs. Johnson to Lady Susan.*

Edward Street.

I am gratified by your reference, and this is my advice: that you come to town yourself, without loss of time, but that you leave Frederica behind. It would surely be much more to the purpose to get yourself well established by marrying Mr. De Courcy, than to irritate him and the rest of his family by making her marry Sir James. You should think more of yourself and less of your daughter. She is not of a disposition to do you credit in the world, and seems precisely in her proper place at Churchhill, with the Vernons. But you are fitted for society, and it is shameful to have you exiled from it. Leave Frederica, therefore, to punish herself for the plague she has given you, by indulging that romantic tender-heartedness which will always ensure her misery enough, and come to London as soon as you can. I have another reason for urging this: Mainwaring came to town last week, and has contrived, in spite of Mr. Johnson, to make opportunities of seeing me. He is absolutely miserable about you, and jealous to such a degree of De Courcy that it would be highly unadvisable for them to meet at present. And yet, if you do not allow him to see you here, I cannot answer for his not committing some great imprudence—such as going to Churchhill, for instance, which would be dreadful! Besides, if you take my advice, and resolve to marry

De Courcy, it will be indispensably necessary to you to get Mainwaring out of the way ; and you only can have influence enough to send him back to his wife. I have still another motive for your coming : Mr. Johnson leaves London next Tuesday ; he is going for his health to Bath, where, if the waters are favourable to his constitution and my wishes, he will be laid up with the gout many weeks. During his absence we shall be able to chuse our own society, and to have true enjoyment. I would ask you to Edward Street, but that once he forced from me a kind of promise never to invite you to my house ; nothing but my being in the utmost distress for money should have extorted it from me. I can get you, however, a nice drawing-room apartment in Upper Seymour Street, and we may be always together there or here ; for I consider my promise to Mr. Johnson as comprehending only (at least in his absence) your not sleeping in the house. Poor Mainwaring gives me such histories of his wife's jealousy. Silly woman to expect constancy from so charming a man! but she always was silly—intolerably so in marrying him at all, she the heiress of a large fortune and he without a shilling : one title, I know, she might have had, besides baronets. Her folly in forming the connection was so great that, though Mr. Johnson was her guardian, and I do not in general share *his* feelings, I never can forgive her.

Adieu. Yours ever,

ALICIA.

## XXVII.

*Mrs. Vernon to Lady De Courcy.*

Churchhill.

This letter, my dear mother, will be brought you by
Reginald. His long visit is about to be concluded at
last, but I fear the separation takes place too late to
do us any good. She is going to London to see her
particular friend, Mrs. Johnson. It was at first her
intention that Frederica should accompany her, for
the benefit of masters, but we overruled her there.
Frederica was wretched in the idea of going, and I
could not bear to have her at the mercy of her mother;
not all the masters in London could compensate for
the ruin of her comfort. I should have feared, too, for
her health, and for everything but her principles—there
I believe she is not to be injured by her mother, or
her mother's friends; but with those friends she must
have mixed (a very bad set, I doubt not), or have been
left in total solitude, and I can hardly tell which would
have been worse for her. If she is with her mother,
moreover, she must, alas! in all probability be with
Reginald, and that would be the greatest evil of all.
Here we shall in time be in peace, and our regular
employments, our books and conversations, with exercise, the children, and every domestic pleasure in my
power to procure her, will, I trust, gradually overcome
this youthful attachment. I should not have a doubt
of it were she slighted for any other woman in the
world than her own mother. How long Lady Susan

will be **in town, or** whether **she** returns here again, I know not. I could not be cordial in my invitation, but if she chuses to come no want **of** cordiality **on** my part will keep her away. I could not help asking Reginald if he intended being in London **this** winter, as soon as I found her ladyship's steps would be bent thither; and though he professed himself quite undetermined, there was something in his look and voice as he spoke which contradicted his words. I have done with lamentation; I look **upon the event** as so far decided **that I** resign myself to it in despair. If he leaves **you** soon for London everything will **be** concluded.

Your affectionate, &c.,

C. VERNON.

## XXVIII.

### *Mrs. Johnson to Lady Susan.*

Edward **Street.**

My dearest Friend,—I write in the greatest distress; the most unfortunate event has just taken **place.** Mr. Johnson has hit on the **most** effectual manner **of** plaguing **us** all. **He** had heard, I imagine, by some means or other, that you were soon to **be in** London, and immediately contrived to have such an attack of the gout as must at least delay his journey to Bath, if not wholly prevent it. I am persuaded the gout is brought **on or** kept off **at** pleasure; it was the same when I wanted to join the Hamiltons **to** the Lakes; and three years ago, when *I* had a **fancy for** Bath, nothing could induce him to have a gouty symptom.

I am pleased to find that my letter had so much effect on you, and that De Courcy is certainly your own.  Let me hear from you as soon as you arrive, and in particular tell me what you mean to do with Mainwaring.  It is impossible to say when I shall be able to come to you ; my confinement must be great. It is such an abominable trick to be ill here instead of at Bath that I can scarcely command myself at all. At Bath his old aunts would have nursed him, but here it all falls upon me; and he bears pain with such patience that I have not the common excuse for losing my temper.

Yours ever,<br>ALICIA.

## XXIX.

*Lady Susan Vernon to Mrs. Johnson.*

Upper Seymour Street.

My dear Alicia,—There needed not this last fit of the gout to make me detest Mr. Johnson, but now the extent of my aversion is not to be estimated.  To have you confined as nurse in his apartment !  My dear Alicia, of what a mistake were you guilty in marrying a man of his age ! just old enough to be formal, ungovernable, and to have the gout ; too old to be agreeable, too young to die.  I arrived last night about five, had scarcely swallowed my dinner when Mainwaring made his appearance.  I will not dissemble what real pleasure his sight afforded me, nor how strongly I felt the contrast between his person

and manners and those **of** Reginald, to the infinite
disadvantage **of** the latter. For an hour or two I was
even staggered in my resolution of marrying him,
and though this was too idle and nonsensical an idea
to remain long on my mind, I do not feel very eager
for the conclusion of my marriage, nor look forward
with much impatience **to the** time **when** Reginald,
according to our agreement, is to be **in town.** I shall
probably put off his arrival under some pretence or
other. He must not come till Mainwaring is gone. I
**am** still doubtful at times as to marrying; **if** the old
man would die **I** might not hesitate, but **a** state **of**
dependance on **the** caprice of Sir Reginald will **not**
suit the freedom of my **spirit ; and if** I resolve to wait
for that event, I shall have excuse enough at present
in having been scarcely **ten** months a widow. **I have**
not given Mainwaring **any hint** of my intention, **or**
allowed him to consider my acquaintance with Reginald as more than the commonest flirtation, and he is
tolerably appeased. Adieu, till **we meet ;** I am en-
chanted with my lodgings.

**Yours** ever,

S. VERNON.

## XXX.

*Lady Susan Vernon to Mr. de Courcy.*

Upper Seymour Street.

I have received your letter, and though **I do** not
attempt to conceal that **I** am gratified by your impatience for the hour of meeting, I **yet** feel myself

T

under the **necessity** of delaying that hour beyond the time originally fixed. Do not think me unkind for such an exercise of my power, nor accuse me of instability without first hearing my reasons. In the course of my journey from Churchhill I had ample leisure for reflection on the present state of our affairs, and every review has served to convince me that they require a delicacy and cautiousness of conduct to which we have hitherto been too little attentive. We have been hurried on by our feelings to a degree of precipitation which ill accords with the claims of our friends or the opinion of the world. We have been unguarded in forming this hasty engagement, but we must not complete the imprudence by ratifying it while there is so much **reason** to fear the connection would be opposed by those friends on whom you depend. It is not for us to blame any expectations on your father's side of your marrying to advantage; where possessions are so extensive as those of your family, the wish of increasing them, if not strictly reasonable, is too common to excite surprise or resentment. He has a right to require a woman of fortune in his daughter-in-law, and I am sometimes quarrelling with myself for suffering you to form a connection so imprudent; but the influence of reason is often acknowledged too late by those who feel like me. I have now been but a few months a widow, and, however little indebted to my husband's memory for any happiness derived from him during a union of some years, I cannot forget that the indelicacy of so early a second marriage must subject me to the censure of the world, and incur,

what would **be** still more insupportable, the displeasure
of Mr. Vernon. I might perhaps harden myself **in**
time against the injustice of general reproach, but the
loss of *his* valued esteem I am, as you **well know**, ill-
fitted to endure; and when to this may be added the
consciousness of having injured you with your family,
how am I to support myself? With feelings so poig-
nant as mine, **the** conviction **of** having divided the
**son from** his parents would make me, even **with** you,
the most miserable of beings. It will **surely,** therefore, be advisable to delay our union—to delay **it** till
appearances **are** more promising—till affairs have
taken a more favourable turn. To assist us in such **a**
resolution **I feel that** absence will be necessary. **We**
must not **meet.** Cruel as this sentence may appear,
the necessity **of** pronouncing **it,** which can alone reconcile it **to myself, will** be evident to you **when** you
have considered **our situation in** the light **in** which I
have found **myself imperiously** obliged **to place** it.
You may **be**—you must be—well assured that nothing
**but** the strongest conviction **of** duty could induce me
**to** wound my own feelings **by** urging **a** lengthened
separation, and of insensibility to yours you will
hardly suspect me. Again, therefore, I say that we
ought not, we must not, yet meet. By a removal for
some months from each other we shall tranquillise the
sisterly fears of Mrs. Vernon, who, accustomed herself
**to** the enjoyment of riches, considers fortune as neces-
**sary** everywhere, and whose sensibilities **are not of a**
nature to comprehend ours. Let me hear from you
soon—very soon. Tell me that you submit to my

arguments, and do not reproach me for using such.
I cannot bear reproaches : my spirits are not so high
as to need being repressed. I must endeavour to
seek amusement, and fortunately many of my friends
are in town ; amongst them the Mainwarings ; you
know how sincerely I regard both husband and wife.

I am, very faithfully yours,

S. VERNON.

## XXXI.

### *Lady Susan to Mrs. Johnson.*

Upper Seymour Street.

My dear Friend,—That tormenting creature, Reginald, is here. My letter, which was intended to keep
him longer in the country, has hastened him to town.
Much as I wish him away, however, I cannot help
being pleased with such a proof of attachment. He
is devoted to me, heart and soul. He will carry this
note himself, which is to serve as an introduction to
you, with whom he longs to be acquainted. Allow
him to spend the evening with you, that I may be in
no danger of his returning here. I have told him that
I am not quite well, and must be alone ; and should
he call again there might be confusion, for it is impossible to be sure of servants. Keep him, therefore,
I entreat you, in Edward Street. You will not find
him a heavy companion, and I allow you to flirt with
him as much as you like. At the same time, do not
forget my real interest ; say all that you can to convince him that I shall be quite wretched if he remains

here; you **know my** reasons—propriety, and so forth. **I** would urge them more myself, but that I **am** impatient to **be rid** of him, **as** Mainwaring **comes within** half-an hour.   Adieu!

S. VERNON.

## XXXII.

### *Mrs. Johnson to Lady Susan.*

Edward Street.

My **dear** Creature,—I am in agonies, and know not what to do.  Mr. De Courcy arrived **just** when **he** should not.  Mrs. Mainwaring had that instant entered the house, and forced **herself into** her guardian's presence, though I **did not know** a syllable **of it till** afterwards, for I was out when both she and **Reginald** came, or I should **have** sent him away at all events; but *she* was **shut up with** Mr. Johnson, while *he* **waited** in the drawing-room for **me.  She arrived** yesterday in pursuit of her husband, **but** perhaps you know this already from himself.  She **came to this** house **to** entreat my husband's interference, **and before I** could **be** aware of it, everything that you could wish to be concealed was known to him, and unluckily she had wormed out of Mainwaring's servant that he had visited you every day since your being in town, and **had** just watched him **to** your door herself!  What could I do?  Facts **are such** horrid things!  **All is** by this time known to **De** Courcy, who is **now** alone with Mr. Johnson.  Do not **accuse** me; indeed, it was impossible to prevent it.  **Mr. Johnson has** for some time

suspected De Courcy of intending to marry you, and
would speak with him alone as soon as he knew him
to be in the house. That detestable Mrs. Mainwaring,
who, for your comfort, has fretted herself thinner and
uglier than ever, is still here, and they have been all
closeted together. What can be done? At any
rate, I hope he will plague his wife more than ever.
With anxious wishes,

Yours faithfully,<br>ALICIA.

## XXXIII.

*Lady Susan to Mrs. Johnson.*

Upper Seymour Street.

This eclaircissement is rather provoking. How
unlucky that you should have been from home! I
thought myself sure of you at seven! I am undis-
mayed however. Do not torment yourself with fears
on my account; depend on it, I can make my story
good with Reginald. Mainwaring is just gone; he
brought me the news of his wife's arrival. Silly
woman, what does she expect by such manœuvres?
Yet I wish she had stayed quietly at Langford. Reginald will be a little enraged at first, but by to-
morrow's dinner, everything will be well again.

Adieu!<br>S. V.

## XXXIV.

### *Mr. De Courcy to Lady Susan.*

—— Hotel.

I write **only** to bid you **farewell, the** spell is removed; I see **you** as you **are.** Since we parted yesterday, I have received from indisputable authority such a history of you as must bring the most mortifying conviction of the imposition I have been under, and the absolute necessity of an immediate and eternal separation from you. **You** cannot doubt **to** what I allude. Langford! Langford! that word will be sufficient. I received my information in Mr. Johnson's house, from Mrs. Mainwaring herself. **You** know how I have loved **you; you can intimately** judge of my present feelings, **but** I am not so weak **as** to find indulgence in describing **them to** a woman who will glory **in having** excited their anguish, but whose affection **they have never** been able to gain.

R. DE COURCY.

## XXXV.

### *Lady Susan to **Mr.** De Courcy.*

Upper Seymour Street.

I will not attempt to describe my astonishment in reading the note this moment received from you. I am bewildered in my endeavours to form some **ra**tional conjecture of what Mrs. Mainwaring can have **told** you to occasion so extraordinary **a** change in your **sentiments.** Have I not explained everything to you with respect to myself which could bear a doubtful meaning, and which the ill-nature of the world had interpreted to my discredit? What can you *now* have heard to stagger your esteem for me? Have I ever had a concealment from you? Reginald, you agitate me beyond expression, I cannot suppose that the old story of Mrs. Mainwaring's jealousy can be revived again, or at least be *listened* to again. Come to me immediately, and explain what is at present absolutely incomprehensible. Believe me the single word of Langford is not of such potent intelligence as to supersede the necessity of more. If we *are* to part, it will at least be handsome to take your personal leave—but I have little heart to jest; in truth, I am serious enough; for to be sunk, though but for an hour, in your esteem is a humiliation to which I know not how to submit. I shall count every minute till your arrival.

S. V.

## XXXVI.

### *Mr. De Courcy to Lady Susan.*

—— Hotel.

Why would you write to me? Why do you require particulars? But, since it must be so, I am obliged to declare that all the accounts of your misconduct during the life, and since the death of Mr. Vernon, which had reached me, in common with the world in general, and gained my entire belief before I saw you, but which you, by the exertion of your perverted abilities, had made me resolved to disallow, have been unanswerably proved to me ; nay more, I am assured that a connection, of which I had never before entertained a thought, has for some time existed, and still continues to exist, between you and the man whose family you robbed of its peace in return for the hospitality with which you were received into it ; that you have corresponded with him ever since your leaving Langford ; not with his wife, but with him, and that he now visits you every day. Can you, dare you deny it ? and all this at the time when I was an encouraged, an accepted lover ! From what have I not escaped ! I have only to be grateful. Far from me be all complaint, every sigh of regret. My own folly had endangered me, my preservation I owe to the kindness, the integrity of another ; but the unfortunate Mrs. Mainwaring, whose agonies while she related the past seemed to threaten her reason, how is *she* to be consoled ! After such a discovery as this, you will scarcely affect further wonder at my meaning in bidding you adieu. My understanding is at length restored, and teaches no less to abhor the artifices which had subdued me than to despise myself for the weakness on which their strength was founded.

R. De Courcy.

## XXXVII.

### *Lady Susan to Mr. De Courcy.*

Upper Seymour Street.

I am satisfied, and will trouble you no more when these few lines are dismissed. The engagement which you were eager to form a fortnight ago is no longer compatible with your views, and I rejoice to find that the prudent advice of your parents has not been given in vain. Your restoration to peace will, I doubt not, speedily follow this act of filial obedience, and I flatter myself with the hope of surviving my share in this disappointment.

S. V.

## XXXVIII.

### *Mrs. Johnson to Lady Susan Vernon.*

Edward Street.

I am grieved, though I cannot be astonished at your rupture with Mr. De Courcy; he has just informed Mr. Johnson of it by letter. He leaves London, he says, to-day. Be assured that I partake in all your feelings, and do not be angry if I say that our intercourse, even by letter, must soon be given up. It makes me miserable; but Mr. Johnson vows that if I persist in the connection, he will settle in the country for the rest of his life, and you know it is impossible to submit to such an extremity while any other alternative remains. You have heard of course

that the Mainwarings are to part, and I am afraid
Mrs. M. will come home to us again; but she is still
so fond of her husband, and frets so much about him,
that perhaps she may not live long. Miss Mainwaring is just come to town to be with her aunt, and
they say that she declares she will have Sir James
Martin before she leaves London again. If I were
you, I would certainly get him myself. I had almost
forgot to give you my opinion of Mr. De Courcy; I
am really delighted with him; he is full as handsome, I think, as Mainwaring, and with such an open,
good-humoured countenance, that one cannot help
loving him at first sight. Mr. Johnson and he are
the greatest friends in the world. Adieu, my dearest
Susan, I wish matters did not go so perversely. That
unlucky visit to Langford! but I dare say you did
all for the best, and there is no defying destiny.

Your sincerely attached,<br>
ALICIA.

## XXXIX.

### *Lady Susan to Mrs. Johnson.*

Upper Seymour Street.

My dear Alicia,—I yield to the necessity which
parts us. Under circumstances you could not act
otherwise. Our friendship cannot be impaired by it,
and in happier times, when your situation is as independent as mine, it will unite us again in the same
intimacy as ever. For this I shall impatiently wait,
and meanwhile can safely assure you that I never was

more at ease, or better satisfied with myself and everything about me than at the present hour. Your husband I abhor, Reginald I despise, and I am secure of never seeing either again. Have I not reason to rejoice? Mainwaring is more devoted to me than ever; and were we at liberty, I doubt if I could resist even matrimony offered by *him*. This event, if his wife live with you, it may be in your power to hasten. The violence of her feelings, which must wear her out, may be easily kept in irritation. I rely on your friendship for this. I am now satisfied that I never could have brought myself to marry Reginald, and am equally determined that Frederica never *shall*. To-morrow, I shall fetch her from Churchhill, and let Maria Mainwaring tremble for the consequence. Frederica shall be Sir James's wife before she quits my house, and *she* may whimper, and the Vernons may storm, I regard them not. I am tired of submitting my will to the caprices of others; of resigning my own judgment in deference to those to whom I owe no duty, and for whom I feel no respect; I have given up too much, have been too easily worked on, but Frederica shall now feel the difference. Adieu, dearest of friends; may the next gouty attack be more favourable! and may you always regard me as unalterably yours,

S. VERNON.

## XL.

### *Lady de Courcy to Mrs. Vernon.*

My dear Catherine,—I have charming news for you, and if I had not sent off my letter this morning you might have been spared the vexation of knowing of Reginald's being gone to London, for he is returned. Reginald is returned, not to ask our consent to his marrying Lady Susan, but to tell us they are parted for ever. He has been only an hour in the house, and I have not been able to learn particulars, for he is so very low that I have not the heart to ask questions, but I hope we shall soon know all. This is the most joyful hour he has ever given us since the day of his birth. Nothing is wanting but to have you here, and it is our particular wish and entreaty that you would come to us as soon as you can. You have owed us a visit many long weeks; I hope nothing will make it inconvenient to Mr. Vernon; and pray bring all my grandchildren; and your dear niece is included, of course; I long to see her. It has been a sad, heavy winter hitherto, without Reginald, and seeing nobody from Churchhill. I never found the season so dreary before; but this happy meeting will make us young again. Frederica runs much in my thoughts, and when Reginald has recovered his usual good spirits (as I trust he soon will) we will try to rob him of his heart once more, and I am full of hopes of seeing their hands joined at no great distance.

Your affectionate mother,

C. DE COURCY.

## XLI.

### *Mrs. Vernon to Lady de Courcy.*

Churchhill.

My dear Mother,—Your letter has surprised me beyond measure! Can it be true that they are really separated—and for ever? I should be overjoyed if I dared depend on it, but after all that I have seen how can one be secure? And Reginald really with you! My surprise is the greater because on Wednesday, the very day of his coming to Parklands, we had a most unexpected and unwelcome visit from Lady Susan, looking all cheerfulness and good-humour, and seeming more as if she were to marry him when she got to London than as if parted from him for ever. She stayed nearly two hours, was as affectionate and agreeable as ever, and not a syllable, not a hint was dropped, of any disagreement or coolness between them. I asked her whether she had seen my brother since his arrival in town; not, as you may suppose, with any doubt of the fact, but merely to see how she looked. She immediately answered, without any embarrassment, that he had been kind enough to call on her on Monday; but she believed he had already returned home, which I was very far from crediting. Your kind invitation is accepted by us with pleasure, and on Thursday next we and our little ones will be with you. Pray heaven, Reginald may not be in town again by that time! I wish we could bring dear Frederica too, but I am sorry to say that her mother's errand hither was **to** fetch her away; and, miserable **as it** made **the poor** girl, **it** was impossible to detain her. I was thoroughly unwilling to **let her** go, and so was her **uncle**; and all that **could be urged** we did urge; but Lady Susan declared that as she was now about to fix herself in London for **several** months, she could not be easy if her daughter were not with her for masters, &c. Her manner, to **be** sure, was very kind and proper, and **Mr.** Vernon believes that Frederica will now be treated with affection. I wish I could think so too. **The poor** girl's heart was almost broke **at** taking leave **of** us. I charged her **to** write to me **very** often, and to remember **that if** she **were in** any distress we should **be** always her friends. **I took care** to see her alone, that I might say all **this, and I** hope made her **a little** more comfortable ; **but I** shall not be **easy** till I can go to town and judge of her situation myself. I wish there were a better prospect than now appears of the match which the conclusion **of** your letter declares your expectations of. At present, **it is** not very likely.

Yours ever, &c.,<br>**C. Vernon.**

---

## CONCLUSION.

This correspondence, **by a** meeting between some **of** the parties, and a separation between the others, could not, to the great detriment of the Post-Office revenue, be continued any longer. Very little assistance to the State could be derived from the epistolary intercourse of Mrs. Vernon and her niece; for the former soon perceived, by the style of Frederica's letters, that they were written under her mother's inspection! and therefore, deferring all particular enquiry till she could make it personally in London, ceased writing minutely or often. Having learnt enough, in the meanwhile, from her open-hearted brother, of what had passed between him and Lady Susan to sink the latter lower than ever in her opinion, she was proportionably more anxious to get Frederica removed from such a mother, and placed under her own care; and, though with little hope of success, was resolved to leave nothing unattempted that might offer a chance of obtaining her sister-in-law's consent to it. Her anxiety on the subject made her press for an early visit to London; and Mr. Vernon, who, as it must already have appeared, lived only to do whatever he was desired, soon found some accommodating business to call him thither. With a heart full of the matter, Mrs. Vernon waited on Lady Susan shortly after her arrival in town, and was met with such an easy and cheerful affection, as made her almost turn from her with horror. No remembrance of Reginald, no consciousness of guilt, gave one look of embarrassment; she was in excellent spirits, and seemed eager to show at once by every possible attention to her brother and sister her sense of their kindness, and her pleasure in their society. Frederica was no more altered than Lady Susan; the same restrained manners, the same timid look in the presence of her mother as heretofore, assured her aunt of her situation being uncomfortable, and confirmed her in the plan of altering it. No unkindness, however, on the part of Lady Susan appeared. Persecution on the subject of Sir James was entirely at an end ; his name merely mentioned to say that he was not in London ; and indeed, in all her conversation, she was solicitous only for the welfare and improvement of her daughter, acknowledging, in terms of grateful delight, that Frederica was now growing every day more and more what a parent could desire. Mrs. Vernon, surprised and incredulous, knew not what to suspect, and, without any change in her own views, only feared greater difficulty in accomplishing them. The first hope of anything better was derived from Lady Susan's asking her whether she thought Frederica 'looked quite as well as she had done at Churchhill, as she must confess herself to have sometimes an anxious doubt of London's perfectly agreeing with her. Mrs. Vernon, encouraging the doubt, directly proposed her niece's returning with them into the country. Lady Susan was unable to express her sense of such kindness, yet knew not, from a variety of reasons, how to part with her daughter ; and as, though her own plans were not yet wholly fixed, she trusted it would ere long be in her power to take Frederica into the country herself, concluded by declining entirely to profit by such unexampled attention. Mrs. Vernon persevered, however, in the offer of it, and though Lady Susan continued to resist, her resistance in the course of a few days seemed somewhat less formidable. The lucky alarm of an influenza decided what might not have been decided quite so soon. Lady Susan's maternal fears were then too much awakened for her to think of anything but Frederica's removal from the risk of infection ; above all disorders in the world she most dreaded the influenza for her daughter's constitution !

Frederica returned to Churchhill with her uncle and aunt; and three weeks afterwards, Lady Susan announced her being married to Sir James Martin. Mrs. Vernon was then convinced of what she had only suspected before, that she might have spared herself all the trouble of urging a removal which Lady Susan had doubtless resolved on from the first. Frederica's visit was nominally for six weeks, but her mother, though inviting her to return in one or two affectionate letters, was very ready to oblige the whole party by consenting to a prolongation of her stay, and in the course of two months ceased to write of her absence, and in the course of two more to write to her at all. Frederica was therefore fixed in the family of her uncle and aunt till such time as Reginald De Courcy could be talked, flattered, and finessed into an affection for her which, allowing leisure for the conquest of his attachment to her mother, for his abjuring all future attachments, and detesting the sex, might be reasonably looked for in the course of a twelvemonth. Three months might have done it in general, but Reginald's feelings were no less lasting than lively. Whether Lady Susan was or was not happy in her second choice, I do not see how it can ever be ascertained ; for who would take her assurance of it on either side of the question ? The world must judge from probabilities; she had nothing against her but her husband, and her conscience. Sir James may seem to have drawn a harder lot than mere folly merited ; I leave him, therefore, to all the pity that anybody can give him. For myself, I confess that *I* can pity only Miss Mainwaring; who, coming to town, and putting herself to an expense in clothes which impoverished her for two years, on purpose to secure him, was defrauded of her due by a woman ten years older than herself.

FINIS.

# THE WATSONS.

# PREFACE.

THIS WORK was left by its author a fragment without
a name, in so elementary a state as not even to be
divided into chapters ; and some obscurities and in-
accuracies of expression may be observed in it which
the author would probably have corrected. The
original manuscript is the property of my sister, Miss
Austen, by whose permission it is now published.
I have called it 'The Watsons,' for the sake of having
a title by which to designate it. Two questions may
be asked concerning it. When was it written ? And,
why was it never finished ? I was unable to answer
the first question, so long as I had only the internal
evidence of the style to guide me. I felt satisfied,
indeed, that it did not belong to that early class of
her writings which are mentioned at page 46 of the
Memoir, but rather bore marks of her more mature
style, though it had never been subjected to the filing
and polishing process by which she was accustomed
to impart a high finish to her published works. At
last, on a close inspection of the original manuscript,
the water-marks of 1803, and 1804, were found in the
paper on which it was written. It is, therefore, probable, that it was composed at Bath, before she
ceased to reside there in 1805. This would place
the date a few years later than the composition, but

earlier than the publication of 'Sense and Sensibility,' and 'Pride and Prejudice.'

To the second question, why was it never finished? I can give no satisfactory answer. I think it will be generally admitted that there is much in it which promised well: that some of the characters are drawn with her wonted vigour, and some with a delicate discrimination peculiarly her own; and that it is rich in her especial power of telling the story, and bringing out the characters by conversation rather than by description. It could not have been broken up for the purpose of using the materials in another fabric; for, with the exception of Mrs. Robert Watson, in whom a resemblance to the future Mrs. Elton is very discernible, it would not be easy to trace much resemblance between this and any of her subsequent works. She must have felt some regret at leaving Tom Musgrave's character incomplete; yet he never appears elsewhere. My own idea is, but it is only a guess, that the author became aware of the evil of having placed her heroine too low, in such a position of poverty and obscurity as, though not necessarily connected with vulgarity, has a sad tendency to degenerate into it; and therefore, like a singer who has begun on too low a note, she discontinued the strain. It was an error of which she was likely to become more sensible, as she grew older, and saw more of society; certainly she never repeated it by placing the heroine of any subsequent work under circumstances likely to be unfavourable to the refinement of a lady.

# THE WATSONS.

HE first winter assembly in the town of D. in Surrey was to be held **on** Tuesday, October 13th, **and** it was generally expected to be a very good one. A long list of county families **was** confidently run over **as** sure of attending, and sanguine hopes were entertained that the Osbornes **themselves** would be there. **The** Edwards' invitation **to** the Watsons followed of course. The Edwards were **people of** fortune, who lived in the town and kept their **coach.** The Watsons inhabited **a** village about three miles distant, **were** poor and had no close carriage ; and ever since **there had** been balls in the place, the former were accustomed to invite the latter to dress, dine, and sleep at their house on every monthly return throughout the winter. On the present occasion, **as** only two of Mr. Watson's children were **at** home, and one was always necessary as companion to himself, for he was sickly and had **lost** his wife, one only could profit by the kindness **of** their friends. Miss Emma Watson, who was very recently returned to her family from **the** care of an aunt who had brought her up, was **to make** her first

public appearance in the neighbourhood, and her eldest sister, whose delight in a ball was not lessened by a ten years' enjoyment, had some merit in cheerfully undertaking to drive her and all her finery in the old chair to D. on the important morning.

As they splashed along the dirty lane Miss Watson thus instructed and cautioned her inexperienced sister.

' I dare say it will be a very good ball, and among so many officers you will hardly want partners. You will find Mrs. Edwards' maid very willing to help you, and I would advise you to ask Mary Edwards' opinion if you are at all at a loss, for she has a very good taste. If Mr. Edwards does not lose his money at cards you will stay as late as you can wish for ; if he does he will hurry you home perhaps—but you are sure of some comfortable soup. I hope you will be in good looks. I should not be surprised if you were to be thought one of the prettiest girls in the room, there is a great deal in novelty. Perhaps Tom Musgrave may take notice of you ; but I would advise you by all means not to give him any encouragement. He generally pays attention to every new girl, but he is a great flirt and never means anything serious.'

'I think I have heard you speak of him before,' said Emma, 'who is he ?'

'A young man of very good fortune, quite independent, and remarkably agreeable, an universal favourite wherever he goes. Most of the girls hereabout are in love with him, or have been. I believe I am the only

**one** among them that have escaped with a whole heart;
and yet I was the first he **paid** attention to when he
came into this country six years ago; and very great
attention did **he** pay **me**. Some people say that he
has never seemed to like any girl so well since,
though **he is** always behaving in a particular way to
one or another.'

'And how came *your* heart to be the only cold
one?' said Emma, smiling.

'There was a reason for that,'—replied Miss Watson,
changing colour—'I have not been very well used
among them, Emma, I hope you will **have** better
luck.'

'Dear sister, I beg **your pardon, if** I have unthink-
ingly given you pain.'

'When first we knew **Tom** Musgrave,' continued
Miss Watson, without seeming to hear her, 'I was
very much attached **to a** young **man** of the name of
Purvis, a particular friend of Robert's, who used to
be with us **a** great **deal.** Everybody thought it
would have been a match.'

A sigh accompanied these words, **which** Emma
**respected** in silence; but **her** sister after a short
pause went on.

'You will naturally ask why it did not take place,
and why **he** is married to another woman, while I
am still single. **But you** must ask him—not me—
you must ask Penelope. Yes, Emma, Penelope **was**
at the bottom of it all. She thinks everything fair
for a husband. I trusted her; she set him against
me, with a view of gaining him herself, **and it** ended

in his discontinuing his visits, and soon after marrying somebody else. Penelope makes light of her conduct, but *I* think such treachery very bad. It has been the ruin of my happiness. I shall never love any man as I loved Purvis. I do not think Tom Musgrave should be named with him in the same day.'

'You quite shock me by what you say of Penelope,' said Emma, 'could a sister do such a thing? Rivalry, treachery between sisters! I shall be afraid of being acquainted with her. But I hope it was not so; appearances were against her.'

'You do not know Penelope. There is nothing she would not do to get married. She would as good as tell you so herself. Do not trust her with any secrets of your own, take warning by me, do not trust her; she has her good qualities, but she has no faith, no honour, no scruples, if she can promote her own advantage. I wish with all my heart she was well married. I declare I had rather have her well married than myself.'

'Than yourself! yes I can suppose so. A heart wounded like yours can have little inclination for matrimony.'

'Not much indeed—but you know we must marry. I could do very well single for my own part; a little company, and a pleasant ball now and then, would be enough for me, if one could be young for ever; but my father cannot provide for us, and it is very bad to grow old and be poor and laughed at. I have lost Purvis, it is true; but very few people marry their first loves. I should not refuse a man because he **was not Purvis.** Not that I can ever quite forgive Penelope.'

Emma **shook her** head in acquiescence.

'Penelope, **however,** has had her **troubles,'** continued **Miss** Watson. 'She was sadly disappointed in **Tom** Musgrave, **who** afterwards transferred **his** attentions from me **to her,** and **whom** she was **very** fond of; but he never **means** anything serious, and when he had trifled **with her long enough,** he began **to** slight her for **Margaret, and poor Penelope was** very wretched. **And** since then, **she has been** trying to make some **match** at Chichester—she **won't** tell us with **whom; but** I believe **it is a** rich old Dr. Harding, uncle to **the** friend she goes to **see;** and she has taken a vast deal **of trouble** about **him, and** given up **a great** deal **of time to no purpose as yet.** When she went away the **other day, she said it** should be **the** last **time.** I suppose **you did not know what her** particular business was **at** Chichester, **nor** guess at the object which could take her **away from** Stanton just **as** you were coming home after **so** many years' absence.'

'**No** indeed, **I** had not the smallest suspicion of it. I considered her engagement to Mrs. Shaw just at that time as very unfortunate for me. I had hoped to find all my sisters **at** home, **to be** able to make an immediate friend **of** each.'

'I suspect the Doctor **to** have had **an** attack of the **asthma,** and that she **was** hurried **away** on that account. The Shaws are quite on her side—at least, **I** believe **so;** but she tells me nothing. She professes to keep her own counsel; she says, and truly enough, that "Too many cooks spoil the broth."'

'I am sorry for her anxieties,' said Emma; 'but I do not like her plans or her opinions. I shall be afraid of her. She must have too masculine and bold a temper. To be so bent on marriage—to pursue a man merely for the sake of situation, is a sort of thing that shocks me; I cannot understand it. Poverty is a great evil; but to a woman of education and feeling it ought not, it cannot be the greatest. I would rather be teacher at a school (and I can think of nothing worse), than marry a man I did not like.'

'I would rather do anything than be teacher at a school,' said her sister. '*I* have been at school, Emma, and know what a life they lead; *you* never have. I should not like marrying a disagreeable man any more than yourself; but I do not think there *are* many very disagreeable men; I think I could like any goodhumoured man with a comfortable income. I suppose my aunt brought you up to be rather refined.'

'Indeed I do not know. My conduct must tell you how I have been brought up. I am no judge of it myself. I cannot compare my aunt's method with any other person's, because I know no other.'

'But I can see in a great many things that you are very refined. I have observed it ever since you came home, and I am afraid it will not be for your happiness. Penelope will laugh at you very much.'

'That will not be for my happiness, I am sure. If my opinions are wrong I must correct them; if they are above my situation, I **must** endeavour to conceal them; but **I** doubt whether ridicule—has Penelope much wit?'

'Yes; she **has** great spirits, and never cares what she says.'

'Margaret is more gentle, I imagine?'

'Yes; especially in company; she **is** all gentleness and mildness when anybody is by. But she is a little fretful and perverse among ourselves. Poor creature! She is possessed with the notion of **Tom** Musgrave's being more seriously in love with her **than** he ever was with anybody else, and is always expecting him to come to the point. This is the second **time** within this **twelvemonth that** she **has gone** to spend **a** month **with Robert and Jane on** purpose to egg him **on by her** absence; **but I am sure** she is mistaken, and that he will no **more** follow her to Croydon now than he did last March. He will never marry unless **he** can marry somebody **very great**; Miss Osborne, perhaps, **or** somebody **in that style.'**

'Your account of this Tom Musgrave, Elizabeth, gives me very little inclination for his acquaintance.'

'You are afraid of him; I do not wonder at you.'

'**No,** indeed; I dislike and despise him.'

'Dislike and despise Tom Musgrave! No, *that* you never can. I defy you **not** to be delighted with him if he takes notice of you. I hope he will dance **with** you; **and** I dare say he will, unless the Osbornes come with **a** large party, **and** then he will not speak **to** anybody else.'

'He seems to have most engaging manners!' said

Emma. 'Well, we shall see how irresistible Mr. Tom Musgrave and I find each other. I suppose I shall know him as soon as I enter the ball-room ; he *must* carry some of his charms in his face.'

'You will not find him in the ball-room, I can tell you ; you will go early, that Mrs. Edwards may get a good place by the fire, and he never comes till late ; if the Osbornes are coming, he will wait in the passage and come in with them. I should like to look in upon you, Emma. If it was but a good day with my father, I would wrap myself up, and James should drive me over as soon as I had made tea for him ; and I should be with you by the time the dancing began.'

'What! Would you come late at night in this chair ?'

'To be sure I would. There, I said you were very refined, and *that's* an instance of it.'

Emma for a moment made no answer. At last she said—

'I wish, Elizabeth, you had not made a point of my going to this ball ; I wish you were going instead of me. Your pleasure would be greater than mine. I am a stranger here, and know nobody but the Edwards; my enjoyment, therefore, must be very doubtful. Yours, among all your acquaintance, would be certain. It is not too late to change. Very little apology could be requisite to the Edwards, who must be more glad of your company than of mine, and I should most readily return to my father ; and should not be at all afraid to drive this quiet old creature home.  Your **clothes I** would undertake **to** find means **of** sending **to you.'**

'My dearest Emma,' **cried** Elizabeth, warmly, '**do** you think I would do such **a** thing?  Not for the universe!  But **I** shall never forget your goodnature **in** proposing it.  You must have a sweet temper indeed! I never met with anything like it!  **And** would you really give up the ball that I might be able to go **to it?**  Believe me, **Emma, I am** not **so** selfish **as** that comes to.  No; though **I** am nine **years** older than you are, **I** would not be the means **of** keeping you from being seen.  You are very pretty, and it would **be very hard that** you should not have **as fair a** chance **as we have all had to make your fortune.  No,** Emma, **whoever** stays at **home this** winter, it **shan't** be you.  **I am sure I should never** have forgiven **the person** who kept me **from a ball** at nineteen.'

**Emma** expressed **her gratitude, and for** a few minutes they jogged **on in** silence.  **Elizabeth first** spoke :—

'You will take notice **who Mary Edwards** dances **with ?'**

'**I** will remember her partners, if **I can ;** but you know they will be all strangers to me.'

'Only observe whether she dances **with** Captain Hunter more than once—I have my fears in **that** quarter.  **Not that** her father or mother like officers ; but **if** she does, you know, **it is** all over with poor **Sam.  And I have** promised to write him word **who** she dances with.'

'Is Sam attached **to Miss** Edwards ?'

x

'Did not you know *that?*'

'How should I know it? How should I know in Shropshire what is passing of that nature in Surrey? It is not likely that circumstances of such delicacy should have made any part of the scanty communication which passed between you and me for the last fourteen years.'

'I wonder I never mentioned it when I wrote. Since you have been at home, I have been so busy with my poor father, and our great wash, that I have had no leisure to tell you anything; but, indeed, I concluded you knew it all. He has been very much in love with her these two years, and it is a great disappointment to him that he cannot always get away to our balls; but Mr. Curtis won't often spare him, and just now it is a sickly time at Guildford.'

'Do you suppose Miss Edwards inclined to like him?'

'I am afraid not: you know she is an only child, and will have at least ten thousand pounds.'

'But still she may like our brother.'

'Oh, no! The Edwards look much higher. Her father and mother would never consent to it. Sam is only a surgeon, you know. Sometimes I think she does like him. But Mary Edwards is rather prim and reserved; I do not always know what she would be at.'

'Unless Sam feels on sure grounds with the lady herself, it seems a pity to me that he should be encouraged to think of her at all.'

'A young man must think of somebody,' said Elizabeth, 'and why should not he be as lucky as

Robert, who has got a good wife and six thousand
pounds?'

'We must not all expect to be individually lucky,'
replied Emma. 'The luck of one member of a family
is luck to all.'

'Mine is all to come, I am sure,' said Elizabeth,
giving another sigh to the remembrance of Purvis. 'I
have been unlucky enough; and I cannot say much
for you, as my aunt married again so foolishly. Well,
you will have a good ball, I daresay. The next turning will bring us to the turnpike: you may see the
church-tower over the hedge, and the White Hart is
close by it. I shall long to know what you think of
Tom Musgrave.'

Such were the last audible sounds of Miss Watson's
voice, before they passed through the turnpike-gate,
and entered on the pitching of the town, the jumbling
and noise of which made further conversation most
thoroughly undesirable. The old mare trotted heavily
on, wanting no direction of the reins to take the right
turning, and making only one blunder, in proposing
to stop at the milliner's, before she drew up towards
Mr. Edwards' door. Mr. Edwards lived in the best
house in the street, and the best in the place, if Mr.
Tomlinson, the banker, might be indulged in calling
his newly-erected house at the end of the town, with
a shrubbery and sweep, in the country.

Mr. Edwards' house was higher than most of its
neighbours, with four windows on each side the door;
the windows guarded by posts and chains, and the
door approached by a flight of stone steps.

'Here we are,' said Elizabeth, as the carriage ceased moving, 'safely arrived, and by the market clock we have been only five-and-thirty minutes coming; which I think is doing pretty well, though it would be nothing for Penelope. Is not it a nice town? The Edwards have a noble house, you see, and they live quite in style. The door will be opened by a man in livery, with a powdered head, I can tell you.'

Emma had seen the Edwards only one morning at Stanton; they were therefore all but strangers to her; and though her spirits were by no means insensible to the expected joys of the evening, she felt a little uncomfortable in the thought of all that was to precede them. Her conversation with Elizabeth, too, giving her some very unpleasant feelings with respect to her own family, had made her more open to disagreeable impressions from any other cause, and increased her sense of the awkwardness of rushing into intimacy on so slight an acquaintance.

There was nothing in the manner of Mrs. and Miss Edwards to give immediate change to these ideas. The mother, though a very friendly woman, had a reserved air, and a great deal of formal civility; and the daughter, a genteel-looking girl of twenty-two, with her hair in papers, seemed very naturally to have caught something of the style of her mother, who had brought her up. Emma was soon left to know what they could be, by Elizabeth's being obliged to hurry away; and some very languid remarks on the probable brilliancy of the ball were all that broke, at intervals, a silence of half-an-hour, before they were

joined by the master of the house. Mr. Edwards
had a much easier and more communicative air than
the ladies of the family ; he was fresh from the street,
and he came ready to tell whatever might interest.
After a cordial reception of Emma, he turned to his
daughter with—

'Well, Mary, I bring you good news: the Osbornes
will certainly be at the ball to-night. Horses for two
carriages are ordered from the White Hart to be at
Osborne Castle by nine.'

'I am glad of it,' observed Mrs. Edwards, 'because
their coming gives a credit to our assembly. The
Osbornes being known to have been at the first ball,
will dispose a great many people to attend the second.
It is more than they deserve ; for, in fact, they add
nothing to the pleasure of the evening : they come so
late and go so early ; but great people have always
their charm.'

Mr. Edwards proceeded to relate many other little
articles of news which his morning's lounge had
supplied him with, and they chatted with greater
briskness, till Mrs. Edwards' moment for dressing
arrived, and the young ladies were carefully recommended to lose no time. Emma was shown to a very
comfortable apartment, and as soon as Mrs. Edwards'
civilities could leave her to herself, the happy occupation, the first bliss of a ball, began. The girls, dressing
in some measure together, grew unavoidably better
acquainted. Emma found in Miss Edwards the show
of good sense, a modest unpretending mind, and a
great wish of obliging ; and when they returned to the

parlour where Mrs. Edwards was sitting, respectably attired in one of the two satin gowns which went through the winter, and a new cap from the milliner's, they entered it with much easier feelings and more natural smiles than they had taken away. Their dress was now to be examined: Mrs. Edwards acknowledged herself too old-fashioned to approve of every modern extravagance, however sanctioned; and though complacently viewing her daughter's good looks, would give but a qualified admiration; and Mr. Edwards, not less satisfied with Mary, paid some compliments of good-humoured gallantry to Emma at her expense. The discussion led to more intimate remarks, and Miss Edwards gently asked Emma if she was not often reckoned very like her youngest brother. Emma thought she could perceive a faint blush accompany the question, and there seemed something still more suspicious in the manner in which Mr. Edwards took up the subject.

'You are paying Miss Emma no great compliment, I think, Mary,' said he, hastily. 'Mr. Sam Watson is a very good sort of young man, and I dare say a very clever surgeon; but his complexion has been rather too much exposed to all weathers to make a likeness to him very flattering.'

Mary apologised, in some confusion—

'She had not thought a strong likeness at all incompatible with very different degrees of beauty. There might be resemblance in countenance, and the complexion and even the features be very unlike.'

'I know nothing of my brother's beauty,' said

Emma, 'for **I** have not seen him since he was seven years old ; **but** my father reckons us alike.'

'Mr. Watson!' cried Mr. Edwards; 'well, you **astonish me.** There is not the least likeness in the world ; **your** brother's eyes are grey, yours are brown ; he has a long face, and a wide mouth. My dear, do *you* perceive the least resemblance?'

'Not the least: Miss Emma Watson puts me very much in mind of her eldest sister, and sometimes I see a look of Miss Penelope, and once or twice there has been a glance of Mr. Robert, but I cannot perceive **any** likeness to Mr. Samuel.'

'I see the likeness between her and Miss Watson,' replied **Mr.** Edwards, **'very** strongly, but I am not sensible **of the** others. **I do** not much think she is like **any of the family** *but* **Miss** Watson ; but I **am** very sure there **is** no resemblance between her **and** Sam.'

This matter was settled, **and** they went to dinner.

'Your father, Miss Emma, is one **of** my oldest friends,' said Mr. Edwards, as he helped her to wine, when they were drawn round the fire **to** enjoy their dessert. 'We must drink to his better health. It is a great concern to me, I assure you, that he should be such an invalid. I know nobody who likes a game of cards, in a social way, better than **he** does, and very few people who play a fairer rubber. It is a thousand pities that he should **be** so deprived of the pleasure. For now, we have a quiet little Whist Club, that meets three times a week at the White Hart ; and if he could but have his health, how **much** he would enjoy it!'

'I daresay he would, sir; and I wish, with all my heart, he were equal to it.'

'Your club would be better fitted for an invalid,' said Mrs. Edwards, 'if you did not keep it up so late.' This was an old grievance.

'So late, my dear! What are you talking of?' cried the husband, with sturdy pleasantry. 'We are always at home before midnight. They would laugh at Osborne Castle to hear you call *that* late; they are but just rising from dinner at midnight.'

'That is nothing to the purpose,' retorted the lady, calmly. 'The Osbornes are to be no rule for us. You had better meet every night, and break up two hours sooner.'

So far the subject was very often carried; but Mr. and Mrs. Edwards were so wise as never to pass that point; and Mr. Edwards now turned to something else. He had lived long enough in the idleness of a town to become a little of a gossip, and having some anxiety to know more of the circumstances of his young guest than had yet reached him, he began with—

'I think, Miss Emma, I remember your aunt very well, about thirty years ago; I am pretty sure I danced with her in the old rooms at Bath the year before I married. She was a very fine woman then, but like other people, I suppose, she is grown somewhat older since that time. I hope she is likely to be happy in her second choice.'

'I hope so; I believe so, sir,' said Emma, in some agitation.

'Mr. Turner had not been dead a great while, I
think?'

'About two years, sir.'

'I forget what her name is now.'

'O'Brien.'

'Irish! ah, I remember; and she is gone to settle
in Ireland. I do not wonder that you should not
wish to go with her into *that* country, Miss Emma;
but it must be a great deprivation to her, poor lady!
after bringing you up like a child of her own.'

'I was not so ungrateful, sir,' said Emma, warmly,
'as to wish to be anywhere but with her. It did not
suit Captain O'Brien that I should be of the party.'

'Captain!' repeated Mrs. Edwards. 'The gentleman is in the army then?'

'Yes, ma'am.'

'Aye, there is nothing like your officers for captivating the ladies, young or old. There is no resisting
a cockade, my dear.'

'I hope there is,' said Mrs. Edwards gravely, with
a quick glance at her daughter; and Emma had just
recovered from her own perturbation in time to see a
blush on Miss Edwards' cheek and in remembering
what Elizabeth had said of Captain Hunter, to wonder
and waver between his influence and her brother's.

'Elderly ladies should be careful how they make a
second choice,' observed Mr. Edwards.

'Carefulness and discretion should not be confined
to elderly ladies, or to a second choice,' added his
wife. 'They are quite as necessary to young ladies in
their first.'

'Rather more so, my dear,' replied he; 'because young ladies are likely to feel the effects of it longer. When an old lady plays the fool, it is not in the course of nature that she should suffer from it many years.'

Emma drew her hand across her eyes, and Mrs. Edwards, in perceiving it, changed the subject to one of less anxiety to all.

With nothing to do but to expect the hour of setting off, the afternoon was long to the two young ladies; and though Miss Edwards was rather discomposed at the very early hour which her mother always fixed for going, that early hour itself was watched for with some eagerness. The entrance of the tea-things at seven o'clock was some relief; and, luckily, Mr. and Mrs. Edwards always drank a dish extraordinary and ate an additional muffin when they were going to sit up late, which lengthened the ceremony almost to the wished-for moment.

At a little before eight o'clock the Tomlinsons' carriage was heard to go by, which was the constant signal for Mrs. Edwards to order hers to the door; and in a very few minutes the party were transported from the quiet and warmth of a snug parlour to the bustle, noise, and draughts of air of a broad entrance passage of an inn. Mrs. Edwards, carefully guarding her own dress, while she attended with yet greater solicitude to the proper security of her young charges' shoulders and throats, led the way up the wide staircase, while no sound of a ball but the first scrape of one violin blessed the ears of her followers; and

Miss Edwards, **on** hazarding the anxious enquiry of whether there were many **people** come yet, was told by the waiter, as she knew she should, that Mr. Tomlinson's family were in the room.

In **passing** along **a short** gallery **to the** assembly **room,** brilliant in lights before them, they were accosted by a young man in a morning-dress and boots, who was standing in the doorway of **a** bedchamber apparently on purpose to see them go by.

' Ah ! Mrs. Edwards, how do you do ? **How** do you do, Miss Edwards ?' he **cried, with an** easy air. ' You are determined to be in good time, **I** see, as usual. The candles are but this moment lit.'

' I like to **get** a good seat **by** the fire, you know, Mr. Musgrave,' replied Mrs. Edwards.

**'I am** this moment going **to** dress,' said he. **'I** am waiting for my stupid fellow. We shall have **a** famous ball. The Osbornes are certainly coming ; **you** may depend upon *that*, **for I was** with Lord Osborne this morning.'

The party passed on. Mrs. Edwards' satin gown swept along the clean floor of the ballroom **to the** fireplace at the upper end, where one party only were formally seated, while three or four officers were lounging together, passing in and out from the adjoining card-room. A **very** stiff meeting between these near neighbours ensued, and as soon as they were all duly placed again, Emma, in a low whisper, which became the **solemn** scene, said to Miss Edwards :—

' The gentleman we passed in the passage was Mr.

Musgrave, then ; he is reckoned remarkably agreeable, I understand ?'

Miss Edwards answered hesitatingly, ' Yes ; he is very much liked by many people ; but *we* are not very intimate.'

' He is rich, is not he ?'

' He has about eight or nine hundred a-year, I believe. He came into possession of it when he was very young, and my father and mother think it has given him rather an unsettled turn. He is no favourite with them.'

The cold and empty appearance of the room, and the demure air of the small cluster of females at one end of it, began soon to give way. The inspiriting sound of other carriages was heard, and continual accessions of portly chaperones, and strings of smartly dressed girls, were received, with now and then a fresh gentleman straggler, who, if not enough in love to station himself near any fair creature, seemed glad to escape into the card-room.

Among the increasing number of military men, one now made his way to Miss Edwards with an air of empressment which decidedly said to her companion, 'I am Captain Hunter ;' and Emma, who could not but watch her at such a moment, saw her looking rather distressed, but by no means displeased, and heard an engagement formed for the two first dances, which made her think her brother Sam's a hopeless case.

Emma in the meanwhile was not unobserved or unadmired herself. A new face, and a very pretty one, could not be slighted. Her name was whispered from one party to another, and no sooner had the signal been given by the orchestra's striking up a favourite air, which seemed to call the young to their duty and people the centre of the room, than she found herself engaged to dance with a brother officer, introduced by Captain Hunter.

Emma Watson was not more than of the middle height, well made and plump, with an air of healthy vigour. Her skin was very brown, but clear, smooth, and glowing, which, with a lively eye, a sweet smile, and an open countenance, gave beauty to attract, and expression to make that beauty improve on acquaintance. Having no reason to be dissatisfied with her partner, the evening began very pleasantly to her, and her feelings perfectly coincided with the reiterated observation of others, that it was an excellent ball. The two first dances were not quite over when the returning sound of carriages after a long interruption called general notice!—' The Osbornes are coming!' 'The Osbornes are coming!' was repeated round the room. After some minutes of extraordinary bustle without and watchful curiosity within, the important party, preceded by the attentive master of the inn, to open a door which was never shut, made their appearance. They consisted of Lady Osborne; her son, Lord Osborne; her daughter, Miss Osborne; Miss Carr, her daughter's friend; Mr. Howard, formerly tutor to Lord Osborne, now clergyman of the parish in which the castle stood; Mrs. Blake, a widow sister, who lived with

him ; her son, a fine boy of ten years old ; and Mr.
Tom Musgrave, who probably, imprisoned within his
own room, had been listening in bitter impatience to
the sound of the music for the last half-hour.   In
their progress up the room they paused almost immediately behind Emma to receive the compliments
of some acquaintance, and she heard Lady Osborne
observe that they had made a point of coming early
for the gratification of Mrs. Blake's little boy, who
was uncommonly fond of dancing.   Emma looked at
them all as they passed, but chiefly and with most
interest on Tom Musgrave, who was certainly a
genteel, good-looking young man.   Of the females
Lady Osborne had by much the finest person ; though
nearly fifty, she was very handsome, and had all the
dignity of rank.

Lord Osborne was a very fine young man ; but
there was an air of coldness, of carelessness, even of
awkwardness about him, which seemed to speak him
out of his element in a ball-room.   He came in fact
only because it was judged expedient for him to
please the borough ; he was not fond of women's
company, and he never danced.   Mr. Howard was an
agreeable-looking man, a little more than thirty.

At the conclusion of the two dances, Emma found
herself, she knew not how, seated amongst the Osborne's set ; and she was immediately struck with
the fine countenance and animated gestures of the
little boy, as he was standing before his mother, considering when they should begin.

'You will not be surprised at Charles's impatience,'

said Mrs. Blake, a lively, pleasant-looking little woman of five or six and thirty, to a lady who was standing near her, 'when you know what a partner he is to have. Miss Osborne has been so very kind as to promise to dance the two first dances with him.'

'Oh, yes! we have been engaged this week,' cried the boy, 'and we are to dance down every couple.'

On the other side of Emma, Miss Osborne, Miss Carr, and a party of young men were standing engaged in very lively consultation; and soon afterwards she saw the smartest officer of the set walking off to the orchestra to order the dance, while Miss Osborne passing before her to her little expecting partner, hastily said, 'Charles, I beg your pardon for not keeping my engagement, but I am going to dance these two dances with Colonel Beresford. I know you will excuse me, and I will certainly dance with you after tea;' and without staying for an answer, she turned again to Miss Carr, and in another minute was led by Colonel Beresford to begin the set. If the poor little boy's face had in its happiness been interesting to Emma, it was infinitely more so under this sudden reverse; he stood the picture of disappointment with crimsoned cheeks, quivering lips, and eyes bent on the floor. His mother, stifling her own mortification, tried to soothe his with the prospect of Miss Osborne's second promise; but, though he contrived to utter with an effort of boyish bravery, 'Oh, I do not mind it!' it was very evident by the unceasing agitation of his features that he minded it as much as ever.

Emma did not think or reflect; she felt and acted. 'I shall be very happy to dance with you, sir, if you like it,' said she, holding out her hand with the most unaffected good-humour. The boy, in one moment restored to all his first delight, looked joyfully at his mother; and stepping forwards with an honest, simple 'Thank you, ma'am,' was instantly ready to attend his new acquaintance. The thankfulness of Mrs. Blake was more diffuse; with a look most expressive of unexpected pleasure and lively gratitude, she turned to her neighbour with repeated and fervent acknow-ledgements of so great and condescending a kindness to her boy. Emma with perfect truth could assure her that she could not be giving greater pleasure than she felt herself; and Charles being provided with his gloves and charged to keep them on, they joined the set which was now rapidly forming, with nearly equal complacency. It was a partnership which could not be noticed without surprise. It gained her a broad stare from Miss Osborne and Miss Carr as they passed her in the dance. 'Upon my word, Charles, you are in luck,' said the former, as she turned him; 'you have got a better partner than me;' to which the happy Charles answered 'Yes.'

Tom Musgrave, who was dancing with Miss Carr, gave her many inquisitive glances; and after a time Lord Osborne himself came, and under pretence of talking to Charles, stood to look at his partner. Though rather distressed by such observation, Emma could not repent what she had done, so happy had it made both the boy and his mother; the latter of whom was continually making opportunities of addressing her with the warmest civility. Her little partner she found, though bent chiefly on dancing, was not unwilling to speak, when her questions or remarks gave him anything to say ; and she learnt, by a sort of inevitable enquiry, that he had two brothers and a sister, that they and their mamma all lived with his uncle at Wickstead, that his uncle taught him Latin, that he was very fond of riding, and had a horse of his own given him by Lord Osborne ; and that he had been out once already with Lord Osborne's hounds.

At the end of these dances, Emma found they were to drink tea ; Miss Edwards gave her a caution to be at hand, in a manner which convinced her of Mrs. Edwards' holding it very important to have them both close to her when she moved into the tea-room ; and Emma was accordingly on the alert to gain her proper station. It was always the pleasure of the company to have a little bustle and crowd when they adjourned for refreshment. The tea-room was a small room within the card-room ; and in passing through the latter, where the passage was straitened by tables, Mrs. Edwards and her party were for a few moments hemmed in. It happened close by Lady Osborne's casino table ; Mr. Howard, who belonged to it, spoke to his nephew ; and Emma, on perceiving herself the object of attention both to Lady Osborne and him, had just turned away her eyes in time to avoid seeming to hear her young companion exclaim delightedly aloud, 'Oh, uncle !

do look at my partner ; she is so pretty !' As they were immediately in motion again, however, Charles was hurried off without being able to receive his uncle's suffrage. On entering the tea-room, in which two long tables were prepared, Lord Osborne was to be seen quite alone at the end of one, as if retreating as far as he could from the ball, to enjoy his own thoughts and gape without restraint. Charles instantly pointed him out to Emma. 'There's Lord Osborne, let you and I go and sit by him.'

'No, no,' said Emma, laughing, 'you must sit with my friends.'

Charles was now free enough to hazard a few questions in his turn. 'What o'clock was it ?'

'Eleven.'

'Eleven! and I am not at all sleepy. Mamma said I should be asleep before ten. Do you think Miss Osborne will keep her word with me when tea is over ?'

'Oh, yes! I suppose so ;' though she felt that she had no better reason to give than that Miss Osborne had *not* kept it before.

'When shall you come to Osborne Castle ?'

'Never, probably. I am not acquainted with the family.'

'But you may come to Wickstead and see mamma, and she can take you to the castle. There is a monstrous curious stuffed fox there, and a badger, anybody would think they were alive. It is a pity you should not see them.'

On rising from tea there was again a scramble for

the pleasure of being **first** out of the room, which happened **to** be increased by one or two of the card-parties having just broken up, and the players being disposed to move exactly the different way. Among these **was** Mr. Howard, his sister leaning on his arm; **and no** sooner were they within reach **of** Emma, than **Mrs.** Blake, calling her notice by **a** friendly touch, said, 'Your goodness **to** Charles, **my** dear Miss Watson, brings all his family upon **you.** Give me leave to introduce my brother.' Emma curtsied, the gentleman bowed, **made** a hasty request for the honour of her hand in the two next dances, to which as hasty an affirmative was given, and they were immediately impelled in **opposite** directions. Emma **was** very well **pleased** with **the** circumstance; there was a quietly cheerful, **gentlemanlike** air **in** Mr. Howard which suited her; **and in a** few minutes afterwards the value of her engagement increased, **when,** as she was sitting in the card-room, somewhat screened by a door, she heard Lord Osborne, who was lounging on a vacant table near her, call Tom Musgrave towards him and say, 'Why do not you dance with that beautiful Emma Watson? I want you to dance with her, and I will come and stand **by** you.'

'**I** was determined on it this very moment, my lord; I'll be introduced and dance with her directly.'

'Aye, **do; and if you find** she does not want much talking to, you may introduce me **by** and **by.'**

'Very well, my lord; **if she** is like her sisters she will only want to be listened to. I will go this moment.  I shall find her in the tea-room.  That stiff old Mrs. Edwards has never done tea.'

Away he went, Lord Osborne after him; and Emma lost no time in hurrying from her corner exactly the other way, forgetting in her haste that she left Mrs. Edwards behind.

'We had quite lost you,' said Mrs. Edwards, who followed her with Mary in less than five minutes. 'If you prefer this room to the other there is no reason why you should not be here, but we had better all be together.'

Emma was saved the trouble of apologising, by their being joined at the moment by Tom Musgrave, who requesting Mrs. Edwards aloud to do him the honour of presenting him to Miss Emma Watson, left that good lady without any choice in the business, but that of testifying by the coldness of her manner that she did it unwillingly.  The honour of dancing with her was solicited without loss of time, and Emma, however she might like to be thought a beautiful girl by lord or commoner, was so little disposed to favour Tom Musgrave himself that she had considerable satisfaction in avowing her previous engagement.  He was evidently surprised and discomposed.  The style of her last partner had probably led him to believe her not overpowered with applications.

'My little friend, Charles Blake,' he cried, 'must not expect to engross you the whole evening.  We can never suffer this.  It is against the rules of the assembly, and I am sure it will never be patronised by our good friend here, Mrs. Edwards; she is by much too nice a judge of decorum to give her license to such a dangerous particularity ——'

'I am not going to dance with Master Blake, sir!'

The gentleman, a little disconcerted, could only hope he might be fortunate another time, and seeming unwilling to leave her, though his friend, Lord Osborne, was waiting in the doorway for the result, as Emma with some amusement perceived, he began to make civil enquiries after her family.

'How comes it that we have not the pleasure of seeing your sisters here this evening? Our assemblies have been used to be so well treated by them that we do not know how to take this neglect.'

'My eldest sister is the only one at home, and she could not leave my father.'

'Miss Watson the only one at home! You astonish me! It seems but the day before yesterday that I saw them all three in this town. But I am afraid I have been a very sad neighbour of late. I hear dreadful complaints of my negligence wherever I go, and I confess it is a shameful length of time since I was at Stanton. But I shall *now* endeavour to make myself amends for the past.'

Emma's calm curtsey in reply must have struck him as very unlike the encouraging warmth he had been used to receive from her sisters, and gave him probably the novel sensation of doubting his own influence, and of wishing for more attention than she bestowed. The dancing now recommenced; Miss Carr being impatient to *call*, everybody was required to stand up; and Tom Musgrave's curiosity was appeased on seeing Mr. Howard come forward and claim Emma's hand.

'That will do as well for me,' was Lord Osborne's remark, when his friend carried him the news, and he was continually at Howard's elbow during the two dances.

The frequency of his appearance there was the only unpleasant part of the engagement, the only objection she could make to Mr. Howard. In himself, she thought him as agreeable as he looked; though chatting on the commonest topics, he had a sensible, unaffected way of expressing himself, which made them all worth hearing, and she only regretted that he had not been able to make his pupil's manners as unexceptionable as his own. The two dances seemed very short, and she had her partner's authority for considering them so. At their conclusion, the Osbornes and their train were all on the move.

'We are off at last,' said his lordship to Tom; 'How much longer do you stay in this heavenly place?—till sunrise?'

'No, faith! my lord; I have had quite enough of it, I assure you. I shall not show myself here again when I have had the honour of attending Lady Osborne to her carriage. I shall retreat in as much secrecy as possible to the most remote corner of the house, where I shall order a barrel of oysters, and be famously snug.'

'Let me see you soon at the castle, and bring me word how she looks by daylight.'

Emma and Mrs. Blake parted as old acquaintance, and Charles shook her by the hand, and wished her goodbye at least a dozen times. From Miss Osborne and Miss Carr she received something like a jerking curtsey as they passed her; even Lady Osborne gave her a look of complacency, and his lordship actually came back after the others were out of the room, to 'beg her pardon,' and look in the window-seat behind her **for** the gloves which were visibly compressed in his hand. As Tom Musgrave was seen **no** more, we may suppose his plan to have succeeded, and imagine him mortifying with his barrel of oysters in dreary solitude, or gladly assisting the landlady in her bar to **make** fresh negus for the happy dancers above. Emma could **not help** missing the party by whom she had been, though **in some** respects unpleasantly, distinguished, and the two dances which followed and concluded the ball **were rather** flat in comparison with the others. Mr. Edwards having played with good luck, they were some of the last in the room.

'Here we are back again, I declare,' said Emma sorrowfully, as she walked into the dining-room, where the table was prepared, and the neat upper maid was lighting the candles.

'My dear Miss Edwards, how soon it **is** at an **end**! I wish it could all come **over** again.'

**A great** deal of kind pleasure was expressed in her having enjoyed the **evening** so much; and Mr. Edwards was as warm as herself in the praise of **the** fulness, brilliancy, and spirit of the meeting, though **as** he had been fixed the whole time at the same

table in the same room, with only one change of
chairs, it might have seemed a matter scarcely perceived; but he had won four rubbers out of five, and
everything went well.  His daughter felt the advantage of this gratified state of mind, in the course of
the remarks and retrospections which now ensued
over the welcome soup.

'How came you not to dance with either of the
Mr. Tomlinsons, Mary?' said her mother.

'I was always engaged when they asked me.'

'I thought you were to have stood up with Mr.
James the two last dances; Mrs. Tomlinson told me
he was gone to ask you, and I had heard you say two
minutes before that you were *not* engaged.'

'Yes, but there was a mistake; I had misunderstood.  I did not know I was engaged.  I thought it
had been for the two dances after, if we stayed so long;
but Captain Hunter assured me it was for those very
two.'

'So you ended with Captain Hunter, Mary, did
you?' said her father.  'And whom did you begin
with?'

'Captain Hunter,' was repeated in a very humble
tone.

'Hum!  That is being constant, however.  But
who else did you dance with?'

'Mr. Norton and Mr. Styles.'

'And who are they?'

'Mr. Norton is a cousin of Captain Hunter's.'

'And who is Mr. Styles?'

'One of his particular friends.'

'All in the same regiment,' added **Mrs.** Edwards. ' Mary was surrounded by red-coats all **the** evening. I should have been better pleased to see her dancing with some of our old neighbours, I confess.'

' **Yes, yes;** we must not neglect **our** old neighbours. But **if** these soldiers are quicker than other people **in** a ball-room, what are young ladies **to** do ?'

' I think there is no occasion for their engaging themselves so many dances beforehand, Mr. Edwards.'

' No, perhaps not; but I remember, **my dear,** when you and I did the same.'

Mrs. **Edwards** said no more, and Mary breathed again. **A good** deal **of** good-humoured pleasantry followed, **and Emma** went **to bed** in charming spirits, her head full **of Osbornes, Blakes,** and Howards.

The next morning **brought a** great many visitors. **It** was the way of the **place** always to call on Mrs. Edwards the morning after a **ball,** and **this** neighbourly inclination was increased in the present instance by a general spirit of curiosity on Emma's account, as everybody wanted to look again **at the girl** who had **been** admired the night before by Lord Osborne. Many were the eyes, and various the degrees of approbation with which she was examined. Some saw no fault, and some no beauty. With some her brown skin was **the** annihilation **of** every grace, and others could never be persuaded that she was half so handsome as Elizabeth Watson had been ten years ago. The morning passed quickly away **in** discussing the merits of the ball with all this succession of company,

and Emma was at once astonished by finding it two
o'clock, and considering that she had heard nothing
of her father's chair.  After this discovery she had
walked twice to the window to examine the street
and was on the point of asking leave to ring the bell
and make enquiries, when the light sound of a carriage driving up to the door set her heart at ease.
She stepped again to the window, but instead of the
convenient though very un-smart family equipage
perceived a neat curricle.  Mr. Musgrave was shortly
afterwards announced, and Mrs. Edwards put on her
very stiffest look at the sound.  Not at all dismayed,
however, by her chilling air, he paid his compliments
to each of the ladies with no unbecoming ease, and
continuing to address Emma presented her a note,
which 'he had the honour of bringing from her sister,
but to which he must observe a verbal postscript from
himself would be requisite.'

The note, which Emma was beginning to read
rather before Mrs. Edwards had entreated her to use
no ceremony, contained a few lines from Elizabeth
importing that their father, in consequence of being
unusually well, had taken the sudden resolution of
attending the visitation that day, and that as his road
lay quite wide from D. it was impossible for her to
come home till the following morning, unless the
Edwards would send her, which was hardly to be
expected, or she could meet with any chance convey-
ance, or did not mind walking so far.  She had
scarcely run her eye through the whole, before she

found herself obliged to listen to Tom Musgrave's further account.

'I received that note from the fair hands of Miss Watson only ten minutes ago,' said he; 'I met her in the village of Stanton, whither my good stars prompted me to turn my horses' heads. She was at that moment in quest of a person to employ on the errand, and I was fortunate enough to convince her that she could not find a more willing or speedy messenger than myself. Remember, I say nothing of my disinterestedness. My reward is to be the indulgence of conveying you to Stanton in my curricle. Though they are not written down, I bring your sister's orders for the same.'

Emma felt distressed; she did not like the proposal—she did not wish to be on terms of intimacy with the proposer; and yet, fearful of encroaching on the Edwards, as well as wishing to go home herself, she was at a loss how entirely to decline what he offered. Mrs. Edwards continued silent, either not understanding the case, or waiting to see how the young lady's inclination lay. Emma thanked him, but professed herself very unwilling to give him so much trouble. 'The trouble was of course honour, pleasure, delight—what had he or his horses to do?' Still she hesitated—'She believed she must beg leave to decline his assistance; she was rather afraid of the sort of carriage. The distance was not beyond a walk.' Mrs. Edwards was silent no longer. She enquired into the particulars, and then said, 'We shall be extremely happy, Miss Emma, if you can give us the pleasure of your company till to-morrow; but if you cannot conveniently do so, our carriage is quite at your service, and Mary will be pleased with the opportunity of seeing your sister.'

This was precisely what Emma had longed for, and she accepted the offer most thankfully, acknowledging that as Elizabeth was entirely alone, it was her wish to return home to dinner. The plan was warmly opposed by their visitor—

' I cannot suffer it, indeed. I must not be deprived of the happiness of escorting you. I assure you there is not a possibility of fear with my horses. You might guide them yourself. Your sisters all know how quiet they are; they have none of them the smallest scruple in trusting themselves with me, even on a race-course. Believe me,' added he, lowering his voice, '*you* are quite safe—the danger is only *mine*.'

Emma was not more disposed to oblige him for all this.

' And as to Mrs. Edwards' carriage being used the day after a ball, it is a thing quite out of rule, I assure you—never heard of before. The old coachman will look as black as his horses—won't he, Miss Edwards ?'

No notice was taken. The ladies were silently firm, and the gentleman found himself obliged to submit.

' What a famous ball we had last night,' he cried, after a short pause ; ' How long did you keep it up after the Osbornes and I went away ?'

' We had two dances more.'

'It is making it too much of a fatigue, I think, to stay so late.  I suppose your set was not a very full one.'

'Yes; quite as full as ever, except the Osbornes. There seemed no vacancy anywhere; and everybody danced with uncommon spirit to the very last.'

Emma said this, though against her conscience.

'Indeed! perhaps I might have looked in upon you again, if I had been aware of as much; for I am rather fond of dancing than not.  Miss Osborne is a charming girl, is not she ?'

'I do not think her handsome,' replied Emma, to whom all this was chiefly addressed.

'Perhaps she is not critically handsome, but her manners are delightful.  And Fanny Carr is a most interesting little creature.  You can imagine nothing more *naïve* or *piquante*; and what do you think of Lord Osborne, Miss Watson ?'

'He would be handsome even though he were *not* a lord, and, perhaps, better bred; more desirous of pleasing and showing himself pleased in a right place.'

'Upon my word, you are severe upon my friend! I assure you Lord Osborne is a very good fellow.'

'I do not dispute his virtues, but I do not like his careless air.'

'If it were not a breach of confidence,' replied Tom, with an important look, 'perhaps I might be able to win a more favourable opinion of poor Osborne.'

Emma gave him no encouragement, and he was

obliged to keep his friend's secret. He was also obliged to put an end to his visit, for Mrs. Edwards having ordered her carriage there was no time to be lost on Emma's side in preparing for it. Miss Edwards accompanied her home; but as it was dinner hour at Stanton stayed with them only a few minutes.

'Now, my dear Emma,' said Miss Watson, as soon as they were alone, 'you must talk to me all the rest of the day without stopping, or I shall not be satisfied; but, first of all, Nanny shall bring in the dinner. Poor thing! You will not dine as you did yesterday, for we have nothing but some fried beef. How nice Mary Edwards looks in her new pelisse! And now tell me how you like them all, and what I am to say to Sam. I have begun my letter; Jack Stokes is to call for it to-morrow, for his uncle is going within a mile of Guildford next day.'

Nanny brought in the dinner.

'We will wait upon ourselves,' continued Elizabeth, 'and then we shall lose no time. And so you would not come home with Tom Musgrave?'

'No, you had said so much against him that I could not wish either for the obligation or the intimacy which the use of his carriage must have created. I should not even have liked the appearance of it.'

'You did very right; though I wonder at your forbearance, and I do not think I could have done it myself. He seemed so eager to fetch you that I could not say no, though it rather went against me to be throwing you together, so well as I knew his tricks; but I did long to see you, and it was a clever

way of getting you home. Besides, it won't do to be
too nice. Nobody could have thought of the Edwards letting you have their coach, after the horses
being out so late. But what am I to say to Sam?'

'If you are guided by me you will not encourage
him to think of Miss Edwards. The father is decidedly against him, the mother shows him no favour,
and I doubt his having any interest with Mary. She
danced twice with Captain Hunter, and I think
shows him in general as much encouragement as is
consistent with her disposition, and the circumstances
she is placed in. She once mentioned Sam, and certainly with a little confusion; but that was perhaps
merely owing to the consciousness of his liking her,
which may very probably have come to her knowledge.'

'Oh! dear, yes. She has heard enough of *that*
from us all. Poor Sam! he is out of luck as well as
other people. For the life of me, Emma, I cannot
help feeling for those that are crossed in love. Well,
now begin, and give me an account of everything as
it happened.'

Emma obeyed her, and Elizabeth listened with
very little interruption till she heard of Mr. Howard
as a partner.

'Dance with Mr. Howard. Good heavens! You
don't say so! Why he is quite one of the great and
grand ones. Did you not find him very high?'

'His manners are of a kind to give me much more
ease and confidence than Tom Musgrave's.'

'Well, go on. I should have been frightened out

of my wits to have had anything to do with the
Osborne's set.'

Emma concluded her narration.

'And so you really did not dance with Tom Musgrave at all; but you must have liked him—you must
have been struck with him altogether.'

'I do *not* like him, Elizabeth.  I allow his person
and air to be good; and that his manners to a certain
point—his address rather—is pleasing.  But I see
nothing else to admire in him.  On the contrary, he
seems very vain, very conceited, absurdly anxious for
distinction, and absolutely contemptible in some of
the measures he takes for being so.  There is a ridi-
culousness about him that entertains me; but his
company gives me no other agreeable emotion.'

'My dearest Emma!  You are like nobody else in
the world.  It is well Margaret is not by.  You do
not offend *me*, though I hardly know how to believe
you; but Margaret would never forgive such words.'

'I wish Margaret could have heard him profess his
ignorance of her being out of the country; he declared
it seemed only two days since he had seen her.'

'Aye, that is just like him; and yet this is the
man she *will* fancy so desperately in love with her.
He is no favourite of mine, as you well know, Emma,
but you must think him agreeable.  Can you lay
your hand on your heart, and say you do not?'

'Indeed, I can, both hands; and spread them to
their widest extent.'

'I should like to know the man you *do* think
agreeable.'

' His name is Howard.'

' Howard !  Dear me ; I cannot think of him **but** as playing cards with Lady Osborne, and looking proud.  I must own, however, that it is a relief to me to find you can speak as you do of Tom Musgrave. My heart did misgive me that you would like him too well.  You talked so stoutly beforehand, that I was sadly afraid your brag would be punished.  I only hope it will last, and that he will not come on to pay you much attention.  It is a hard thing for a woman to stand against the flattering ways of a man when he is bent upon pleasing her.'

As their quietly sociable little meal concluded, Miss Watson could not help observing how comfortably it had passed.

' It is so delightful to me,' said she, ' to have things going on in peace and good-humour.  Nobody can tell how much I hate quarrelling.  Now, though we have had nothing but fried beef, how good it has all seemed.  I wish everybody were as easily satisfied as you ; but poor Margaret is very snappish, and Penelope owns she would rather have quarrelling going on than nothing at all.'

Mr. Watson returned in the evening not the worse for the exertion of the day, and, consequently, pleased with what he had done, and glad to talk of it over his own fireside.  Emma had not foreseen any interest to herself in the occurrences of a visitation ; but when she heard Mr. Howard spoken of as the preacher, and as having given them an excellent sermon, she could not help listening with a quicker ear

'I do not know when I have heard a discourse more to my mind,' continued Mr. Watson, 'or one better delivered. He reads extremely well, with great propriety, and in a very impressive manner, and at the same time without any theatrical grimace or violence. I own I do not like much action in the pulpit; I do not like the studied air and artificial inflexions of voice which your very popular and most admired preachers generally have. A simple delivery is much better calculated to inspire devotion, and shows a much better taste. Mr. Howard read like a scholar and a gentleman.'

'And what had you for dinner, sir?' said his eldest daughter.

He related the dishes, and told what he had ate himself.

'Upon the whole,' he added, 'I have had a very comfortable day. My old friends were quite sur·prised to see me amongst them, and I must say that everybody paid me great attention, and seemed to feel for me as an invalid. They would make me sit near the fire; and as the partridges were pretty high, Dr. Richards would have them sent away to the other end of the table, "that they might not offend Mr. Watson," which I thought very kind of him. But what pleased me as much as anything was Mr. Howard's attention. There is a pretty steep flight of steps up to the room we dine in, which do not quite agree with my gouty foot, and Mr. Howard walked by me from the bottom to the top, and would make me take his arm. It struck me as very becoming in so young a man, but **I am** sure I had no claim to expect it, **for** I never **saw** him before in my life. By the by, he enquired after one **of** my daughters, but I do **not** know which. **I** suppose **you** know among yourselves.'

**On the** third day after the ball, **as Nanny**, at five minutes before three, was beginning **to** bustle into the parlour with the tray and knife-case, she was suddenly called to the front door by the sound **of as** smart a rap as the end of a riding whip could give; and though charged by Miss Watson **to** let nobody in, returned in half a minute with a look **of** awkward dismay to **hold** the parlour **door** open for Lord Osborne **and Tom** Musgrave. The surprise **of the** young ladies **may be imagined.** No visitors would have been **welcome at such** a moment, but such visitors as these—such **an one as** Lord Osborne at least, a nobleman and **a** stranger, was really distressing.

He looked a little embarrassed himself, as, on being introduced by his easy voluble friend, **he** muttered something of doing himself the **honour** of waiting upon **Mr. Watson.** Though Emma could not **but** take the compliment of the visit to herself, she was very far from enjoying it. She felt all the inconsistency of such an acquaintance with the very humble style in which they were **obliged** to live; and having **in** her aunt's family **been used** to many of the elegancies of life, was fully sensible of all that must be open to **the** ridicule of richer people **in** her present home. Of the pain of such feelings, Elizabeth knew very little. Her simple mind, or juster reason, saved her from such mortification; and though shrinking under a general sense of inferiority, she felt no particular shame. Mr. Watson, as the gentlemen had already heard from Nanny, was not well enough to be down stairs. With much concern they took their seats; Lord Osborne near Emma, and the convenient Mr. Musgrave, in high spirits at his own importance, on the other side of the fireplace with Elizabeth. *He* was at no loss for words; but when Lord Osborne had hoped that Emma had not caught cold at the ball he had nothing more to say for some time, and could only gratify his eye by occasional glances at his fair companion. Emma was not inclined to give herself much trouble for his entertainment, and after hard labour of mind, he produced the remark of its being a very fine day, and followed it up with the question of, 'Have you been walking this morning?'

'No, my lord, we thought it too dirty.'

'You should wear half-boots.' After another pause: 'Nothing sets off a neat ankle more than a half-boot; nankeen, galoshed with black, looks very well. Do not you like half-boots?'

'Yes; but unless they are so stout as to injure their beauty, they are not fit for country walking.'

'Ladies should ride in dirty weather. Do you ride?'

'No, my lord.'

'I wonder every lady does not; a woman never looks better than on horseback.'

'But **every woman may not have the** inclination or the means.'

'If **they** knew **how** much **it** became them, they would **all** have the inclination; and I fancy, Miss Watson, when once they had **the** inclination, the **means** would soon follow.'

'**Your** lordship thinks we always have our own way. *That* is a point on which ladies and gentlemen **have** long disagreed; but without pretending to decide it, I may say that there are some circumstances which even *women* cannot control. Female economy will do **a great** deal, my lord, **but it cannot turn a** small income **into a** large one.'

**Lord Osborne** was silenced. Her manner had **been neither** sententious **nor** sarcastic, but there **was** a something **in its mild** seriousness, as well as **in the** words themselves, **which made his** lordship think; and when he addressed **her again, it** was with a degree of considerate propriety totally unlike the half-awkward, half-fearless style of his former remarks. It **was** a new thing with him to wish to **please a** woman; it was the first time that he had **ever felt** what was due to **a** woman in Emma's situation; but as he was wanting **neither** in sense nor a good disposition he did not **feel it** without effect.

'You have **not been** long in this country, I understand,' said he, in the **tone** of a gentleman. 'I hope **you** are pleased with **it.**'

He was rewarded **by a** gracious answer, and a more liberal full view **of her face** than **she** had yet bestowed. Unused to exert himself, and happy in contemplating her, he then sat in silence for some minutes longer, while Tom Musgrave was chattering to Elizabeth; till they were interrupted by Nanny's approach, who, half-opening the door and putting in her head, said—

' Please, ma'am, master wants to know why he be'nt to have his dinner ? '

The gentlemen, who had hitherto disregarded every symptom, however positive, of the nearness of that meal, now jumped up with apologies, while Elizabeth called briskly after Nanny to take up the fowls.

' I am sorry it happens so,' she added, turning good-humouredly towards Musgrave, 'but you know what early hours we keep.'

Tom had nothing to say for himself, he knew it very well, and such honest simplicity, such shameless truth, rather bewildered him. Lord Osborne's parting compliments took some time, his inclination for speech seeming to increase with the shortness of the term for indulgence. He recommended exercise in defiance of dirt ; spoke again in praise of half-boots ; begged that his sister might be allowed to send Emma the name of her shoemaker ; and concluded with saying, ' My hounds will be hunting this country next week. I believe they will throw off at Stanton Wood on Wednesday at nine o'clock. I mention this in hopes of your being drawn out to see what's going on. If the morning's tolerable, pray do us the honour of giving us your good wishes in person.'

The sisters looked on each other with astonishment when their visitors had withdrawn.

'Here's an unaccountable honour!' cried Elizabeth at last. 'Who would have thought of Lord Osborne's coming to Stanton? He is very handsome; but Tom Musgrave looks all to nothing the smartest and most fashionable man of the two. I am glad he did not say anything to me; I would not have had to talk to such a great man for the world. Tom was very agreeable, was not he? But did you hear him ask where Miss Penelope and Miss Margaret were, when he first came in? It put me out of patience. I am glad Nanny had not laid the cloth however, it would have looked so awkward; just the tray did not signify.' To say that Emma was not flattered by Lord Osborne's visit, would be to assert a very unlikely thing, and describe a very odd young lady; but the gratification was by no means unalloyed; his coming was a sort of notice which might please her vanity, but did not suit her pride, and she would rather have known that he wished the visit without presuming to make it, than have seen him at Stanton.

Among other unsatisfactory feelings it once occurred to her to wonder why Mr. Howard had not taken the same privilege of coming, and accompanied his lordship, but she was willing to suppose that he had either known nothing about it, or had declined any share in a measure which carried quite as much impertinence in its form as good breeding. Mr. Watson was very far from being delighted when he heard what had passed; a little peevish under immediate pain, and ill-disposed to be pleased, he only replied,

'Pooh! Pooh! what occasion could there be for

Lord Osborne's coming?   I have lived here fourteen
years without being noticed by any of the family.   It
is some fooling of that idle fellow, Tom Musgrave.   I
cannot return the visit.   I would not if I could.'
And when Tom Musgrave was met with again, he
was commissioned with a message of excuse to
Osborne Castle, on the too sufficient plea of Mr.
Watson's infirm state of health.

A week or ten days rolled quietly away after this
visit before any new bustle arose to interrupt even for
half a day the tranquil and affectionate intercourse of
the two sisters, whose mutual regard was increasing
with the intimate knowledge of each other which such
intercourse produced.   The first circumstance to break
in on their security was the receipt of a letter from
Croydon to announce the speedy return of Margaret,
and a visit of two or three days from Mr. and Mrs.
Robert Watson, who undertook to bring her home,
and wished to see their sister Emma.

It was an expectation to fill the thoughts of the
sisters at Stanton and to busy the hours of one of
them at least ; for, as Jane had been a woman of
fortune, the preparations for her entertainment were
considerable ; and as Elizabeth had at all times more
goodwill than method in her guidance of the house,
she could make no change without a bustle.   An
absence of fourteen years had made all her brothers
and sisters strangers to Emma, but in her expectation
of Margaret there was more than the awkwardness
of such an alienation ; she had heard things which
made her dread her return ; and the day which brought

the party to **Stanton**, seemed to her the probable conclusion **of** almost all **that** had been comfortable **in** the house.

Robert Watson was an attorney at Croydon **in a** good way of business; very well satisfied with himself **for the** same, **and** for having married the only daughter of the attorney to whom he **had** been clerk, **with a** fortune of six thousand pounds. Mrs. Robert **was not** less pleased with herself for having had that **six** thousand pounds and for being **now in** possession of a very smart house in Croydon, where she gave genteel parties and wore fine clothes. **In her** person there **was** nothing remarkable; **her** manners were pert and conceited. Margaret was not without beauty; **she had a** slight **pretty** figure, and rather wanted **countenance than good** features; **but the** sharp and anxious expression **of** her face made her beauty in general little **felt. On** meeting her long-absent sister, as on every occasion of show, her manner was all affection and her voice all gentleness; continual smiles and a very slow articulation being **her** constant resource when determined **on** pleasing.

She was now 'so delighted to see dear, dear Emma,' **that** she **could** hardly speak a word in **a** minute.

'I am **sure** we shall be great friends,' she observed with much sentiment **as** they were **sitting** together. Emma scarcely knew **how to** answer such a proposition, and the manner in **which** it was spoken she could not attempt to equal. **Mrs.** Robert Watson eyed her with much familiar curiosity and triumphant compassion; **the** loss of the aunt's fortune was uppermost in her mind at the moment of meeting ; and she could not but feel how much better it was to be the daughter of a gentleman of property in Croydon than the niece of an old woman who threw herself away on an Irish captain. Robert was carelessly kind, as became a prosperous man and a brother ; more intent on settling with the post-boy, inveighing against the exorbitant advance in posting, and pondering over a doubtful halfcrown, than on welcoming a sister who was no longer likely to have any property for him to get the direction of.

'Your road through the village is infamous, Elizabeth,' said he ; 'worse than ever it was. By heaven ! I would indict it if I lived near you. Who is surveyor now ?'

There was a little niece at Croydon to be fondly enquired after by the kind-hearted Elizabeth, who regretted very much her not being of the party.

'You are very good,' replied her mother, 'and I assure you it went very hard with Augusta to have us come away without her. I was forced to say we were only going to church, and promise to come back for her directly. But you know it would not do to bring her without her maid, and I am as particular as ever in having her properly attended to.'

'Sweet little darling,' cried Margaret. 'It quite broke my heart to leave her.'

'Then why was you in such a hurry to run away from her ?' cried Mrs. Robert. 'You are a sad shabby girl. I have been quarrelling with you all the way we came, have not I ? Such a visit as this I never heard of ! You know how glad we are to have any of you with us, if it be for months together; and I am sorry (with a witty smile) we have not been able to make Croydon agreeable this autumn.'

'My dearest Jane, **do not** overpower me with your raillery. **You** know what inducements I had to bring me home. Spare me, I entreat you. **I am** no match for your arch sallies.'

'**Well,** I only beg you will not set your neighbours **against** the place. Perhaps Emma **may be** tempted **to** go back with us and stay till Christmas, if you don't put in your word.'

Emma was **greatly** obliged. 'I assure **you we** have very good society at Croydon. I do not much attend the balls, **they** are **rather** too mixed ; but our parties are **very select and good.** I had seven tables last week in my drawing-room.'

'Are you fond of the country ? How do you like Stanton **?'**

'Very much,' replied Emma, who thought a comprehensive answer most to the purpose. She saw that her sister-in-law despised her immediately. Mrs. Robert Watson was indeed wondering what **sort of a** home Emma could possibly have been used **to in** Shropshire, and setting it down as certain that the aunt could never have had six thousand pounds.

'How charming Emma is,' whispered Margaret to Mrs. Robert **in** her most languishing tone. **Emma** was quite distressed by such behaviour; and she did **not** like **it** better when **she** heard Margaret five minutes afterwards say to Elizabeth in a sharp, quick accent, totally unlike the first, 'Have you heard from

Pen since she went to Chichester?   I had a letter the other day.   I don't find she is likely to make anything of it.   I fancy she'll come back 'Miss Penelope,' as she went.'

Such she feared would be Margaret's common voice when the novelty of her own appearance were over; the tone of artificial sensibility was not recommended by the idea.   The ladies were invited upstairs to prepare for dinner.

'I hope you will find things tolerably comfortable, Jane,' said Elizabeth, as she opened the door of the spare bedchamber.

'My good creature,' replied Jane, 'use no ceremony with me, I entreat you.   I am one of those who always take things as they find them.   I hope I can put up with a small apartment for two or three nights without making a piece of work.   I always wish to be treated quite "en famille" when I come to see you. And now I do hope you have not been getting a great dinner for us.   Remember we never eat suppers.'

'I suppose,' said Margaret rather quickly to Emma, 'you and I are to be together; Elizabeth always takes care to have a room to herself.'

'No.   Elizabeth gives me half hers.'

'Oh!' in a softened voice, and rather mortified to find that she was not ill-used.

'I am sorry I am not to have the pleasure of your company, especially as it makes me nervous to be much alone.'

Emma was the first of the females in the parlour again; on entering it she found her brother alone.

'So Emma,' said he, 'you are quite a stranger at home. It must seem odd enough for you to be here. A pretty piece of work your Aunt Turner has made of it! By heaven! A woman should never be trusted with money. I always said she ought to have settled something on you, as soon as her husband died.'

'But that would have been trusting *me* with money,' replied Emma, 'and I am a woman too.'

'It might have been secured to your future use, without your having any power over it now. What a blow it must have been upon you! To find yourself, instead of heiress of 8,000*l.* or 9,000*l.*, sent back a weight upon your family, without a sixpence. I hope the old woman will smart for it.'

'Do not speak disrespectfully of her ; she was very good to me, and if she has made an imprudent choice, she will suffer more from it herself than I can possibly do.'

'I do not mean to distress you, but you know everybody must think her an old fool. I thought Turner had been reckoned an extraordinarily sensible, clever man. How the devil came he to make such a will ?'

'My uncle's sense is not at all impeached in my opinion by his attachment to my aunt. She had been an excellent wife to him. The most liberal and enlightened minds are always the most confiding. The event has been unfortunate, but my uncle's memory is, if possible, endeared to me by such a proof of tender respect for my aunt.'

'That's odd sort of talking.   He might have provided decently for his widow, without leaving everything that he had to dispose of, or any part of it, at
her mercy.'

'My aunt may have erred,' said Emma, warmly;
'she *has* erred, but my uncle's conduct was faultless;
I was her own niece, and he left to her the power of
providing for me.'

'But unluckily she has left the pleasure of providing
for you to your father, and without the power.   That's
the long and short of the business.   After keeping
you at a distance from your family for such a length
of time as must do away all natural affection among
us, and breeding you up (I suppose) in a superior
style, you are returned upon their hands without a
sixpence.'

'You know,' replied Emma, struggling with her
tears, 'my uncle's melancholy state of health.   He
was a greater invalid than my father.   He could not
leave home.'

'I do not mean to make you cry,' said Robert,
rather softened—and after a short silence, by way of
changing the subject, he added : 'I am just come from
my father's room ; he seems very indifferent.   It will
be a sad break up when he dies.   Pity you can none
of you get married !   You must come to Croydon as
well as the rest, and see what you can do there.   I
believe if Margaret had had a thousand or fifteen
hundred pounds, there was a young man who would
have thought of her.'

Emma was glad when they were joined by the

others ; it was better to look at her sister-in-law's finery than listen to Robert, who had equally irritated and grieved her. **Mrs.** Robert, exactly as smart **as** she had been at her own party, came in with apologies **for** her dress.

'I would not make you wait,' said **she,** 'so I put **on the** first thing I met with. I am afraid I am a sad figure. My dear Mr. W. (addressing her husband), **you** have not put any fresh powder in your hair.'

'**No, I** do not intend it. I think there is powder enough in my hair for my wife and sisters.'

' Indeed, you ought to make some alteration in your dress before dinner when you are out visiting, though you do not at **home.'**

' Nonsense.'

'It **is very** odd **you do not** like to do what other gentlemen do. Mr. Marshall **and** Mr. Hemming change their dress **every day of** their lives before dinner. And what was the use of my putting **up** your last new **coat,** if you are never to wear **it ? '**

' **Do** be satisfied with being fine yourself and **leave** your husband alone.'

**To put** an end to this altercation and soften the evident vexation of her sister-in-law, Emma (though in no spirits **to** make such nonsense easy), began to admire her gown. **It** produced immediate complacency.

' Do you like it **? '** said **she.** ' I am very happy. **It** has been excessively admired, but sometimes I think **the** pattern too large. **I shall wear** one to-morrow which I think you will **prefer** to this. Have you **seen** the **one** I gave Margaret **? '**

Dinner came, and except when Mrs. Robert looked at her husband's head, she continued gay and flippant, chiding Elizabeth for the profusion on the table, and absolutely protesting against the entrance of the roast turkey, which formed the only exception to 'you see your dinner.' 'I do beg and entreat that no turkey may be seen to-day. I am really frightened out of my wits with the number of dishes we have already. Let us have no turkey I beseech you.'

'My dear,' replied Elizabeth, ' the turkey is roasted, and it may just as well come in as stay in the kitchen. Besides, if it is cut, I am in hopes my father may be tempted to eat a bit, for it is rather a favourite dish.'

'You may have it in, my dear, but I assure you I shan't touch it.'

Mr. Watson had not been well enough to join the party at dinner, but was prevailed on to come down and drink tea with them.

'I wish he may be able to have a game of cards, to-night,' said Elizabeth to Mrs. Robert, after seeing her father comfortably seated in his arm-chair.

'Not on my account, my dear, I beg. You know I am no card-player. I think a snug chat infinitely better. I always say cards are very well sometimes to break a formal circle, but one never wants them among friends.'

'I was thinking of it's being something to amuse my father,' said Elizabeth, 'if it was not disagreeable to you. He says his head won't bear whist, but perhaps if we make a round game he may be tempted to sit down with us.'

'By all means, my dear creature, I am quite at your service, only do not oblige me to choose the game, that's all. Speculation is the only round game at Croydon now, but I can play anything. When there is only one or two of you at home, you must be quite at a loss to amuse him. Why do you not get him to play at cribbage? Margaret and I have played at cribbage most nights that we have not been engaged.'

A sound like a distant carriage was at this moment caught; everybody listened; it became more decided; it certainly drew nearer. It was an unusual sound for Stanton at any time of the day, for the village was on no very public road, and contained no gentleman's family but the rector's. The wheels rapidly approached; in two minutes the general expectation was answered; they stopped beyond a doubt at the garden-gate of the parsonage. Who could it be? It was certainly a postchaise. Penelope was the only creature to be thought of; she might perhaps have met with some unexpected opportunity of returning. A pause of suspense ensued. Steps were distinguished along the paved footway, which led under the window of the house to the front door, and then within the passage. They were the steps of a man. It could not be Penelope. It must be Samuel. The door opened, and displayed Tom Musgrave in the wrap of a traveller. He had been in London and was now on his way home, and he had come half-a-mile out of his road merely to call for ten minutes at Stanton. He loved to take people by surprise with sudden visits at extraordinary seasons, and, in the present instance, he had the additional motive of being able to tell the Miss Watsons, whom he depended on finding sitting quietly employed after tea, that he was going home to an eight o'clock dinner.

As it happened, he did not give more surprise than he received, when, instead of being shown into the usual little sitting-room, the door of the best parlour (a foot larger each way than the other) was thrown open, and he beheld a circle of smart people, whom he could not immediately recognise, arranged with all the honours of visiting round the fire, and Miss Watson seated at the best Pembroke table, with the best tea-things before her. He stood a few seconds in silent amazement. 'Musgrave,' ejaculated Margaret, in a tender voice. He recollected himself, and came forward, delighted to find such a circle of friends, and blessing his good fortune for the unlooked-for indulgence. He shook hands with Robert, bowed and smiled to the ladies, and did everything very prettily, but as to any particularity of address or emotion towards Margaret, Emma, who closely observed him, perceived nothing that did not justify Elizabeth's opinion, though Margaret's modest smiles imported that she meant to take the visit to herself. He was persuaded without much difficulty to throw off his great coat and drink tea with them. For 'whether he dined at eight or nine,' as he observed, 'was a matter of very little consequence;' and without seeming to seek he did not turn away from the chair close by Margaret, which she was assiduous in providing him. She had thus secured

him from her sisters, **but it** was not immediately in
her power to preserve him from her brother's claims;
for as he came avowedly from London, and had left
**it only four** hours ago, the last current report as to
public news, and the general opinion of the day, **must
be** understood before Robert could **let** his attention
**be** yielded to the less rational and important demands
**of the** women. At last, however, he was at liberty to
**hear** Margaret's soft address, as she spoke her fears of
**his** having had a most terrible cold, dark, dreadful
journey—

'Indeed, you should not have set out so **late.**'

'I could not be earlier,' he replied. 'I **was detained**
chatting at **the** Bedford **by a** friend. All hours **are**
alike to me. **How** long have **you** been in the country
Miss Margaret?'

'**We only** came **this** morning; my kind brother
**and** sister brought me **home** this very morning. 'Tis
singular—is not it?'

'**You were** gone a great **while, were not** you? A
fortnight, I suppose?'

'*You* may call a *fortnight* a great **while,** Mr. Musgrave,' **said Mrs.** Robert, sharply; '**but** *we* think a
*month* very little. I assure you **we bring her** home
at the end **of a** month much against our **will.**'

'A month! Have you really been gone a month?
'Tis amazing how time **flies.**'

'You may imagine,' said Margaret, in a sort of
whisper, 'what are my sensations in finding myself
**once** more at Stanton; **you** know what a sad visitor I
make. **And I** was so excessively impatient to see

Emma ; I dreaded the meeting, and at the same time
longed for it.　Do you not comprehend the sort of
feeling ?'

'Not at all,' cried he, aloud ; 'I could never dread
a meeting with Miss Emma Watson, or any of her
sisters.'

It was lucky that he added that finish.

'Were you speaking to me ?' said Emma, who had
caught her own name.

'Not absolutely,' he answered ; 'but I was thinking
of you, as many at a greater distance are probably
doing at this moment.　Fine open weather, Miss
Emma—charming season for hunting.'

'Emma is delightful, is not she ?' whispered Margaret ; 'I have found her more than answer my
warmest hopes.　Did you ever see anything more
perfectly beautiful ?　I think even *you* must be a con-
vert to a brown complexion.'

He hesitated.　Margaret was fair herself, and he
did not particularly want to compliment her ; but
Miss Osborne and Miss Carr were likewise fair, and
his devotion to them carried the day.

'Your sister's complexion,' said he, at last, 'is as
fine as a dark complexion can be ; but I still profess
my preference of a white skin.　You have seen Miss
Osborne ?　She is my model for a truly feminine complexion, and she is very fair.'

'Is she fairer than me ?'

Tom made no reply.　'Upon my honour, ladies,'
said he, giving a glance over his own person, 'I am
highly indebted to your condescension for admitting

me in such dishabille into your drawing-room. I
really did not consider how unfit I was to be here, or
I hope I should have kept my distance. Lady Osborne would tell me that I was growing as careless as
her son if she saw me in this condition.'

The ladies were not wanting in civil returns, and
Robert Watson, stealing a view of his own head in an
opposite glass, said with equal civility—

'You cannot be more in dishabille than myself.
We got here so late that I had not time even to put
a little fresh powder into my hair.'

Emma could not help entering into what she supposed her sister-in-law's feelings at the moment.

When the tea-things were removed, Tom began to
talk of his carriage ; but the old card-table being set
out, and the fish and counters, with a tolerably clean
pack brought forward from the buffet by Miss Watson,
the general voice was so urgent with him to join their
party that he agreed to allow himself another quarter
of an hour. Even Emma was pleased that he would
stay, for she was beginning to feel that a family party
might be the worst of all parties; and the others were
delighted.

'What's your game?' cried he, as they stood round
the table.

'Speculation, I believe,' said Elizabeth. 'My sister
recommends it, and I fancy we all like it. I know
you do, Tom.'

'It is the only round game played at Croydon now,'
said Mrs. Robert ; 'we never think of any other. I
am glad it is a favourite with you.'

'Oh! *me*,' said Tom. 'Whatever you decide on will be a favourite with *me*. I have had some pleasant hours at speculation in my time; but I have not been in the way of it for a long while. Vingt-un is the game at Osborne Castle. I have played nothing but vingt-un of late. You would be astonished to hear the noise we make there—the fine old lofty drawing-room rings again. Lady Osborne sometimes declares she cannot hear herself speak. Lord Osborne enjoys it famously, and he makes the best dealer without exception that I ever beheld—such quickness and spirit, he lets nobody dream over their cards. I wish you could see him over-draw himself on both his own cards. It is worth anything in the world!'

'Dear me!' cried Margaret, 'why should not we play vingt-un? I think it is a much better game than speculation. I cannot say I am very fond of speculation.'

Mrs. Robert offered not another word in support of the game. She was quite vanquished, and the fashions of Osborne Castle carried it over the fashions of Croydon.

'Do you see much of the parsonage family at the castle, Mr. Musgrave?' said Emma, as they were taking their seats.

'Oh! yes; they are almost always there. Mrs. Blake is a nice little goodhumoured woman; she and I are sworn friends; and Howard's a very gentleman-like good sort of fellow. You are not forgotten, I assure you, by any of the party. I fancy you must have a little check-glowing now and then, Miss

Emma. Were not you rather warm last Saturday about nine or ten o'clock in the evening ? I will tell you how it was—I see you are dying to know. Says Howard to Lord Osborne——'

At this interesting moment he was called on by the others to regulate the game, and determine some disputable point ; and his attention was so totally engaged in the business, and afterwards by the course of the game, as never to revert to what he had been saying before; and Emma, though suffering a good deal from curiosity, dared not remind him.

He proved a very useful addition at their table. Without him it would have been a party of such very near relations as could have felt little interest, and perhaps maintained little complaisance, but his presence gave variety and secured good manners. He was, in fact, excellently qualified to shine at a round game, and few situations made him appear to greater advantage. He played with spirit, and had a great deal to say ; and though no wit himself, could some-times make use of the wit of an absent friend, and had a lively way of retailing a common-place, or say-ing a mere nothing, that had great effect at a card-table. The ways and good jokes of Osborne Castle were now added to his ordinary means of entertain-ment. He repeated the smart sayings of one lady, detailed the oversights of another, and indulged them even with a copy of Lord Osborne's overdrawing him-self on both cards.

The clock struck nine while he was thus agreeably occupied; and when Nanny came in with her master's basin of gruel, he had the pleasure of observing to Mr. Watson that he should leave him at supper while he went home to dinner himself.  The carriage was ordered to the door, and no entreaties for his staying longer could now avail; for he well knew that if he stayed he would have to sit down to supper in less than ten minutes, which to a man whose heart had been long fixed on calling his next meal a dinner, was quite insupportable.  On finding him determined to go, Margaret began to wink and nod at Elizabeth to ask him to dinner for the following day, and Elizabeth at last, not able to resist hints which her own hospitable social temper more than half seconded, gave the invitation—'Would he give Robert the meeting, they should be very happy?'

'With the greatest pleasure,' was his first reply.  In a moment afterwards, 'That is, if I can possibly get here in time; but I shoot with Lord Osborne, and therefore must not engage.  You will not think of me unless you see me.'  And so he departed, delighted in the uncertainty in which he had left it.

Margaret, in the joy of her heart, under circumstances which she chose to consider as peculiarly propitious, would willingly have made a confidante of Emma when they were alone for a short time the next morning, and had proceeded so far as to say, 'The young man who was here last night, my dear Emma, and returns to-day, is more interesting to me than perhaps you may be aware;' but Emma, pretending to understand nothing extraordinary in the words, made some very inapplicable reply, and jumping up, ran away from a subject which was odious to her. As Margaret would not allow a doubt to be repeated of Musgrave's coming to dinner, preparations were made for his entertainment much exceeding what had been deemed necessary the day before; and taking the office of superintendence entirely from her sister, she was half the morning in the kitchen herself, directing and scolding.

After a great deal of indifferent cooking and anxious suspense, however, they were obliged to sit down without their guest. Tom Musgrave never came; and Margaret was at no pains to conceal her vexation under the disappointment, or repress the peevishness of her temper. The peace of the party for the remainder of that day and the whole of the next, which comprised the length of Robert and Jane's visit, was continually invaded by her fretful displeasure and querulous attacks. Elizabeth was the usual object of both. Margaret had just respect enough for her brother's and sister's opinion to behave properly by *them*, but Elizabeth and the maids could never do right; and Emma, whom she seemed no longer to think about, found the continuance of the gentle voice beyond calculation short. Eager to be as little among them as possible, Emma was delighted with the alternative of sitting above with her father, and warmly entreated to be his constant companion each evening; and as Elizabeth loved company of any kind too well not to prefer being below at all risks; as she had rather talk of Croydon with Jane, with every inter-

ruption of Margaret's perverseness, than sit with only
her father, who frequently could not endure talking
at all, the affair was so settled, as soon as she could
be persuaded to believe it no sacrifice on her sister's
part. To Emma the change was most acceptable and
delightful. Her father, if ill, required little more than
gentleness and silence, and being a man of sense and
education, was, if able to converse, a welcome companion. In *his* chamber Emma was at peace from
the dreadful mortifications of unequal society and
family discord; from the immediate endurance of
hard-hearted prosperity, low-minded conceit, and
wrong-headed folly, engrafted on an untoward disposition. She still suffered from them in the contem-
plation of their existence, in memory and in prospect,
but for the moment she ceased to be tortured by their
effects. She was at leisure; she could read and think,
though her situation was hardly such as to make reflection very soothing. The evils arising from the loss
of her uncle were neither trifling nor likely to lessen ;
and when thought had been freely indulged in con-
trasting the past and the present, the employment of
mind and dissipation of unpleasant ideas, which only
reading could produce, made her thankfully turn to a
book.

The change in her home society and style of life,
in consequence of the death of one friend and the
imprudence of another, had indeed been striking.
From being the first object of hope and solicitude to
an uncle who had formed her mind with the care of a
parent, and of tenderness to an aunt whose amiable

temper had delighted **to** give her every indulgence; from being the life **and** spirit of a house where **all** had been comfort **and** elegance, and the expected heiress **of** an easy independence, **she** was become of importance to no one—a burden on those whose affections **she could not** expect, an addition in a house **already** overstocked, surrounded by inferior minds, **with little** chance of domestic comfort, and as little **hope of** future support. It was well **for** her that she **was** naturally cheerful, for the change **had been** such **as** might have plunged weak spirits in despondence.

She was very much pressed by Robert and **Jane to** return with them **to** Croydon, and had some difficulty in getting **a** refusal accepted, **as** they thought **too** highly of **their own** kindness **and** situation to suppose the **offer could** appear **in less** advantageous light **to** anybody **else.** Elizabeth **gave** them her interest, though evidently against **her** own, in privately urging Emma to **go.**

'**You** do not know what **you** refuse, Emma,' said she, '**nor what** you have to **bear at home.** I would **advise you by** all means to accept **the** invitation; **there is always** something lively going on **at** Croydon. You will **be in** company almost every day, and Robert and Jane **will** be very **kind to** you. As for me, I shall be no worse off **without** you than I have been used to be; **but** poor Margaret's disagreeable ways **are** new to *you*, and they would **vex** you more than **you** think for, if you stay **at** home.'

Emma was of course uninfluenced, except to greater

esteem for Elizabeth, by such representations, and the visitors departed without her.

---

When the author's sister, Cassandra, showed the manuscript of this work to some of her nieces, she also told them something of the intended story; for with this dear sister—though, I believe, with no one else—Jane seems to have talked freely of any work that she might have in hand. Mr. Watson was soon to die; and Emma to become dependent for a home on her narrow-minded sister-in-law and brother. She was to decline an offer of marriage from Lord Osborne, and much of the interest of the tale was to arise from Lady Osborne's love for Mr. Howard, and his counter affection for Emma, whom he was finally to marry.

J. D. & Co.

PRINTED BY
SPOTTISWOODE AND CO., NEW-STREET SQUARE
LONDON